THE STONE MOVERS

PATRICIA MULLEN

A Time Warner Company

WARNER BOOKS EDITION

Copyright © 1995 by Patricia Mullen
All rights reserved.

Aspect is a trademark of Warner Books, Inc.

Cover design by Don Puckey
Cover illustration by Tim Hildebrant

Warner Books, Inc.
1271 Avenue of the Americas
New York, NY 10020

W A Time Warner Company

Printed in the United States of America

First Printing: January, 1995

10 9 8 7 6 5 4 3 2 1

FINAL DAYS OF THE FIVE TRIBES

OGRES: Fierce and gentle unicorn riders, the Shaggy Ones tell the ancient prophecies.

ELVES: The Queen is mad, protected by her husbands—until disaster looms, and a strong leader is needed.

DWARFS: Master craftsmen and warriors who owe allegiance only to Honor and Duty.

PESKIES: Followers of the herds, they will lose everything if their lands are overrun.

HUMANS: A race of villains and heroes, those who betray, enslave, and slaughter—and those who fight back fiercely.

* * *

"Full of high magic, high intrigue, very believable characters, and the most basic conflicts of civilization....A labor of love, and quite an accomplishment for a first novel."

—R. A. Salvatore, *New York Times* **bestselling author of** *The Legacy*

"A grand parable of love, magic, treachery—and racial tolerance. [Mullen's] heroes, heroines, elves, trolls, ogres and villains are stunningly complex and thoroughly believable creations. *THE STONE MOVERS* is that literary rarity—a sweeping fantasy epic profoundly relevant to our land and times."

—**Marvin Kaye, author of** *Fantastique*

Dedicated to Spot, Hudson, and the others
who showed me Magic

With thanks to
Marvin Kaye, Donald Maass,
the Ladies of the Roundtable,
and special gratitude to K. Marx
for promises kept

Straits of Kythra

BEACON'S KEEP

Cranberry Bogs

Trollurgh Mountains

Fendown Plain

Argontell Plain

LONGHILE RIVER

FLEAN

100 Miles

Inset map:

Argontell

Argontell

CHILE RIVER

LONG

DUNNAIRE

BOOK ONE

"Think of the island as a beast, Your Eminence, the north is the head, the south the body," The Tyrant's minister was saying. "If you can, with politics, cut off the head, I can, with force, occupy the unprotected farmland." Eacon Gleese and the minister were bent over the map of Morbihan like boys over a game board. They used spice bowls and a salt shaker for pieces, moving them, pondering, then moving them again. Nearby, the servant Fryd hovered silently, almost stealthily, anticipating their needs as he served the warm brew and fresh-baked honey cakes that The Eacon had called for.

"In the wintertime the mountains cut off the two halves well enough," The Eacon mused, "and The Tyrant's fleet controls the shipping to both sides of the island." He paused, his hand fluttering over the map with excitement and indecision.

The two men sat in a private room in the heavily guarded citadel that was the summer residence of The Seventh Tyrant of The Perime of Moer. The Tyrant's minister was called Lothen. He was a man of middle years, his powerful shoulders tapering down to a compact waist. Like all The Tyrant's ministers, he was also a priest, and devout. He sat at ease, his dark cloak draped about his shoulders, a darker air hovering about him. He towered by half a head over his companion yet he was so perfectly proportioned that his height seemed normal.

On the other hand, Eacon Gleese was a tall man whose great obesity made him seem shorter than he was. His chair groaned under his weight as he considered. "But no," he sighed finally, with reluctance. "We can do nothing while Telerhyde and Fallon live."

The minister was careful not to let his impatience show. Instead, he bared his teeth in an expression that was nothing like a smile. "Telerhyde!" he repeated softly. "I would enjoy meeting him on the field of combat." His hand caressed the hilt of his sword and a chill breeze ruffled the tablecloth.

The Eacon's double chin shook like a chicken's wattle. "No, Lothen," he scolded, "you wouldn't enjoy that at all. I have tried it, and believe me when I tell you that's precisely what we're trying to avoid. Besides, it's not just Telerhyde; it's his cursed collaborator, Fallon. The two of them are hand in hand. You think of Telerhyde because he leads the armies, but the real power is Fallon and his Magic. They are unremitting enemies of The Tyrant, loved by Human and devil alike. Together they unite Morbihan against us." He sighed, reaching for another honey cake.

"Then we must destroy them."

"Destroy Telerhyde!" The Eacon laughed, leaning back in his chair until his great weight threatened to tumble him backward. "He's protected day and night. His vigilance is legendary! And Fallon's Magic . . ."

"Nevertheless," said Lothen smoothly, with emphasis, "our Master desires Morbihan for his own, and you advise me that with Telerhyde and Fallon alive we cannot take it."

The Eacon frowned at the tablecloth, finally at a loss for words. In the silence, Fryd stepped to the table with the quiet skill of one who knows the needs of other men, placing goblets of neat wine at the edge of the map. He swept up the plates left from lunch and brushed crumbs from the table.

The minister sipped his wine, savoring its deep, rich flavor, spiced by the tang peculiar to the vineyards of Morbihan. He found it pleasant to disconcert The Eacon. "I know that as The Tyrant's sole representative on Morbihan, you have done your best," he went on at last, "and The Tyrant appreciates your efforts. But he has lost patience and commanded me to find a strategy that will conquer. Here in Moer I have met a Human who can help us. He's one of their own, who has expressed hatred for The Old Faith and its ways."

The Eacon arched one eyebrow, his blue eyes flinty and hard. "I should like to meet this man," he said stiffly. He made a welcoming gesture with his hand, and in doing so he overturned his goblet.

Fryd leaped forward, seizing the fallen cup, dabbing with a soft cloth at The Eacon's robe.

"You clumsy fool!" roared The Eacon, rising to his feet. "How dare you place that cup in my way, you bumbling moron!" He struck Fryd in the face.

Stunned, the servant lurched away with a cry of pain. Recovering himself, he hastened forward, bobbing in an awkward bow as he finished mopping the mess. Beneath his linen rag the map of Morbihan was stained dark red, as though already drowning in blood.

Chapter 1

It was not any beast that Morbihan resembled. In ancient times the great prophetess Kythra determined that, if viewed from the air, the Isle of Morbihan was the shape of a snarling wolf's head. The shape was fitting because, like a huge sentinel, Morbihan guarded the eastern approach to the Outer Isles from The Perime of Moer.

Morbihan was never a gentle land. Along the sea-shattered northern coast which formed the wolf's ears and snout lay the cold, rocky Plain of Kythra. There the hardy Lords of the North had carved out their domains. In the south, from the wolf's jowl to curling ruff, generations of Human farmers had settled the more fertile Fensdown Plain, and even begun to venture across the swift waters of the Longhile River to the borders of the sacred Argontell Plain. But the greater part of the island lay between these ancestral Human strongholds. In a wide swath from jaw to base of skull spread the vast expanse of mountain, wood, and bogland known as Harkynwood, homeland to the Others.

In ancient times Magic had prospered the island. Each village boasted its own wizard and there was little need for trade. But centuries passed and the port towns grew into cities, swollen with commerce. Many of the Human inhabitants came to love prosperity more than freedom, and there was but one Master Wizard for all of Morbihan.

Just before the darkest of these days, a lone rider traveled through the foothills of the Trollurgh Mountains in the north-

ern borderlands of Harkynwood. By late afternoon he neared
an isolated village nestled beside the great ravine called
Kythra's Chasm, where the River Dark flowed from the
mountains to the plain. The Dwarfin children saw him first
and fled across the stony ground on their bowed legs toward
their homes, calling out with excitement. The inhabitants of
the village stirred and gathered at their windows and doors to
watch him pass, but no one reached for an ax or short sword.
The Dwarves of the village of Knot, like the rest of Morbihan, had been at peace for eighteen years.

The lone rider was young, Human, and rode a nimble-
footed mare, which he rested often as the path grew steeper
and more narrow. Although he was only of middling height
for a Human, to the Dwarfin children he seemed absurdly
tall. The summer sun was behind him, making him seem
even larger than he was, highlighting his brown hair with
streaks of gold. The double dragon of the House of Crowell
was sewn into the sleeve of his jacket and an empty sword
scabbard hung from his saddle. Except for these, he rode
without arms or ornament. Yet there was no disguising the
Elfin-tooled quality of his boots and bridle, nor the fluid ease
with which he sat the sweat-stained horse. He reined to a
stop before the swarm of giggling, shrieking children and
asked directions.

Following their pointing fingers, he spurred the mare up
the stony path until, just beyond the village, he came to a
neat house and barn. From the side of the barn extended a
shed with a bronze ax head painted on its side, faded and
peeling with time and weather. At the door, on a level path
of ground, an iron anvil stood on the stump of a once-mighty
tree. Inside was a forge, complete with a huge bellows oper-
ated by a long pole. Above the forge, the air shimmered with
heat, making the shed's occupant seem more like someone
caught in a shapechanger's spell than a blacksmith of flesh
and blood.

He was a Dwarf, tall for his tribe, with massive shoulders.
He was a head shorter than the Human and almost twice as
wide. His hair was tied in a knot by a thong on the top of his
head, and his long, steel-grey beard, parted in the middle,
was draped backward over his shoulders. His bulging eyes

seemed to be glaring out of a massive coil of grey rope as he meticulously fashioned a pair of iron hinges.

"Smith?" the Human greeted him politely, sliding from the saddle.

The smith did not look up. With the absorption of a skilled craftsman, he continued to work, using iron tongs to hold up the red-hot hinges. He measured their angle by eye, then laid them across the anvil to strike them again. At length he dropped them into a vat of water, where they hissed and boiled. Only then did he turn to the visitor.

"Yes?"

"Excuse me, are you Broderick of Knot?"

"Yes."

"I have come from Crowell."

"Ah," the Dwarf said, nodding toward the empty scabbard. "A new manling."

The Human nodded his head. He was a handsome young man, not tall, but strongly built with a straight nose and light grey eyes which were bright with excitement. "Master Smith," he said formally, following the ritual of the occasion, "I have come to claim my sword."

"You come on a fine day," the Dwarf said. "It was on such a day that I made Snitch, Telerhyde's great sword. Even finer than the day when I made the sword for his son, Brandon." He stepped closer, looking up into the young man's face. "Who are you?"

"I'm Nyal of Crowell, Telerhyde's youngest son. By our custom, my father has sent me to seek my sword from the one who forged his own."

The Dwarf regarded him for a moment, a deep frown lining his face. "I honor any emissary from Telerhyde, but I cannot make your sword, Nyal."

For a moment the young Human was without words. Sword making was an important ritual for both Human and Dwarf, and Broderick's refusal was shocking. "But Father has invited guests to my Sword-Naming!" he protested. "Smith, I can't go home empty-handed!"

"I'm sorry," the Dwarf shrugged, "my helper is gone for the day. Even if he were here, it would not be possible. I cannot."

"Cannot? You must! You are a Naerlundg, and a Dwarf of your family has been Crowell's smith since Kythra's day!"

"Watch your tongue, manling!" the Dwarf's words cracked like a wagon driver's whip. "You sound like a New Faith bigot! I'm not 'Crowell's smith,' nor anyone's but my own! A bond of affection ties my family and yours, and don't you forget it! I cannot make your sword, so begone!"

It occurred to the Human that he was being tested. "I'm sorry, Master Smith. No one supports the strength of the Naerlundg more than the sons of Telerhyde." Mollified, the Dwarf grunted and Nyal went on contritely. "Allow me to be your helper, then," he said. "I have a little experience in making iron from helping with the horseshoeing at home. I'll pump the bellows, I'll make charcoal. I'll do whatever you need done."

"I'm sorry, I have to finish my work." Shaking his head with an air of finality, the smith turned from the young man and sank his hand into the water vat to pull out the cooled hinges.

"I have gold," Nyal said. "I'll pay you." The Dwarf paused. Quickly the Human unbuckled the empty scabbard from his waist. "Here, see this ornament? The double dragon of Crowell, given to me by my father."

Broderick examined the heavy gold piece, his scarred and callused fingers delicately working it loose from the thongs which bound it to the leather scabbard. "This is excellent," he murmured. When it was free, he turned it over and over in his hands. "The workmanship is extraordinary. It must be very old."

"It's yours."

Broderick tossed the golden ornament back to Nyal, startling the mare, who threw up her head. "Take your gold; one day you'll have better use of it."

Nyal stepped into the shadows of the shed, anger twisting his mouth. "But why? I'll work! I'll pay you! Why won't you honor the bond between our families?"

In the darkness of the shed, Broderick felt something pulse with a white heat hotter than any forge. He recoiled from the young man instinctively, gasping.

Mistaking the Dwarf's reaction, Nyal's resolve faltered

and his face softened like a child's. He turned toward his horse, humiliated. "Very well," he said stiffly, "but my father will hear of this."

"Stop!" cried Broderick. When Nyal turned back to him, the heat was gone. Human and Dwarf faced each other in the cool shadows of the shed. "Feed and water your horse," Broderick commanded, "then return. I'll need you to bring a cartload of charcoal from the barn. I hope you're strong enough to pump the bellows. The fire must be hot to forge a charmed sword."

When Nyal returned from the barn, the smith had chosen three heavy iron ingots and laid them on the coals of the forge. "It's the mix that gives iron strength and flexibility," said the Dwarf. "For a keen edge, I'll use an ingot from The Perime of Moer, curse them. An ingot from the Argontell Plain will bend and overcome strength greater than its own. And this," he held up an oddly black and heavy piece of iron, "this is from the Dwarfin mine here in the Trollurgh Mountains. It will bind the others together and give this sword its life."

The bellows, massive and old, was reluctant to be pumped. Nyal stripped off his tunic and grasped the long bellows pole, pushing and pulling, already sweating from the heat of the forge.

When the ingots glowed dully, the smith removed them from the fire and beat each one until it was long and thin. Then he cleverly stacked them, one upon the other, and laid them on edge in the coals. "Now pump the bellows with a will, manling of Crowell!" he said. "The metal must sing in the fire." Nyal pumped until the forge roared.

The irons were glowing cherry red, hissing and sparking, when the smith finally snatched them from the fire. Laying the three together on the anvil, he swung his huge hammer. Sparks flew and the air was filled with smoke. The irons folded together like cloth until they took the shape of one slender strip of metal, glowing darkly.

"Pump!" Broderick commanded. When the length of iron began to sing and spark again, the Dwarf pulled it out with his tongs and folded it over once more, his hammer ringing out a powerful rhythm on the huge anvil.

Nyal watched, grey eyes large in his sweat-drenched face, reflecting the fire's glow. Again and again Broderick folded the iron over with sure blows, hammering it flat. The heat was overwhelming and Nyal leaned back, shielding his eyes from the glowing metal. Each time the iron cooled and ceased to spark, Broderick cast it back into the fire and Nyal threw his weight against the bellows pole once more.

They worked for hours. Gradually the metal bar took on a long and graceful shape beneath the smith's hands. At last Broderick nodded. "Rest," he told Nyal. "I'll need you again very soon." The Dwarf laid the blade on the ground and cooled it with a spadeful of fresh earth.

Nyal staggered from the smithy. To his surprise, night had already fallen and a three-quarter moon hung over the roof of the shed. A cloud dimmed the moon's profile, darkening the yard. Nyal had never been so tired in his life. His clothes were soaked with sweat and blackened with sooty smudges. He stumbled, setting a bucket clanging across the yard as he leaned against the wall of the barn, grateful for the cool air. He slid down the wall to the ground, letting his tired arms fall to his sides.

Why was Broderick treating him this way? It was as puzzling as Telerhyde's reluctance to send him here in the first place. Nyal's brother, Brandon, had not had to work or wait for his sword. Only weeks after his eighteenth birthday Brandon had found Broderick, taken a room with a Dwarfin family, and feasted on goat pie and hurly cakes until his sword was finished. Nyal tried to remember what Telerhyde had told him of Snitch's creation. Certainly the great warrior had not taken a hand in making his own sword. But Nyal had little time to rest or wonder before the smith called and he dragged himself to his feet.

Inside, the shed was brightly lighted by the forge. The long, flat piece of iron lay upon the anvil, roughly shaped like the sword it was soon to become. Sweat plastered Broderick's hair to his head and his great ears fanned out like small wings. He said not a word, only nodded for Nyal to begin work again. Once more the bellows wheezed and the forge shimmered with heat. The smith constantly turned the blade with his long tongs until the steel glowed bright red. At last he smiled with satisfaction and slid the blade, boiling and hissing, into a trough of water.

"Not a crack or warp, very good," Broderick announced, examining the cooled metal. "It's passed the first test! Now, we must temper it to find its strength." He gestured toward the forge once again, but Nyal's arms were so heavy that he could hardly lift them to the pole.

"I can't, I have to rest," he pleaded.

"This is not the time to rest!" the Dwarf barked. "Now the real work begins, manling! If you would have this sword, you must give me all your strength!"

Nyal reluctantly stumbled to the bellows. The heat was searing and sweat poured from his body. The bellows pole seemed to grow stiffer with each thrust. Blisters formed on his hands, then burst, then bled. He wheezed and gasped and the bellows fought him, groaning and roaring in protest. He would have cried but for the Dwarf's eyes upon him. Instead, he arched his back, pulling, pushing, lifting, sinking. His breath came in little cries, his arms shuddered with their own strength.

In the fire, the blade glowed crimson, then orange. "More!" called the smith, protecting his face from the heat with his hands. The blade grew lighter, glowing deep gold as the angry hiss of the bellows blew the coals blue, then white. The smith turned the blade again and again, making certain the glow was even from one end of the sword to the other. The deep gold grew brighter, then brighter still.

Nyal could no longer feel his body. He no longer felt pain or exhaustion, only the sense that he was now a part of the bellows, that he had always been here in the fierce glow of the forge, always would be. The blade began to shimmer, vibrating and pulsating in the coals. And something else within the shadows of the shed was vibrating, glowing with energy. As though surrounded by a silent chord of music, Nyal shone with a clarity brighter than any light. The Dwarf, who saw, smiled with satisfaction.

The iron was glowing a pale shade of gold when at last the master smith cried "Yes!" snatched the blade from the fire, and cast it into the water vat. Steam filled the shed as the water boiled. Outdoors, a flash of lightning made Nyal jerk in surprise. A clap of thunder rolled across the hills.

"It calls forth a great storm," observed the smith. Swiftly he fashioned the hilt and handle from metal scraps which lay on the floor. Nyal stared dully as the storm displayed its power over the countryside.

Assembled at last, the sword lay dark and heavy on the anvil. Outside, the storm continued to rage, rain cascading across the barnyard. Broderick wiped sweat from his forehead and gestured at the stone wheel beside the forge. "Crank the sharpening wheel, Nyal, and we'll give your blade its sting."

Nyal was beyond protest, moaning softly as he cranked the handle to turn the great sharpening stone. The scream of steel on stone was deafening, but soon the blade gleamed in the Dwarf's hands, growing more and more slender as he ground away metal to create the edge.

The storm had passed and the sky was lightening with dawn when at last the smith nodded for Nyal to rest. The young Human slumped against a wall, his face glazed with exhaustion. As Broderick wrapped the handle in cowhide, a look of troubled concern softened his face. Nyal lay where he had fallen, crumpled in a corner, mind and body empty of thought and feeling. Finally the sword was finished, bright and gleaming.

"I know that Human custom demands that you return to your family for celebrations as soon as the sword is completed," the Dwarf said, prodding Nyal gently with his foot. "So saddle your horse."

Nyal moved as though in a dream. "Whoa, Lady, whoa," he soothed, as the mare shied from the forge. Soot caked and grimy, he slumped in the saddle. The Dwarf stood before him, solemnly holding the new sword.

"I have forged the swords of Malrech, of Malrech's son, Telerhyde, and of Telerhyde's son, Brandon," the Dwarf said slowly. "As my father before me, and his father before him, each sword I have dedicated to the strength of the House of Crowell. I have made this sword for you in the same spirit, yet I cannot dedicate it in the same way."

Despite his exhaustion, Nyal's patience came to an end.

"Broderick, I've worked like an Ogre for this sword! Have the decency to dedicate it, at least! I am Telerhyde's son and it's my right!"

"Telerhyde and I were Sword-Companions during the war," Broderick said. "I was with him in Harkynwood and I followed him all the way to the Stone Moving on Wolf's Fang. I knew him well. Well enough to know you are not his son."

"What?" Nyal sat upright. He had heard whispers all his life, but no one had ever said it to his face.

"You are not Telerhyde's son," Broderick repeated gently. "Have you never suspected this? You were born of Magic and betrayal. Your birth lies heavy on you, Nyal. The light of Magic and the shadow of betrayal will lead you throughout your life."

"But you're wrong, I *am* Telerhyde's son. He would have told me . . ."

Broderick shrugged. "It is not for me to judge what you think to be true. Nor is it for you to question what I know." He held up his hand before the astonished young man could say more. "But even as Telerhyde has honored you and raised you as his own, I am honored to dedicate your sword." He held the sword above his head and the light from the forge transformed the blade into soft gold.

"*I dedicate this sword to the destiny of* all *the Tribes of Morbihan, Other, and Human, mighty and despised.* I warn you, Nyal, this is not a sword like other swords. It has been tempered in your own sweat and blood. It is called Firestroker and it is Broderick the Dwarf's finest work." Bowing his head, which was as much of a flourish as one might expect from a Dwarf, he sheathed the sword and handed it to Nyal.

The young man's hands were bleeding, wrapped in rags. His fingers were stiff and painful as he grasped the hilt, still warm from the fire. He slid the sword from its scabbard to test its balance. The steel was light and quick, the leather wrapped hilt fit snugly in his hand. Swinging it in an arc, he felt the blade bite the air, humming with a fine vibration. He felt a rush of emotion, like joy and grief all run together. "My thanks," he said. "It is a fine sword."

"Ride home now, and begone. May Firestroker serve you

in whatever way you need. And deserve." The smith turned away, walking toward the house, his square shoulders drooping in sudden exhaustion.

Chapter 2

Crowell was once a ring-fort, built at an earlier time by Ogres as protection from marauding Humans and Peskies. The ancient circular wall was constructed with great stones in the massive style of Ogre masonry. Outside the fortress, a small group of cottages clustered within a network of roads and paths which led out to the surrounding fields. The hollow center of the old fort was so large that it accommodated not only Crowell Manor, with its great hall and many rooms, but also the stable, three apple trees, a large garden, and a spacious courtyard, paved in bluestone, which stretched between the Manor's front door and the heavy wooden gate of the fort.

Crowell Manor itself, a large, two-story keep of stone and timber, was built by Humans long after the Ogres had been driven from their fortress. On the southeast side, which faced the courtyard, Crowell's massive walls were riddled with windows made of the finest Elfin glass. Telerhyde loved to look out on distant, unspoiled Harkynwood. Under Telerhyde's guidance, Crowell had become an important center, and upon the occasion of Telerhyde's youngest son's Sword-Naming, visitors and well-wishers had arrived from all of Morbihan.

On the night that Nyal's sword was forged, Crowell was filled with guests, both Human and Other. The surrounding fields and meadows were crowded with great ceremonial tents which well-to-do guests pitched outside the fort walls. Even Nyal's groom, Tymeryl, had given up his own room to share the high-vaulted, sweet-smelling hayloft above the stable with the Dwarf, Ruf Nab.

Tym was small for a Human although strong for his size. His slight body seemed to be made not of bone and muscle, but of knotted cord. Like everyone else, he had been up late celebrating Nyal's approaching Sword-Naming. Well into the night, he was awakened by the sound of violent pounding. He listened, a frown creasing his usually bland and pleasant face. His thinning, blond hair was matted and tangled with hay stalks, making him scratch furiously. Seeing the feeble light which passed through the cracks between the boards of the walls, he knew that it was just before dawn. And when the thumping came again, he knew exactly what it was. He swore under his breath.

Beside him, a mound of hay stirred. A knobby, muscular arm and hand appeared, scratching reddish hair and pulling hay clumps from oversized ears. "Is that the wild stallion again?" Ruf Nab grumbled crossly.

Tym nodded. "He's got the stable manners of a unicorn. I haven't had a decent night's sleep since The Wizard brought him. I'll pitch him some hay, maybe he'll be quiet."

He climbed down the stout ladder from the hayloft and moved quickly between rows of stalls to where the pounding of hooves sounded. "Whoa, you big ox! Settle down and let folks sleep!" he commanded. It was dark in the stable. Tym could barely see the fine lines of the stallion's head. He squinted, peering into the gloom, unsure whether it was sight or imagination which revealed the gleam of the stallion's eyes and the sharp-tipped ears laid back. The white blaze on the horse's face seemed to be suspended in the air, motionless for an instant, then sped like a dart for Tym's arm.

Tym realized what was happening too late to save himself. He felt the iron grip of the horse's teeth on his forearm. He cried out in surprise and pain, pummeling the stallion's head with his free arm.

"Whoa!" Ruf Nab's voice thundered. Standing in the doorway, the Dwarf snatched up a pitchfork and waved it in the horse's face. Distracted, the stallion released Tym, snapping his teeth, nostrils flaring. Tym, who had been trying to wrench himself away, fell in a heap on the floor and felt Ruf Nab's powerful arms dragging him to safety.

In the tack room, the Dwarf lit a lantern and pulled back the torn sleeve of Tym's shirt. On Tym's lean forearm were two perfect semicircles, each horse-tooth perfectly outlined in dark blue and swelling rapidly. "You're lucky, there's no blood. Can you move your arm?"

"A little." Tym flexed his fingers and winced.

"There's nothing broken," the Dwarf observed after some cautious probing and bending. "You should see The Wizard."

"I don't need a wizard; I'll heal." Tym cradled his arm against his chest and rocked back and forth, more in spent fear than in pain.

"Suit yourself." The Dwarf kindled a fire in the hearth and put on water for a brew. They sat together—the slender Human rocking in his chair, towering by a head over the broad, powerful Dwarf—and listened to the stallion kicking at the sides of his stall.

"What kind of present is this for Nyal?" Tym wanted to know, his teeth chattering slightly. "An untrained stallion! It takes four of us just to tie him down to groom him. Nyal's too hotheaded for a horse like this. He's a good boy," he hastened to assure Ruf Nab, who nodded in agreement, "and a hard worker, too. Good with animals. But he doesn't often think before he gets himself into trouble. He needs a mount that's dependable and a bit on the cautious side." These were qualities which Tym also valued in himself.

"Aye, but The Wizard has the wisdom of Magic," Ruf Nab objected. "Mayhap he has a purpose in mind."

"Mayhap he's just a bad judge of horseflesh," Tym grumbled, and lapsed into silence. He was not from Morbihan. His youth and young manhood had been spent as a seafarer far to the north. He had a healthy respect for the gods of the sea, sky, and sail, for he had known them at work. But he was skeptical about Morbihan's wizards and Magic.

However, as the day wore on the slightest movement of Tym's hand shot bolts of pain up his forearm. He tried to enlist the stable boys to help him groom the horse, but each one glanced at Tym's arm, listened to the stallion fretting in his stall, and suddenly remembered something urgent he had to do. Concerned that the horse would look shabby when he was presented to Nyal at the ceremonies, Tym reluctantly sought out Fallon the Wizard.

Tym found the man on a bench in the courtyard, soaking

up the afternoon sun. Known to followers of The Old Faith as the Shapechanger and Fallon the Twice-tested, he was Morbihan's only Master Wizard. He was even skinnier than Tym himself and had a sensible look about him, which gave Tym hope that he knew his business. Like Telerhyde, he was past his middle years. Large pockets drooped beneath his eyes and his once-sandy hair was streaked with white. His beard curled across a sky-blue robe.

At The Wizard's side sat a young woman also clad in the sky-blue robe of a Magic worker. Her straight black hair was pulled back severely and gathered at the nape of her slender neck with a rough clasp of bone. Her eyes were large and dark green, the color of a winter sea. She regarded Tym curiously as he stood before them.

"Excuse me, sir," Tym said. He bowed shyly. "My Lady."

"Is something wrong?" The Wizard's eyes startled Tym. Like the Magic's robes, they were pale blue and they radiated light like the summer sky.

"I'm Nyal's man, sir. I'm taking care of the horse you brought for him. He's a spirited one." Tym shifted uneasily before The Wizard's look of alarm. "You'll be glad to know he's fine, sir. But he's bitten me. I wouldn't bother you with it, but I can't move my fingers to pitch hay or groom the beast. All the stable boys are afraid of him, sir. I was hoping you could heal me so I can clean him up before Nyal gets home."

"Sit down, fellow. Let me see."

Self-consciously, Tym rolled up his torn sleeve and presented his arm. Fallon frowned, turning to the young woman at his side. "Cyna, take a look at this."

"Yes, Master Fallon." Her voice was deep, husky, almost a whisper. Her fingertips were cool as she traced the outline of the bite on Tym's arm. "Is this sore?" she asked, pressing on a welt.

"Ah!" Tym yelped. "Yes, Your Ladyship. Indeed it is."

"You must be more gentle, Cyna," The Wizard cautioned. "First observe. See the swelling, the bruises?"

Cyna nodded.

"Second, gather information, but take care not to complicate the injury. Fellow," Fallon said to Tym, "can you move your arm?"

"Yes, sir," Tym replied, energetically flexing his elbow. "It's just a horsebite, Your Grace." He wished he could simply be healed and go back to work.

"Patience, fellow, let my apprentice have a look. Cyna?"

After a long silence, Cyna said thoughtfully, "Well, it's not broken."

"How do you know?" demanded Fallon.

"The way he moves it," she replied.

"It's just a horsebite," Tym repeated impatiently. "It's a bit sore. Maybe you've got a little liniment I could use?"

"Cyna?" The Wizard urged again, watching her closely.

"It's sprained," she said, finally. "And badly bruised."

"That is correct," Fallon confirmed. "Now, how shall we treat it?"

"A poultice," she replied, sounding more confident. "Mugwort and comfrey will take out the soreness."

"Very good!" Fallon exclaimed. "You may take it from my herb chest. A pinch of tansy, too, to take the swelling down. But just a pinch."

An ancient wooden box with leather handles lay on the ground beside him. Cyna lifted the lid, her fingers lovingly stroking its polished surface. Inside were many tiny compartments filled with bottles and small linen bags. Tym smelled the fragrance of unfamiliar herbs and spices.

"I'll get boiling water from the kitchen," Cyna said and disappeared through a door.

"You're a groom at the stable?" Fallon asked Tym.

"No, sir, I'm Nyal's man. I mind his business and keep his equipment in shape. I watch after him, you might say, and coach him in hunting and combat."

Fallon nodded thoughtfully. "He has come late to his Sword-Naming."

"It's not his fault, sir. Telerhyde's been busy all spring with those lords from the cities. Nyal's a good boy, he'll be a fine lord."

The Wizard watched him curiously, but said no more. Tym sat uncomfortably in silence until Cyna returned with a kettle of steaming water. Beneath The Wizard's watchful eyes, the young woman sprinkled herbs into the water. When they had steeped, she dipped a rag into the boiling pot, pulled it out with a stick, and laid it on Tym's bare arm. Tym gasped, gritting his teeth, feeling sweat break out on his forehead.

"No, no, Cyna!" exclaimed The Wizard. "You're trying to heal him, not poach him. Wave the rags about to cool them before you lay them on."

Tym wished mightily that he had tended to himself in the stable. But he sat for a long time, feigning patience, while Cyna applied the poultice under Fallon's tutelage. At last The Wizard nodded. "Good. Now you know how to prepare a poultice on a real live Human."

"Yes, Master Fallon."

"But even more important, what are your thoughts?"

"To observe, to gather information," she recited, "to diagnose . . ."

"Yes, of course. But when you have diagnosed and determined a treatment, what are your thoughts?"

"To choose the herb. No. To boil water?" She was floundering. Tym tried not to smile.

"To heal, your thoughts must be pure," Fallon said emphatically. "You must think of this fellow not as he is—horse bitten and in pain. As you apply the cure, you must think of him healthy, with full use of his arm restored. Only when you can see that clearly in your mind, is the healing complete. Healing does not lie in potions and herbs, but in the thoughts of the Healer. Do you understand?"

"Yes, Master Fallon," Cyna replied.

"Do so."

Cyna closed her eyes. The Wizard did, too, and Tym sat between them, feeling embarrassed.

"Can you see him healed?" Fallon inquired after a long silence.

"Yes, Master."

"Good. Take off the poultice now. Fellow, give me your arm." He took Tym's hand and held it firmly for a moment. A cool tingling seemed to flood Tym's fingers and spread up to his shoulder. "Yes, it's already better," Fallon said. "Take a nap this afternoon. You'll be as good as new by this evening."

Tym was relieved that Fallon was right. By afternoon the bruises were fading. Unsure when Nyal would return from his journey, Tym invoked Telerhyde's name and commanded half a dozen reluctant stable boys to help him cross-tie the stallion between the two strongest apple trees in the courtyard.

The horse was a bright chestnut with white forelegs stained dark by his kicking in the stall. Tym dodged a threatening hoof and applied a currycomb and rags with vigor. The stallion snapped his teeth near Tym's ear. "Here, watch it!" Tym barked, rapping the horse sharply between the eyes with the back of a brush. "Whoa, you mangler!"

Ears laid flat, teeth bared, the horse threw up his head. Restrained by the ropes, he was forced to stand, his hide quivering as Tym brushed it. When the groom was finished, the stallion's coat gleamed like polished copper. Tym covered him with a light rug and cross-tied him in his stall so that he would cause less disruption. Later, Tym napped in the quiet warmth of the hayloft. It was almost evening when the sound of trumpets brought him to the stable door.

He was hoping to witness Nyal's return. Instead, a small procession was halted at the gate. Ten or twelve horsemen and several heavily burdened packhorses escorted a large covered cart, richly carved with strange symbols and decorated with polished bronze fittings. Guards were shouting and Tym glimpsed Ruf Nab, his hand resting on the hilt of his sword, arguing with a horseman.

A hush fell over the crowd as the door of the great hall burst open. In the doorway stood Telerhyde, tall for a Human, thick chested and powerful. His once-black hair now shone silver like the hilt of his sword. His scarlet cloak swept the ground behind him as he strode across the bluestones of the courtyard to the gate, his own men stepping back respectfully. "Who goes here?" he demanded.

"Eacon Gleese wishes shelter, M'Lord." Ruf Nab's voice was almost a snarl.

As he spoke, the ornate cart heaved and creaked, groaning under a great load. The curtains parted and bejeweled fingers appeared. Tym was amazed by the Human who emerged. He was huge not only in height, for there he stood as tall as Telerhyde himself, but in girth. *He's as big as a horse!* thought Tym in shocked disbelief that all the tales he had heard were true.

Eacon Gleese wore a splendid purple robe caught at his bulging throat with a large gold clasp. His hair was cut short and curled about his face in the fashion popular in The Perime of Moer, making his head seem small in comparison to his spectacular body. Tym edged across the courtyard to see better. Crowning that incredible bulk were the most beautiful features Tym had ever seen on a man—large, deep-set eyes, a long, aquiline nose, and full, rounded lips. As the lips parted in a generous smile, Tym felt a tremor of fear, as though a snake were loose in the hayloft.

"My dear Lord Telerhyde!" The Eacon spoke in a melodious voice, but there was no warmth in Telerhyde's tone.

"Eacon Gleese."

"Forgive me for this unannounced visit, but I heard in Elea that your youngest son has reached his Sword-Naming. I thought I should come by and offer my heartfelt congratulations."

"Thank you," Telerhyde replied, with a stiff dignity.

"That is your youngest son, isn't it? The one born in Harkynwood?" Before Telerhyde could reply, Eacon Gleese went on. "Also, I'm afraid, I must throw myself upon your mercy. I'm returning from an errand in The Perime. We landed this morning after a rough crossing, and at this late hour we find ourselves without shelter. I would rather not have to bother you on such an occasion, but I have a child with me." He pulled the curtains with a meaty hand to reveal a delicate, pretty girl, blond and fair-skinned. Too old to be a child, Tym observed, nor yet a woman, either. She shrank back from the men in the courtyard, hiding her face. "She's my poor dead sister's daughter, Melloryth. I would not have her sleeping in a field."

His words, simple as they were, had an odd effect on Tym. Although he knew better, he felt a rush of compassion for the blond girl and her large companion.

"You are welcome to what we have," Telerhyde said, his

voice a mask of courtesy. "Ruf Nab, find a room for The Eacon and the child. His men can stay in the stable." He turned back to The Eacon. "We dine late tonight, at moonrise. You are welcome to join us in the great hall."

"You are most gracious, Lord Telerhyde," The Eacon replied, bowing as deeply as his large girth would permit.

Chapter 3

Melloryth waited until the baggage was brought in before she slipped through the door.

"Melloryth! Curse her. Where is that girl?"

She clapped her hands over her ears and ran, her bare feet slapping softly on the cold stone floor of the corridor. If she couldn't hear her uncle, she couldn't disobey him. If she didn't disobey him, she would remain pure and good. Which she would rather be, since anything else made him so excited and angry. But she wanted to see the mountains.

She had not minded the sea voyage, for she had grown up by the sea and felt comfortable with it, although the roll and lurch of the ship had reminded her of the terrible insecurity she had felt since her parents' deaths. She wept often, but she had her own compartment on the ship and no one paid her much attention. But the trip overland found her closed within the curtains of the bumpy cart, constantly in the presence of her uncle. There was little room and she had to fight to keep from sliding down the pillows and bumping into his huge, soft body. The sweet scent he wore made her dizzy in the close confines of the cart.

She was exhausted upon her arrival at Crowell. As The Eacon threw aside the curtains and revealed her to Telerhyde, she had caught a glimpse of something distant, so huge that it filled the horizon for as far as she could see. As one who had spent all her short life by the sea, she understood instantly that here was something that could make a difference to her. The mountains of Morbihan were the first mountains she had ever seen.

At the end of the hall, the door to the courtyard was ajar and she slipped through, her uncle's voice lost in the squeak of door hinges. The late-afternoon sun lighted the four stone towers which rose up above her, leaving the courtyard shadowed beneath a bright sky. To one side, a flight of stairs led upward and Melloryth gathered up her skirt and sprinted up them, scrambling, desperate that her uncle not find her before she saw the mountains again.

Atop the ramparts, the glare of the sun made her squint. She turned away and gasped. In the distance the Trollurgh Mountains rose up amber and purple before her. They were serene, powerful, and it seemed to her that they were the pillars and arches that supported the sky. All the dread and loneliness that she had felt in the past months were lifted by the sight of them. She leaned against the protective wall of the tower and exclaimed softly, "Ah!"

Nearby, a movement caught her eye. She had thought the ramparts empty, but one of the men who had argued with her uncle stood near her. He leaned, as she did, against the wall, gazing into the distance. The late-afternoon breeze quickened and stirred the folds of his red cloak. She watched him warily, but he seemed oblivious to her presence. She turned her attention to the mountains again and felt her heart exulting in her chest, soaring up as the peaks soared up above her. She leaned out over the wall and felt the clean bite of cool air against her cheeks.

"You can feel the glacier in the air," a voice said.

"What?" she gasped. The man was looking at her now. He seemed tall and stern, but his voice was kind.

"The cold breeze. Even in midsummer, you can feel the glacier."

"What's a glacier?" she asked.

"A great river of ice that's trapped in the mountains." He waved an arm at the snowy peaks. "It never melts, but flows slowly into the sea. Can you feel it?"

She nodded, leaning out again to catch the chill breeze on her face, imagining the frozen, sluggish river flowing slowly to the sea. "Have you been to the mountains?" she asked. "Who lives there?"

"I've been there many times," he replied. "All the animals there are white. Wolves and goats, foxes and bears—trolls live there, too, and clothe themselves in the white skins of animals."

She nodded, for it seemed she had known that. For a moment she imagined herself beautiful, clothed in a handsome white fur robe.

"What's your name, child?" the man asked. He spoke to her in a kind way and her shyness melted before him.

"I am Melloryth." She curtsied.

"And I am Telerhyde." He bowed low.

"Eacon Gleese is my uncle," she said, hoping to impress him.

"Yes, I know Eacon Gleese." He said the name in a curious way that made her shudder.

"My uncle came to visit and took care of me when my mother sickened. She has died and now I am my uncle's ward. He said I must leave The Perime of Moer and live here with him."

"I'm very sorry for your loss," Telerhyde said. "I hope you'll be happy in Morbihan."

"My uncle says this is a very evil place, which must be cleansed by fire and sword."

"Oh, I'm sure he does," Telerhyde said so quietly that Melloryth looked up at him questioningly. "But he's wrong. This is a wonderful place. Look," he pointed toward the beckoning mountains. "Those are the Trollurgh Mountains. They divide Morbihan right down the middle like a great wall. And see the Great Escarpment—that reddish cliff that rises up there in the distance? How the deep green laps about the foot of the mountains like a fine robe?"

"It's very beautiful," she said.

"Oh, it is. That's the Harkyn."

She drew back. "The demons live there."

"There are no demons in Morbihan!" Telerhyde laughed. "The Isle of Morbihan is a family and we Humans are only one set of brothers and sisters. We live here in the meadow-lands along the coast. Our Other brothers and sisters live in

Harkynwood—Elves, Ogres, Peskies. The Dwarves live high
in the foothills, where they find the iron and gold they work
with. And the trolls live higher still, right up on the mountain
peaks."

"Are the trolls the best of all because they are so high?"

"No. Some think the trolls are the least of all, outcasts and
thieves. But I believe we are best when all of us are together.
Then we are The Five Tribes and very powerful. Look, here
comes a Dwarf now. You can see how fine a fellow he is. Up
here, Ruf!" he called.

The powerful figure moved effortlessly up the steps. "My
Lord. I see you've found the child. The Eacon"—again the
word made a shudder weaken Melloryth's limbs—"The
Eacon's like a crazed man, looking for her."

And then her uncle was there, laboring up the stairs, sweat
beading his forehead, the gold rings that encircled his fat fingers gleaming as he reached out to her. "My child, you must
not abuse the hospitality of our host! I feared I had lost you."
He pulled Melloryth to him in a hug, patting her shoulder,
holding her hand. The sweet scent he wore rose up around
her, overpowering the keen, glacier-filled breeze. His great
bulk blotted out the mountains.

Chapter 4

"To the kitchen, quick!" cried the cook's assistant. "We've
so many guests for dinner that Cook needs help!"

Tym enjoyed working in the kitchen on the rare times he
was called to it, and this night was no exception. The arous-
ing aroma of food delighted him and during the evening he
managed, when no one was looking, to taste the contents of
each pot. He set tables, found extra chairs, and burned his
fingers taking bread from the oven. Juggling the hot loaves,
he bumped into Ruf Nab at the kitchen door. The Dwarf
frowned dourly.

"Here, what are you so gloomy about?"

"Didn't you see who's come?"

"Aye, The Eacon. Small difference he'll make. There's so many guests now, they're sleeping in tents in the cow pasture, some of them."

Distaste curled Ruf Nab's lips. "Telerhyde gave him shelter. *I'd* give him a cold sword."

"Now, Ruf, Telerhyde knows what's best. Besides, The Eacon doesn't seem like he's such a bad fellow, these days. Hold the door, will you? And carry a few of these, but watch it, they're hot."

Ruf Nab gingerly accepted two loaves of bread that were as long as he was tall. "Telerhyde tries too hard to be fair," he complained as he followed Tym into the kitchen. "One can't afford fairness when you're dealing with New Faith bigots like Gleese. You didn't live in Morbihan when he tried to rule, Tym. You don't remember the burnings."

"I heard," Tym said. "They called them Brownie Roasts."

"Brownie Roasts!" The Dwarf looked as though he wanted to spit. "Eacon Gleese and the rest of those bigots can call it what they want; it was murder! Dwarfin wives and children forced into the cranberry bogs with hundreds of Elves and Peskies . . ."

Tym shuddered. Thousands of Others had been killed. The soldiers of The Perime had tried to keep the mass murders a secret, but the peat had caught fire and the bogs had smoldered for months. "I know . . ."

"Then you know that The Tyrant of Moer decreed the death or enslavement of all who weren't Human. And he still calls for it, Tym! Eacon Gleese is faithful to The Tyrant, believe me! He hates The Five Tribes. All this trade with The Perime just conceals his real goals. He'd be dressing me in chains and trading slaves right now if it weren't for Telerhyde and Fallon . . ."

"I do know, Ruf!" the north seaman argued as they deposited the loaves of bread on Cook's table. "I know that we won the war twenty years ago!" The Brownie Roasts had occurred during Tym's youth. As a child busy building toy galleys to launch in the bright blue bay on the Outer Isle of Snipe, his childhood had been carefree. But the tales of the outrages on Morbihan reached him as he listened to his fa-

ther talking with other sailors. The horror of it sent him crying to his mother's arms with bad dreams, for when The Perime of Moer savaged Morbihan, everyone in the Outer Isles
trembled with fear.

Eacon Gleese had fought for The Tyrant of Moer, flying
the banners of The New Faith. He had led a huge force of
Perime raiders as they pillaged and murdered the citizens of
Harkynwood. Believers in The Old Faith, Human and Other,
fell to sword and flame. As Tym grew to manhood, he
dreamed of joining with the forces that fought for freedom.
But the battle never touched Snipe Isle's shores and by the
time Tym had joined Telerhyde's service, a young Wizard
named Fallon had proved the power of The Five Tribes' Law
by raising the ancient stone on Wolf's Fang, the first Stone
Moving in a generation. With Magic strong again, Telerhyde's army of lords and Others had swept out of Harkynwood, driving The Perime's forces before them. Morbihan
was free, Eacon Gleese all but imprisoned in The Eacon's
Keep. "You can't go on fighting, Ruf. It's a new time."

"I wonder if The Eacon knows that," Ruf Nab snapped.
"He's an evil Human. He corrupts everything he touches. It's
not a good sign, him arriving on the eve of Nyal's Sword-
Naming."

Before Tym had time to worry about this, he heard a voice
calling his name. "The brandy! Tym, get out there and serve
the brandy!" cried Cook.

Tym sampled it first, found it excellent, and filled the tall
flagon used for formal occasions. Elfin brandy is powerful
stuff, to be sipped, not quaffed. After the first few toasts, it
was slow work. Yet there were so many gathered in the
hall—all the spare tables had been set out—that there was no
time to rest.

The guests were jovial, for a Sword-Naming was a happy
occasion in a Human household, the public proclamation of a
young man's coming of age. In the dedication of his sword
was the first oracle of what his life might become. The prosperous and the not-so-prosperous, the mighty lords and the
simple farmers of Fensdown Plain, the Humans and Others
who were all Telerhyde's friends had come to celebrate with
him. They had brought their families (the children were

being fed separately in the courtyard that adjoined the kitchen, under the watchful eyes of Cook's daughters and some village girls), and all were attired in their finest clothes and on their best behavior. As was Telerhyde's custom, Human sat with Other, rich dined with poor, and all enjoyed the bounty of Crowell's wealth.

Tym was excited and anxious that everything about Nyal's Sword-Naming go just right. He observed that a large amount of brandy was being drunk at the table of several young Humans, sons of the Lords of the North. "Perhaps you want some water, sir?" he suggested to Nedryk of Fanstock, but was met with a derisive laugh.

"Pour the brandy, boy," Nedryk said. Turning to a friend, he added, "Telerhyde runs a strange household. In Fanstock we don't let the kitchen boys tell us how much to drink!"

Tym, who had known Nedryk for years, and had even courteously held the young lord's horse that morning, ignored the offense. He was used to being overlooked, mistaken for someone else, or simply unrecognized. In part, it was his bland, agreeable face. But it was also his determined effort not to stand out. In Tym's opinion, those who stood out often did more work than those who didn't. He filled Nedryk's glass half-full and then moved on, obstinately pretending that he did not see the young lord's repeated gestures that he fill it to the brim.

From across the great hall, Telerhyde summoned him with a glance. When Tym had filled his chalice, Telerhyde nodded his head toward the Ogre who sat by his side. "And would you see to His Majesty."

Tym was fond of Ogres. The largest Other of all the members of The Five Tribes, they were hairy, shaggy fellows. In their native state they usually went about naked but for their dense, dark fur which covered their entire body. This one wore a short kilt about his wide waist in honor of the public occasion. Beside him an older female, her mane aged silver halfway down her back, wore a baggy tunic. She rested the fingertips of her huge hand on the lip of a large bowl of iced strawberries and mint leaves, Ogre delicacies.

He was Ur Logga, king of the Harkynwood Ogres, a favorite of Tym's because of his patient manner and predilection for storytelling. Muscles bulged in his shoulders as he leaned back to let the slight Human closer to the table. He smiled, revealing long canine teeth. "My thanks," he murmured with a growl. She was Bin Laphet, elder of the same clan. She covered her cup and shook her head when Tym turned to her.

"As I have told you many times," Telerhyde was saying to Eacon Gleese, who sat across the table from him, "this is a Human problem. Humans must solve it with their own resources." Tym paused to listen. Lord Landes, Telerhyde's chief advisor, leaned forward attentively. Fallon pushed himself back from the table and waved away Tym's brandy, frowning.

The Eacon nodded vigorously until several chins shook. "But you must agree with me that a solution is essential. The very quality of Human life is at stake."

"That's New Faith exaggeration," Landes objected.

"Nay, My Lord!" said The Eacon so sharply that his honey-sweet voice stilled the boisterous voices at nearby tables. "This is not my faith against yours, no matter how you wish it were. This is life or death for Humankind!"

Again Tym felt that strange rush of feeling, like a sense of kinship toward the fat man.

"Oh come, Gleese," muttered Fallon, half to himself.

"Humans need land!" The Eacon continued with passion. Heads turned at other tables. "The cities are crowded beyond bearing. Humans sicken and die there. Little children grow up in unimaginable squalor! Yet in our heartland are thousands of acres of uninhabited land!"

Telerhyde put up a restraining hand. "This is not conversation for a dinner gathering," he said in a low tone. Tym melted back into the shadows. A hush fell over the dinner guests as everyone turned to the central table.

The Ogres were clearly visible from every corner of the room, for they were head and shoulders taller than any Human at the banquet. Bin Laphet looked away in embarrassment. Ur Logga's face darkened, taking on a purple cast. "The Harkyn is the sacred heart of Morbihan," he said softly. "I would not have anyone suffer, but since the days of Kythra, the forest has remained untouched by Humans."

The Eacon did nothing to conceal his contempt for the Ogre. "I am asking the question of Telerhyde," he insisted.

"Since you are too rude to listen to my guest, it is a question I will answer yet again," Telerhyde said, evenly. "For one thing, as you well know, the problem exists in only two cities—Flean and Elea, the ports open to trade with The Perime."

"The only towns in Morbihan worthy of being called cities!" The Eacon retorted. "Human cities are the cradle of art and culture, the bedrock of prosperity for any nation. The rest of Morbihan is nothing but provincial towns, farms, and forest. Believe me, I have the interests of Morbihan at heart . . ."

"Our culture comes from the strength of The Five Tribes, Eacon."

Eacon Gleese snorted. "A little Elfin leather work? Dwarfin metallurgy? You call that culture? Or art? The natives of The Perime bring with them the ability to organize a nation! To make it strong and follow the natural destiny of Humans! Where you see a forest, they see timbers for ships! Where you see a bogland, they see a prosperous farm!"

Telerhyde cut him off with a gesture of his hand. "Where I see refugees from The Perime, I see poverty and misery and ignorance. I feel sorry for the poor Humans trapped in the cities—and they are poor! The poverty in Elea is heartbreaking—but the poor are refugees from The Tyrant of Moer, not citizens of Morbihan."

"Have you no compassion? History tells us that all Humans came originally from Moer," The Eacon objected.

"Centuries ago, Eacon. Morbihan has shaped us, cradled us in The Old Faith. We are Morbihanians now, our allegiance is to The Five Tribes. Too many of The Tyrant's refugees bring with them The New Faith. They want freedom for themselves, yet think it is their holy duty to destroy the freedom of the Others. They have to learn to respect our customs. Besides, Morbihan is not big enough to be home to all who flee the masters of The Perime. Many will have to return to The Perime or travel on to the Outer Isles."

"There is more than enough room!" exclaimed The Eacon. "The forest could be home to ten thousand souls!"

"And let Morbihan fall under the sway of The New Faith?" jeered a Peskie from a nearby table.

"How long before the fires would be burning again?" called Ruf Nab. "How long before we're in another war?"

"Eacon, we are not fools!" Landes said. "When The New Faith rules, subjugation by The Perime of Moer is close at hand!"

The Eacon shook his head. "No, no, My Lord. That is old prejudice! To hold faith in The New Faith, as you call it, is not always to be loyal to The Perime. These poor Humans are but helpless refugees, seeking only that we open our homeland to them."

"You all miss the point!" Telerhyde slammed down his chalice, staining the tablecloth with drops of brandy. "The Harkyn is not ours to give away! The forest is the home of the Others—sacrosanct to them. Those who would take it from them are as much thieves as those who would take Crowell from me! We fought a war about this once, My Lord Eacon."

"And finally we come to the truth!" The Eacon cried, his voice ringing through the hall. "You insist on putting Brownies before Humans! Letting Humans suffer while demons flourish!" With a flourish he pointed a finger at the Ogres. "You set a place at your table for demons! Is this how The Old Faith has corrupted Morbihan?"

Tym glared at the brandy pitcher, blaming its contents for his confusion. The Eacon's words were hateful, yet his golden tone of voice was compelling.

"Gleese, sit down," Fallon said sharply. "What a tiresome bore you've become." He turned to Ur Logga, who was staring at his lap in an agony of embarrassment. "Forgive The Eacon, Your Majesty. Although he would rather forget, I can remember the time before he became an apostle of The New Faith. He and I studied Magic together when we were both young."

"We have all made mistakes, Fallon," The Eacon hissed.

"That was before he found his New Faith so profitable. He was earnest about Magic in those days," The Wizard went on, loudly enough so that all could hear. "He wanted nothing more than to receive a Gift. In fact, when I received my own

Gift, Gleese confided in me that he wished to be a great wizard." An appreciative titter filled the room. "And listening to you this evening, it is clear you *have* received a Gift. Your eloquence, which you ignorantly turn against The Law."

"If I possess eloquence, it is to serve The Tyrant, to be used in his glory," The Eacon murmured, dabbing wine from his lips.

"If that is how you prefer to believe," Fallon said mildly, "so be it. But be careful, Gleese. If a Gift is used against The Law, it will turn upon its user."

"The only law is the law of The Perime!" The Eacon proclaimed. "Others are spawned by the evil one and must give way before The New Faith!"

Telerhyde rapped the table with his knuckles. "You violate The Peace with such talk, sir!" He turned to the Ogres, who were staring miserably at their dinner plates. "Your Majesty, Elder Bin, please accept my apologies. I am mortified that you had to hear such drivel in my house."

"I apologize if my beliefs have offended," Gleese said smoothly, not looking at the Ogres. "But one day Humans will have to answer the questions you refuse, Lord Telerhyde!"

It seemed to Tym that a smile of triumph lighted the greedy face of the corpulent Eacon as he signaled for more brandy. The rest of the meal was finished in uneasy silence, each guest lost in solitary thought.

Chapter 5

Ever since the Battle of Harkynwood had established an uneasy peace in Morbihan a generation before, Lord Telerhyde, Lord Landes, and Fallon the Wizard had guided Human policy in Morbihan. Lord Landes, who was Cyna's father, was Telerhyde's staunchest friend. A stocky, powerful Human, he was more suited to the directness of combat than the subtleties of peace. He took great pride that he was often called

Telerhyde's right hand, just as Fallon was indifferent that he was known as Telerhyde's left. Throughout the Harkyn it was felt that, without Fallon's power and wisdom, Morbihan would have been lost to The Perime years before.

Cyna enjoyed being Fallon's only student. She particularly enjoyed the privileged time which she spent alone with him. As his apprentice, it was her right to ask questions concerning all she did not understand. While often she felt she understood a great deal, the events of the previous night had aroused her curiosity.

"It's true," Fallon told her as he sat having his lunch beneath the apple tree in the courtyard. "Gleese and I apprenticed together. I always thought he had more talent than I, but who can tell these things? He was certainly more ambitious and his ambition has spoiled him."

"But how did a wizard become an eacon of The New Faith?" Cyna's stormy eyes were dark and troubled.

Fallon loved to talk of Magic and The Law. He cut a chunk of cheese and waved it like a teaching-stick. "As you are learning, Cyna, to become a wizard—or a witch—one must receive a Gift. All Gifts come from the power of The Law and are magical. But I think that Gleese, because of his great talent, had expectations of a great Gift.

"When I received my Gift of shapechanging, he scoffed at me. Shapechanging to him was a trick to entertain children— he aspired to clairvoyance or even prophecy! Yet, more and more it became clear that his Gift was eloquence. Which is a fine Gift, but he thought it even more lowly than shapechanging and was ashamed. He left his apprenticeship and I think he spent some years in The Perime. I saw little of him until he began to preach The New Faith and the hatred with which he twists Human minds. It is a dark side of Humans, Cyna, that often, if we cannot have what we desire, we will try to destroy it."

She thought about that while Fallon lavished butter upon thick brown bread and spread it with honey. "What did you mean when you said a Gift will turn on its user, Master?"

"The Law is very strict; it is not an arbitrary figurehead. Gleese believes his Tyrant rules by the will of The Vorsai, a great force that he thinks of as being like a man who bestows

favors upon those he approves and ill luck upon those he
hates. But that is too petty a way for the universe to run. The
Law does not approve or dislike anyone or anything. To The
Law, it matters not whether a being believes or not, or even
is good or bad, by our lights. The Law works for The Eacon
and The Tyrant of The Perime as well as it works for me or
for that snail crawling on a leaf. And to receive the power of
The Law through a Gift, and then to turn the Gift into a tool
of hatred and destruction, will create only hatred and destruction for the hater."

"Which is why you always say a Gift must be expressed
with compassion and creativity?"

"Correct, if compassion and creativity are what you wish
for your life. But later on you will understand more. When
you receive your Gift, you will know the guiding force of the
universe firsthand. All your questions will be answered.
Until then, go and meditate upon the success of the ceremonies tonight, for I believe Nyal will return this afternoon."

"Yes, Master Fallon."

In the great hall she passed her father, who was talking
with a group of Humans.

"Cyna, you pretty thing," called Landes fondly, "do you
know Lord Adler? My daughter, Cyna."

"My Lady." Lord Adler bowed low. Mindful of the pres-
tige inherent in her sky-blue witch's robes, Cyna merely
nodded her head in his direction. Although she was still an
apprentice, she enjoyed the privilege that Magic workers
held over others. Adler was a handsome young man with a
hawklike face and great piercing eyes. Although he was not
much older than her brother Nedryk, he was a powerful lord
of the North, whose land holdings included the city of Elea,
known to the inhabitants of Harkenwood as The Wolf's Eye.
"Nedryk has told me much about you," Adler said, smiling at
her.

"All of it untrue, I assure you," Cyna smiled, her eyes
darting toward her brother, who stood slightly apart as usual,
watching from the perimeter of the group. He was darkly
handsome, Cyna's masculine counterpart. On the third finger
of his right hand he wore a heavy gold ring.

"I hope not, Lady, for he has said wonderful things."
Adler bowed again.

Cyna smiled, but Adler's flattery left her with an uncomfortable feeling. Mouthing polite phrases, she left them, eager suddenly for the quiet of meditation.

"Cyna, wait!"

"Ned!" She waited while he caught up to her.

"You've hardly said hello," he said accusingly.

"You seemed very busy."

He caught her by the hand and led her to an empty room where sun streamed through the window. "You're still angry with me?"

"I have nothing to be angry about, Ned," she said coolly. "You must live your life in your own way."

"You don't mean that. You think I should have stayed with Fallon. That I should have waited even longer for my Gift. I'd be the oldest apprentice in the history of Morbihan, Cyna!"

She sighed and sat on the cold stones of the window ledge. "No I don't really think that, not anymore. I'm awaiting my own Gift, Ned, I know how you must have felt." She held his left hand up so that the sun reflected off his gold ring and made bright circles of light on the ceiling of the room. "But you had won your Healer's ring, you were working with the greatest wizard of our age—you might have had a little more patience, not thrown away your whole future."

"You've been waiting for only two years, Cyna. I waited nearly four!"

Cyna shook her head. She had argued with Ned before and always felt he only half listened to her. "Your ring is on the wrong hand," she said, drily.

"Yes, I know. I'm not a Healer any more."

"Fallon still says you were his best student."

"He does? Too bad he never told me, when it might have done some good. But enough of grumpy old men, how are you? I understand from Father—speaking of grumpy old men—that you've been in the woods living with Ogres!" He made a mock roar, lurching toward her with what was a fair imitation of an Ogre's embarrassed smile.

"Ned stop that!" Cyna cried, but his mimicry was so exact

that she fell back laughing. She tousled his hair fondly, then moved aside on the narrow windowsill, patting it where she wanted him to sit. "My, how dignified you've become," she mocked him gently. "And someone told me that you'd gone to The Perime and taken on airs!"

"But it's true," he said, dropping his Ogre imitation and nimbly sitting beside her so that his legs hung outside the window into the courtyard. "I've been traveling a lot, back and forth from Fanstock to Elea. When I finally left Fallon, I went away for a time. Then, last fall, Father commissioned me to supervise the cargo trains from Fanstock. Other lords have joined us and now I'm a cargo master. I gather the goods, take them by the wagons to the city, bargain for the fairest price, then see them shipped to The Perime."

"How exciting," Cyna said sarcastically.

"That's not fair, Cyna. It's honest work."

"But I thought you talked of studying statecraft with Telerhyde!"

"No, that's for Brandon. I'm an honest tradesman now. I spend half my time in Elea."

"How can you stand to be in a city?"

"I like it. At least I'm never alone. And you? How are your studies with Master Fallon?"

She made a face. "As I said, I'm still awaiting my Gift."

Ned laughed, throwing his head back. "Of course you are! As I'm still waiting for mine! Has he told you to stop asking questions yet?"

"No. He says that my questions will be answered when I receive my Gift."

Ned nodded. "Well, I hope so, Cyna, for your sake. But it's not fair. I studied with him for almost four years, listening to those promises. I think Gifts are Old Faith myths. Fallon encourages them just to keep his apprentices working for him."

"Ned, you've become a cynic!" Cyna scolded, wondering at the shadow that clouded his handsome face for a moment. She searched his eyes. "You like what you're doing and you're doing it well. Perhaps, in a sense, you've found your Gift."

"Oh, Cyna!" For just a moment, Ned's voice held a note

of despair. "It's not like a Gift. It's settling for what I can do. I would give every penny I make in trade for a true Gift!"

Later, when Cyna knelt upon the stone floor of her chamber to meditate, she remembered the pain in Nedryk's clear, blue eyes. She embraced him with her thoughts, wishing him well.

Chapter 6

Nyal rode through the night until the moon set and the way threatened to become too dark. Then he tethered his horse beside a small stream where lush grasses grew, wrapped himself in his cloak, and lay down on the bare ground. But despite his exhaustion, sleep refused to come. The voice of Broderick returned again and again, tormenting him with questions. How could it be that Telerhyde, renowned for his honesty, had lied to everyone and raised a son who was not his own? And if Telerhyde was not his father, who was?

By first light Nyal was in the saddle again, giving the mare her head down the steep foothills and through the northern reaches of Harkynwood. He occasionally dozed in the saddle, jerking himself upright whenever the mare's pace stumbled or faltered. A distant trumpet sounded as Nyal crested Unicorn Tor, late in the afternoon of the second day.

He rode down the sloping meadow to within sight of Crowell's low-roofed hamlet. The Human farmers left Crowell's fields and forests to line the side of the road. They cheered as he passed, waving their hats in the air, marveling at his smudged face and filthy clothes. He had looked forward to this procession since he was a small boy, yet now he scarcely noticed it as he spurred his weary mount toward Crowell Manor.

Telerhyde greeted him just inside the gate. The old soldier's huge hands grasped Nyal's shoulders as he dismounted in the courtyard. "Greetings, warrior!" Telerhyde said, hugging him in a fierce embrace. Brandon came forward eagerly, cuffing Nyal on the shoulder with brotherly affection. Brandon's wife Gwenbar, plump and swollen with their first child, leaned forward to kiss Nyal's grimy cheek. "Welcome, brother," she whispered demurely. "Seven cheers for Nyal!" cried Cook from the pantry. The kitchen workers, peering through the windows and spilling into the yard, began to applaud, some beating kettles with wooden spoons.

"Father—Telerhyde—" Nyal stammered as he slid from his horse, "I must talk with you."

"Of course, my boy. But look at you, you're filthy! Go and clean off some of that grime from the road so you'll be presentable for our guests."

Nyal was too impatient to wait for Tym to heat water on the kitchen hearth. Instead he scrubbed himself from a bucket of cold water in the alley behind the stable. When his skin glowed pink and he was dripping in suds, Tym poured another bucket of cold water over his head. He gasped and whooped, the cold water clearing his head. His tunic was still unlaced and his boots unbuckled when he hurried across the courtyard and climbed the staircase that led to Telerhyde's private chambers. He found Telerhyde in his room talking with Brandon, gazing out over the fields that were Crowell's fortune.

"Sir, Broderick the Dwarf said I'm not your son," he said, without waiting for formalities.

Brandon glanced up in surprise, but Telerhyde only looked at Nyal soberly, waiting for him to go on.

"He said I was born of Magic and betrayal. That the light of Magic and the shadow of betrayal would shape my life. Is it true?"

"Is this the first time you've heard this?" Telerhyde asked.

"No. Ned used to tease me when I was little. And the cook's boy."

"Yes, I knew about the cook's boy. And I had him beaten for it. I didn't know about Nedryk. Brandon, have you heard this?"

Heir to Telerhyde's size and strength, Brandon shrugged his shoulders. "There's always gossip, Father."

"Sit down, Nyal." Telerhyde gestured toward the narrow

bed and Nyal perched on the edge, heart hammering in his chest.

Telerhyde was silent for a moment, as though searching for a way to begin. "When I was young, your mother and I loved each other very much. We had Brandon and your sisters, and we were happy together, here in Crowell. I would have remained here with her all my life and died a happy man, but it finally dawned on me that Others were not so happy, that terrible suffering was happening in Morbihan. You know all this." Nyal nodded.

Those days had been a time that was told again and again in song and story. A time that had become a part of the very fabric that bound The Old Faith and The Five Tribes together. Nyal had grown up hearing of the unspeakable Brownie Roasts, of Telerhyde's heroism in the desperate fight against Eacon Gleese and The New Faith. How Telerhyde escaped into Harkynwood with only one companion, Lord Landes, and emerged a year later with an army composed of the Lords of the North, Fallon the Wizard, and all the Others, united for the first time in a hundred years as The Five Tribes. How the desperate allies were driven to Wolf's Fang, their backs against the sea. And how finally, rallied by Telerhyde and guided by Fallon, The Five Tribes performed the first Stone Moving in generations and defeated The Eacon's forces. "I know," Nyal said.

They were a rich contrast. The older man was dark and powerful—the very air around him was charged with gravity. Beside him, Nyal seemed slight and pale as he leaned forward, taut with intensity.

"Much happened in that year in the forest," Telerhyde continued softly. "There was confusion, separation, and long months when I was alone. It is natural for rumors to cling to great times."

"Yes, sir," said Nyal. "But am I your son? The Dwarf said . . ."

"I know what the Dwarf said! And you know as well as I do that Dwarves never lie. No, Nyal, you are not my son. But know this: until the day she died, I loved your mother as I love my life. And she loved me." Nyal had paled as Telerhyde spoke. The warrior reached out and grasped his shoulder with rough gentleness. "You are as dear to me as she was. Never doubt that! If you *were* my own son, I could not love you more."

"Who was my father?"

"I swore to your mother and to him that I wouldn't tell you that. Perhaps someday he will tell you himself. Remember that it was an extraordinary time, and extraordinary events happened every day. You were one of them."

Nyal nodded, unable to speak. Brandon reached out to touch Nyal's shoulder, his face grave with concern. Without a word, Telerhyde drew both young men to him, holding them in a fierce embrace as a great oak will shelter its saplings beneath its branches. After a moment, he spoke. "Be silent about this, both of you. It's only fuel for Eacon Gleese's gossip, and if the truth were known, you would have powerful enemies, Nyal."

Nyal stepped back. "But, sir, Broderick wouldn't dedicate my sword to Crowell." Nyal quickly related Broderick's refusal and Firestroker's strange dedication. "When I repeat his words at the Sword-Naming, everyone will know."

" 'To all the Tribes,' " Telerhyde repeated, frowning.

"That's not such a bad dedication, when you think about it," Brandon observed, holding Firestroker up and examining its keen blade and simple hilt by the fading light from the window. "But he might have made the sword with a little more care. It has a nice balance, but no decoration. It's as plain as a poor woodsman's sword. Or a troll's."

"Curse Broderick!" Telerhyde said angrily and both young men looked at him in surprise. "Things are strained enough with The Eacon and the lords of the cities clamoring for space. This is not the time! You can't use that dedication, Nyal."

"But sir . . ."

"No. You'll use the Crowell dedication as Crowell men always have. Say not a word of this to anyone."

"Yes, sir."

"Don't look so worried! This is nothing worth spoiling the occasion of your Sword-Naming! Buckle your boots, for Dragon's sake, boy. Brandon, help him to get ready. He still doesn't know how to dress!"

Brandon winked as he laced up Nyal's tunic. But looking from his brother's dark head to Telerhyde's broad shoulders, Nyal was painfully aware of being very different.

Nyal pondered Telerhyde's reply all afternoon. Father or not, he loved the man and trusted him absolutely. Yet he couldn't help but wonder if his real father would be in the hall this evening, to watch an unknowing son being accepted into The Dragon's service.

That evening, as custom decreed, Nyal entered the great hall after all the guests were assembled. He was dressed simply in a dark green tunic just as The First Warrior had been when he sought The Dragon, his unruly, sun-bleached hair combed and plastered to his head with water by Tym's fierce ministrations. He encountered Fallon near the kitchen door. They exchanged greetings and in a ritualistic motion, Fallon traced a pentagram in the air with his hand to harmonize Nyal with The Law for the ceremony ahead. "You know my apprentice?" Fallon nodded to Cyna, who stood beside him, tall and regal in her sky-blue robe. Her dark hair fell down her back in a heavy braid woven with silver threads.

"My Lady," Nyal stammered.

"Nyal," Cyna replied, nodding her head. The distracted expression on his face stopped her. "Nyal? Don't you remember me?"

"No—I beg your pardon—"

"Nyal! It's me! Cyna!"

"Cyna?"

"Has so much time passed that you've forgotten me?"

"Forgive me, Lady, you've changed."

"And so have you, but I recognized you, nevertheless."

"Forgive me."

Brandon intervened. "Ignore my brother, Lady," he said smoothly. "The libations have gone to his head." He gripped Nyal's elbow and steered him across the room toward the hearth, where Telerhyde stood. "Don't worry about the dedication, brother," he whispered. "Father's right; it would only cause gossip and concern among our city allies. Ned's sister is attractive, isn't she?"

"Who?" asked Nyal.

"Here, Father, take him. He's Elfed-out on hard cider, I'm afraid."

"I am not Elfed-out!" Nyal protested. "I'm sober as The Dragon herself!"

Telerhyde silenced Nyal with a glance.

In the center of the room, Finn Dargha, the leader of the Peskie tribe, entertained. A short fellow, he was strongly built like all Peskies. He was plainly dressed in a tight-fitting brown tunic with boots and hat made of brown felt. A companion plucked a tune on a shalkleon, a stringed instrument made of bone and rosewood. Finn doffed his hat and was greeted by cheers and whistles from the guests.

"Sing!" cried The Snaefid of the Dwarves, and Ur Logga the Ogre king applauded.

"To blast a hearth
Into a heap,
To break your heart
And make you weep,
Marry a witch
And try to keep
Her as a wife.
Ruin your life!"

The Peskie's voice was a rich, high tenor and he sang with relish, pausing to roll his eyes, making his audience laugh.

"The sky will thunder
The earth will quake
Blown asunder
The stones will shake
If you dare
A marriage make
Of a wizard's son
To a Gifted One."

Banging their mugs on the tabletops, the guests joined him for the last verse.

"But power will
To power breed

And might and Magic's
Passions feed
To fall like rain
Upon the seed
Of Kythra's plan
For Morbihan!"

As the cheers and clapping died away, Telerhyde nodded toward a raised platform by the hearth, and Nyal stepped onto it, facing the guests. "Let the Sword-Naming begin!" Telerhyde said. At his gesture, Ruf Nab, hidden behind the kitchen door, began a roll on a drum. The guests fell silent.

"Who goes here?" Telerhyde spoke the formal Human dialect, reciting words that Human males had repeated since they first came to Morbihan, more than a millennium before.

"I am Nyal of Crowell," Nyal intoned. "I seek to serve The Dragon."

Telerhyde turned to the guests. "A new warrior stands before us. Who among you will sponsor him?"

"By the grace of The Dragon's wisdom, I will," Landes proclaimed. He raised an arm in a theatrical gesture, his voice rising in a singsong cadence. "Nyal of Crowell, I call upon you to put aside youth and folly."

"I am ready," Nyal said.

"In accordance with the laws and customs of the Humans of Morbihan, have you a token of your manhood?"

Nyal drew Firestroker from its scabbard. The blade gleamed in the torchlight and the hilt was warm in Nyal's hand. He swung the sword and its passage through the air made a tearing sound. "I hold in my hand the token of my new state," he said clearly, "wrought by a master smith for my hand only."

"It's as ordinary as a pitchfork!" whispered a young farmer in the back of the hall.

Nyal stood rock-still, a flush slowly creeping up his neck and face. He cleared his throat and began to recite with the Human love of ritual. "Broderick the Dwarf dedicated this sword——" His voice faltered, then went on. "He dedicated this sword to the strength and prosperity of Crowell. To the fertility of the fields, of the flocks, of the Humans who tend them."

In ancient days, a Sword-Naming was a week-long ceremony in which the sword was plunged into the earth, used to sacrifice cows and ewes, and finally worn by the new warrior in a heated and public ceremonial marriage. But Humans were nothing if not thrifty, and the gentle wisdom of The Old Faith had mellowed this ceremony. Now, no livestock were lost and feasting and the giving of presents were all that remained of the old days. Nyal held the sword aloft. "Broderick has made this sword and he named it Firestroker."

"May Firestroker carve your destiny, Nyal," Landes cried. "Whenever your deeds are spoken, may Nyal and Firestroker bring honor upon the Warriors of The Dragon and the Humans of Morbihan."

"My thanks, noble sponsor," Nyal intoned. "I will strive to uphold the honor of The Dragon." In a rich tenor voice, he began to sing "The Song of Dragon." From around the room, the deep and resonant voices of the other lords joined him. When they were done, he held Firestroker up for a moment more, than returned the sword to its scabbard.

"Congratulations!" Landes said heartily. The guests applauded politely.

Nyal felt strangely empty. Firestroker, which had vibrated like a living thing in his hand at the forge, felt cold and heavy in the great hall of Crowell.

Telerhyde's voice rose to the booming roar that had so often rallied his loyal followers. "My boy," he declared, "in celebration of your new state, the badge of seneschal is yours." With a swift motion Telerhyde leaned forward and hung a small golden seal about Nyal's neck. "Be the keeper of my stockyard and fields."

"Thank you, sir." Nyal flushed with pleasure.

A shout of approval filled the hall, for it was unusual for so high a position as seneschal to be bestowed upon one as young as Nyal.

Beaming, Landes waited for the hall to quiet, then held out a shield made of oak and iron. On the shield's face were incised the twin dragons of Crowell. "May this be a fitting companion to your sword."

The gift givers formed a line. Each present was displayed and applauded with typical Human delight in possessions. From Brandon he received a helmet. From Ruf Nab, a gold drinking cup. Ur Logga presented a beautifully carved stone urn.

Cyna stepped forward. "An Elf-knit cloak to keep you warm." It was rust-colored and handsome. Green leaves were embroidered along the edges of the cowl.

"Thank you, My Lady." His fingers brushed hers as he took the cloak.

Fallon was the last of the guests. He smiled broadly, torch-light gleaming in his bright blue eyes. "Nyal, behold!"

At the sound of hooves, everyone turned. Tym appeared in the doorway with the chestnut stallion. Torchlight made the horse's coat gleam, reflecting off his mane and tail like a shower of sparks. Muscle swelled his arched neck and his hooves rang on the stone floor. Nervous at the sight of so many people, he pranced sideways. He would have shied out the door, but Tym held him tightly. A murmur of admiration swept the guests. Nyal had stepped down from the platform and the crowd parted to let him through.

"Be careful, My Lord," Tym cautioned. "He bites."

But Nyal was oblivious, stroking the horse's head, brushing the forelock back from his dark eyes. "He's magnificent!" he exclaimed. "Thank you, Master Fallon."

"I'm glad you like him. He has a fine spirit, though he's not trained yet. He's wild-bred from the forest herds near Tooth Bay," Fallon said. "The Peskies caught him in their shalk nets a few months ago. They called him Avelaer—the Wind Thief."

"Avelaer," Nyal repeated.

"Ride him, Nyal," called Landes.

"He's half-broken, sir, be careful," Tym cautioned again as he led the stallion into the courtyard. It was dusk. As the guests filed out to watch, they carried their brandy cups and took up torches which threw long, flickering shadows across the stones.

Still holding the reins, Tym gave Nyal a leg up. For a moment he thought all would be right. Then Lord Adler thrust his torch aloft and shouted, "Seven cheers for the new war-

rior!" and everyone cried out at once, applauding. In the enclosed courtyard, the sound was like a blow. Made frantic by
the waving torches Avelaer spun away from the noise. He
galloped across the courtyard, seeking escape.

"Runaway!" cried Tym, yanked off his feet and losing his
hold on the reins. The chestnut slipped on the smooth stones
of the courtyard, a shower of sparks lighting the ground beneath his feet. Nyal clung to his mane, his balance shaken.
"Sea Prissies save him!" Tym implored.

"Put out your torches! Stand quiet!" Telerhyde commanded. His guests complied, watching in the dim light as
the fear-crazed animal careened across the yard.

Half-unseated, Nyal did not struggle for balance as a lesser
rider might. Instead, as the stallion swerved to avoid a stack
of kegs near the kitchen, Nyal reached forward and seized
the horse's bridle, then let himself fall. He landed on his feet
with one hand on the bridle and an arm firmly wrapped
around the horse's neck. The Human's unexpected weight
jolted the chestnut to a lurching halt. He reared, seeking to
throw off the restraining burden, but Nyal clung to him,
lifted high off the ground. Shaking his head, teeth bared, the
horse stumbled sideways into the kegs and was frightened
afresh as they fell and rolled across the stones.

The horse fought desperately, but Nyal's weight was
firmly attached to his head, Nyal's words whispered into his
ear. At last he slowed, then stopped, head low, sides heaving.
"Good boy," said Nyal, patting his neck. "Easy boy. Stay
back!" he commanded in a low voice as Tym stepped forward. "Stay back and keep everyone quiet." He soothed the
horse a moment longer, and let him look at the barrels. The
stallion snorted, ready to be afraid again, but Nyal spoke to
him and the horse quieted. When he was still, Nyal smoothly
vaulted onto his back. The stallion started, but stood still.

"Good, Nyal, good," said Telerhyde, watching from the
door. "The rest of you, be silent and don't move until he's
finished."

Sitting lightly, Nyal guided the horse about the courtyard,
stroking his neck.

"How did he do that?" marveled Landes.

"Nyal has a way with animals," Fallon observed, smiling.

"Yes, sir," Tym agreed, proudly.

When the horse had circled the yard, stopped, turned, and even taken a few steps backward, Nyal finally stopped beside the stable door and slid off. "Here, Tym, take him now." Dragging Tym behind him, Avelaer bolted into the safety of the barn. Nyal grinned, took a step forward, and nearly crumpled to the ground.

Telerhyde and Brandon carried him into the great hall and sat him on a bench before the lazy summer fire which flickered in the hearth.

"My ankle twisted when we hit the kegs," Nyal said between his teeth.

Fallon bent over him. With quick, gentle fingers he stripped off the boot and cupped Nyal's ankle in his hands. "It's not broken," he said at last.

Telerhyde let out his breath. "Thank The Law."

"But I'm afraid the full moon will come round again before it bears your weight, Nyal," Fallon said.

"The stallion will bear my weight well enough until then," Nyal said.

Landes shook his head. "You should mend first, Nyal. Let your horsetamer geld him and take the edge off his spirit."

"Geld him!" Nyal howled.

Brandon laughed. "Nyal is our horsetamer here at Crowell, Lord Landes. And if I know my brother, he has plans that call for a stallion."

"He's too skittish for a war-horse," Landes said disapprovingly. "He'll never stand for the clash of arms."

"If I were a warrior, I might agree, sir," Nyal said. "But I'm a farmer. Let me breed his hot blood to our cool-headed mares here at Crowell. In a few years you'll pay a fortune to own his colts!"

"Enough about horses," Fallon reproved. "Your ankle swells in the heat of the fire. You need to rest, Nyal. Your Sword-Naming is over."

"But Master Fallon, I can't miss the feast—the drinking . . ."

"You can." The Wizard was abrupt. "Cyna, see he gets put to bed and wrap that ankle."

Cyna was startled. "Master Fallon, perhaps you should see to it. I'm not sure that I . . ."

"Nonsense. You can tend sprains, now. You healed that stable boy well enough. Go."

Nyal ceased his protest and Cyna followed Ned and Brandon as they carried him from the hall.

Chapter 7

Cyna found it difficult to concentrate with her brother and Brandon whispering and joking. Nyal smiled, grey faced, from his narrow cot along the wall.

"Hurry up and give this warrior his healing," Ned said. "He has his sword now, he'll want his pick of maidens." Ned and Brandon giggled like drunken Elves.

"Get out!" Cyna blazed. "Both of you, get out!"

"Cyna, it's just a joke," Brandon objected. "Besides, you can't throw me out of my own brother's room . . ."

"Get out!" she repeated, more loudly. "How can I heal him with the two of you braying like jackasses! Go!" She pointed to the door. With shrugs and raised eyebrows, Brandon and Ned left, Ned glancing over his shoulder to roll his eyes at Nyal. Cyna closed the door firmly behind them.

There was a knock.

"Stay out!" Cyna exclaimed as she jerked it open.

Tym stood stunned in the doorway, The Wizard's herb chest in his arms. "Begging your pardon, Lady," he said indignantly, "I'm only doing The Wizard's business."

"Oh, come in," Cyna said crossly. "Thank you," she added as she took the chest from him.

The fragrance of herbs filled the air as she brushed a fingertip across the tiny bags and bottles, her forehead tense in concentration. She loved herbs. She felt immense satisfaction in knowing that a brew of strawberry leaves would cure an Ogre or Human of diarrhea, or that tormentil, well diluted, would soothe an Elf's inflamed throat. She had memorized the properties of all the known roots and berries and herbs, and now felt confidence well up within her.

Her fingers paused over a small bottle filled with a greenish liquid. "Mother of thyme," she murmured. "Fellow," she said to Tym, who was watching her uneasily from the doorway, "get me something to bind his ankle. Make sure it's strong. And bring another kettle of boiling water from the kitchen."

Nyal watched her, his grey eyes clouded. "Does it hurt very much?" she asked him.

"No," he said. But he flinched and bit his lip as she touched his foot. The ankle was already swollen. He shifted his weight and flinched again. "It does hurt a little," he admitted.

Within the herb chest was a latched door and on it, painted in perfect detail, was the skull of an Ogre. Cyna hesitated for a moment. Carefully, she opened the tiny door. Within, four tiny bottles lay wrapped in cloth. She took the one marked "Henbane" and shook two drops into a mug. She filled the mug with steaming water from the kettle. "Drink this," she ordered Nyal. "It will ease the pain."

Tym returned with long strips of grey Peskie-felt. Cyna waited until the henbane was having its effect, then tightly wrapped the felt around Nyal's ankle. Nyal's eyelids were drooping as she pulled the last strip tight. "Does that hurt?"

"No, it's much better," he smiled.

"You'll sleep now," she told him. "When you awaken, you'll feel better."

"Sleep," he repeated. "I've not slept since Broderick forged my sword. Curse him!" His eyes opened wide and he stared about the room. Alarmed, Cyna knelt beside him. She had never seen it happen before, but she knew from Fallon that sometimes dangerous herbs, like nightshade and henbane, could have the opposite effect from that intended.

"Curse him!" Nyal repeated. He seized Cyna's hand as she leaned close to look into his eyes. "Why can't Dwarves lie?" he demanded.

"They never do," she replied, masking her surprise. "It's part of being a Dwarf." His eyes were dilated and unfocused. The herb was working.

"Curse me," he said weakly. He struggled to stay awake. "Curse me," he said again. "I'm not Telerhyde's son!"

"Here, sir, you're out of your head!" Tym said sharply.

"Shhhhhhh," soothed Cyna. "It's a bad dream." She held Nyal's hand and felt him fighting sleep.

"A stranger's son," he said, and lost the battle, his fingers twitching as though gripping a dream-sword.

She put her ear to his chest. His heartbeat was strong, his breathing rhythmical. She sighed in relief. "I gave him a strong herb," she explained to Tym, who stood, aghast, at the foot of the bed. "It can cause strange dreams. He'll sleep till morning."

"I'll stay by him," Tym said.

"No, I'll stay," Cyna said firmly. "Go back to the stable. Come to me at first light, for I'll need your help to soak his ankle." Tym was reluctant and finally Cyna had to order him out the door.

The truth was, she had forgotten to perform Fallon's teaching of the day before. When Tym was finally gone, she knelt by Nyal's felt-wrapped ankle, deep in meditation. Fanned by the evening breeze, a single candle threw moving shadows on the wall and ceiling. Cyna tried to picture Nyal walking, strong and healthy, but her imagination rebelled. The best she could do was to see him riding the chestnut stallion at a furious pace. Firestroker hung at his side and her father's gift, the shield, was slung on the pommel of the saddle. He rode in pursuit, pursued. "Now, why did I think that?" she wondered, and then chastised herself for making up stories rather than doing the business of healing. But no other images would come to her and finally she, too, fell asleep.

Tym disregarded Cyna's instructions and spent the night sleeping in the hall outside Nyal's door. Although he felt uneasy that the apprentice witch had usurped his duties, the late-night celebrating (as well as the flask of brandy which Ruf smuggled up to him) ensured that he had a sound sleep. When he awoke, he was lying on the floor where sunshine streamed through the window, blinding him and making the inside of his head feel like steel scraping stone. He shielded his eyes with his arm and tried to burrow into the warm floor.

"Tym!" came Nyal's voice through the door.

"Sir!" he cried, leaping to his feet. He slicked down his hair with spit on his palm and tugged the biggest wrinkles from his tunic. "Sir!" he said again and opened the door to Nyal's room.

Dressed only in the trousers he had worn the night before, Nyal stood beside his bed. He hopped on one leg, the other held up stiffly, its felt wrapping loose and draped across the floor. "Tym, get me my clothes," he ordered.

"Fetch Fallon, Tym," said Cyna. She stood between Nyal and the door, her fists clenched.

"Tym!" roared Nyal.

"Sir!" Tym entered the room, trying to slide past Cyna to the chest where Nyal's clothes were kept. Cyna seized his arm.

"Tym, your master has had a powerful herb and is not of sound mind. He's been hurt and he wishes to hurt himself further. Pay no attention to him." To Nyal she said in tones usually used to reason with a child, "Ned and Brandon will be right up to carry you wherever you wish to go."

Tym hesitated, looking from one to the other.

"I will not be carried about like a baby!" Nyal said between clenched teeth. "This is my Sword-Naming. There are guests to thank, there are pledges to be made! I will not"— and he hopped around the bed toward the chest—"I will not ruin the ceremony!"

"Your sword is named and you are already pledged," Cyna snapped, "and your ankle is swollen as big as your head! The rest of the ceremony can do very well without you. Now, either go to bed or wait for Ned and Brandon to carry you down! Tym, help me."

"Tym!" There was a warning edge in Nyal's voice that made Tym hesitate, torn between them. He trusted Cyna's healing powers and was inclined to think she was right, yet habit and devotion drew him to Nyal.

"Fetch Fallon," Cyna said quietly, and Tym, grateful for the compromise, fled.

He found The Wizard in his chamber, dressing for breakfast. "Master Fallon, they need you upstairs. Lady Cyna's told Nyal he can't come down by himself. She wants Ned and Brandon to carry him, and he's in a terrible state of mind, sir. They're carrying on like trolls. Lady Cyna wants you right away."

Fallon reached beneath his long linen underrobe to scratch his scrawny chest. "Of course they're carrying on. Did you call Ned and Brandon? Good. Don't bother. Fetch me a little warm water in a bowl, would you?"

When Tym returned The Wizard was still dressed in his underrobe and stood fluffing his beard before the bronze mirror that hung on the wall. "Thank you. This will help." He splashed the water on his face and fumbled for a towel. "Yes, that's better." He took up a comb and began to straighten his hair and beard, glancing at Tym, who stood impatiently by the door. "Glad to see you, fellow. How's your arm?"

"It's fine, sir. The lady's a fine Healer, even if I had my doubts at first."

"Let me see."

"But sir, they're going at each other up there . . ."

"Of course. But let me see your arm."

Tym shifted uneasily while The Wizard carefully inspected his horsebite. The tooth marks had faded to a yellowish green bruise and the joint moved easily without soreness. "Excellent," observed Fallon. "Now, help me dress."

It seemed a waste of time to Tym, for Fallon had but two robes, both exactly alike, sky-blue and belted at his waist. But he held out each one while The Wizard pondered over which to wear. Then Fallon had him dust his sandals and rub tallow on the straps. When he was at last ready, he strolled with agonizing slowness toward Nyal's chamber, pausing at each window to exclaim over the beauty of the view and pausing at length in the hall to explain to Tym how to keep the torches from smoking up the ceiling.

At last they neared Nyal's chamber and Tym heard Nyal's voice raised in anger. Tym cracked open the door and he and The Wizard peeked in. Cyna held a bundle of clothes under her arm. Nyal hopped on one leg and she nimbly avoided him.

"Dragon Fire, give me my clothes!" Nyal cried, hopping to corner her between the window and the bed.

"Take them if you're so strong!" Cyna retorted and leaped across the bed to the other side of the room. Nyal hurled himself upon the bed after her and howled in pain. Cyna saw Fallon at the door and gasped.

In the silence that followed, Fallon stepped into the room. "Cyna, is this the way you care for your patients?"

"Master, I . . ."

He ignored her, turning to Nyal who had sat up on the bed, holding his ankle. "Is this how you listen to your Healer? Have you no respect for Magic?" He looked sternly from one to the other. "Listen," he said. "Listen to each other." He turned to Tym. "Come fellow, show me the way to the great hall, I want breakfast." But once out in the corridor he contradicted himself again and waved Tym away. "On second thought, stay here. Fetch them whatever they need. I would not get between them, however."

Tym agreed. He would have rather gotten between a pair of angry unicorns.

"See what you've done to your ankle," Cyna chided Nyal. "You've twisted it again. You're lucky you didn't break it, carrying on that way. I'll have to strap it up again." Nyal winced as she pulled the felt strips tight. Cyna was feeling rather smug. "As your Healer, I must recommend that you rest."

Nyal sighed and held his head in his hands. "All my life I've looked forward to this day and now that it's here, I wish it weren't."

"But Nyal, that's foolish. People will understand. Let Brandon and Ned help you to the great hall and everything will go on as it should."

He shook his head. "You don't understand. I've just taken my oath of manhood." His eyes were dark and shadowed. "Today is the first day of my life as a man. How can I appear carried in the arms of other men?"

"I'm sorry."

"It's all right. It doesn't seem sensible to you—a witch who reads The Law. You think I'm foolish."

"No." She had so a moment before, but now she looked at him thoughtfully. "A passage from *The Kythrian Predictions* reads: 'Now I begin as I finish, now I start as I stop. From the lowest to the bottom, from the highest to the top.' Fallon has often said that any undertaking must be begun as you would have it finish."

"That's exactly how I feel. First mouthing the words of that oath, now being carried about like a cripple. Is this what my life is going to be like?"

"But that was a beautiful oath." Cyna didn't see Nyal's troubled frown. "And you don't have to be carried in. I only meant that you had to spare your ankle. We could get a pair of stout sticks and you could go to the ceremonies on a pair of crutches."

"At least that's a little better."

"Yes, that's much better. You'll start your new life strong, independent, and healing from an honorable injury."

Chapter 8

A few of Telerhyde's guests remained at Crowell after the rest departed. Fallon, Landes, and Benare were there, along with Adler and other lords of the troubled cities. Each morning they met with Telerhyde in his study, closed the doors, and discussed the problems that confronted Morbihan. The problems of immigration and overcrowding, particularly in the two major ports, Elea and Flean, were great and would not go away. Every ship that arrived from The Perime brought another stowaway.

Lord Landes favored rounding up all the refugees and shipping them back to The Perime. Lord Benare and many of the country lords and farmers supported him. Telerhyde had favored that solution for a time, but now, he argued, there were too many, and more coming every day. To close the harbors would strangle trade.

Fallon spoke often and emphatically. "We fail our land

and its people!" he argued. "Humans grow rich by trade with The Perime, and the cities grow like abscesses."

Landes leaned forward. "Lord Adler, speaking of cities, Elea has been causing some concern among some of us. The Snaefid tells me that Others are in danger of being stoned in the streets. Kidnappings and murder are commonplace!"

"With all due respect, it's a port city, M'Lord. Life in any port is inclined to be rowdy."

"Rowdy!" Fallon exclaimed. "Finn Dargha told me that a Peskie caravan was attacked within the city gates. Not only robbed, but jeered as Brownies!"

"Horrible!" Landes shuddered.

"It's hard in a city to keep the peace, My Lords," Adler said smoothly. "Elea has become a haven for refugees from The Perime. Most are good people, looking for freedom. A few may be Perime agents or spies, but a single incident has been exaggerated out of all reality. My men-at-arms patrol constantly. Just ask Ned. He brings a caravan through at least once a month. Would he trade in a city that wasn't safe?"

"My son enjoys risk," Landes observed.

Telerhyde rapped the table with his knuckles to get their attention. "Lord Adler, I was in Elea not a month ago. It's a dirty, violent place. I don't know how Others feel there, but I know that I didn't feel safe, even surrounded by my men-at-arms."

"It can be very difficult to keep order," Adler admitted. "But it's the price we pay for trade."

"That is what's intolerable," Fallon said. "Some of us insist on trading with an enemy who is opposed to everything we are! I say that Eacon Gleese must go. Exile him and all the rest back to where they came from."

"We live by trade!" Lord Faryll objected. "There's no harm in a little healthy exchange."

"There's harm in believing that trade is more important than the rights of Others," Fallon flared.

"Are you calling me a bigot?" Adler's hawklike face was flushed with indignation.

"I call you a young fool who doesn't know how to run his own city! Your father knew the risks. He kept order in Elea, fed the people, and limited the number of immigrants."

"My father never had these problems," Adler grumbled. "There's just no room left within the walls of the city. Refugees come over impoverished, can't find work, and lie about fomenting trouble. What am I to do, slaughter them?"

Faryll shook his head. "They'll be killed by The Tyrant if we force them to go back. Instead, why not move them out of the cities into the countryside?"

"Settle them in the cranberry bogs near Tooth Bay," Adler urged. "There's plenty of land."

"It's a part of Harkynwood," Fallon objected.

"The Peskies graze the shalk herds there a few weeks each year! The land goes to waste!" insisted Adler.

Telerhyde shook his head. "We'll not touch Harkynwood," he said firmly.

"Then there's no solution," Faryll said with poorly masked exasperation.

"Send them back where they came from, if you can't control them," Landes said. "Only Elea has such outrages."

"Not true," Farryl said, "the city of Flean is just as bad. I hear that Ham Urbid's Ogres refused to enter the city because of the danger of Perime thugs."

"Disgraceful," Landes muttered. The arguments continued through the afternoon and into the evening.

It was part of Cyna's apprenticeship to learn statecraft from Fallon, but long discussions of politics left her bored and exhausted. Healing Nyal became her project. She met with him first thing in the morning to wrap his ankle tightly in strips of coarse Peskie-felt. Often she walked with him to the stables, letting him lean on her to keep his weight off the ankle. He was proud of his new title of seneschal and diligent as he supervised the care of the horses and the milking of the cows.

In the mornings, while the lords argued over the fate of Morbihan, Nyal rode in a cart to the fields outside Crowell and supervised the cutting and gathering of the hay crop. In the afternoons he spent long hours beneath the shade trees in the courtyard, propping up his leg on a stool, talking with Cyna. "You love Crowell, don't you?" she observed.

"It's my home." He thought seriously for a moment. "More than anything, I want to breed the strongest, fastest horses in Morbihan. There's no better place in the world for it than right here. The grass grows so thick up by the Escarpment that we could easily pasture twenty more horses. Even the winters are perfect. The snow lies deep and the days are short, so it's easy to keep the mares quiet before they foal." A smile narrowed his eyes and he reached over his head to pluck an apple from the tree. It was still green, but he bit into it, savoring its sharp tang. "Morbihan is the most beautiful place in the world, and Crowell is the finest part of Morbihan."

Cyna laughed. "Have you seen all the world?"

"I haven't even seen all of Morbihan, but I know I'm right. Don't you think of Fanstock that way?"

But Fanstock, on the tip of Ear Peninsula on the northernmost end of the island, was a cold place with rocky beaches and thin soil. Cyna did not miss the harsh winters or the constant struggle her father waged to feed and clothe his people.

"What is it like to study with Fallon?" Nyal asked her a few days later.

"Difficult. Fallon travels all the time, so it's like being without a home. He's very exacting, but he's a patient teacher. Perhaps because he's always learning. He's studying herbology right now with the Ogres, so we've been staying at Ur Logga's den. Ogres are nice when you get used to their shyness. But it's strange to live underground."

"I hear Ogre cooking is terrible," Nyal said.

"Worse than that, it's boring! How they get so large living on nothing but fruit and lumpy porridge is a mystery even Fallon can't unravel. But Ur Logga is kind. He loves Fallon and he's a thoughtful host. I'm learning a great deal."

"So you'll be a witch?"

She nodded, her eyes shining. "I hope to heal. Fallon says I have talent. My mother was a wonderful Healer. I hope to become as good as she was."

Each morning before the horses were fed and groomed, Nyal offered Avelaer a handful of grain. Before long, the horse stopped shying from his hand and began to greet his arrival at the barn with pricked ears. Nyal and Cyna spent afternoons together, talking.

But on one morning when the air was heavy with summer,

Cyna fell strangely silent as she rewrapped Nyal's ankle. As usual, she accompanied him to the barn. The sun was just up and the courtyard filled with the droning sound of bees at work in the garden that grew outside the kitchen door. Although Nyal's ankle no longer hurt him, the wrapping was tight and he limped with his arm about Cyna's shoulder, leaning a little on her. She walked beside him, her light yellow gown loosely belted at the waist and falling to her ankles.

From the stable came the hammering sound of Avelaer impatiently striking the sides of his stall with a hoof. As they entered, the horse stopped and thrust his nose toward them, whickering softly.

"Wind Thief, you're getting like an old pet living in the stable!" Nyal scolded him gently, stroking the velvet nose.

Cyna said nothing, only watched as Nyal limped toward the tack room. He called Tym, roused the stable boys, and soon the courtyard was humming with activity. Nyal was in fine spirits, joking with Tym as the small man ponied Avelaer around the paddock for exercise.

"It'll be good when *you* can ride him sir," Tym remarked. He hated working with the half-wild horse, constantly alert to hooves and teeth and unexpected attacks.

"I'll ride him whenever Cyna says I'm ready." Nyal pulled himself to the top of the fence, balancing cleverly, enjoying the strength of his arms. He turned to see if Cyna were impressed. But the shady spot beside the stable where she usually sat was empty. "Cyna? Where did she go?" he wondered out loud. He hurried through the morning's work, delegating Tym to supervise the cow milking. He could not find Cyna in the kitchen or garden. The tightly strapped Peskie-felt forced him to walk with a double-hop as he hurried down the corridors of Crowell Manor, glancing in each room as he passed.

"Have you seen Cyna?" he asked Brandon, whom he found sitting alone in the dining hall with a stack of documents, looking tired and cross.

"She's with Fallon. They've started the meeting late because she asked to talk with him."

Nyal felt a strange sense of dread as he hobbled toward the

Wizard's quarters. The door was closed, so he waited on a carved bench in the hall, absentmindedly tracing the finely chiseled Dragon and her warriors with his fingertips. After a long time, the door opened and Fallon appeared.

"Nyal," The Wizard said, as though he had expected to find him waiting in the hall.

"Cyna's with you, Master Fallon?"

"She is, but she's meditating right now."

"Is she all right?"

"She's fine. We had a matter concerning her apprentice-ship to discuss. How's the horse?"

"Coming along, sir. He has great spirit."

"Great spirit! Yes, he does. You like creatures with spirit, don't you, Nyal?"

Nyal nodded. "Will Cyna be out soon?"

"Soon enough. Have patience, my boy. Were you happy with your Sword-Naming?"

Nyal was distracted. "Yes . . ."

"And the dedication?"

Nyal remembered Broderick's words. Fallon's blue eyes seemed to bore through him. "Master Fallon . . ."

"Yes? What is it?" Fallon prompted after a moment.

"Nothing." Nyal stood in silence.

"Don't you have hay to get in?" Fallon asked finally.

"The fellows will do just as well without me. I'll wait for Cyna. I have something to tell her."

"Very well." The Wizard gathered his robe about him and departed. Nyal settled down on the bench. It seemed a long time before the door to Fallon's room creaked open. Cyna was surprised that he was there. "Nyal! Well, come in. We have to talk."

"What's wrong?" He limped into the room. It was filled with Fallon's possessions, chests and boxes stacked in neat piles by the wall.

"Sit down." Cyna opened a small chest and drew out a sharp knife with a short, slender blade. Her long, dark hair was loose. As she knelt beside him, it fell past her cheek, shielding her face. Without a word, she began to cut away the tight felt wrap.

"Cyna, what are you doing? Why did you disappear this morning?"

"I'm going to miss you," she said, eyes intent on the knife and the felt. "Ogres are interesting, but I'm going to miss you and Crowell very much."

"You're leaving?"

She nodded. "In a few days. Fallon says that the meetings are deadlocked. There's nothing more to be done here, so we're returning to Ur Logga's den."

Nyal was silent for a moment. He felt as though the wind had been knocked from his body. He stared at the curve of Cyna's neck and the graceful line of her head and shoulders. Forcing himself to take a deep breath, he said, "I don't want you to go."

"By The Law!" she swore.

"What's wrong?"

"Nothing."

She finished cutting the felt, folding and refolding it neatly as she turned away from him toward the window. He waited. He was surprised that his hands were shaking and he held them tightly behind his back, so she wouldn't see.

When she finally spoke, she still did not look at him. "I have to tell you something. Something I don't like. All this time that I've been healing you, I've lain awake nights wishing you wouldn't get well so fast. I should have taken that wrap off days ago, but I was afraid that if you knew you were well, you'd be off in the fields all day. And I wanted to go on seeing you." She turned to face him and Nyal saw a tear trickling down her cheek. "Fallon trusted me to heal you, but the better I've gotten to know you . . ." She paused, shaking her head. "Forgive me, Nyal, I've been a bad Healer, thinking only of myself."

Nyal stood up, testing his foot and ankle. They held his weight. "You're not a bad Healer! Look at me. I'm strong as a unicorn, thanks to you!"

She shook her head. "I've taken an oath to heal and help. But I almost broke that oath with you. Fallon says I must rededicate myself to Magic."

"Cyna, I have something I must tell you," Nyal said

abruptly, his grey eyes clear and intense. "I am not Telerhyde's son. I don't even know who my real father was."

Startled, she looked into his face. "Why . . ."

"You have to understand that because of what I'm about
to tell you. I don't want you to go. Ever since the night of my
Sword-Naming, even if Fallon himself had said I was well,
I'd have limped and called for you to help me—I'd have broken both legs if that were the only way to keep you with
me!" He took a deep breath. "I have no rights, since I don't
even know the name of my father. But I love you, Cyna."
She watched him like a half-wild animal, unsure whether to
flee or come to his hand. Thinking that she didn't understand, he repeated, "I love you!"

She cried out as though he had wounded her and he felt
her arms, quick and strong about his neck. He held her
tightly, shocked to feel, mixed with his joy, the sting of his
own tears.

That evening, Cyna stood beside Nyal as he knocked impatiently on the door of Telerhyde's private study. It was a
large room with an oaken worktable and chairs arranged so
that Telerhyde could look out the windows at the mountains
in the distance. Landes and Fallon were with Telerhyde, talking in the glow of two lanterns.

"Yes, Nyal?" Telerhyde asked, frowning slightly. He
hated to be interrupted at work.

Nyal was nervous, gripping Cyna's hand tightly. "Forgive
me, sir, but we must speak with all three of you."

"Yes, my children, what is it?" Landes welcomed any di-
version from the intense sessions about problems he pri-
vately feared were hopeless.

Nyal stepped into the center of the room. His voice
cracked slightly. "My Lords, Cyna and I would like your
permission to marry."

"Marry! You and Cyna! Well!" Landes exclaimed. "Well!
What can I say! Telerhyde, did you know of this?"

Telerhyde shook his head, frowning.

"We have fallen in love," Nyal said.

"Isn't this a bit impulsive?" Telerhyde asked. "How long

have you really known each other? A few weeks? Summer's passion often wilts like picked flowers."

"Oh, no, sir, we're in love."

Telerhyde and Fallon exchanged glances and Nyal thought he saw something dark cross Telerhyde's face. "Father?" he asked.

Landes rose. "For my part, I would be glad to have Cyna join you here at Crowell."

"Thank you, Lord Landes," Nyal beamed. Landes and Cyna embraced.

Fallon cleared his throat. Remembering, Nyal turned to him. "Excuse me, Master Wizard. I wish to marry your apprentice."

Fallon was silent a long moment, thoughtfully tugging on a tuft of his beard. "Cyna, you are only an apprentice. No one—not I, not you—knows yet whether you will, with your talents, be a Healer, or if you have the capacity to be something more. You await your Gift. Now, there's no rule in The Old Faith which prohibits a Healer from marrying—certainly, many marry and live happy lives. But if you should receive a more significant Gift—well. Remember the song?"

" 'Marry a witch and try to keep
Her as a wife. Ruin your life!' " Landes whistled the tune.

"There's truth in that," Fallon said. "To be a great witch takes total dedication."

"And Nyal," Telerhyde said gently. "You have new duties here and much to learn. Perhaps this is not the best time."

"I agree," Fallon said, nodding. "Cyna, you have seen how difficult loving and healing are together. In view of the conflicts we discussed this afternoon, I must charge you to put from your mind this new feeling you have for Nyal." He put up a hand as she began to object. "Only for a little while, however. Wait until you either receive your Gift or finish your term of apprenticeship. If no Gift comes and you still wish to, then marry, and you will have my blessings! If, however, you receive a Gift, we will need to talk again."

"And if you truly love each other," Telerhyde offered, "time will only make it sweeter."

"But how long must we wait?" Nyal asked.

"Cyna pledged to me three years ago, come the next Stone Moving. Unless she receives a Gift first, after that she is free."

Nyal was aghast. "That's not until next spring!"

"You will live, Nyal, believe me," Telerhyde said dryly.

Landes, looking disappointed, turned to Fallon. "A little waiting is sweet, a long wait hard. But I suppose you're right. What are the chances of her receiving a major Gift?"

The Wizard shrugged. "There are very few great witches and wizards born in a generation. Those few belong not to themselves, but to The Old Faith and The Five Tribes. Since the days of Kythra, Morbihan has survived because of her witches. Cyna," he went on, "believe me, I know how you feel. You love Nyal, I have seen that. But trust me when I tell you that although a Gift and a great love can feed each other, there is great risk. If you prove unworthy of either, both die. Dare double profit, risk double loss. So, for now, be patient and put your trust in The Law."

Cyna gripped Nyal's hand tightly as she said, "I'm sworn to you until my time is up, Master. I'll honor my pledge."

Later that night, a full moon rose high over the mountains, bathing Crowell with its stark light. Fallon crossed the courtyard alone, feeling stiff and weary from the long day's discussions. He sat on the bench beneath the apple tree, enjoying the cool night air. When he had sat for a long time, his head nodded forward and a hand fell loosely by his side. Cook, who had banked the fires in the kitchen and was on his way to his home in the hamlet, thought The Wizard napped.

In the dark, no one noticed a momentary shimmering of the air around Fallon, or the cat who sat beside his nodding body when the shimmering ceased. The cat yawned and stretched, hopping off the bench to roll luxuriously on the bluestones, which were still warm from the afternoon sun. It was a small cat, fine boned and delicate. Its coat was sleek, the color of a wild thing. It was a perfect cat, except for one thing. Its eyes were pale blue and they radiated light like a summer sky.

A faint rustle came from the garden. Curious, the cat in-

vestigated. It moved silently among the herbs and vegeta-
bles, savoring the rich odors. By the old fort's wall, the
moonlight lay in shimmering pools. Cyna and Nyal stood
close together, talking. The cat paused to watch. Splendored
in moonlight, molten with despair, they kissed. Nyal traced
his fingers across Cyna's brow like a blind man fixing his
beloved's face in his mind.

"It's so much time apart. Are you afraid?" Nyal whispered.

"No," Cyna replied. "You heard Fallon—it's rare to receive a true Gift. Ned wanted to work Magic more than anything, yet he received nothing! I only want a small talent for
healing; I won't receive a Gift. I love you, Nyal, and nothing
can change that!"

In the dark, the air around Fallon shimmered so violently
that the leaves of the apple tree shook as though from a gust
of wind. The cat was gone. The Shapechanger jerked and sat
upright, fighting for breath. For a moment, the memory of a
lost love ravaged him and all his Magic was shaken before it.
Then the memory faded.

Looking across the garden with Human eyes, he could not
make out Cyna or Nyal, only hear the rustling of their whispers. Fallon felt a wave of sadness. He was a Master Wizard
and too knowledgeable about the law of cause and effect to
feel regret. Yet while he had no Gift for prophecy, he knew
that Nyal and Cyna would never again stand in Crowell as
they were this night—young, in love, brave in the face of the
future. Even the full moon above them was fading, and when
it came around again, everything would be different.

BOOK TWO

Lothen secretly brought the convert to The Eacon's Keep on Wolf's Fang late at night.

"He says he is moved by the suffering of Humans," Lothen said.

"That is not a recommendation," Eacon Gleese replied testily. "I want to know what he is moved to do. Bring him to me."

Lothen stepped into the hall to summon the convert. "Do as he says," he whispered. Their boots sounded a sharp rhythm on the grey stones of the floor.

"Your Worship."

"Don't bow to me like that. Only my own followers bow to me. What do you want?"

"I wish to serve The Tyrant." The Eacon's snort of disbelief was like a slap and the convert flushed. "I have studied for a long time, sir, in search of the truth. I have come to believe as you do, that the greatest virtue resides in The Vorsai."

"Have you? And why do you come to me? Why not pray to The Vorsai for mercy and be done with it?"

"I wish to serve His cause."

"Of course you do. And you expect me to believe you? What sort of fool do you think I am?"

"But, sir . . ."

"*You, an heir of The Old Faith, come to me and urge me to condemn myself by telling how I would have you serve The Vorsai? Get out.*"

"*Please, sir! I'm telling you the truth! I loathe Magic. I will no longer be a part of that which rules with lies and false promises!*"

"*I don't believe you.*"

"*You must! I will do anything you ask to prove myself!*"

Chapter 9

Three weeks after Cyna left Crowell, following Fallon back to the forest, Nyal had heard nothing from her. There was no way to post messages in Morbihan other than the network of Peskie nomads who traveled constantly, trading goods and livestock and carrying information. They reported only that Fallon and his apprentice had safely reached Harkynwood. Nyal was glad that she was safe and he was busy, for he believed Cyna when she told him that nothing would change.

And yet it already had. The sharp-edged mountains that towered in the distance were no longer the first thing he longed to see when he awoke. Tym noticed that even when that year's crop of colts were weaned, Nyal often seemed distracted.

Visitors came and went from Crowell, seeking Teler-hyde's counsel. Ned returned from a trading caravan and stayed at his father's request to sit in on the endless meetings and offer what he had learned of the cities' problems.

The summer had been bountiful, providing a generous harvest, but the days were growing shorter. Each day Nyal drove himself and the farmers to gather what the fields provided.

One afternoon, the sky to the north grew ominous with thunderheads and the air felt warm and heavy. Hoping that the rain would hold off until he could bring in the hay crop from the high meadow near Unicorn Tor, Nyal ignored the tired ache in his shoulders. He wore stout farmer's boots and

trousers as protection from the nettles and thistles that grew
with the hay. The summer sun had plastered his shirt to his
chest with sweat, and grasshoppers leaped from the grass before him. He swung his scythe in an easy rhythm, the dark
tenor of his voice rising and falling. Behind him, like a V of
geese, Tym and the hearty farmers of Crowell swung their
scythes and raised their voices in the age-old song of the harvest.

Still well before noon, Nyal paused to wipe the sweat off
his brow and was surprised to see the leader of the Peskies,
Finn Dargha, racing over the stubble of the field toward
them. The farmers, sensing Nyal's loss of rhythm, rested
their scythes and looked up.

Finn's forest-green cap was clutched in his hand and he
waved it as he vaulted the stone fence that surrounded the
meadow and puffed up to the sweaty group. Although he
came only up to Nyal's armpit, his brown eyes gave the impression of boundless energy and goodwill. "Telerhyde's
missing!" he cried. "His horse has just returned with an
empty saddle!"

"Dragon's Breath!" swore Nyal. In the rough terrain near
Harkynwood, the footing could be perilous and dead tree
limbs could knock an unwary rider from the saddle. Even
Nyal had more than once been thrown by his mare and
forced to walk home, dreading the amused smiles of Brandon and Ruf Nab. Telerhyde loved to ride there, and while
the Master of Crowell rarely lost a mount, even he was not
immune to the hazards of wild country. "Fellows," Nyal
called to the farmers. "We've lost our lord, and we'll have to
find him. Tym, finish this acre and if we're not back in an
hour, you'd better join the hunt."

"Yes, sir."

Avelaer was grazing nearby, tied to a tree by the edge of
the lane. He laid back his ears, prancing sideways as Nyal
mounted, then moved briskly down the lane toward Crowell
as Finn trotted beside him. "Brandon said he would ride with
Landes and Ned along the low road to the River Dark. You
take the wood road and meet them at the lightning-blasted
oak," the Peskie said. "My troop will fan out through the

woods and keep in touch with both of you. And Brandon said to hurry, you know how Telerhyde hates to walk!"

"Done!" Nyal laughed. A quarter of a mile from the hay meadow, he pulled Avelaer to a stop before a high wooden gate. The Peskie waved and continued to jog swiftly toward Crowell. The Wood Road was used by the farmers to cart firewood from the fringes of Harkynwood. Recent rains made it rutted and swampy, and Nyal had ordered the gate closed to carts until it dried out. The road was still muddy and Avelaer moved carefully over the ruts, his head low. Nyal gave him free rein, leaning to the side to look for signs of a horseman's passage. He did not look carefully, for even when the Wood Road was dry and easily passable, Telerhyde preferred to ride the long way round, through the meadows. To his left, Nyal heard the sounds of the Peskies, communicating with whistles and birdcalls.

The road climbed a little and the ground became firmer. On either side, meadows and brush gave way to trees and saplings. Avelaer stretched out his head and whinnied, breaking into a trot. Nyal let him go. The land here alternated between forest and meadow, as it did in the wooded glades where the wild horse herds roamed. The afternoon sun found its way through the canopy of leaves overhead and cast dappled shadows on the road before them. Nyal's thoughts strayed to Cyna.

As the road descended the bluff above the river, distant thunder rumbled over the mountains and clouds began to gather overhead. Nyal could tell by the sudden breeze that the storm was coming. Avelaer shook his head impatiently as Nyal slowed the horse to a cautious walk. If Telerhyde had ridden here, a slip on the steep slope could have unhorsed him. Nyal scanned the trees and brush on each side.

He had almost reached the bottom of the bluff when Avelaer stopped, head up, ears pricked, and nostrils flaring. The Peskie birdcalls fell silent and it seemed as though even the trees were straining to hear. Nyal nudged the stallion forward and the horse moved gingerly down the hill, his neck arched, poised to bolt at any moment. Following the horse's riveted gaze, Nyal glimpsed what had upset his mount. "Ho!" he cried.

Telerhyde sat leaning against the blasted oak. Avelaer shied away and Nyal impatiently pulled the stallion's head around again and set his spurs. The horse pranced sideways, throwing up his head. "Father!" Nyal called. "Are you all right?"

Telerhyde sat with his back to Nyal, his legs outstretched. One hand rested beside him, the other was clutched at his chest. Nyal thought the old warrior had been thrown and would catch his breath and rise to his feet, laughing. Rain began, a fine mist sweeping across the clearing. Telerhyde was motionless, and Nyal was suddenly unnerved by the silence of the scene. "Telerhyde?" he called again, his voice a whisper. As he forced the unwilling horse closer, the hair on the back of his arms prickled. Nyal threw himself from Avelaer's back and stumbled through the tangled grass.

Telerhyde had been murdered. No effort had been made to hide his body; he lay where he had fallen by the side of the road. Brought by the sound of Nyal's anguished cries, Peskies gathered by the edge of the clearing. Brandon came, his face ashen as he slid from his horse. The sounds of weeping brought Landes and Ned.

Landes was the first to gather himself together, rousing the shocked brothers to look for the murderer's tracks beside the road. There was nothing to see, for in their confusion, both Humans and Peskies had carelessly trampled the ground. Yet the wounds on Telerhyde's body told much. Struck hard from behind, his sword arm had been rendered useless. He had whirled to face his attacker and taken several blows on his shield before a single thrust smashed through his guard and split his heart.

Brandon bowed his head and wept as Landes and Ned lifted the body to lay it across a horse. "Wait," Ned said. "What's this?"

They laid Telerhyde on the ground again and with trembling fingers Landes touched the gaping wound. A stone spearhead was lodged in the flesh. Landes pulled it free and held it up.

"That's from a Peskie spear," Finn said in a toneless whisper.

Ned drew his sword menacingly. "Traitor!"

Nyal was beside him, Firestroker cold and heavy in his hand. "Why?" he demanded of the Peskie leader. "Why kill the best of Morbihan?"

"Nyal, no!" cried Finn. "Telerhyde was my friend!" The Peskies drew close to their leader, fingering their short bows. "We came to honor you and to trade shalk pelts for grain. Why would we harm the Human who saved us from The New Faith?"

"Put down those swords!" Brandon stepped between them, his face tear-stained and pale. "My father had nothing to fear from Others. And Finn Dargha's troop carried no spears when I met them at the gate last night. They were armed only with the bows they carry now."

"Thank you, My Lord," murmured Finn Dargha.

Ned stepped back, clearly disappointed. "It was trolls, then," he said. "Mati Redcloak and his trolls."

"Bandits! Scum!" said Landes like a curse. "The dregs of all our tribes. They've never come so far from the mountains before."

"Why would trolls murder Telerhyde?" Nyal wanted to know.

"Bring the spearhead," Brandon commanded. He motioned to Nyal and together they lifted Telerhyde's body to a horse. The mournful procession started home.

Chapter 10

News of Telerhyde's death traveled swiftly. Those who were able hurried to Crowell to pay their last respects to the Human who had been the shield of The Old Faith. Throughout Morbihan, scattered communities of Others performed their rituals of grief according to their customs. They were frightened and uneasy. Many Humans shared those feelings. Yet, as with the passing of any great man, there were some who secretly rejoiced.

The funeral pyre was built at the top of Unicorn Tor. It

was necessary to await Fallon's arrival, and the rituals that attended the death of a great hero were observed. A profound silence fell over Crowell even as the mourners began to arrive.

The sharp birdcalls of the Peskies carried the news to Fallon, and the long strides of the Ogre's unicorns brought him to Crowell at midafternoon, two days after the murder. Fallon's legs stuck out from the unicorn's sides like a small child's on a huge horse. He clung to the fur of Ur Logga's back. Wizard, Ogre, and unicorn were soaked in sweat from the swift journey from Harkynwood. Fallon found Brandon tight-lipped and smoldering beneath his formal greeting. At his side Nyal was softer, grieving and distant.

The funeral pyre stood ready. It was a small procession that followed the winding path to the top of the tor. Except for Ned and Landes, Adler and Benare were the only Lords of the North to hear the news in time to attend. They had ridden day and night from Elea, Adler's city on the coast, to reach Crowell. Finn Dargha was there with his Peskie troop, shooting a volley of arrows into the air as Fallon kindled the torch fire. Ur Logga knelt beside The Wizard, twirling the fire-stick with his long fingers. When the fire blazed, each mourner lit a torch and laid it upon the pyre.

Cyna stood silently beside Nyal as the fire burned steadily through the afternoon and into the twilight. When the moon rose, she left him to assist Fallon in reading the coals. She knelt beside The Wizard throughout the night, her own tears shocked away by his. At dawn she brought him bread and a little brandy. "What did you see, Master?" she asked.

"I have no Gift of prophecy," he replied in a hollow voice. "I saw nothing."

The last ceremony was The Leave-Taking, held traditionally at the mouth of The Mother-Dragon's lair high in the Trollurgh Mountains. The Old Girl's Cave was a deep cleft in the blue-grey rock from which issued forth billows of sulfurous steam. It was thought that the flame of her breath kept the stones surroundings the cave warm, and ice never formed there, even in the dead of winter. Dark and small, the entrance was not large enough for three Ogres to stand abreast. The wide ledge before it was far too narrow to accommodate the many scores of mourners who had come from every corner of Morbihan. Peskie families, ragged wood Elves, and solemn Ogres mingled with prosperous Human farmers and well-to-do Dwarves. They crowded before the warm rocks at the entrance and straggled down the jagged path which cut across the cliff face. Before the cave's entrance, colorful banners snapped in the wind, punctuating the hushed stillness which gripped the mountains.

Brandon, the new lord of Crowell, knelt before the dark opening in the rock. Only his lips moved as he whispered the sacred words that told The Dragon of the hero's death. He was haggard but stiffly erect. Just behind him knelt Nyal, his head bowed as though lost in thought. A stride behind the brothers, where the ledge widened, knelt the Royal Others and the Lords of the North. Brandon finished the sacred words. He turned, reaching for his brother's hand. Nyal, startled from a tearful reverie, moved to Brandon's side.

"I swear," Brandon whispered hoarsely, "by my life and my brother's life, I swear to you, Immortal Dragon, that my father's death will be avenged!" His eyes blazed with intensity, and only a few lords in the first row noticed that his grip on Nyal's hand was so fierce that the younger man winced.

Brandon rose, carrying Telerhyde's heavy shield, which still bore the scars of the attack. The arms of Crowell, twin dragons on a maroon field, glared balefully at the watchers as he hung the shield on a carved post before the mouth of the cave. Brandon bowed his head for a moment longer before he turned to face the rest of the lords.

Nyal was first to step forward, dropping to one knee. "I recognize you as the rightful lord of Crowell, and I pledge to you my sword and my life." Brandon clasped Nyal's hand and pulled him to his feet.

Wilting beneath his spreading paunch, Landes stepped across the stony ground, limping slightly from an old wound suffered at the Battle of Harkynwood. He clasped Brandon's hand, his voice a hoarse whisper. "Brandon, I recognize you as the new lord of Crowell. I pledge you my friendship and support."

"Thank you, Lord Landes," Brandon said. They embraced.

Ned followed. "Lord of Crowell," he pledged formally.

His blue eyes glowed like gemstones in his handsome face as he grasped Brandon's hand.

One by one the remaining lords acknowledged Brandon and took their place in a rank on his right. In the funeral week just passed, they had repeatedly given ritualistic as well as deeply felt condolences. The Leave-Taking was the final ceremony in which the mourners turned to face the future.

All fell silent as Fallon approached the new lord. Closer to Nyal's stature than Brandon's, he gazed up into Brandon's face and made the arcane movements with his hands that harmonized Brandon's life with The Law. Then without a word he took his place at Brandon's left, one lone Wizard balancing the score of lords on his right.

As a rule, only Human males participated in The Leave-Taking, for only Humans held The Dragon to be a warrior's sacred guardian. But Telerhyde had been not only a Human hero, but the first War Leader of The Five Tribes.

Quick and intense as always, Finn Dargha strode forward. "Greetings, new lord of Crowell," he said, his high voice ringing clear. "The Peskies of Morbihan support you."

A silver trumpet sounded and The Meg of the Elves crossed the narrow stones to the mouth of the cave, her tiny face swollen with teras. Her flowing golden hair was braided with yellow and orange ribbons, the Elfin colors of mourning. Petite even for an Elf, she moved with a stately grace almost absurd in one who stood barely taller than a Human waist is high. She was the first female of any tribe to participate in this ceremony. "Dear, dear Brandon, poor son! Poor orphaned son!" she cried.

Brandon politely stooped down to her and was surprised by her lingering kiss on his cheek. He smelled the quick odor of Elfin brandy on her breath.

Murdock, Snaefid of the Dwarves, came next. He said little, his feelings expressed by his grim face and dark eyes. Of all the Tribes, Humans and Dwarves were closest in customs and bellicosity. Murdock and his son, Ruf Nab, had been dearer to Telerhyde than many Humans.

The two Ogre kings were the last of the Others, looming over everyone, their thick fur groomed and shiny. In the custom of Ogres, their eyes never left the ground as they rose to greet Brandon. With a nod, each politely deferred to the other and neither stepped forward. An awkward pause fell over the ceremony. Brandon sighed and held out his hands to them both. "Your Majesties," he said, solving their dilemma.

"My condolences," murmured Ur Logga, the taller of the two. He was attired in his ceremonial kilt, holding a symbolic broken branch in his hand. His companion was Ur Banfit, king of the mountain Ogres from near Fensdown Plain. Slightly shorter than Ur Logga, he had fur which held a hint of auburn as was common for the southern branch of the tribe. He politely stared away as he spoke, but he was startlingly direct for an Ogre. He acknowledged Brandon's new title then leaned down to whisper, "We are stricken with grief. Your father was a great hero whom we held in esteem and affection. We sincerely hope it is not the beginning of The Dracoon."

Now there was a shifting in the crowd, even a fluttering of alarm. Eacon Gleese rose from where he'd been sitting, his crimson-and-gold robe shimmering in the light, emphasizing his enormous bulk. His size made him seem like a member of another tribe, a creature apart from the rest. "My dear Lord of Crowell," he intoned. His resonant voice filled the mouth of the cave and spilled out onto the uneasy crowd of Humans and Others on the path below. There were a few Humans who listened and were secretly charmed, but his words were chilling to the Others and those who loved The Law.

"Your father was, in the end, my friend. He was a great man, a man of vision, a man of courage, a man who ensured that The New Faith would live in peace alongside The Old Faith of his fathers." The honeyed voice rolled on. A faint smile froze Brandon's lips, a mixture of politeness and disdain.

Nyal searched The Eacon's eyes and found only the feral look of a hungry animal. The Eacon rejoiced in Telerhyde's death, Nyal was sure. He examined the group of Humans and Others that surrounded him, his face masking all emotion but his grief. He stepped closer to Brandon, guarding his back. The brothers of Crowell would need every ounce of diplo-

macy and wit they could muster to discover the murderer and
his motives.

An Elfin trumpet sounded a lingering note. The week-long
ceremonies that marked Telerhyde's funeral were over. The
Dragon had been notified of the hero's death, the new heir
recognized by all. The Humans of The Old Faith now hoped
that their dragon would look for Telerhyde among the next
Gathering of Fallen Warriors.

The multitudes that thronged the treacherous path to the
Old Girl's Cave began to break apart. A few struggled on toward the cave to catch a glimpse of the Royal Others and
Telerhyde's lords, the rest turned back. Most of the Others
would return to their homes in Harkynwood, the Humans to
their fiefs and farms along the coast. All of The Five Tribes
crowded the narrow trail, united in their grief and their long
tradition together. By the cave entrance, the Royal Others
and the lords waited for the crowd to thin before making
their way down from the mountainside.

Landes came by, pressing Brandon's hand. "Come spring
we'll take a troop up into the mountains and eliminate every
troll we find. We'll avenge him, Brandon, and be rid of the
murderous pests."

Brandon shook his head. "There are many things to consider, Lord Landes. I'm not convinced it was trolls."

"We need to put an end to rumors. The fat Eacon would
love for Humans to think that proper Peskies had a role in
this. We must be clear that only trolls would be so low."

When he was gone, Brandon leaned back against the rock
ledge, soaking up the hazy autumn sunlight. Nyal sat on one
side of him and on the other stood Ruf Nab. Brandon's tutor
since he was a boy, Ruf Nab now sat alert, his strong right
hand resting on the hilt of his dagger, watching everyone
who passed. His vigilance did not cease as Fallon stopped for
a moment beside the two brothers.

"Master Fallon," Brandon greeted him. "Have you read
the signs?"

Fallon kept his pale blue eyes on the dwindling crowd. "I
have, but I need no signs to tell me that Eacon Gleese is at
the root of this, My Lord."

"Aye, I think you're right, though I wish I could be sure.

Landes thinks it was trolls. Proof, Master, can you give me proof? I need the hand that did it as well as the head that planned it."

"I can tell you this," replied Fallon. "Look close at home. A friend brought him to his death. No enemy could have approached his back while he lived."

Brandon nodded, unsurprised. "And the future?"

Fallon sighed. "You too, Brandon? Everyone's asking me about the future. I'm a Wizard, not some prophesying charlatan. Move over, Nyal, let me sit down."

"You read my father's ashes. What did you see?"

"I saw turmoil and confusion. But whether it was mine or Morbihan's, I can't say. Prophecy is not my strength."

"Very well," said Brandon, rising. Beside him, keen as a terrier, Ruf Nab sprang to his feet. "Nyal," Brandon's voice held the edge of command. "Call your man to saddle the horses. I want to be back in Crowell as soon as possible. We have work to do."

"Brandon!" Fallon's voice stopped Brandon in midstride. Nyal turned to listen. "Be patient. The hand that holds the weapon may be so close that you can't see it."

"Is that a prediction, Master Fallon?" Brandon asked.

"Of course not! I'm advising you to cover your rump and watch your step," Fallon replied. "It doesn't take Magic to know it was no clumsy stranger who took your father. It was one who may well be your match, too. If you seek revenge, you must have patience."

"Thank you, Shapechanger. If it takes patience to avenge my father, I'll have it."

"Go in harmony with The Law, then, Brandon."

Brandon closed his eyes and turned away. "How can you believe in all that, Master?" he asked, his voice a harsh whisper.

"In all what?" Fallon frowned.

"The Law. If any man ever lived in harmony, it was father. If there's a Law, why is he dead?"

"Brandon!" said Nyal.

"Nay, let him speak." The Wizard laid his hand on the young man's shoulder. "Nothing is outside The Law, Brandon, even Telerhyde's death. When we are hurt, the wise man looks more deeply and tries to understand."

Brandon bit his lip. "Can you tell me why Telerhyde was murdered?"

Fallon shook his head. "Who knows how a man's life will end? The web of cause and effect has entangled us all, even Telerhyde. But The Law works within you whether you believe in It or not. I hope for your sake you are in harmony with Its Principles." He made a quick, light movement in the air, tracing a pentagram before Brandon's forehead. "Go in harmony with The Law," he repeated. "You too, Nyal."

Brandon turned away, striding swiftly away from the mouth of the cave. Nyal followed him, away from where Telerhyde's shield glowed in the afternoon light.

Chapter 11

Just after the midwinter solstice, a wild unicorn, driven by winter hunger from its customary range near the Cranberry Bogs, broke through the low stone wall by the river and destroyed a large supply of grain. The next night it returned and badly battered a man-at-arms who tried to chase it from the barn.

Throughout that long autumn, Brandon had not forgotten Fallon's advice. He considered every Human in Morbihan with doubt, those who had supported Telerhyde as well as those who had opposed him. Although it was against his nature, he sought subtle ways to test everyone who came before him, asking questions that were veiled with double meaning. He confided his darkest suspicions to no one, not even the beautiful Gwenbar, who had borne him a son only days after The Leave-Taking. Brandon named him Telerhyde. Young Tel, the child came to be called.

Visitors streamed through Crowell's gates. Others came, eager to see the new baby and seek counsel from Brandon. Lords came, some to test the new lord of Crowell, to see what would happen now that Telerhyde was gone. Brandon followed his father's policies, doing nothing to harm trade with The Perime, but firmly opposing those who clamored for the right of Humans to settle Harkynwood. As he greeted each visitor, he searched their eyes and words for a clue to his father's murderer.

Some of the lords tried to convince Brandon that Telerhyde had died at the hands of their longtime irritant, the trolls. They cited the stone spearhead and the season, when trolls were said to roam far from the Trollurgh Mountains. Ned was one of those against the trolls. He visited frequently, calling for an armed excursion to rid the mountains of the pests.

As the months passed, cold storms laid a light blanket of snow across the fields and foothills which surrounded Crowell. Imprisoned by ice and cold, Brandon became even more intense and angry, chafing at the lack of information. "It was not the work of trolls, I swear it," he muttered to Nyal, warming his hands by the hearth while the tapestries on the wall swayed in the winter draft. "No Other would have harmed him, not even a troll. It was one of our own. Or a New Faith bigot. But who?"

Nyal wavered, sometimes convinced his brother was right, sometimes sure trolls were the criminals. Too often his thoughts strayed to Cyna or farm matters. He tried to escape the bitter cloud of mourning that hung over Crowell by preparing for the farm's upcoming breeding season.

The wild unicorn attack cheered everyone up. Farmers and sturdy men-at-arms left their homes and built bonfires in the fields to keep the shaggy beast away. They gathered in large groups, glad to be worried about the simple threat of a wild animal rather than the shadowy hazards of an assassin. While Nyal took a group of men to rebuild the stone wall, Brandon brooded alone in the great hall, watching the fires through the large windows. Even he seemed shaken from his dark lethargy. At last he put patience aside.

That night, Peskies carried invitations to every inch of Morbihan. The Royal Others, the Lords of the North, Fallon, and Eacon Gleese were invited to a unicorn hunt. The replies came quickly. The Eacon declined but sent his lieutenant,

Tyrll. The Meg of the Elves sent a delegation of her Husbands. The Ogres declined and sent a note of protest, and in sympathy with them, Fallon sent Cyna in his place. She delivered the Ogres' protest against hunting in general (and the hunting of unicorns in particular) with tact and sympathy, conveying the Ogres' hatred of hunting without offending the Humans who were present.

Despite the loss of grain, Nyal managed the supplies so that the table was set sumptuously. Breakfast was held before dawn, torchlight illuminating the faces of the guests as they consumed steaming meat pies and rich hunter's soup. The Royal Elfin Husbands gathered by the foot of the table and led a rousing hunting song. The Snaefid of the Dwarves banged his mug, keeping rhythm. Brandon moved freely among the guests, occasionally stopping to whisper a few words into someone's ear. He smiled, but the jovial mood sobered wherever he passed.

Nyal sat with Cyna near the fire, his eyes bright, holding her hand beneath the table. Cyna laughed at something he said and bent her head toward his until their foreheads touched. He whispered and she laughed again. Brandon appeared at Nyal's side.

"Excuse me, My Lady," he said. "I need my brother for a moment."

"Of course." Cyna smiled at Brandon but beneath the table she gripped Nyal's hand tightly, holding him in his chair.

"Nyal!" said Brandon sharply, turning away.

"Coming!" Nyal reluctantly pulled away from Cyna's hand.

A small room off the great hall was lighted by a wavering torch. Brandon stood impatiently, flanked by Ruf Nab and Tym.

"Nyal!" he said again.

"I'm coming, I'm coming!" Nyal was cross. Although Cyna had been in Crowell for more than a day, he hadn't been able to be alone with her for more than a few minutes at a time.

Brandon closed the door and turned to face them. His face was thinner than it had been in the flush of summer, and his eyes were dark and shadowed. "Today we catch the man who murdered Father. I need each one of you to be on his guard," he said. "Ruf, I want you to keep an eye on Lord Landes."

"Don't tell me you suspect him?" complained Nyal. "He's going to be my father-in-law!"

"I suspect everyone," Brandon replied. "Trust no one, Nyal. No one! You are to watch Tyrll. Father would never have turned his back to The Eacon's henchman, but Tyrll knows the hand we seek, I'm sure. Watch to whom he speaks and whom he avoids. Tym, be wary of the lords from the cities, Adler, Benare, and their companions. It's far bigger game than unicorns we're after. Father's murderer is in this house right now, I'm sure.

"As Master of the Hunt, I'll ride in the lead. Nyal, keep your distance, but guard my back. Ruf, once the hunt is on, you and Tym will flank Nyal. Let anyone who wishes approach me, but don't let him out of your sight." Brandon's eyes were cold and expressionless, as they had been all winter. "I've spread the rumor that I know the assassin's identity and will reveal him after the hunt. The murderer will strike at me."

"It's not safe," Ruf Nab grumbled. "I don't like you making yourself a target."

"A trap needs bait. Stay sharp and we'll have our man by nightfall."

Nyal had no time to return to Cyna before the bugles blew and the hunters assembled in the courtyard.

Cyna spent the day indoors, playing with Young Tel and talking with Gwenbar. She felt a heaviness in the air, a melancholy. Gwenbar seemed pale and distracted. Even Young Tel was affected, fussing and crying until his nurse took him off for a nap. "You're a witch?" Gwenbar asked Cyna.

"Not yet."

"But you know healing? Mayhap you would stay a few days and look at Brandon; he's not well. Since his father was killed, he's like a crazed man. He doesn't eat, he hardly sleeps."

"What does your Healer say?"

"She's a dolt!" Gwenbar was peevish, her pretty face lined by worry. "She gives him potions that only make him tired. He won't see her anymore."

"I'll do what I can," promised Cyna. She herself had not slept the night before. Despite her joy at seeing Nyal again, she had felt a sense of dread.

It was dark when the hunters finally rode through the gates of Crowell, carrying the wounded dogs across their saddles. They were muddy and tired but bursting with stories. The unicorn had charged out of the woods, almost trampling several Peskies. The dogs were released too soon and when they brought the unicorn to bay in the foothills on the far side of the River Dark, the horsemen were miles away, still struggling to cross the ford. The unicorn had broken free, lumbering back to Harkynwood, from which winter had driven it.

A deep cold settled in and ice was forming in the corners of the water trough. Cyna wrapped herself in her heavy brown woolen cloak and joined Nyal in the stable. While Tym held a torch aloft, she directed the care of the dogs, applying herbal ointments to their wounds as Fallon had instructed her. The most grievously wounded was an old hound, one of Telerhyde's favorites. Although he whimpered in pain, he quieted as Nyal murmured to him. Cyna sewed up a raw and bleeding gash that exposed the dog's ribs. When she was finally done, she stroked his grizzled head. "Good dog," she said, gently. He licked her hand. In the lamplight, his wolfish eyes were large and soft with shock.

"Cursed unicorn!" swore Nyal.

"The unicorn was only defending himself," Cyna said as she rinsed the dog's blood from her hands. "The unicorns which the Ogres ride are always gentle. They're tethered on a rope and Ogre kits play about their feet."

"This unicorn almost killed one of our men. Should we have let Young Tel play about his feet?" Nyal's tone surprised them both.

"Anything attacked will fight back, Nyal. You can't curse a unicorn for being what it is!"

"I know. I'm sorry, Cyna." He reached out to her and she threw her arms about his neck, anxious that nothing harsh or angry come between them.

A sound startled them. It was Tym, peering in from the door, clearing his throat. "Beg your pardon, sir, but it's dinnertime. They'll be needing you."

Cyna hurried to her chamber to change. It was hard keeping clothes nice while apprenticing to a wizard, particularly when one was forced to live in an Ogre den, but she had brought her last good dress. It was Elf-spun of a fine wool, and she liked it because it was dyed with dandelion to a color almost matching the maroon of Crowell's crest. Over this she spread her sky-blue cloak. Nyal had given her a burnished bronze mirror, and she frowned into it, smoothing her long black hair with a wooden comb. The dark green eyes that looked back at her from the mirror were troubled. "I will not let this place make me sad!" she said out loud. And then she laughed, for it seemed ridiculous that a place, particularly one where she had been so happy, could have that power.

She saw little of Nyal at dinner. He sat beside Brandon at the great table. Good conversation flowed freely and the ox was done to perfection. The high, light loaves of bread for which Crowell grain was famous were washed down by gallons of applejack from the local orchards. Nyal and Ruf Nab remained sober as the guests became increasingly jovial. Brandon smiled coldly as he watched everyone enjoy their meal. He drank only water from a silver jug.

Late that night, Cyna dreamed. It seemed that Fallon asked her a question and she would not answer. A rapping sound awakened her. She covered herself with her blue cloak and groped through the dark to the door. By torchlight she recognized Tym.

"Brandon's taken sick, My Lady. Nyal asked that you please come quickly!"

Still rumpled from sleep, she followed Tym along the corridors to the upper halls, where the family lived. Some guests lingered by the door of Brandon's rooms. Her father gave her a worried smile and at his side Adler bowed low as she passed.

Ned met her at the door. "He began to feel sick soon after dinner," he whispered. "He doesn't know where he is." Inside, Brandon lay on his bed. Gwenbar, her golden hair loose and tangled, knelt on the floor beside him, holding his hand in both of hers. Nyal comforted her, his arm resting on her shoulder.

Cyna knelt beside the bed. "Brandon?" she said. "What's wrong?"

He turned his eyes toward her. Despite the torch which Ned held near his face, his pupils were large and dark. Shadows lined his face like purple bruises. He breathing was labored and rapid. "Brandon," she repeated, "it's Cyna. What's wrong?"

"Cyna," he whispered. "Where's Nyal?"

"Right here."

"Gwen?"

"Here, too."

"I can't feel my arms," he whispered. "I'm floating up off the bed."

"You're on the bed. And Gwenbar's holding your hand—squeeze it tight, Gwenbar. Feel it?"

"Nyal—father's murderer—Ned . . ." His voice rattled in his throat and a great spasm shook him.

"Brandon!" cried Nyal in alarm.

Gwenbar began to cry.

Cyna called for hot water to prepare a brew. Her hands shook as she searched through the small collection of herbs which she had brought with her. She snatched up a pouch of sage, her fingers fumbling with the knot.

But Brandon lay senseless on the bed, his jaw slack. He could not swallow when the brew was finally prepared. The door to his room was closed and a few guests spent the night outside in the cramped corridor. Inside, Cyna battled, wrapping his cold limbs with blankets, filling the air with smoke as she burned nettle stalks to rouse him. But his limbs grew colder and his breath more shallow as the night wore on. He died as dawn lighted the bright winter sky.

Chapter 12

Late in the spring, a wild Elf called Slipfit, one of the solitary nomads of the forest, crouched motionless near a grove of ancient oak trees deep in Harkynwood. He peered through the rain and gloom of twilight, his large ears straining for a sound. The object of his attention was a Human who stood beneath the central oak, his head thrown back as though he were waiting for the tree to speak.

The Elf had been around for many years and he recognized Fallon the Shapechanger when he saw him, even in this thickening half-dark. It was said that if one witnessed a shapechanger at his work, one's greatest wish would come true. It was almost certainly superstition, but like most Elves, this one was very superstitious.

Fallon was prophesying. Or rather, he was attempting to. As every witch and wizard has a Gift, each also has crafts which are difficult. Shapechanging was Fallon's Gift and it came as naturally to him as breathing. Prophecy was another matter. Prophecy was the time-honored function of Magic-Keepers ever since Kythra had revealed it as *her* Gift. But for Fallon it was a grueling discipline, one he dreaded.

He needed to glimpse the tapestry of time. The threads of the present felt ominous and his position as Master Wizard decreed that he use his powers, such as they were, for the protection of The Five Tribes. Recently a strong sense of unease had settled upon him. Although the winter had been unseasonably mild, no one in Morbihan could fail to notice that spring was a long time in coming.

Even after the sun had climbed halfway to the solstice, the jagged mountains which towered over the forest were still steadfastly cloaked in snow. In the foothills, angry, frigid storms from the peaks met the warm winds from the coast and together they tore at the land. Alternately freezing and thawing, swollen rivers flooded their banks. Tree buds swelled only to be frozen by ice storms. Shoots of new grass drowned in rain-soaked meadows. Creeks became rivers, roads became muddy streams. Humans and Others with any sense stayed home and nurtured whatever dry firewood they had left.

After Brandon's death, Fallon had fasted for a week without catching a glimpse of a vision. Now he had been without food for three days and without sleep for two. Fallon hated to abuse his body but, when dreams would not come, this was the only way he knew of forcing visions. As a last resort, he was exposing himself to the unceasing storms.

He stood beneath the giant oak, eyes closed and sight turned inward. It was miserably cold. An occasional pellet of sleet stung his skin. The night deepened and a raw wind swept the rain across the oak grove. The wild Elf shivered and found shelter within a hollow tree. Fallon resisted the desire to give in to his Gift, to step out of his frozen, hungry, exhausted old man's body and be comfortable again. *A wolf,* the thought came to him unbidden, *with thick fur and a full belly. And then we could nestle together, my wolf-self and I, and I would warm myself.*

A gust of wind tore across the rise of earth upon which the old man stood. Above the roar, he heard a rending sound. A limb from a nearby tree was thrown violently at his feet, branch tips lashing his face. He swore out loud. Another gust tugged at him, blowing his beard straight out to the side. He stared up into the darkness. "Kythra! Give me a sign!" he cried. But the shudders which convulsed his thin shoulders were from cold, not from the elemental energy he sought. His tears mixed with the rain and were blown off his cheeks. "Founders! Let me see!" He could hardly hear his own voice over the wind. He closed his eyes. Exhaustion closed over him like an icy wave, but with it at last came something else. His body jerked as though he were about to fall, and he let himself be taken into the vision.

Through a rising mist, he glimpsed water tumbling in foamy abandon over rocks and ledges. A man in the full regalia of a Master Wizard waited beside a riverbank. A sharp stab of fear assaulted Fallon. Even as he fought to waken, he felt himself swept up. The earth became a tiny speck beneath him, and then he was rushing toward it again at a dizzying speed.

A fire flared against a grey sky. The Snaefid of the Dwarves leaned on one knee, head bowed. Nearby, Ruf Nab stood beside a wild Elf. Fallon glimpsed the faces of the Lords of the North and The Meg of the Elves. Finn Dargha stood at the head of a Peskie troop and Ur Logga glowered from the rear. Cyna, hollow-eyed, held a torch. A tear trickled down her cheek as she gazed at a still figure that lay in the midst of the fire. She spoke words he could not hear over the crackling of the flames, casting her torch into the inferno. A Master Wizard lay motionless upon the funeral pyre.

And then, louder than the roaring river, louder than the flames, he heard another sound. From the distance the din of battle reached him. The deep bass roar of Humans, the sharp cry of Peskies and Elves punctuated by the clash of steel.

Even as he strained to see, the vision became faint. The sounds of the battle became muted, the bright scene dimmed and flickered out. "Thunder and sour cheese," he swore. Numbed with cold, he toppled over.

The wild Elf had heard his oath. Holding his faded felt cap firmly on his head, he peered out from his shelter. In the dim light, he could just make out the tangled heap of The Wizard collapsed at the foot of the tree. As he started up to aid the fallen Human, a movement caught his eye. A haze settled about The Wizard. Slipfit approached gingerly, curiosity overriding his customary Elfin caution. The haze thickened abruptly. With a flush of horror he realized he was staring at a huge timber wolf with eyes so blue they glowed even in the dark. The Elf drew back with a gasp, gripping the hilt of his dagger.

Oblivious to the terrified Elf, the wolf shook itself and lay beside the crumpled shape of The Wizard, covering him with its fur. The Elf hardly dared breathe. For a long time the wolf sheltered the Human figure from the wind. Then abruptly there was a shimmer of light and the wolf was gone. Fallon rose to his feet, blew on his hands, and pulled his ragged cloak tightly about him. He strode from the oak grove straight for where the Elf was concealed.

"Na!" exclaimed the frightened Other, but he was cornered in the bole of the tree.

Hearing the sound, The Wizard paused, glaring about him, looking for the source. "Hello!" he said suddenly, peering into the hollow tree. "What are you doing here?"

"Na! Get back! Leave me be!" The Elf waved his knife and tried to look threatening.

"Who are you? Are you hungry? Would you like to come inside with me and get warm?"

"Get back!" The Elf waved his knife and when The Wizard stepped back he sprang from the hollow tree and scrambled backward toward the deeper forest, holding his weapon menacingly before him. "You'll not have me, you shapechanging Elf eater!"

"Wait!" The Wizard thundered, and the Elf paused, shocked by the old Human's power. "I know you." Fallon took a step closer and looked into the Elf's eyes. "Slipfit? I just had a dream and saw you in it. Don't you remember me? I'm Fallon. We knew each other in the Harkyn."

"Fallon the wolf," Slipfit muttered.

"Yes, the Shapechanger. Where have you been? Your family needs you."

"Begone!" cried the Elf, suddenly enraged. "Begone and leave me be!"

"Ah, well." Fallon was again shuddering from the cold. "I'll see you again," he said, and stumbled toward the Ogre barrow.

For some time afterward Slipfit trembled, whether from cold or fright he wasn't sure. He had never felt so alone. For the first time since he had deserted The Meg's palace many years before, he wanted desperately not to be a wild Elf, a Solitary wandering Harkynwood. He wanted to be someone with friends and a warm place to live.

Fallon hurried through the forest, his thoughts more chilling than the driving wind. Years before, when he first entertained the desire to become a Master Wizard, he had gone to his teacher for a prophecy. Staring into the hearth-fire through a quartz crystal as big as a man's head, she had told him: "You will be thrice tested. Once, to defy your own nature. Second, to defy love. Third, to defy death."

He had been disappointed by the prophecy at the time, but it had proven right, so far. The discipline of Magic had demanded a great struggle against his own nature. To ride with Telerhyde at the Battle of Harkynwood, he had defied love, although not without a sad, sweet struggle. To defy death still lay before him, but it drew closer. He had sensed it even before Telerhyde's murder. If he should merely die like other men, he would not be disappointed, for to master two out of three great tests was no disgrace. Neither was he frightened, for he was old and it was often given to a Magic-Keeper to foresee his own death. If Morbihan were strong, The Five Tribes free, he could leave without a qualm. But his wizard's sense told him things were not right.

He shuddered, not from the cold this time, but from a feeling of unease. *Dis-ease,* he mused, trying to distract himself from the cold. An evil was loose, the land gripped in a kind of fever. But what are the elements of the healing? Cyna's Gift had better come soon, he thought grimly. Morbihan could not stand for long without Magic.

He fought the wind, making his way toward a rise of ground. This part of Harkynwood was rolling land, broken occasionally by rocky ledges, and covered by ancient oak trees. Hidden among a group of natural hills, the earthen mound was remarkable only in that the great oaks grew smaller upon it. A well-defined footpath ended at one end of this odd hill. To an unobservant eye it simply disappeared, but closer examination revealed an entrance formed by two enormous boulders topped by a massive stone lintel. The doorway was wide enough for two oxen to enter easily, and two Humans high. It was Urden Barrow, the ancestral home of the Harkynwood Ogres.

Deep within the earth, warm in a high-vaulted chamber near the center of the barrow, Cyna was calculating. She bent over the smooth stone floor near the fire in the center of the room, absently chewing a strand of her long, dark hair much the way she had seen Fallon nibble his beard when lost in thought.

In stone chambers all around her, the Ogre community slept. In fact, she suspected, most creatures in the forest slept. But dreams, her allies when life had seemed more pleasant, plagued her. Night after night dreams of Nyal riding his chestnut wildly through the night awoke her, seized her in a nameless fear. She was thinner than she had been the summer before, and her face had a pinched look about it. Her skin was pale from the long winter and longer spring spent underground with the Ogre community, yet on this night her cheeks were flushed, her dark eyes flashing green in the firelight.

Her marking stone was too small for the project and a confusion of symbols spilled across the floor. Her forehead was furrowed in concentration as she subtracted the summer solstice from the lunar phases and entered the sum in its proper space with a charcoal stick. She felt a small but keen flutter of excitement. According to the marking stone there would soon be a total lunar eclipse. Methodically she went over the figures, double-checking each formula. Smudged and persistent, the same prediction appeared again.

She rose and stretched, her mind restlessly throwing off the weariness of her body. The fire had burned down during the night and now she stoked it, staring into the coals. Ancient wise ones like Kythra had seen the future in fire, but the glowing coals told Cyna nothing. She turned away to glance at her handiwork. She loved the power of a craft which allowed her to foretell the future in the skies while she was buried deep within the shadows of the earth. Now that the work was done she felt drained, chilled. Loneliness enveloped her and she thought again of Nyal, alone in the mourning-draped corridors of Crowell. She settled closer to the fire, wrapping herself in a torn woolen cloak. Resting her head on her arm, she dozed.

Even in her sleep she felt Fallon when he returned, a wave of power and energy that invaded her dreams and tugged her toward wakefulness. He stood in the middle of the room, surveying her marks on the floor. He was soaked to the skin, his white hair clumped in long tufts hanging soggily to his shoulders. Despite Cyna's many attempts to patch his cloak, it hung in threadbare strips to the floor. As he examined her work, the cloak dragged behind him, erasing precious formulas as he moved about.

"Master Fallon," she stammered, starting up from sleep.

He waved his hand at her, sending an arc of water droplets through the air. "Pardon, Cyna, I didn't mean to waken you. You've been hard at work, I see."

"Yes, Master," she replied, rising and pulling her cloak about her. "Have you any news of Nyal?"

"Not a word. Don't worry about him, he's fine."

She stifled a yawn and watched The Wizard with concern. "You've been out in the storm again," she observed.

He grunted, neither an admission nor denial, merely acknowledging the question. "What is this?" he asked, eyes still following the course and logic of her calculations.

"An attempt to predict an eclipse," she replied.

"Ah." Engrossed, his lips moved slightly as he checked her figures. He crossed to the end of the formula, his cloak mopping the floor clean behind him. After a long time he murmured "Ah," again. "Good. Quite good." He turned to her. "You have a talent for numbers. I did not teach you all this."

Cyna blushed at the compliment. "No, Master. But something you said to Ur Logga the other day made me think . . . well, I thought I would try it."

"Very good," he said again. "Although it's easier to predict eclipses by the age-old custom, within a stone circle. But it's good to know that with a run of bad weather like we've been having, you can predict what's happening in the heavens. You have made the calculation quite straightforward. What do you predict?"

"Four days after the Stone Moving there will be a lunar eclipse."

"Will there, now?" He gazed at her speculatively for a moment, then turned toward the fire. She realized he was shivering.

"Master, you should get out of those wet clothes!" Beneath his soggy cloak Cyna was surprised to see that he wore nothing to cover his bare chest. She took the kettle from its customary perch near the hearth and poured warm water into a bowl with a pinch of willow bark. A tremor shook him. She waited until it was past to offer the brew, wrapping her blanket around him. "You mustn't go out like this. You'll catch your death of cold!" she scolded.

"Yes, perhaps," he agreed, savoring the cup. "But there's much work to do. And the signs are so odd. I don't understand them." He was silent for several moments and Cyna sat beside him respectfully, staring into the fire. "How could I forget?" he asked abruptly. "I have something for you." He took from his neck the soft leather pouch he always wore and gave it to her. It felt strangely heavy in Cyna's hand. Inside was a Healer's ring. "You should have had this some time ago. I asked The Snaefid to cast it," Fallon said. "A passing Peskie finally brought it this morning."

It was heavy and gleaming, shaped like an endless chain of seven links. Inside each link was the symbol for each of The Seven Principles of The Law. "Oh, Master, thank you!" She slipped it on the third finger of her left hand and held it out, admiring the way it gleamed in the firelight. A dark thought cast a shadow across the room. "I'm not sure I deserve to wear this," she said softly.

"You have been ready ever since you healed Nyal. The midwifery you have done with the Ogres has prepared you even more." He frowned, seeing more in her expression than he expected. "You're thinking of Brandon again? You must stop. He was not the last patient you'll lose, I'm afraid. Healers can mend, but not defy death." That reminded him of the prophecy and he frowned absently, wondering how it might be accomplished.

A courteous rumbling sound came from the doorway. Ur Logga towered there, his hands smeared in mud, his shaggy forearms and head dripping water.

"Your Majesty!" Fallon said, bowing his head respectfully. "Don't tell me you've been out in the storm?"

"There's another leak," the Ogre grumbled. "We've patched it for now, but I don't know how long it will last."

Cyna presented him with a basin of clean water and a cloth.

"Thank you, Lady Cyna." The Ogre sat before the fire and washed his hands.

"Have you any news from Crowell, Your Majesty?"

"No news from anywhere," the Ogre grumbled, shaking his shaggy head. "Even the Peskies have given up their travels and wait for drier weather in their tents. We're almost out of firewood, Master Fallon. Can we expect spring soon?"

"I certainly hope so," The Wizard replied, "but I'm no fortune-teller." The Ogre continued to stare at him, his great eyebrows arched in a question. "I have seen nothing, yet," Fallon added, examining his cup of brew with great interest.

"You have seen The Final Days," the Ogre reproved gently.

"Nothing like that!" Fallon protested. "I've seen disturbance, true, but I am not a prophet."

"It is The Dracoon," murmured the Ogre. "I have dreamed it."

"The Dracoon?" asked Cyna.

"An element of Ogre mythology," Fallon explained. "They believe that Kythra made prophecies about the end of Morbihan."

"When Kythra lived in Harkynwood, she foresaw The Final Days and she called it The Dracoon," Ur Logga explained. "Certain warnings will precede the end of our world."

"What are they?" Cyna prompted when Fallon remained silent.

"First, there is the death of a hero," Ur Logga said. "Then, the rise of a traitor."

Cyna's eyes widened, flashing bright green in the firelight. "You think that Telerhyde's murder was a warning?"

"That's nonsense!" Fallon said sharply. "Each of us must die sometime."

"The third sign is the confusion of seasons," the Ogre went on doggedly. "And this spring season is not like spring at all, but like a strange autumn."

"We are not strangers to late springs in Morbihan," Fallon objected. "You must be careful not to become pessimistic, Your Majesty."

"What are the other warnings?" Cyna asked.

"There are seven." The Ogre took a breath and began to recite. Ur Logga was a renowned Singer, and his voice resounded in the stone room.

A traitor rises,
A hero dies.
Confusion tears apart the skies
Twisting seasons out of order.

A stone is shattered,
A moon consumed,
The shards of Kythra's heart entombed
For love and faith are splintered.

The final sign
That all is lost
And heart and mind must pay the cost
Magic dies alone.

When all of this
Has come to be,
Darkness will cover all we see.
The Law is hidden from our sight."

His deep voice rose in a melancholy wail:

"Liars and fools call likes their opposite,
Seeking cause beyond themselves."

"This is very obscure Ogre folklore!" Fallon objected, "and open to interpretation."

"This is Kythra's legacy to us!" Ur Logga insisted softly. "Her *Teachings from the Tower.* Ogres have faithfully preserved her words for generations."

"You believe this is happening, Your Majesty?" Cyna asked.

"A great hero has been slain," the Ogre replied. "And who but a traitor would murder Telerhyde? I fear the confusion of seasons is upon us. The barrow roof has never leaked before."

"That's three out of seven signs," Cyna mused. "And in a short while, all of The Old Faith will gather for the Stone Moving."

" 'A stone is shattered,' " repeated the Ogre, nodding his head emphatically. "Master Fallon, what of 'a moon consumed'?"

"With all respect, Your Majesty, leaky roofs are discouraging, but not the end of our world, and eclipses are but a natural phenomenon," Fallon protested. "Besides, how can I read an eclipse without a cloudless night and a stone circle?"

"But Master," exclaimed Cyna, "my figures——"

Fallon made a sharp gesture with his hand. Although he was across the room, Cyna felt a soft blow strike her chest, driving her words away.

"What figures?" inquired the Ogre.

"Nothing," Cyna stammered. "A foolishness."

"You have foreseen an eclipse?" Ur Logga insisted. He reached down and gently touched Cyna's shoulder. She felt a warm current of thought tugging at her mind. The Ogre's eyes widened. "You have foreseen the sign! Then The Dracoon is upon us." A tone of dread colored the Ogre's voice.

"That's nonsense!" Fallon said impatiently. "Cyna merely experiments with figures; she can't be sure of what she says. Besides, an eclipse, if it comes, was due from the beginning of time, Your Majesty. It is the movement of the sun and moon, and that is as constant as The Law Itself."

"But Lady Cyna believes it will come . . ."

"Lady Cyna is an apprentice! It's only a short time ago that she needed luck not to poison her patients when they came to her with a cold. She has talent and she shows a surprising affinity for figures, true, but she knows little yet of true Magic."

Cyna flushed, retreating to stir the embers in the hearth.

The Ogre was silent for a moment, then went on, timidly. "But the weather is confused, Master Fallon, you cannot deny it. And what of the Death of Magic? Are you not afraid, my friend?"

"I fear only careless rumors. Magic will not die as long as we dare to love our lives."

The Ogre scratched his shaggy head. The look of worry subsided into an expression of permanent puzzlement around his wide brown eyes. After a moment he smiled at Cyna, his canines gleaming in the firelight. "It's a lovely ring. You are a Healer now? Congratulations."

"Thank you, Your Majesty." Cyna traced the endless links with the tip of her finger. It felt warm and comfortably heavy on her finger. Ur Logga rose to leave, nodding diffidently as both Humans bowed to him.

When he was well out of the chamber, Fallon turned to Cyna. "The Royal Others must not be upset by rumors!"

"But Master, I never told him."

"I know, I know. But be careful around him, for Ogres have a way of knowing. Their Gift, perhaps. You must tell no one else. I must discourage these thoughts from taking hold in the Ogre community."

"But why? Surely the Tribes should be warned."

Fallon shook his head impatiently. "I don't want everyone talking about it, worrying about it! The Dracoon—or any disaster—won't descend upon us from Moer, imported by The Eacon. Disasters rise out of us. We create them with our own lack of faith. Kythra told us, 'Think not on mischief or you will achieve it.' You must not say a word about this to anyone, do you understand me?"

"Yes, Master Fallon. But may I speak with you?"

"Of course. When have I ever denied you that?"

"Considering the weather and Telerhyde's death, isn't it strange that the Stone Moving and a full eclipse occur so close together?"

He frowned, his pale eyes darkened by the shadows of the room. "Say what you're thinking, Lady Cyna."

She held her breath for a moment, choosing her words carefully. "Could these be four of the Ogres' signs?"

The roar from The Wizard startled her. "Four? Where do you see four signs, Lady? By the greatest stretch of the imagination—assuming your calculations about the eclipse are correct—I see only three possible signs here."

"I only meant—I am only suggesting that, at the Stone Moving, if The Stone should fall, it would be the fourth . . ."

"If!" snorted The Wizard. "Are you making prophecy your Gift?" He went on before she could answer. "Being a witch entails certain responsibilities, among them not to project thoughts of disaster! Even if you should foresee some tragedy, a witch's work is to avert it—in act, in words, and in thought! Cause begets effect!"

"Master, I was only asking . . ."

"And the answer is no! I see only three random events here and nothing more! Eacon's Breath!" he swore. Cyna had never seen him so upset. "You are not to indulge in projections of this kind, do you understand me?"

"But . . ."

"No buts!" He traced a mysterious pattern in the air as he spoke. "I place the Bond of Silence upon you!" he said fiercely. "You are forbidden to speak of The Dracoon to any-one, do you understand?"

She felt the restrictions of the Bond settling on her lips and breath. "But Master, that's not fair!"

Fallon regarded her with surprise. It was the first time in her apprenticeship that she had protested openly to him. "Apprenticeship is not fair, Cyna. It's hard work and doing what you're told. When you receive your Gift, it will tell you what you must do. But for now, obey *me*."

Her lower lip trembled. "Mayhap I have already received my Gift." As he arched an eyebrow, she rushed on in a flurry of words. "You said I have a talent for figures and logic. If the eclipse comes, and I'm sure it will, I will have used that talent for prediction. By logic I can foresee that with three other signs present, the Stone Moving is critical this year! Could this not be my Gift?"

"Logic and a knack for figures?" Fallon was aghast. "You equate these with a Gift? Lady Cyna, prediction is as different from prophecy as a torch is from a bolt of lightning! Both cast light, but how can you compare them? Do not bother me with trivial nonsense at a time like this. When you truly receive your Gift you will not need to ask if you have it. You will know!"

BOOK THREE

Lothen bore the long days of waiting in concealment with patience. He held himself aloof from his host. The Eacon, he sensed, wished to form a bond, even a friendship. But Lothen was friend to no one. He had never been. He saw others as tools and agents for The Tyrant's will, just as he saw himself. That the convert had become a disciple, a ready tool, pleased him as honing the edge of his dark blade pleased him. Tools for The Tyrant, converts for The Vorsai.

Lothen watched as The Eacon and the convert walked along the path that followed the side of the temple, sheltered from curious eyes by the high wall, far from listening ears. The convert had become the trusted disciple, walking a half-step behind his mentor, his hands in plain sight by his sides. The Eacon gestured with his, underscoring a point with a jabbing finger, leading the way to a conclusion with a triumphant fist.

"There were no Brownie Roasts!" The Eacon was saying. "That is their great lie. Oh, a few mass immolations, perhaps, spontaneous outpourings of Human emotion. But there was no official policy as such. There is—there was—no need for such policies. With sufficient numbers of The Vorsai's believers to guard them, the demons are useful to us. They

99

will be forced to cut and burn the forest, till and harvest the land for their Human masters. That is the natural order of things, for Humans to rule and take from the land and its creatures the bounty that is our due. Do you remember the holy words?"

The disciple spoke eagerly, the words tumbling from his lips. " 'Ye are the sons of The Vorsai, pride of my loins. I have put you in my place to rule the world and purify the gross.' "

"Excellent. Those words are our commandment. To be worthy of The Vorsai's love and tolerance, we must rule Morbihan and purify it of its foul inhabitants. Do you believe this?"

"With all my heart."

"Good. Yet do not think that The Vorsai's love is easily won. I love you and trust you for what you have already done. But The Vorsai demands more deeds. He feeds on acts of love. He would test your devotion."

"I am ready."

"Very well."

Lothen smiled as he watched them walk, the trusted disciple a respectful half-step behind, their voices drifting about the temple courtyard, spinning The Tyrant's dreams.

Chapter 13

"I want you to ride with us," Ned was saying. "It will cheer you up. The younger lords are all coming—Adler, Combin, Farryl—but I don't trust them like I trust you. I'd like you to be my lieutenant, Nyal."

"Lieutenant!" Nyal shook his head. "I'm only Crowell's seneschal. I can't give orders to lords!"

"I should think you'd want to ride; it's your father we're avenging," argued Ned. "Don't be squeamish!"

"I'm not squeamish; I just don't think killing trolls is the best way to avenge Telerhyde." Nyal rode in the vanguard beside Nedryk. They both moved with the unconscious grace of born horsemen, bending toward each other as they talked. Ned rode a large and powerful black gelding, Nyal sat easily astride Avelaer, mufflered against the weather in the rust-colored cloak from Cyna.

The horsemen who splashed along the road behind them were so thickly wrapped in woolen cloaks and canvas water-proofs that they resembled a group of prosperous merchants, except for the ends of their long swords protruding from beneath their cloaks and the occasional ring of sleet striking armor. As was their custom, the Lords of the North had gathered together to ride to the Eacon's Keep for the Stone Moving. The most important of all The Five Tribes' annual celebrations, Stone Moving celebrated the first time Kythra had moved the great stone Argontell, one thousand years before. The journey had the excitement of a great tradition.

101

Heavy fog obscured the coast while inland the grim and ceaseless rain held a hint of sleet. That morning the puddles had been edged in ice crystals and even now, in late afternoon, the horses were steaming.

Lord Landes rode toward them, his horse's hooves splashing up the mud of the road. "Here, boys, I need to talk to you."

Avelaer threw up his head and challenged the new arrival with a snort. Nyal reined him to one side so that Landes could ride between them. "M'Lord," he said respectfully.

"So, Nyal, you're going troll hunting with Ned?" Landes asked.

"He'll come, but he won't accept a command," Ned said resignedly.

"You may have to, like it or not, Nyal," Landes said, wiping mud from his face with a callused hand. "I've decided to put your title up before the Council of Lords."

"My title? I have no title, sir."

"You're standing in for your father and brother in the ceremonial procession, aren't you? I'm only suggesting we make it official. These are strange times, Nyal. Your family has always been in the center of difficult times. We need a lord of Crowell."

"Young Tel will grow into that soon enough," Nyal said.

Landes shook his grizzled head. "Not so. I would take nothing from Brandon's son, but the Others need to see a lord of Crowell riding in the vanguard if we're to keep up the strength of The Five Tribes. No one will deny you the right to be Telerhyde's successor."

"My Lord, I cannot!" Nyal protested. "By all that's right, it goes to Young Tel when he's able. And besides . . ." he paused, seeking words.

"When Young Tel is old enough, you can relinquish the title and return it to him. I'm not suggesting you usurp your nephew's rights. But we need a man to govern Crowell, not a tiny baby. Surely you see the sense in that."

"There's that other matter," Nyal said. "I have no right to be lord of Crowell."

"Your paternity?" Landes leaned forward in his stirrups to cuff Nyal lightly on the shoulder. "My boy, don't think about it! Telerhyde accepted you as his son and the other lords can do no less! It's settled as far as I'm concerned. Now, are you still planning to marry my daughter?"

For a moment, worry slipped from Nyal's face. "As soon as she leaves Master Fallon, M'Lord."

"Well, you can't rush a Gift, as we all know." Nedryk's cheeks flushed red as Landes went on. "Her time of apprenticeship is almost over. I thought we could announce your engagement at the Council of Lords. What do you say?"

"Most definitely!" Nyal agreed.

"Good, assuming she has no Gift by then, you'll publicly pledge to each other the last day of the ceremony. You'll be the married lord of Crowell—hunting trolls with Ned by summer! No more objections!" He beamed through the rain at both young men.

They rode in companionable silence for a few miles. Avelaer fretted and pulled the bit, impatient with the slow pace.

"Why are trolls always Others?" Nyal asked. "Are there no Human rogues?"

"Others have more tendency for evil," Ned observed.

"Here, that's nonsense, Ned!" his father exclaimed. "Humans have never lacked for rogues. I'll wager that in knavery we Humans outstrip all the tribes, except for Peskies, and they don't think of their taking of livestock as 'stealing.' But an Other who commits a crime has nowhere to run except to the mountains. A Human outlaw can find safety in The Perime of Moer. No matter what evil a Human's done, The Tyrant will welcome him as a New Faith convert and hero!"

"But a real troll preys on everyone, while a New Faith Human preys mostly on Others," Ned protested.

"Yes, that's true," Landes agreed. "I say a pox on them both."

"Why did Telerhyde always insist upon respecting the trolls' rights to the mountains?" Nyal persisted.

"Because your father was a man who respected the rights of every citizen of Morbihan, even the lowest. He couldn't know the trolls would murder him."

Nyal bit his lip. "Strange how Brandon never believed that, M'Lord."

"Brandon tortured himself with suspicions," Ned said. "I

should have seen what was happening to him. I'll never forgive myself for not offering him better counsel in those last months."

"He wouldn't have listened," Nyal said, awkward with his own grief as he tried to comfort his brother's friend. "He was suspicious of everyone."

"Except you," Ned said.

Nyal was surprised. "Except me." Avelaer threw up his head. "Whoa, boy," Nyal said soothingly. With an irritated squeal the stallion sank his teeth into the neck of Landes's horse.

"Here, watch it!" cried Landes.

"Hold him!" shouted Ned.

"Whoa, Avelaer, whoa!" Nyal snatched back the reins and Avelaer pranced sideways, glaring at Landes's bay and gnashing his teeth. "He's fretful with the slow pace, M'Lord," Nyal said. "I'll ride ahead and work it out of him."

"He's never going to learn manners unless you make him behave!" Landes shouted after him, but Nyal was already letting the chestnut stride ahead.

He soothed the horse as he watched the sides of the road for a familiar landmark, some key to jog his memory. Mist shrouded the fields. He couldn't be sure if the surrounding country were hilly or flat. He rode for some time, grateful for the silence and solitude. The road turned downward. Avelaer slid for a stride and stopped. Without warning, the road disappeared, swallowed by a raging stream. Behind him, Nyal heard the lord's horses drawing closer.

"Here, Nyal!" exclaimed Landes as they glimpsed each other. "Thought you'd been Ogred up." He peered through the thickening mist. Beneath the old lord's thick muffler, the curse of later middle age was straining at the seams of his chain mail.

"Stream's too high to cross here," said Nyal.

"Don't you remember your father's ford?" Landes gestured downstream. "A thousand men crossed without a wet backside among them. It was spring then, too, and high water. Follow me, boys!"

The path to the ford was narrow, barely wide enough for one horse. The tree branches were so heavy with rain that the riders had to bend low over their horses' necks to avoid being drenched by the frost-withered leaves. Nyal was not impressed by the ford. The river widened and the churning rapids quieted, but it still raced swiftly, tearing at its banks as it roiled before them. "There'll be some wet backsides today, by the look of it," he said.

"It is a little high," Landes admitted as the horsemen milled uncertainly at the riverbank.

"Someone should try it," Ned suggested.

"Excellent idea," Landes said. "Let's have someone who can swim! Here, you! What's-your-name, come here!"

"Me, sir?" Tym splashed up from the rear on his sturdy brown palfrey. Behind him, glaring uneasily at the churning rapids, Ruf Nab rode a cobby Elfin pony.

"You've no armor on. Try the ford," Landes said.

Tym threw an appealing glance at Nyal. "I can't swim, sir."

"No matter," Landes said, "we'll get a rope and haul you out if there's trouble."

"Try it, Tym," Nyal urged. "If you get stuck, we'll pull you out."

"Let me go," Ruf Nab said.

But Landes had already produced a rope from his saddlebag and tossed it to Nyal. Nyal tied it tightly through the tree of Tym's saddle while Ned took the other end and made it fast to a large tree. Squaring his shoulders, Tym urged the palfrey toward the riverbank. At the edge, the gelding threw up his head to refuse, but Tym swung his hickory stick smartly and the horse splashed chest-deep into the racing current. Nyal held his breath as he paid out the coils of rope, keeping the line free. Horse and rider carefully moved deeper. Then they were halfway across.

"See? It's perfectly safe!" said Adler.

"I'm with him!" Ruf Nab cried. His pony needed no urging, but leaped into the water, swimming strongly. "I'll beat you across!" Ruf shouted as his pony's head neared the palfrey's rump. Just then the palfrey's head disappeared beneath the water. Tym gave a strangled cry which was cut off as he, too, disappeared, only to bob up a second later. The rope was yanked from Nyal's hands, stretching taut as the palfrey was swept downstream.

Tym was tangled for a moment with his horse, thrashing and trying to free himself. Then the rope snapped and the frightened animal was swept like an ice floe past a large rock in the middle of the stream. He disappeared into the rapids beyond as Tym found a handhold on the rock and cried out "Help!"

"Hold on!" cried Ruf, reaching out his hand for the frightened Human, but the pony was no match for the strong current in the middle of the stream. Still swimming furiously, pony and Dwarf were carried down the river.

Nyal tore his helmet from his head, threw his lance and shield to the ground, and set spurs to the chestnut. With a leap he was midstream and beneath him he could feel the stallion's legs churning against the current. As though he were a child again, riding his pony in the millpond, Nyal slid off the horse's back and paddled beside him, holding the pommel tightly. The shock of the icy brown water took his breath, but the chestnut was a strong swimmer and obeyed the hand that still held the reins. Swept by the current toward Tym, Nyal called out, "Grab hold!"

Tym released his desperate hold on the rock to reach for the saddle and came up clutching the heavy iron stirrup. For a moment the force of the river gripped them, sweeping horse and men into the rapids below the rock. Then Tym felt the explosive power of Avelaer as the stallion found bottom and lunged for the shore. Breathing more water than air, too numb from cold to feel the blows of the boulders on his legs and belly, Tym's grip was weakened. As the horse dragged both men toward the riverbank, the groom lost his hold and fell into a shallow pool of water, safe from the current. He was dimly aware that, only a few feet farther on, Avelaer stumbled to a stop, his sides heaving and legs trembling. Nyal, gulping for air, staggered upright and waved across the water at the horrified band of horsemen on the opposite bank.

Landes waved frantically. "I can't hear you!" Nyal shouted, shaking his head. Landes continued to wave, his lips moving as his words were swallowed by the raging stream. Tym struggled up from the pool of water in which he shivered and saw that downstream, where the river widened and the current slackened, Ruf's pony had gained the river-bank. He watched as Ruf, dripping water and out of breath, urged the little horse along the riverbank. Avelaer whinnied a greeting. "Pardon me, sir, but you seem half-drowned," the Dwarf called to Nyal, trying hard to mask a roguish grin.

"More than half," Nyal replied. "Tym, are you hurt?" Still gasping for breath, Tym shook his head. "The lords don't show any enthusiasm about following us," Nyal observed. "We'll have to go on by ourselves to The Eacon's. What do you think, Ruf, can we make it by nightfall?"

Ruf nodded. "With a little luck. Here, Tym, don't stand around in the water! You'll chill yourself."

Tym roused himself, stumbling across the rocks to high ground. In the mud of the riverbank Avelaer stood, breathing hard. For once the horse made no attempt to bite as Tym rubbed his neck and flanks with the tail of his soggy coat.

Nyal turned again to the far shore. "Go by way of Maoleen's Bridge!" he shouted, waving his arms. "If it's held against the current, they'll be able to join us at Eacon's Keep the day after tomorrow," he told Ruf. "Maoleen's Bridge!" he shouted again over the roar of the water, making the shape of a bridge with his arms. At last Landes, a smile of understanding lighting his face, turned his horse away from the riverbank. Ned hurled Nyal's helmet and lance across the water. Adler threw his shield. Made of heavy oak reinforced with iron, it fell short and was swept downstream, barely floating.

"Ogre turds," Tym heard Nyal exclaim in disgust. The lords on the other side of the river turned to follow Landes and disappeared into the mist. Tym loosened the girth and pulled off Avelaer's saddle, smoothing the soggy saddle pad. The bedroll and all the extra food and grain that Nyal had carried had been torn loose by the river. "We've no lunch," Tym complained, as he saddled the stallion again. "And nothing for the horses." A chill swept him, making his teeth chatter.

"Ruf," Nyal ordered, "make a fire and warm Tym. I'll find my shield, if Adler hasn't lost it forever." He took the time to lead Avelaer a few steps to be sure he was sound. Then he vaulted into the saddle and rode into the trees that followed the riverbank.

"I've my own fire, Ruf," Tym said. His hands shook with cold as he pulled a pewter flask from his soggy pocket and drank deeply. The Elfin brandy warmed him as he huddled beneath a great oak. Ruf patiently struck sparks off his flint lucky piece with his dagger blade into soggy moss. Together they shielded the thin flame from the wind and rain with their bodies. The rain lightened, and a thick, cold fog obscured the road. It seemed to Tym that he was keeping the fire warmer than it was keeping him.

They could hear Nyal long before they saw him. He materialized suddenly in the mist, leading the brown palfrey, his shield hung triumphantly from the pommel of his saddle. "Here Tym, I found your horse!" His grin was larger than Tym had seen in months. "We're on our own now!"

"Aye, and alone on the open road, sir." Ruf Nab's voice was heavy with warning.

But Tym, too, felt relieved that the Lords of the North had left them. "It's Stone Moving time, Ruf," he said. "We'll be safe and warm by sundown." He gingerly stepped close enough to Avelaer to take the palfrey's reins from Nyal's outstretched hand. The stallion's ears flashed flat to his head and he snapped his teeth. Nyal checked him sharply. "Mount up, we've a good day's travel before us." Nyal turned the chestnut toward the road.

Tym drummed his heels on the palfrey's sides and the tired horse began a reluctant trot. Tym could feel a rivulet of cold water running down the back of his neck and he cursed the day he'd forsaken sailing a warm and sunny sea for adventures among peculiar folk in inclement places. Ruf Nab's pony cantered beside him. Three horse lengths ahead, barely visible in the thick fog, Avelaer trotted easily. *Just wait*, grumbled Tym to himself. *In another hour you won't prance so well with your fetlocks full of frozen mud.*

They rode in a silence punctuated only by hoofbeats and the sharp sounds Avelaer made as he tossed his head, pulling on the bit. "Whoa," Nyal said soothingly. "Whoa, good boy." Cold rain streamed down his cheeks and his helmet glistened in the grey light. "By The Old Girl, he spoils me, this horse. Nothing like a bit of spirit to keep you on your toes."

Or on your back, thought Tym. The activity of riding began to warm him, and the memories of cold water and raging rapids faded from his mind. If Avelaer could keep up this pace, they would make The Eacon's Keep well before nightfall. If the roads didn't get worse. Or the palfrey give out. Tym was mulling over other possible complications when Avelaer stopped with a sharp snort.

Nyal urged Avelaer forward, but the chestnut refused, shaking his head and prancing in a circle in the muddy road. *Now he's balking,* thought Tym angrily, but before the thought was out of his head he heard a soft noise from the thick fog to his right.

Nyal heard it, too. "Hello?" he shouted. Avelaer whinnied deep in his throat and an answering sound come from the thick mist. "Hello!" cried Nyal again.

A strangely hoarse voice (so close it made Tym jump) called, "Who goes there?"

Avelaer, in a froth of excitement, danced sideways, shaking his head, trying to seize the bit. "Nyal of Crowell," Nyal managed to shout, pulling the horse's head around, "with his man, Tymeryl, and Ruf Nab the Dwarf. Whoa!" With a violent jerk on the reins he managed to still the chestnut for a moment. "I thought everyone was on the road with Lord Landes."

"Nyal of Crowell!" said the voice softly.

The fog was so thick that Tym could see nothing clearly past the palfrey's ears. A peculiar chill, colder than the river, swept over him. "Sir, be careful!" he said.

"The mongrel of Crowell and his Brownies!" jeered the voice.

Ruf Nab stiffened. "A New Faith bigot!" he hissed. Tym made out the dim figure of a horseman on the road ahead of him.

"Watch your tongue!" Nyal cried out.

"Sir, be careful," cautioned Tym again.

"You'd best swallow your pride, Nyal," Ruf Nab hissed. "We're alone in this forsaken fog."

"Take back those words!" Nyal raged. "Or I'll school you in manners!"

A deep laugh seemed to echo, as though from the depths of a dark crypt. "School! Crowell's mongrel would teach me manners!" The sound of steel on brass cut through the swirling mist as an unseen sword was drawn from its scabbard.

"Oh, sir, be careful!" Tym pleaded.

"I'm this bigot's match!" Nyal reached to unbuckle Firestroker as Avelaer reared with excitement. Nyal jerked him to a standstill, peering into the mist before him. "Show yourself, New Faither!" he challenged.

"A lesson!"

The words sounded in Nyal's ear only a split second before the edge of a sword crashed against his helmet. Reeling and dazed, he fumbled for Firestroker as he lifted his shield to fend off the next blow. Avelaer trumpeted, whirling to meet the attack.

"New Faith treachery!" shouted Ruf Nab. His Elfin pony was swift and brave, but the Dwarf's broadax was not designed for mounted combat. He attacked the horseman, a tall figure on a grey horse, his black shield gleaming in the lightly falling rain.

With a cry, the Human spurred forward, the jeweled hilt of his sword held high, the blade lost for a moment in the fog. The force of the blow was shattering, crumbling the Dwarf's great strength, knocking the ax from his hand. The pony went down, struggling in the grass.

Tym drew his short sword as the horseman turned toward him. He thrust it with desperate abandon at the vulnerable area between helmet and shoulder. The stranger parried and the air was ripped by the long sword's passage as it narrowly missed Tym's ear. Without helmet or armor, the groom sought to retreat, but the brown palfrey was awakened by battle. Neighing in a poor imitation of Avelaer, he laid back his ears and kicked viciously at the grey horse, bringing Tym within sword range again. Tym saw the flash of the jeweled hilt and tried to duck.

Luckily, the palfrey's maddened attack unbalanced the horseman and the blow was landed with the flat of the sword, which surely saved Tym's life. The impact took his breath and he felt all his life's heat sucked from his body. With a sudden longing for peace, he tumbled from his horse's back. "Run, sir!" he cried, lying as though dead on the muddy road. The clash of arms surged above him. He closed his eyes so as not to see the horse's hooves hammering the soggy turf on either side of his head.

Nyal had freed Firestroker from its sheath. Avelaer screamed and reared. Nyal pulled him down and set his heels, driving his horse forward. He swung Firestroker with all his strength, but he was no match for the tall horseman. Each blow weakened him, numbing his arm, chilling his thoughts. A flash of the blade knocked the breath from his body. Another sent him reeling to the ground, where he fell across Tym. As he struggled to rise, the point of the heavy sword caressed his throat.

"Be still!" the hoarse voice barked. The horseman towered above Nyal. He leaned down, pressing the sword tip deeper. Nyal gasped and braced himself.

"I'll not kill you yet, mongrel puppy," said the hoarse voice. "You'll need seasoning if you're to die as well as Telerhyde. I trust you'll see fit to teach me even more when next we meet. Roth Feura!" He saluted the fallen Human with a sweep of his sword, touched his horse with a spur, and was gone.

Tym lay quietly, listening to the sound of hooves receding. "Tym?" came Nyal's voice. "Tym?" He felt himself pulled up from the mud. Cautiously, he tested his legs and arms. Everything worked. "Dragon's Breath, I thought you were killed!"

"Me too, sir," Tym agreed.

"Ruf?"

"Here!" came a cry. Together they followed the sound of the Dwarf's voice through the fog.

They found the pony first, dead where it had fallen. "Brave little beast," murmured Nyal. Ruf was leaning against a tree, his leg extended before him. Tym knelt beside him and brushed away the mud and sand. There was a deep wound in Ruf's knee. Nyal tore a strip from his tunic. "Why did you let him get away?" Ruf asked ruefully.

"Get away?" Tym exclaimed. "We're lucky we're still alive! I've never felt a blow like that fellow struck! It chilled me to the bone."

"I thought I was going to join The Dragon right here in the mud," Nyal said ruefully. He was not practiced in field surgery, but he stopped the flow of blood and bound the wound tightly. Then he sat beside Ruf and leaned against the tree, feeling the dazed reverie that often follows combat.

"I don't like it," growled Ruf. "First Telerhyde is attacked on the road, and now Nyal. The House of Crowell has a treacherous enemy."

"So why are we alive?" asked Tym. "He didn't spare us out of mercy." His teeth began to chatter again.

"We'd best be on the road," Nyal said abruptly. "Ruf, you'll ride behind Tym. We've a long ride to reach Eacon's Keep tonight."

But Ruf Nab's wound slowed their pace. Despite Nyal's best efforts, the saddle grew red with blood.

Tym shivered in apprehension at every turn in the road. "I wish the sun would burn off this cursed fog," he said several times.

Chapter 14

Melloryth awoke instantly, like a wild thing, consciousness flooding her like a bell pealing an alarm. She lay perfectly still, invisible among the quilts and blankets that covered her, listening. The eaves dripped outside her window and a rooster crowed and flapped in the yard. From the barn came the hollow sound of a wooden bucket dropped on stone and a soft curse. But The Eacon was not awake yet, for all about her The Keep was silent. She rolled over on the soft feather-stuffed mattress, hugging a pillow to her belly for her ritual daydream.

Ever since she had come to live with her uncle, the dream had been the same. She saw herself homeless, wounded, brave, and beautiful but driven to despair in some foul dungeon or dark wood. Sinister figures tortured her, tried in vain to make her speak, to betray her love. When all hope seemed lost, *he* came, like a bright ray of sunshine, fighting his way to her dungeon. He freed her from the dark demons and carried her away to the mountains, close to the sky, where everything was white and pure. There he nursed her back to health, grateful that she hadn't betrayed him, loving her above everyone else. He was strong, tall, and powerful. His kindness to her was equaled only by his ferocity toward her enemies. But try as she might, in her dreams he never had a face.

A sharp rap on the foot of the bed shattered her dream. "Get up, girl! He'll be up in no time. Get up and scrub your face!" Ethyl was an old woman, always in a state of alarm, always rushing about leaving tasks half-done. Melloryth trusted her because by trying to avoid The Eacon's anger, Ethyl made sure that Melloryth did nothing to provoke it. Although she saved herself, in this way she also made Melloryth's waking life more bearable.

Melloryth rose reluctantly and dressed, combing her long blond hair so that it fell free over her shoulders and down her back. Ethyl selected a forest-green frock, yanking the belt roughly about the girl's thin waist. The crone frowned and clucked over Melloryth's small, budding breasts, pulling the fabric into folds that gave the illusion of flatness. "Slump over, girl. There, that's better." Ethyl shook her head, brushing Melloryth's hair with impatient fingers. "I've done my best with you," she sighed in exasperation as she pinched Melloryth's cheeks to redden them.

Ethyl started as a bell rang in the courtyard. "Vorsai damn them!" she exclaimed. "They'll be waking *him* up and we'll all be in trouble!" Melloryth followed the old nurse to the window to peek at the scene below. Men-at-arms raced toward the gate, grasping spears and swords. Four archers scrambled up the steps to the ramparts. One was half-dressed and hopped frantically as he sought to run while he pulled up his drawers. Melloryth laughed and Ethyl cuffed her into silence.

The gatekeeper arrived, barrel chested and strutting with

importance. He hurried along, impeccably dressed in his short cloak and displaying his badge of office proudly. A ragged and skinny boy trotted at his side. Everyone in the yard froze in position. The bell fell silent. At the top of the ramparts, the gatekeeper peeked over the wall. "Open the gate!" he cried. The ragged boy scrambled to swab the pulley and rope with tallow as the drawbridge lowered smoothly. With much ceremony and great creaking and groaning, the gate was raised as the drawbridge lowered. A horseman galloped across, his horse's hooves making a sound like thunder in the quiet courtyard. He was clad in full armor and carried a shield painted black. He rode straight to the great door of The Keep in the center of the courtyard.

"There's another for breakfast! Why doesn't anybody ever tell me!" Ethyl bolted from the room, her hands flapping in alarm.

Melloryth followed her down the dark and twisting stairs to the great hall. It was a large room on the second floor of The Keep, with a smoky fireplace in one corner. At its center stood a rectangular table surrounded by massive chairs. Here Melloryth took three meals a day with her uncle. Here he instructed her in the behavior appropriate for an Eacon's niece and taught her to worship the Vorsai. Usually it was a place of whispers, but this morning it was filled with muted cries and curses as half-dressed Human men and women rushed back and forth, readying the hall for the unexpected guest.

Moments later The Eacon hurried in, pulling his crimson robes around his great girth. His hair was still rumpled from sleeping and a morning beard darkened his chin. He stood at the center of the room, directing preparations with sharp commands. At a glance from him, Melloryth slunk to her chair. Bread crumbs and the remains of the roasted lamb from the previous night covered the table.

The sound of footsteps rang on the stairs and through the door strode the man. Melloryth recognized Lothen at once. He wore his armor as lightly as another man might wear a woolen cloak. Although he was clean-shaven, to Melloryth it seemed that the darkness of his cloak and armor shrouded his face. He crossed the room quickly, greeting The Eacon as an equal. "Roth Feura! I have done my part, our project has begun," he said. "It only needs a little time, like good cheese. In a few weeks, I will lead an army to the south to begin the final conquest of Morbihan."

"Excellent, Lothen, excellent!" The Eacon exclaimed, a wide smile creasing his handsome face. "By that time, the lords of the North will be leaderless, fighting among themselves. The land will be open to your cleansing sword."

Melloryth nibbled at cold lamb, her lips curling back in distaste from the congealed fat that clung to it. She kept her eyes properly downcast.

"I met Telerhyde's mongrel puppy," Lothen said as he pushed back his cowl and sat with The Eacon at the table. "I found him on the road with his Brownies. If all Morbihan's lords fight as he did, there will be no sport."

"You didn't kill him?" The Eacon asked anxiously.

Lothen spat on the floor. "No. You have said you had a use for him."

The Eacon rubbed his finger across his lips. "He will be my tool to disrupt the lords." He poured wine into golden chalices. "How fitting it is that now, even as Brownies and their Human protectors descend upon us to celebrate their victory of the past, we toast their approaching defeat!"

After they had toasted, Lothen said, "Telerhyde's mongrel will be close behind us."

"You must be safely hidden when they arrive. Fryd!"

The servant slunk from behind the door. "Yes, Your Grace?"

"Be sure Lord Lothen's horse is walked till it's cool and the saddle marks brushed out. And escort my guest to the crypt of the chapel. Secure the bolts on the door and make sure no one approaches him! Guard him with your life."

"Yes, Your Grace."

Lothen bowed, then turned to follow Fryd through the door.

The Eacon looked at Melloryth when Lothen had gone. She was picking at the bread before her. It was stale from being out all night and crumbled in her fingers. The Eacon glared. "Must you always make so much noise? How can I think?"

Melloryth shrank away from him. "I'm sorry, Uncle."

He continued to regard her intently. "The demons will begin to arrive soon, and I don't want you exposed to Old Faith decadence. The thought of what the vile creatures would do with one of your innocence makes me shudder." He picked up a pheasant leg and chewed in his rapid, businesslike way as he watched her. She was unnerved, for he rarely addressed her at the table except to correct her manners.

"What vile creatures are they?" she stammered, stupidly.

"Monsters of The Old Faith! Consort with them and you will become as low as they! Do you understand? If you disobey me you will become loathsome and scaly!" exclaimed The Eacon seriously. "You are not to talk with any of The Old Faith, ever! Into the chapel now, and ask The Vorsai to protect you."

Her breakfast half-eaten, Melloryth fled from the great hall. The demons were coming to Eacon's Keep!

Ethyl passed her on the stairs. The girl shrank away from her, stumbling, made awkward by the irregular stone of the steps. When the old woman was out of sight up the curving stairwell, Melloryth ran the rest of the way to the bare dirt courtyard outside The Keep. A few chickens fluttered at her breathless entrance before resuming their picking and stalking. She stood among them, unsure what to do next.

"Melloryth is a Brownie-lover!" She whirled about at the sound of the jeering voice. The gate boy was no taller than she, his dark hair wild and tangled. Tallow from the gate rope covered his hands and clothing and his dark eyes flashed in his narrow, dirt-caked face. He was Ethyl's boy, one of the few children who lived in The Keep. He was a rowdy boy who threw rocks at chickens and delighted in tormenting Melloryth when there was no adult around to protect her. "Brownie-lover! I'll tell The Eacon! He'll burn you with the demons! Melloryth's a demon lover! Troll!"

"Leave me alone! I'll tell your mother! I'll tell my uncle!" But she wouldn't, for she feared The Eacon's anger even more than she dreaded the gate boy's derision. She turned away, determined to ignore him and make her way to the temple that nestled at the back of The Keep. He followed her, taunting. Suddenly it was too much. Without warning, she raced across the courtyard. The chickens ran before her, flapping and clucking in chickenlike terror. She knew he dared not openly chase her in the courtyard. She raced once completely around The Keep and when she glanced back, he was nowhere in sight. She leaned against the cool stones and scowled away the tears that swam in her eyes. Holding her lips tightly so that they would not quiver, she imagined the gate boy on his knees before her hero, pleading, lying. She nodded and her hero swung his sword, avenging her with a mortal blow. She had rested only a few minutes when the bell rang at the gate.

"Riders ho!" cried the watchman. Melloryth turned toward the gate, her blue eyes narrowing as she watched the gate boy again follow the gatekeeper across the courtyard.

The group that rode across the drawbridge made her gasp. She saw the demon first, for it was grotesque and horrible beyond her belief. It was no taller than she was, with a broad face, red hair, and huge, gnarled hands. It wore armor, but that did nothing to disguise its squat body and long, misshapen limbs. Melloryth shrank back against the stones, her heart beating so loudly that she feared the demon would hear. With the Other rode two Humans. One was pale and thin, and rode behind the demon. The second was astride a prancing chestnut.

She recognized instantly that he was different from all the rest. Although he was begrimed by the mud of the road, his eyes were wide set and gentle, his face fine and intelligent. He moved with grace and dignity. He wore a deep blue tunic and a cloak the color of new rust with lovely green leaves embroidered about the front. The scabbard of the sword which hung from his waist was heavily tooled, an ornamental gold dragon twining its full length. Melloryth's heart leaped up with the beauty of him.

He dismounted, brushing his hair back from his face. Melloryth shrank back against the chapel wall. The demon slid from his horse, leaving a long streak of blood on the saddle. She gasped and darted away. In the soft mud of the courtyard she slipped.

"Here, My Lady, let me help you." The handsome Human reached out his hand and steadied her. For a moment he grasped her waist, then gently set her on her feet. "I am Nyal of Crowell," he said to Tyrll, who approached them. "Tell The Eacon I'm here!"

"My Lord, The Eacon awaits you." Tyrll bowed and gestured toward The Keep.

"I'm sure he does," Nyal replied. "Tym, see to Ruf's wound." He swept away from her, striding across the mud to The Keep's door. She stared after him, stunned. Behind her the demon groaned as he was led toward the stable.

With startling grace, she darted around the corner of the temple and ran to The Keep. She paused only long enough to be sure no eyes were watching before lightly scrambling all the way up the slanted stones to the wide ledge that ran beneath the windows of the great hall, a full lance length above the ground. Here she inched her way along on her hands and knees. Beneath a glassless window, she pressed her back against the familiar rock. By lying flat, she was concealed from both the eyes in the courtyard below and anyone looking out the window from the great hall. She often hid here, for she could survey the courtyard and be warned of the approach of the gate boy or other enemies.

Inside, Nyal stood in the doorway of the great hall. She crept closer to the window, and heard his voice. It was rich and vibrant, ringing with strength. She dreamed her dream again, and this time the hero had a face. It was Nyal who rescued her. In league with her fat uncle, the gate boy called up a legion of demons to torment her. Undaunted, Nyal fought through all the Ogres, trolls, Peskies, sorcerers and witches of the north until he faced The Great Dragon, The Old Girl of the Mountain who held Melloryth captive.

The Eacon sat at the table, huge and brilliant in his red robes. As Nyal strode through the door, The Eacon thrust his great bulk back from the table and rose. "The new lord of Crowell!" he said. "How good of you to come to see me." He held out his hand as Nyal stepped before him.

"I am not lord of Crowell, Eacon," Nyal said. He ignored the outstretched hand and declined the chair which The Eacon indicated.

"Welcome to my home. Are you sure you won't sit? You

must be weary, traveling in this dreadful weather. You are very brave, traveling alone. The roads are dangerous."

"Yes, they are," Nyal agreed, stiffly. "My party was attacked."

"No!" The Eacon's eyes widened as he sat back, his chair groaning under his weight. "Attacked! How terrible! I must agree with some of the lords, I'm afraid. The trolls must be eliminated. No one is safe until they are."

"Not trolls. A Human horseman."

The Eacon frowned, shaking his head. "You're not telling me that the Lords of the North attacked you?"

"Of course not." Nyal regarded The Eacon steadily, watching for a flinch, for a sign of wavering.

"My Lord, I fail to understand." The Eacon returned his gaze, cold eyes wide in seeming puzzlement.

"A horseman hailed us—a bigot, to judge by his greeting. He insulted us and attacked with no warning. The Dwarf Ruf Nab was wounded and lost his pony saving my life."

"Well, this is terrible. Attacked you! Whoever could he be?"

"I think you might know," Nyal said evenly. "He swore New Faith oaths and his shield was black without heraldry."

"Oh, dear." The Eacon shook his head. "You think that I have had something to do with this unfortunate incident?"

Nyal said nothing, watching.

The Eacon leaned forward earnestly. "I have many followers in this country, but by the terms of the Peace of Harkynwood, I am allowed only the few armed retainers who protect my walls. Tyrll rides on my errands with only a dagger to protect himself. If you believe that I was the source of the attack, then you must also think that I sent my altar tenders and novices to carry it out."

"I think it has become dangerous for your enemies to travel the roads," Nyal said quietly.

The Eacon raised his eyebrows in surprise. "I was told you lacked diplomacy. You certainly say what's on your mind." His large lips pursed. "If I may, Your Lordship," he said, "there may be an answer to your question. As you know, your father never prohibited me from preaching the faith of The Vorsai, and I do preach. I spread the word with all my heart. I have many followers, more each year, and there may be lords amongst them. I don't count a Human's rank, only his humanity. But I have no control over what my followers do. If any of them have been the source of this trouble, then I promise that I will expound against such violence from my pulpit. But that is the only power I have. Is that sufficient?"

"The arrest of my father's murderers and of the men who attacked me will be sufficient."

"Of course. We all hope for that," the golden voice purred. Laboriously, The Eacon rose to his feet. "I forget myself. I wish to extend my sympathy over the loss of your brother. Terrible to be swept away like that, so young, such a bright future before him. Terrible, so soon after your father's death. Your father had won my respect and admiration, you know. I grieve with you."

Nyal said nothing.

"They say he conquered me, but your father was my teacher, wasn't he, Tyrll?" The Eacon laughed. "That was a time! You're too young to remember, but we old men were all young, then. Young and hot-blooded, each with our cause, our passion." He leaned toward Nyal, looking him in the eye. "Your father was a fine man. A great mediator. He cooled my passions so that I'm no longer a warring missionary. I have become a peaceful pastor. I live in peace with the Other folk." He paused for a moment. "Yes, I was sorry to hear that your father was dead. Not that I expect you to believe me, of course."

Nyal colored, a ruddy flush that crept from his collar to the roots of his hair. "I believe you're glad that Telerhyde is dead. And I believe that he was a great man who taught you much," he said.

The Eacon laughed. "What a refreshing change. An Old Faither as direct and honest as a Moerian centurion!"

"I am a farmer. I don't have fancy words for common things. I wish only to avenge my father's and brother's deaths and get home for planting."

"Avenge your brother's death? I thought he died of sickness."

Nyal stammered and cursed himself. He had not meant to

mention Brandon to The Eacon. The golden voice had lulled him for a moment. "My father's, I meant."

"How very interesting!" The Eacon smiled and Nyal was reminded of a wolf. "But there are happier events in your life, are there not? You will marry soon, I hear."

Nyal shifted uncomfortably. He did not like discussing Cyna with this man. "I am pledged," he admitted. "Lord Landes will announce my engagement to Lady Cyna of Fanstock at the Council of Lords." He sensed a commotion at the window, but when he glanced up, there seemed to be nothing there.

"You won't believe this, but I wish to drink to your health and your long life, Your Lordship." The Eacon smiled as he poured wine.

Nyal didn't drink. As he told Tym later, he suddenly couldn't swallow. For some reason he was thinking of Brandon's silver flask.

Melloryth had heard. A terrible aching in her throat and the sharp sting of tears held her frozen on the window ledge. Nyal was not hers! He was pledged to another! A blind rage shook her and she saw him helpless beneath a dragon's great claws, calling out for her. She spurned him and he pleaded with her, crying out for her mercy. Feeling somewhat better, she cautiously inched along the window ledge until she could gain a handhold on the angled rock that led to the floor of the courtyard.

There the seneschal, a portly man who had a daughter of his own just that age, smiled at her. "Careful, my little lady, you'll scrape your knees!" he called merrily. To the gatekeeper he chuckled. "That age and they don't know if they wants to be ladyloves or young jacks!" They both laughed.

Melloryth's ears flamed. She strode across the courtyard, chickens scattering before her. They would regret this. For a moment the castle stood in ruins before her, smoldering. Nyal lay senseless before her new hero, a faceless knight dressed in white with a long gleaming sword. The seneschal cowered before her wrath. Another chicken squawked and she jerked herself from her dream.

There were visitors at the drawbridge. The gatekeeper was

running toward the gate with the gate boy scrambling behind him. The foot soldiers were straightening their helmets. Melloryth watched the new arrivals with interest. It was a gathering of immense demons who rode across the drawbridge proudly, like a conquering army. At their head was an old Human man on a pony and beside him was a great, hairy, almost manlike beast mounted on a huge, shaggy unicorn. The unicorn's dim eyes stared suspiciously about and its huge, stumplike feet rang on the drawbridge. The timbers sagged under its weight. Behind rode more hairy, manlike creatures. Bringing up the rear by herself strode a tall, dark-haired Human girl only a little older than Melloryth.

"Hear ye!" bellowed the sergeant-at-arms. "Give greeting to our guests! Master Fallon, Seventh-Degree Wizard; His Majesty Ur Logga, king of the Harkynwood Ogres; Lady Cyna of Fanstock, Apprentice Witch! Make way!"

Chapter 15

The Eacon's Keep rose up dark and foreboding from a rocky promontory at the base of the peninsula known as Wolf's Fang. It was remote from Human settlement, bordering Harkynwood on one side and the raging Northern Sea on the other. In Kythra's time, the area had been settled by Elves and for long was a prosperous Elfin community. The black granite keep and the outer ramparts dated from this era, as shown by their lofty, sky-embracing lines. Over the centuries, the encroaching sea had undercut the cliffs until at high tide The Keep was cut off from the mainland. Once, on the occasion of a High Meg-Feast, the cliff had crumbled and part of the outer wall had fallen into the sea. For generations the Elfin castle lay deserted.

After the Battle of Harkynwood, the leaders of The Five Tribes decided it made a fine place to confine Eacon Gleese and The New Faith. The Keep was reroofed and a drawbridge built across the chasm carved by the sea. The Eacon had reconstructed the outbuildings and raised a temple to The Vorsai within the rampart walls.

Despite a light drizzle, Cyna glimpsed The Keep through the trees that edged the muddy road from more than a mile away. The low, spreading castle of Fanstock Manor and the underground halls of Urden Barrow had left her unprepared for an architecture which soared up with lofty arrogance against the sky. The tower balanced high over the cliffs, the rain-darkened granite gleaming like a black fissure in the wide expanse of sky and sea.

The procession halted for a short rest not far from The Keep. The Ogre Honor Guard climbed down from their unicorns to sit, touching each other, their great knobby fingers smoothing each others' hair. Ur Logga moved ceremoniously from Ogre to Ogre. Growling words of encouragement to each one, he accepted from each of his followers the ritual grooming with which Ogres strengthened their communal courage.

Cyna dismounted from where she rode behind Bem Grippon, the commander of the Ogre Honor Guard. By the side of the road, she quickly changed out of her brown traveling cloak into the sky-blue robe of a Magic worker. She helped Fallon into his vestments and watched as he fluffed his beard so that it flowed over his chest. Then the party remounted and approached The Keep.

Her senses were made keen by excitement. Each wave in the rain-driven sea stood out in bold relief. The stately rhythm of the unicorn's stride, the smell of damp Ogre hair, and the sight of the great Keep seemed all one delicious feast. Pennants flew from the towers and men-at-arms had assembled at the ramparts. The drawbridge was lowered across the moat. The golden sound of Ogre bugles sweetened the air as Ur Logga and Fallon led the procession into the courtyard. Cyna had not seen so many Humans in one place since leaving Crowell. The Eacon's servants and New Faith followers stepped back apprehensively and she was aware of many eyes following her. She held herself proudly, looking straight ahead.

Before her, Ur Logga and Fallon rode side by side, The Wizard's pony dwarfed by the Ogre's massive unicorn. The

Honor Guard followed in tight formation, like a conquering army. Entering the bastion of The New Faith, the triumphal procession crossed the courtyard through a sea of faces, some filled with hatred, other aloof with disdain.

At the center of the courtyard, between The Keep and the temple, the procession ended. A final bugle note was blown and trailed off into silence, leaving echoes playing between the towers. Before the keep, Eacon Gleese stood at the top of a short flight of steps. Ur Logga and Fallon reined in their mounts. The Ogre ducked his head pleasantly, a polite smile baring his canines, but Cyna was surprised to see the arrogant set of Fallon's jaw and shoulders. The crowd was silent, watching. The Eacon descended the stair slowly and reluctantly. Before the guests he bowed his head and sank to his knees. "I bid you welcome," he said hoarsely, "Master of Magic."

"I am not alone." Fallon's voice cracked like a whip, echoing off the stones of The Keep's walls.

Cyna thought The Eacon would choke. "And his most esteemed majesty, the Ogre king," he managed.

"What about him?" insisted Fallon.

The words came reluctantly, as though he were swallowing a foul brew. "I welcome him to Eacon's Keep."

"Thank you, Gleese," Fallon said, his voice touched with sarcasm. "You must study! Eighteen years and you still don't remember your part in our ceremony! Or your manners. Or perhaps your memory is becoming poor with age. We don't want anyone thinking you're lame of brain, do we?"

The Eacon, looking like a great stranded seal, struggled to his feet. "Age does not temper you, Fallon," he observed.

"Mayhap it makes me more keen," Fallon said dryly. "Surely it seems to make you wider."

The Ogres turned politely away and stared into the distance to publicly protest that they had not heard the insult. The Eacon's retainers and vassals made a light tittering sound of amusement.

The formal welcome for Fallon and the Ogres took only a few more moments. The seneschal led them to their rooms. Cyna was given a small chamber of her own overlooking the sea next to Fallon's quarters. Through the small window, late-afternoon sun illuminated tapestries which draped the walls. They were brightly colored, illustrating scenes of The Vorsai destroying his enemies (which looked suspiciously like Ogres and Dwarves to Cyna). With a sigh she put down her satchel beside the narrow cot. It felt good to be above ground and have a bed, despite The New Faith trappings. She had missed Humans. She knelt upon the rushes covering the stone floor, a prayer for guidance rising to her lips. A knock sounded at the door.

"Yes?" she called. She heard her name called and threw open the door. "Nyal!"

He took her in his arms, whirling her about the room until she was dizzy. Breathless, she pushed him back, her hands on his shoulders. "Nyal!" He stood only slightly taller than she did. His shoulders were broader than she remembered and his hair had lost the gold sheen it took on in the summer. It curled darkly about his forehead, but not enough to conceal a large bruise. She gasped. "What have you done to yourself?" she scolded. "Fallen off that horse again?" In her most professional manner, she sat him on the cot, touching his forehead gently. It was an alarming shade of purple and green and perfectly matched the colors of his tunic.

She rummaged through her parcel of possessions and extracted her herb box, a gift from Ur Logga. Smaller than Fallon's, it was of exquisitely carved rosewood with a leather carrying handle and many small compartments inside. Her slender fingers moved efficiently, extracting just what she needed. A small fireplace stood in one corner of the room and here she encouraged the fire and set a kettle to boil. Nyal leaned back on the narrow bed, smiling as he watched her work.

"You might take a look at Ruf Nab if you get the chance," he said. "He's worse off than I am."

"What happened?" Cyna asked.

"We were attacked on the road by a fellow. Ruf was hurt saving me."

"How terrible! Where were Father and the lords?"

He told her of the crossing of the ford. "They should be here soon."

Cyna applied a compress of dried arnica blossoms to his

forehead. He winced. "Hold still and don't let this drip all over the bed," she told him. "There's so much that's strange happening right now." The Bond of Silence gripped her chest with gentle pressure. She turned away toward the window.

"The strange thing is this fellow could have killed us. And he spoke like he knew who killed Telerhyde. Said I'd need seasoning to die as well."

"Oh, Nyal, be careful."

"I'll be all right. I'd just as soon not meet that fellow alone again, however. He's as strong as a unicorn. My sword arm still aches."

She cleared her mind. Her breathing became easier and she turned back to him. The compress covered half his face, but his left eye regarded her seriously. "Nyal, I have to tell you something. It's about Brandon. I've thought a great deal about his death. About how he could have slipped away like that, how nothing I did helped."

"Cyna, there was nothing you could do."

"No, there wasn't. Fallon has helped me to understand that even the greatest Healer cannot heal everyone. But I keep thinking about what happened."

Nyal shifted the compress of arnica leaves and leaned back against the wall, listening.

"And then a few weeks ago, I was reviewing herbal cures with Ur Logga's wife. Not many Humans know herbs really well. Ogres do, of course, but they guard the knowledge. With Humans, it's strictly Healers' business. And very secret." Cyna sat at the side of the bed and put her herb box between them. Opening the lid, she showed him the linen bags which contained the precious herbs. "In powerful doses, some of these herbs can kill. Fallon is very strict about this and Healers are carefully trained. While an accident is always possible, I don't believe that it's very likely. But if someone wanted to kill deliberately, there are many herbs which can be dangerous if misused. Ur Logga's wife told me of wolfsbane."

"The purple flowers?"

"Yes. The roots can be boiled to extract a powerful poison. It causes great pain and can kill in a few hours. She told me that it numbs the senses and gives the victim the sensation that he's flying. Do you remember what Brandon said to me?"

Nyal sat upright. "He thought he was floating up off the bed. He said that to me, too, when Gwen called me in earlier."

"Nyal, I think he was poisoned. Someone killed him." She lowered her voice. "I shouldn't talk to you about it. Herbology is a Magic art, and laymen—"

"Cyna, I must know!" His wide grey eyes were earnest and intense. "Have you spoken to Fallon about it?"

"Yes. And he listened, but he said there's no way of being sure. Lately, he's concerned with an Ogre prophecy . . ." Her chest constricted. "You must promise not to tell anyone I told you," she whispered.

"I promise."

"Swear, Nyal. Fallon would be furious if he finds out."

"I swear. I'll tell no one that you told me. But it's true, isn't it? Someone at the unicorn hunt poisoned Brandon." He smashed a fist into his palm. "I knew it! Cyna, I swear to The Dragon that I'll find him! Whoever he is, I will find him!"

She shuddered and reached for his hand. "But now you've been attacked!"

"There are strange things going on."

She looked at him appraisingly. "Stranger than you think," she agreed. "I don't know for certain, but I *believe* that your father's death and the weather are all part of something greater. At the Stone Moving . . ." A chill took her breath. "Nyal, I can't tell you. I want to, but I'm sworn. Fallon has placed the Bond of Silence on my lips."

"What do you know?" he insisted.

She gasped for breath, the pressure on her chest unbearable. "Please, Nyal, I'm forbidden."

"Well, I'm not forbidden. Will you answer me if you can?"

She nodded.

"Does your father see The Eacon very often?"

The pressure released. "What a strange question! Father has always been Telerhyde's emissary to Eacon Gleese, to settle arguments, to enforce rules when The New Faith broke them—Nyal! What are you thinking of?"

"I'm only thinking, that's all." He removed the compress from his forehead. "This is cold."

Cyna took it from him. "Hold still while I put on this salve."

While she stroked the salve gently into the bruise on his forehead, he went on. "I talked with The Eacon this morning. He studied Magic; he would know about herbs."

"But how could he have given wolfsbane to Brandon? He was nowhere near Crowell. He's said to hardly ever leave The Keep."

"Someone is helping him. That's why I asked about your father . . ."

She spread the salve more firmly and he yelped.

"Enough, my head is fine." He pulled away from her and stood up. "Brandon suspected who it was, I'm sure. He told me to trust no one . . ."

"He couldn't have meant your family's friends . . ."

"No one," he repeated.

"Well Brandon was wrong!" Cyna flared. "My father has served Morbihan for longer than you've been alive! He loves The Old Faith and he loved Telerhyde! When Ned and I were growing up, he spent more time with your family than he did with us! For you to accuse him of Telerhyde's murder is the most dishonorable thing I've ever heard!"

"Wait, Cyna, I didn't accuse him! But I have to consider everyone."

"Not my father! You might as well accuse Fallon. Or me."

"I'm accusing no one! But there's a traitor among the lords! I will consider everyone until I find the assassin!"

"A traitor . . ." Cyna began, but the Bond gripped her with such violence she could not go on. She turned away to the window.

Misunderstanding her, Nyal said, "I understand why you don't want to talk about this, but I cannot allow even our feelings for each other to interfere with my search for this man. I swore at Telerhyde's Leave-Taking to find his killer, and before you I pledge to The Dragon to find Brandon's. It's not only for the safety of Crowell and Young Tel, Cyna, it's for you and me—perhaps all of Morbihan." When Cyna remained silent he crossed to the door, then turned back. "I almost forgot. Lord Landes suggests that we pledge our love at the close of the Stone Moving ceremonies, before The Stone."

After a moment she heard the door close. It took longer for her to regain her breath. Trembling, she sat on the bed beneath the grinning face of The Vorsai, which leered at her from the tapestried wall.

As he usually did when he was disturbed, Nyal went to the stable. A stray cat followed him there and climbed up on a rafter, following him with its strange blue eyes. The stable was quiet and after a time he led out Avelaer to curry him. He glanced up to check the cat lest it startle his horse, but it had disappeared.

"Cyna's not being very reasonable," he muttered to himself.

"But she is!" a voice replied so close to his elbow that he jumped.

"Master Fallon!" he exclaimed.

"How do you do, my boy? Cyna is always reasonable. That's her greatest obstacle to obtaining wisdom, although I remain hopeful that she'll outgrow it. How was your journey? Ours was dreadful. Wet. Everyone's late. Rotten weather's impossible. You, me, and the Ogres, we're all that's here."

"A lot of farmers have come, sir. And the Peskie troops."

"Well, the just-plain-folks always come, weather or not. They love a good show of Magic. But I hope the lords arrive soon. I don't like being around Gleese without an armed troop with me."

Nyal nodded. "The lords will arrive soon."

"You have the Gift of prophecy?" Fallon's blue eyes twinkled with amusement.

"No, I only meant I *think* they'll arrive soon. If Maoleen's Bridge has held against the current, they'll be here tonight or tomorrow morning."

"I knew what you meant. Are you thinking to delay the ceremonies if they don't arrive? It's customary to begin promptly in order to reenact the ritual at the same time each year."

Nyal's brow furrowed in thought. "I suppose we must start when we must start, no matter who's here. If the lords are merely late, at worst they will miss the ceremonies. But if evil has befallen them, we will have the unity of the Stone Moving behind us to meet whatever happens."

"Well spoken." The Wizard turned to the horse in the stall.

"Be careful, Master, he bites."

"Yes?" said Fallon, petting Avelaer's nose. Avelaer laid back his ears but didn't bite. "I see his spirit is undimmed. You like troublesome spirits, don't you, Nyal? You'll wait long for a peaceful life." Nyal stood beside The Wizard, lost in thought. "What's on your mind?" Fallon prompted.

He was a long time answering. If he asked about poison herbs he would risk Fallon's anger toward Cyna. He proceeded carefully. "Master, I need your help."

Fallon smiled. "Cyna isn't really angry with you, if that's what it is."

"No, sir, it's not. Master Fallon, I'm sure The Eacon had Telerhyde killed. I believe that one of us has turned traitor."

The Wizard arched one eyebrow. "One of the lords? you may be right. I said as much to Brandon. What do you need from me?"

"Can you use Magic to see the traitor?"

Fallon shifted uncomfortably. "To see the past is akin to seeing the future. It is the profound understanding of the principle of cause and effect—I have never fully mastered it, I'm afraid. I will do all I can, Nyal, but in the end you must trust The Law."

Nyal regarded him steadily. "Master, I believe in what I can see, touch, and feel. I'm not a New Faither—I'm devoted to Magic and The Five Tribes. But I've never understood one thing about The Principles and The Law."

"I didn't say understand it, my boy. I said trust it to work for you. Because trust it or not, it will do its work and only you can determine whether it will be for or against you." He looked earnestly into Nyal's face, but whatever he hoped to see there was not forthcoming. "No matter. You will understand in time, I hope. And be assured that wherever Magic can help, I will be there." A commotion sounded in the courtyard. "The lords come. We must prepare to greet them."

But Nyal realized that Fallon was being honest about his prophesying ability, for it was not Lord Landes and the Lords of the North who had arrived at the castle drawbridge, it was Meg Dallo, the Elfin queen of Harkynwood.

She made a splendid entrance, borne by her well-muscled Husbands on an ornate litter and surrounded by musicians and dancers. The Meg held court for a long time while her Elves entertained. They had been settled down for only a little while when the bugle blew again and the heavily armored escort of Murdock, The Snaefid of the Dwarves, arrived. Stray Peskies filed across the drawbridge all afternoon. Finn Dargha and his retinue arrived by torchlight just after dinner.

As the only representative of the lords who was present, Nyal was expected to greet each Royal Other. He was unsure of the ritual, and wished he had paid more attention when Telerhyde was host. He felt awkward and as a consequence tended to be abrupt. He had no time to speak with Cyna, who was busy at Fallon's side.

He spent a sleepless night in the stable, caring for Ruf Nab and comforted by Avelaer's fretting strength. While he composed the speech he would make at the ceremonies the next day, he listened in vain for the arrival of Lord Landes and the rest. When he awoke in the morning, curled in the warm straw of the hayloft, there was still no sign of the Lords of the North.

Chapter 16

The day dawned with drizzle and fog. Always before, Landes had organized the ceremonies which opened the Council. As dawn grew into morning and he still had not arrived, a growing discomfort spread through the followers of The Old Faith. The uncertainty which the murder of Telerhyde had created was stirred again.

Because of his great tact, the Others elected Ur Logga to bring up the problem. He found Nyal in the blacksmith shop near the stable. "Nyal," Ur Logga began, tugging the bristling hairs on his chin, "you need a vassal to ride at your right hand." The flowers with which Ogres customarily festooned themselves for the ceremonies had not bloomed in this cold, springless year. Instead, Ur Logga was festooned in pussy willows interlaced with a few hardy green shoots. Vegetation was symbolically necessary to Ogres, but the effect was unsettling to Nyal.

"Yes, I know. Dragon's Breath, what do you suppose has happened? They should have been here yesterday."

"My cousins, the Northern Ogres are not here, either. And none of the representatives from Fensdown Plain. Master Fallon says we shouldn't worry—the roads are bad, the mountain passes still choked with snow."

"I didn't need a wizard to tell me that." Nyal paced the crowded space beside the cold forge with restless intensity. "Well, how about you, Your Majesty? In honor of your high position, you be my right hand."

The Ogre shook his shaggy head. "It must be a Human, Your Lordship. The vanguard has always been Human. The lord of Crowell in the center, with might on his right and Magic on his left. It's really quite beautiful."

Nyal sighed. At the moment, besides Cyna, Tym, and Fallon, the only Humans at The Eacon's Keep were of The New Faith. "My man, then," he said. "My man, Tym, will ride at my right hand."

When Ur Logga was gone, Nyal turned to study his reflection in a huge, freshly cast brass bell which rested on the floor of the smithy. Telerhyde's ceremonial armor and Snitch, the ornate long sword, had disappeared with Landes and the lords. Nyal was dressed in the armor and breastplate in which he had traveled to this place. Although Tym had stayed up all night burnishing the fittings, the armor was scratched and dull. Nyal placed his dented helmet on his head and frowned. Over the breastplate hung the rust-colored cloak which Cyna had presented him at his Sword-Naming. With Firestroker's plain hilt at his side, he looked like a poor soldier, not the powerful lord of Crowell. He wondered if his real father had looked like this, a simple man-at-arms, perhaps one of Telerhyde's followers from Harkynwood.

Tym was already busy in the stable with Ruf Nab. The Dwarf's limp was worse. Although he greeted Nyal with a grin and a deep bow, his cheeks were flushed and he seemed grateful to sit on a crude stool, holding his leg stiffly out before him, while Tym saddled the horses.

"Good morning, sir," Tym said, scowling. "A strangely hairy fellow wrapped in sticks just roused me from my bed and told me I am to be your right hand. Can't you find someone else, sir? I'm not good at speaking in public." Nyal caught a whiff of brandy on his breath.

"This is an important occasion," he cautioned the groom. "You must stand in for Lord Landes."

"Yes, sir," Tym agreed, the worried expression becoming more pronounced as he tried to replace it with a look of sober dignity. Tym's patchwork armor glistened in the morning mist. It was old and worn, but respectable.

Nyal cast a last glance toward the courtyard, but there was no sign of the lords. Fallon came by.

"Are you ready, Nyal? Do you remember the words?"

"I hope so, Master. Tym will be my right hand. Is that all right?"

"If that's what you've chosen. Fate has tied herself in knots to bring you here today, Nyal. Trust her."

Mounted, Nyal felt better. He was relieved, he realized, that his armor was his own. Telerhyde's armor was too big and he had dreaded the secret comparison he was sure everyone would make. Avelaer chewed the bit and tossed his head, sending the stable grooms scurrying for cover. Tym accepted Ruf's slow help in mounting the palfrey. "May The Old Girl be with us," Nyal whispered fervently. Ruf tossed him his lance.

The crowd, a mixture of Humans, Peskies, Ogres, Elves, and Dwarves of all ages were dressed in their best clothes. They fell back as the stable doors opened and Avelear bolted forward. Blocked by the wall of folk, Nyal was able to restrain the stallion and turn him toward the open gate. The horse pranced impatiently, his hooves loud on the drawbridge.

Outside the castle, the crowd was even larger. They lined the road and a ragged cheer went up as Nyal appeared at the castle gate. He noticed a brightly colored tent to one side where enterprising Elves were selling honey pies. A Dwarf near the gate was selling tiny replicas of Snitch, Telerhyde's sword.

But Fallon was directly in front of him. Wrapped in a splendid midnight-blue cloak shot through with spun gold, he sat astride a milk-white Elfin mare. At the sight of the mare, Avelaer snorted softly and pranced a little higher. The ceremony began.

"Who be Ye?" cried a voice from the crowd.

A silence fell and Fallon's voice, strangely deep and large for such an old man, boomed, "I am the Fire."

"Who be Ye?" shouted more voices as their expectant faces turned toward Nyal.

"I am the Hammer," he shouted, "forged by Fire." Behind him he heard the sound of the palfrey's hooves on the draw-bridge.

"Who be Ye?"

Tym was silent. *Little Gods, he doesn't know the ceremony!* thought Nyal.

"Who is that?" a ragged Peskie matron demanded.

"Who be Ye?" thundered the crowd.

"I be the Anvil," answered Tym, an uncertain quaver in his voice.

"You be the Anvil struck by the Hammer forged by Fire!" corrected the Dwarf by the gate.

"Yes," said Tym weakly, "I am."

The drawbridge was raised. The crowd cheered again and an avenue opened up. Keeping a tight rein on Avelaer, Nyal rode forward. Fallon fell in at his left and Tym at his right. They circled the castle. At the rear, where The Eacon's Keep faced the sea, the crowd thinned until the three riders were alone on a narrow path. The castle wall, ancient at this place, rose two lance lengths above them and faces, mostly Human, cheered them from the top. On the other side, scant inches from the hoofprints Tym's horse left, the brown turf fell away down the granite cliff into the pounding surf.

The narrow path widened as it turned away from the sea.

The Elves waited there, led by Meg Dallo, who reclined in her litter, bejeweled and swathed in gossamer fabrics. Her Husbands held the litter proudly on their shoulders.

"Who be Ye?" shouted the crowd as Nyal drew near.

Indolently, The Meg arose until, standing on the litter, she was within a head as tall as any Human in the crowd.

"I am Dallo, The Meg of the Elf folk. I come to mingle my powers with those of the Fire, the Hammer, and the Anvil."

"I rejoice," shouted Nyal, his voice lost in the shouts of the crowd.

"What did he say?" shrilled an excited Dwarflet by his stirrup.

"I rejoice!" Nyal bellowed.

The Meg curtsied and held her pinkies out in balance as her Husbands carefully stepped forward to join the procession. The rest of the Elfin dignitaries followed, blowing on their silver flutes and dancing as they came.

The ground and the castle wall both sloped downhill, curving gently toward the main gate. Halfway down the slope, Murdock and his band of Dwarves waited, beating on their black oak drums. They repeated the familiar greeting at the prompting of the crowd.

Before the gate, Ur Logga and his oddly dressed Honor Guard were assembled. They, too, repeated the venerated words and joined the march. Then Finn Dargha and his band of Peskie archers. Now the crowd broke its formal role as Questioner, and many joined the procession. Nyal raised his voice in The Song of Victory and was joined by the high, clear voices of the Elves and Peskies and the low, rumbling tones of the Ogres and Dwarves. Around the castle they marched twice more, the songs and shouts rising in volume and excitement.

The third time they came to the huge gate and drawbridge, they stopped. "Who be Ye?" the crowd roared and the air itself was filled with sound.

Nyal took a huge breath and shouted out over the clamor, "We are the Defenders of The Old Faith, the Warriors of The Dragon, the Movers of The Stone. United, we command you to open these gates and give room within to Life and Na-

ture!" He struck the drawbridge with his lance and was rewarded with a hollow echo.

"Who be Ye?"

A near silence fell. "Speak up, Eacon!" a querulous voice
said far back in the ranks.

"I am the Protector of The New Faith," came The Eacon's
voice, softly, from the other side of the drawbridge. The
ropes groaning, the drawbridge started down.

Fallon urged the white mare forward. "I call upon you to
witness the power of Magic and to acknowledge The Law!"

The Eacon rode a mule, its ears draped in embroidered tas-
sels. Behind him stood ranks of grim-faced men-at-arms.
Abruptly it occurred to Nyal that he and Tym were the only
armed Humans of The Old Faith present. A cold chill swept
him and his hand crept to Firestroker's hilt.

Then the warm, intimate tones of The Eacon filled the
roadway. "I open my gates to the Defenders of The Old
Faith. I forswear war and all violent acts and thoughts. I open
my heart to live in peace."

The crowd cheered ecstatically. The tangled throng led the
way, Humans, Dwarves, Peskies, Elves, and Ogres all crying
out to each other, embracing, clasping hands, and fervently
clapping each other on the back. Finn Dargha was raised high
on the shoulders of two Humans and he began to sing. The
procession dodged the larger puddles as it wound its way off
the road and down the slope of the bowl-shaped meadow
called Curlish Plot. At the bottom of the slope stood a wooden
platform festooned with banners. Nyal dismounted while Ruf
held Avelaer's head. Many hands reached out to him and he
laughed, clasping them in his own. He felt himself lifted up to
the platform. He looked down at their expectant faces.

The entire meadow was filled with Humans and Others
laughing and celebrating. Undaunted by the wet weather,
many had brought brightly wrapped picnic lunches with
them. The Royal Others climbed the platform, each one
cheered lustily by their followers. The last to arrive, The
Eacon stood a little apart from the Others, watching.

"My Friends," Nyal began, "my sisters, my brothers. I am
filled with joy to see you all today. We join in a mighty celebration." The drizzle had stopped and several Human and

Elfin families were spreading out blankets and exclaiming over their picnic victuals. Nyal raised his voice.

"Eighteen years ago, Telerhyde forged the peace that prospers us now. He led the followers of The Old Faith in victory over forces of hatred and intolerance. He created a community where he hoped we could *all,* Old Faith and New Faith, live in peace, harmony, and mutual friendship. He established this day as a celebration of victory, but also as a reminder that those among us who hate must never again be allowed to lead.

"But now, a generation later, is a different time. Telerhyde is cruelly murdered. Evil is loose in the land." As though a pall had fallen over the crowd, all stirring ceased. All eyes fastened on Nyal. His voice rose in strength as he cried, "Some of our friends and family are not here today, and it is a measure of the times that we feel concern for them! Our island must not be allowed to become a place where even armed men travel in fear. We must create a security so strong that all our races may live in safety!"

The sun broke through the clouds in a dazzling illumination that blinded Nyal for a moment. The entire crowd rose, cheering enthusiastically. He held his hands out to quiet them, for he had more to say. Then the sun went behind a cloud and Nyal saw the pennants of the Lords of the North fluttering against the sky. Relieved, he smiled and opened his arms in greeting.

At their head, Landes doffed his helmet and rode through the crowd, nodding and waving. The celebrants of the Eighteenth Annual Convention of the Peace of Harkynwood were shameless in their enthusiasm. Ogre mothers held up their hairy infants, Human men stood at attention and saluted, Elves began to sing "Deep in the Harkyn." From the crowd, Landes plucked up Cyna, leaning forward in the stirrups so that she might ride comfortably behind him. Her hair hung free, richly black against her sky-blue robe. She waved at the crowd and looked pleased. Moments later, followed by Cyna and the Lords, Landes bounded up the platform stairs and stood, waving and bowing to the crowd's heartfelt cheers.

"Welcome, M'Lord!" Nyal shook the older man's hand. "When you didn't arrive, I feared the worst."

"Why would you fear the worst?" Landes shouted above the crowd's roaring. "Who was that who rode in my place?" But the gathering was so noisy that Nyal's answer was swallowed up. Nyal had never heard a noise like the one which swept down upon him from the crowded hill. Voices called out "Lan-des! Lan-des!" Dwarves smashed their fists into their palms in rhythm. Only The New Faith followers who surrounded The Eacon watched silently.

When the cheering finally stopped and all the lords had taken their places on or near the platform, Nyal finished his speech. He called for vigilance and for greater unity. Fallon frowned, absentmindedly brushing the end of his beard across his lips like a paintbrush. Ur Logga listened seriously, a puzzled expression on his wide face. The Meg flirted with two of her Husbands, who flirted back, enjoying her attentions. Finn Dargha and Murdock glanced questioningly at each other. Only The Eacon remained impassive, his hands folded beneath his long vest, his eyes cast down.

When Nyal ended his speech, he drew Firestroker. His voice sounded more vibrant than Cyna had ever heard it. "I pledge my life and this sword to The Peace. May our children flourish and carry on." Cyna blinked and drew her hand across her eyes, for even though the clouds had obscured the sun, it seemed for an instant as if a brilliant light reflected off Firestroker's blade. "Now we merge our minds and move The Stone," Nyal announced, following the ritual of the ceremony. "Eacon, witness the power of The Five Tribes!"

"My dear, Lord of Crowell," replied the Eacon, his dulcet voice carrying to every listener in the field with a special intimacy. "I must respectfully accept." In a softer voice that only the leaders on the platform could hear he added, "Although I pray to The Vorsai to protect my everlasting soul from the company of evildoers and dark forces. Beware your own soul, My Lord."

Ignoring him, Fallon stepped forward and said, "Brothers, sisters, we move The Stone!" The crowd of Humans and Others parted to let The Wizard through. Cyna and her father followed a step behind him, while the leaders of the Others followed with the crowd. "You took your time," Fallon said over his shoulder to Landes.

"Maoleen's Bridge is out," Landes said. "We had to ride all the way to Finn's Crossing."

"You're always late, Landes," Fallon grumbled. "You were late at Harkynwood the day of the battle, too, if I remember."

Landes reddened slightly and slowed his pace, letting Fallon walk ahead. He fell into step beside Nyal. He spoke sharply. "Perhaps you should have waited for us, Nyal. Whatever possessed you to make so pugnacious a speech? Peace means trade with The Perime. Your father and I worked for many years to accomplish what we have, and the diplomacy is complex. Would you destroy The Peace?"

Cyna was surprised at the edge in her father's voice and wondered if, somehow, he knew of Nyal's suspicions. Nyal's reply was lost in the chorus of excited voices. Shrubs and cowpatties in the meadow made it difficult to keep formation and they drifted apart. As she crossed the meadow to the grove of oaks where The Great Stone stood, she sensed Nyal's gaze. She smiled at him and focused her mind on the coming ceremony.

Cyna had moved stones before, but never as an adult. As a child at home she had often enlisted Ned's assistance. She would meet him at the millpond and together they would stare at the pebbles beneath the surface of the pond until one would flip over.

But The Great Stone was different. Cyna had heard of its great size and power all of her life, yet each time she saw it, she was stunned. Although not as great as the fabled stone Argontell, it was huge. Three lance lengths high, she judged, and one wide. Eight Human men stretching out their arms couldn't join hands around it. Old even for a standing stone, it was carved and inscribed on every side with curling decorations and ancient runes.

It stood in the center of a grove of giant oak trees a short distance from The Eacon's Keep. The celebrants of The Peace assembled around it in no particular order. The grey cloud cover was breaking up and occasional patches of sunshine were greeted with cries and rumbles of delight from Humans and Others who had already gotten damp from sitting on the grass of Curlish Plot.

Cyna walked slightly behind Fallon, watching the Ogre

families and the Elfin groups excitedly calling to each other
as they crossed the meadow. Only the followers of The New
Faith, led by The Eacon, were downcast and silent, reluctant
observers of The Old Faith's power.

Ahead of her, Ur Logga stooped to speak to Landes. "Did
you see my relatives on the road?" he inquired. "My cousins,
Ham Urbid and his tribe, have never missed a Stone Moving
before."

"No, Your Majesty, we saw no one."

The Meg, in the swift flowing strides of the Elfin folk,
strode past, holding hands with two of her Husbands and
trailed by the rest. Nyal walked some distance behind them,
watching the backs of the lords, who jostled for a place
around The Stone. Tym walked to his right, Ruf Nab at his
left. Cyna noticed that the Dwarf's cheeks were flushed and
his limp pronounced.

Hundreds of assorted beings assembled around The Great
Stone. First there were more speeches. Ur Logga spoke for a
long time, his Ogre dialect making his vowels sound like
purrs and growls, his consonants popping and snarling. He
praised his Human friends as the organizers of The Peace,
spoke at length about Ogre history, his overwhelming desire
for peace, and his hopes for his tribe's future. Cyna found
her eyelids closing. The harder she tried to listen, the more
her head seemed to fall off her shoulders into sleep.

Meg Dallo spoke about disciplining the younger generation, danced a little, and sat down to enthusiastic applause.
The Snaefid of the Dwarves invited everyone to the Dwarf
tent after the ceremonies. Finn Dargha congratulated everyone for being present and wished them a good year.

Fallon rose. "It is time for the Stone Moving," he said. To
Cyna he whispered, "If The Stone falls, you are still not free
from the Bond of Silence. If it rises safely, perhaps it will encourage you to purge yourself of thoughts of mythical disaster."

"Yes, Master."

Fallon turned to the assembled community. "Thank you all
for participating with me in this celebration. Thank you for
joining with me to demonstrate once more the marvel of The
Law, the power of The Five Tribes working in harmony. I

cannot lift this stone alone. No Human, wizard or witch, can. No Elf, no Peskie, no Dwarf, no Ogre can move this stone. But together, as Kythra taught us, we can move a mountain. Together, let us prove the power of Magic!"

An excited scramble began as the audience found seats on the grass that surrounded The Stone. In the first row stood the leaders of The Old Faith, The Movers. Cyna was beside Fallon. She saw Nyal near the corner of The Stone, still flanked by Tym and Ruf Nab. All three found space between Finn Dargha and Ned.

Fallon spoke again, his voice taking on the deep resonance that so belied his age and size. "In accordance with The Seven Principles of The Law as revealed to us by Kythra and The Founders, I invite the Forces of Creation to join with us as we move this stone. Many paths, one truth, many thoughts, one desire, many tribes, one faith." He took Cyna's hand on one side, The Meg's on the other. Everyone joined hands around The Stone.

Cyna tried to focus her mind. Frowning with concentration, she gripped Fallon's cool, parchment-dry hand more tightly and willed The Stone to rise. Nothing happened. Around her the leaders of The Old Faith stood. Fallon's eyes were closed, his face raised toward the weak spring sun. Cyna closed her own eyes. Her heart raced excitedly. She could not imagine this immense stone broken, but then, neither could she imagine moving it, not even with the combined strength of all the Tribes.

She frowned with effort, but a warning pressure from Fallon's hand stopped her. Uncertain of what to do, she tried to recall the summer afternoons with Ned at the millpond.

It had been easy. They had sat together on lazy summer days, their backs against a tree, watching the pond. The surface of the water would catch the reflections of sky and tree, changing them into ever-shifting patterns of color and light. She would look through that pattern of color into the pond, at the stone they'd chosen, solid and shiny, illuminated by the sunshine passing through the water. She would see the stone, the water, and the reflection of the sky all at once, all different. Holding all those memories of light, water, and time together in her mind, she tried to remember the exact moment when the stone would flip over. There was a murmur of voices behind her.

She felt curiously light and free. In her palm, Fallon's hand was as hot as sun-warmed steel. She opened her eyes. The Stone was rising. It rose not smoothly, but in small shifts and starts. Dirt clung to its sides as it rose from its hole, but she saw that the carved runes continued down its length. With a lurch, it pulled free of the earth and rose into the air.

A sudden cry sounded through the oak grove. Ruf Nab had fallen and lay as still as death, facedown on the ground. As he fell, his hands tore away from Nyal and Ned, breaking the circle. A gasp went up from the crowd. The Stone froze in the air for a moment, trembling like a living thing.

Fallon's hand tightened on Cyna's and she felt as though he were lifting her. The Stone began to quiver violently in the air. Cyna closed her eyes tightly again and willed herself to see the surface of the millpond. Fallon's hand was gentle now, burning in hers, urging her to look through the reflections, through the water to The Stone.

The crowd sighed. When she opened her eyes, Ned held Finn Dargha's hand, completing the circle. The spectators were clearing an aisle for Nyal as he carried the unconscious Ruf toward The Keep. The Stone was still, suspended in the air, its base as high as her head. Although her feet were firmly on the ground, she still felt Fallon lifting her. She closed her eyes and allowed herself to go with him. She knew when the crowd gasped that The Stone was turning in the air. It floated down gently and finally rested again on the earth; not fallen, but whole and safely laid lengthwise across the meadow.

Chapter 17

The celebrating began instantly. Onlookers swarmed over The Stone, and ropes were fetched to pull out the Human children and Ogre kits who tumbled repeatedly into the hole.

Amid congratulations, The Movers strolled to the base of the largest oak tree in the grove, where a banquet had been set out under a tent.

Fallon was laughing, his blue eyes merry. "Well, Your Majesty," he said to Ur Logga, "what do you think of your folklore now?"

"It's a beautiful day!" exclaimed the Ogre. "See, even the sun returns!" He laughed, a deep rumbling sound that rose in pitch as he pointed to a patch of blue sky which had appeared on the horizon.

"Mistress Cyna, how does it feel to be wrong?" The Wizard inquired.

"It feels wonderful!" Cyna exclaimed.

"You're not the least bit sorry we didn't have a disaster?"

"You think I wanted it to fall? I never did!"

Fallon held fast to Cyna's hand as they crossed through the grove. He seated her beside him at the enormous circular table that filled the great green-and-white-striped tent just outside the oak grove. The Meg was already toasting, drinking the ruby-red wine which the Peskie folk had contributed to the festivities, and Finn Dargha had begun carving the joint. Cyna felt a tug at her sleeve. It was Tym.

"My Lady?" he whispered, as though trying to remain invisible to the celebrants at the table. "Nyal wishes you to join him at the stable."

Her father looked up from a conversation with Lord Halbend. His lips compressed slightly at the mention of Nyal's name.

"What?" said Fallon beside her. "What'd the lad say? Speak up, boy!"

Tym colored. He hated making a spectacle of himself. "Nyal asks that Lady Cyna join him at the stable. It's the Dwarf, sir," he added. "He's sick and Nyal needs Her Ladyship for a healing."

Cyna pushed herself back from the table. "May I, Master Fallon?" she asked.

"Of course," he said.

"Can you come soon, Your Ladyship?" mumbled Tym. "Ruf's got fever bad."

"Thank you, Master," she said. She curtsied, and followed Tym from the table.

Outdoors the blue sky had slipped over the horizon and a soft rain had started again. Picnickers scattered for shelter. Only a few dozen of The Old Faith still surrounded The Stone. A Human woman held up a small, undernourished child, murmuring sacred words. A one-legged Ogre hopped beside The Stone, caressing its runic symbols with his great hands. The sick, the injured, and the unfortunate clustered together in the rain, hoping for help. The healings and invocations would go on until The Stone was lowered again into the earth.

Cyna found Nyal in an empty box stall, kneeling beside the senseless form of Ruf Nab. "I told him to see you, but he said he'd rather heal himself. He was better for a while, now he's worse."

Cyna knelt in the straw and touched the Dwarf's forehead. It was hot and oily feeling. His face was pale and his breath was quick and shallow. He shivered in the cool, damp air as Cyna stripped away the cloaks and horse blankets with which Nyal had covered him.

The sword wound on his leg was deep and his entire knee was swollen and hot. On either side of the wound, red streaks ran up and down his leg. "His blood is poisoned," Cyna said, feeling her heart beating with alarm. "He should have sought help days ago."

"Can you save him?" Nyal asked. She glanced up and saw the misery in his eyes. "Fetch Master Fallon," she ordered Tym. "His art of healing is greater than mine. Your Dwarf," she added to Nyal, "is in need of one with a strong art."

"Little Gods," said Nyal fervently.

"I must drain the poisons from his knee," she said aloud, searching her mind for the surest cure. "They mustn't spread farther through his body."

Ruf Nab lay on his back, breathing in a rapid, shallow rhythm. *Heat!* she thought. *Like fights like. Fallon would use heat to cure fever.* She sent a groom to boil water and Nyal ran to her chamber for the chest of herbs. When the herbs and boiling water were before her she made a poultice. She applied it to the Dwarf's knee while willow bark tea steeped in a tin mug. When the brew was strong, she held up Ruf's head and poured a little between his lips. He swallowed and opened his eyes.

"Windmills fart doughnuts," he said conversationally.

"I beg your pardon?" Cyna said, startled.

"Get more torches down here," he mumbled, closing his eyes again. "This tunnel's as dark as a dragon's bowels."

"He's gone mad," said Nyal.

"He's out of his mind with fever," Cyna said, her concern rising. "Go hurry Fallon. There's just so much I know how to do."

When Nyal was gone, she ordered the grooms to wrap Ruf in heavy horse blankets. Outside, rain slashed across the castle courtyard. An aged groom lit a lamp and carefully hung it where it could not fall into the straw that covered the stable floor.

When an hour had passed without a sign of Nyal or Fallon, she changed the poultice. The leg looked worse. Ruf thrashed from side to side, muttering to himself. She placed her hand on his forehead but he threw her off.

"Excuse me, My Lady," said the old groom, pausing by the stall door. "No disrespect, but The Eacon's doctor saved a stable boy with poisoned blood last year."

"Did he?" she asked. She wondered what happened to apprentices who sought help from healers of The New Faith.

"He cut off his arm. Awful sight it was, but it cured him right up. Should I be callin' him? He's prayin' with The Eacon."

"Thank you, no. I'll not cure him with steel. Boil some more water for me, would you?"

"Yes, My Lady," the groom sighed. He shambled down the passage between stalls to the tack room. As he passed Avelaer's stall the horse laid back his ears threateningly, but the groom only made a wide detour and went on.

Ruf Nab shook violently with a chill, teeth chattering, his breath ragged. "Seeds!" he cried, brushing his face desperately with the back of his hand. "I'm covered with swarmy seeds!" Beneath her hand his cheek burned, his very life fluttering like a fire-blinded moth. Brandon's breath had rattled like this just before the end.

A part of her raged at Fallon and the others for not coming. Her hands shook as she bathed Ruf's face. She was glad Nyal and the groom could not see her. She fought to remember Fallon's teachings about herbs. *"Plants don't heal,"* he once told her, *"or else I'd have to wrap myself in wormwood every time I cut my finger. Minds heal. Bodies heal. If the witch works, the herbs will work. If the witch doesn't work, the herbs are poison."*

"This witch works!" she cried out loud. Moaning softly, Ruf threw off his covers. "This witch works. I can heal you, Ruf Nab," she crooned, covering him again and driving away her own dark thoughts. "I am healing you now."

When the groom returned with a steaming kettle, Ruf Nab was still muttering darkly, but Cyna's hands were steady.

"Nonsense, she'll do very well!" Fallon told Tym. "Have a drink, m'boy, it's a holiday!" Tym had drunk two when Nyal arrived at the tent flap, rain-soaked and out of breath. "She can handle it, you'll see," Fallon reassured Nyal, patting his arm and propelling him toward an empty chair at the table. "We've missed you. Have some supper."

Nyal protested, but he was cut off by the shrill blaring of a silver trumpet. An expectant hush fell over the table. In the hollow center, two Dwarves, dressed in traditional brown woolen tweeds with bronze breastplates and helmets, began a Dwarf victory dance. The revelers at the table watched raptly, some beating the rhythm with their spoons on the table as the Dwarves, faces grim and serious, stamped out an ever-quickening tempo accompanied by a single flute.

"Sit down, Nyal," invited Ned, who was half-reclined in a chair.

"I must return to Cyna . . ." Nyal protested.

"Oh, I'm afraid you'll have to send your boy," Ned said. "The lords have called the Council. It won't take long. They'll be calling for us soon."

Tym, hair falling over his forehead, was laughing loudly in a corner with some Ogres. He waved a large mug of Elfin brandy. Nyal gestured to him. "Tym!" he whispered. "Find Cyna in the stable. Tell her Fallon won't come. I'll join her as soon as I can, but the Council needs me for the title change and to announce the wedding."

Tym stared at him blankly.

"Tym!" said Nyal forcefully.

"Yes, sir!" Tym's words were slurred and he was blinking nervously. "Right away." He handed Nyal the mug and turned away, looking for the way out.

Reclined on her well-cushioned sofa, The Meg reached out a diminutive hand and caught Nyal's sleeve. "You beautiful young Human," she said, in her high, clear voice, pulling him toward her. Her golden hair, wound through with real gold and studded with brightly colored gems, had begun to need attention. Damp tendrils clung to her cheeks and clumped at the nape of her tiny, delicately arched neck. "You make me so sad," she murmured. Her breath was heavily scented with Elfin brandy and she spoke very carefully, elongating her vowels.

"Excuse me, Madam, but I must attend the Council," Nyal said, trying to extricate himself.

"Yes, you must!" she said intensely, clutching him more tightly. "Do as your elders tell you, beautiful young Human! Don't be as he was!"

"Who?" asked Nyal. "Be like who was?"

"Have you any idea," said The Meg, "of how it feels to be betrayed by those you love?" A tear slid down her cheek. From nearby several pairs of Peskie eyes began to watch and an Ogre turned politely away.

"No, I don't, Your Majesty," Nyal said, having no idea of what she was talking about. She released his sleeve and gestured to a Husband to refill the golden goblet she held in her hand.

The celebration was at full height. Rain drummed on the tent roof, which leaked steadily around the supporting poles, making muddy patches on the ground. A few Humans and Ogres, the least graceful of the Folk, slipped and fell in the mud, to the riotous enjoyment of their fellows. Elfin and Dwarf musicians, along with a Human harpist, improvised together with a wild, pulsing music. Nyal's head began to ache. The Meg now wept openly, her anxious Husbands vainly trying to comfort her.

"Nyal," Ned appeared suddenly beside him. "The Council wants us. You'd better come."

Rising to follow Ned out, Nyal caught a glimpse of Tym braying drunkenly with a group of Ogres. "Tym!" he shouted. "I told you to go!" But he could not be heard above the pulsating drone of the music.

Trotting through the rain outside, Ned led him through the darkening afternoon to a smaller tent across the grove.

Inside the lords lounged on campaign chairs. Landes, deep in heated conversation with Lord Benare, glanced up.

"M'Lord," Nyal greeted him. "If we could get this over swiftly, I've urgent business."

"Have you?" Landes's face was like granite.

"As you suggested, sir, Cyna and I wish to announce our engagement at the very end of the ceremonies, just before the final toasts."

"Engagement to Cyna?" Adler looked up in surprise from a corner of the tent. "I didn't know." Two red spots flared in his cheeks.

"I would like it if you, Lord Landes, and Master Fallon would lead the toasts," Nyal went on. "Is that agreeable, sir?"

"Yes, yes," Landes said hoarsely. "We'll hold them before The Stone, yes."

Benare thoughtfully tapped his front teeth with a fingernail. "Now that that's settled, Nyal, there's something we must talk about."

"Yes, gentlemen? What is it?" Nyal stood impatiently before them.

Bombaleur cleared his throat. "Nyal, you separated yourself from us on the march."

"Separated myself? Hardly, sir. I pulled my man out of the river."

"Yes, but some of the lords are uneasy about the timing of it."

Nyal frowned. "Timing?"

"And that Dwarf folding up like that. He almost broke The Stone!" Lord Farryl growled.

"That's Ruf Nab!" Nyal chided.

"I don't care who he is, it was almost a disaster out there!"

Farryl, a stocky man only a little older than Nyal, shook his head in disapproval.

Nyal surveyed the lords before him, his eyes moving from face to face. They were prosperous Humans, and each was more resplendent than the last, golden ornaments decorating their armor. They draped themselves across their camp chairs, arrayed before him like a loosely drawn battle line. Adler had turned his face away and glared through the tent flap at the falling rain. Nedryk watched appraisingly from one side. Landes's usual pink-and-white complexion was mottled with blotches, his neck stiff. The rest hung back, shifting with unease, not looking at him directly.

"I'm sorry, M'Lords, I neglected to tell you that soon after leaving you, we were attacked on the road by a strange horseman. Ruf Nab risked his own life to save mine. That is his habit," Nyal went on, wondering at their strange behavior. "The House of Crowell has long been honored by the friendship of his family. Ruf Nab saved my father's life at Harkynwood; now he has saved mine. Do any of you gentlemen find that offensive?"

"Nyal, there's no need to act like the lone champion of the Dwarves," Benare said. "It's just that some of the lords have questions and feel that the ceremonies—our most important political ceremonies—were mishandled today. We'd like to understand what happened." His tone was even and he regarded Nyal with an open gaze.

"Mishandled!" Nyal exclaimed. "You were not here, gentlemen, and the ceremonies had to go ahead."

Nedryk cleared his throat. "I'm sure that Nyal did the best he could."

Landes made a strange sound and all eyes in the tent turned to him. "The best he could? Who was the rascal he rode with?"

"M'Lord, please!" soothed Ned.

"Who rode in my place in the procession?" Landes repeated.

"My man, Tym," Nyal said.

"Your *groom*?" Landes asked indignantly.

Understanding flooded Nyal. "Lord Landes, it was an

emergency. You weren't there and the ceremonies had to go ahead. He in no way replaced you, only represented you—"

"A groom represented me?" The mottled blotches of Landes's face grew more mottled still.

"My Lord—"

"I have never been so insulted in my life!"

"It is a terrible thing to have done," Adler agreed. "A groom!"

"My Lords, you were not here—"

"But we were coming," insisted Adler.

"Could you not wait?" cried Landes.

"I'm sorry, sir, but no!" Nyal replied. "The ceremonies had to go forward. Besides, I was afraid something had happened."

Benare rose to his feet. "What did you fear had happened, Nyal?" he asked.

"I feared you had been attacked as I was."

"How could we have been attacked?" raged Landes. "What could happen to a party of well-armed horsemen? On a holiday, no less? You should have waited!"

"Father, calm down," Ned said.

"Yes, get a hold of yourself," Lord Benare murmured.

"Would that you had not gone off by yourself, Nyal," Adler said.

"Would that you were a better swimmer!" Nyal flashed.

"Or you less rash!" snapped Landes.

Benare gestured impatiently. "This gets us nowhere." He turned to Nyal. "Because you were here while we were not, there are some questions we must ask. You also spoke to the gathering this morning. I didn't hear all of the speech, but leaders of the Others have approached me. The Ogres in particular are quite upset. They are concerned about some prophecy of theirs. They say you proposed that we prepare for another war."

"No. I proposed only that we be more vigilant," he said.

"Why?"

Nyal hesitated. "I have come to believe that The Eacon is responsible for my father's and brother's deaths."

"That is ridiculous!" fumed Landes. "Telerhyde was murdered by trolls and we all saw Brandon die of sickness! How can you claim he was killed?"

Remembering his pledge to Cyna, Nyal bit his lip. "I cannot tell you how I know, but I know. There was a conspiracy and murder."

"What makes you say that your brother was murdered?" Benare demanded.

"Half brother!" Adler corrected him, turning from contemplating the rain. The silence in the tent was like that which follows a thunderclap.

"Is that true?" Benare asked.

A bright flush colored Nyal's neck. "Yes," he replied. "Telerhyde told me before he was killed."

"Your mother must have had an eye for Harkynwood rogues!" Adler smiled.

"Take that back!" Nyal cried.

"Why, if it's true? You're a bastard!" Adler reached for his wine-filled goblet. "Clearly your mother compromised Telerhyde. Apparently our great leader was not as powerful at home as he was among us."

Nyal seized Adler's tunic and dragged him to his feet. "Liar!" he raged. Adler swung a fist to protect himself and they both tumbled to the ground, cursing and flailing at each other. Lords pulled them apart.

This is disgraceful!" thundered Landes. "You have violated the sanctity of the Dragon's Council!"

"I'm sorry, M'Lord," Adler muttered, gingerly touching a bleeding lip. "I beg the Council's pardon."

Ned and Benare had pinned Nyal to the tent-pole. "Come outside and I'll settle you once and for all!" Nyal raged as he struggled against them.

"Enough!" cried Landes. "Nyal, control that temper! Adler, be careful how you insult a man's birth. I move that both of you be confined until the ceremony's end!"

The lords chorused their agreement. "Adler, I'll trust you on your honor to confine yourself. Nyal, you will remain here under guard until your temper cools."

"We can't return The Stone without a representative of Crowell present," Benare said as Nyal quieted. "The Eacon would mark it a triumph."

"Yes, you're right." Landes shook his head in frustration. "Then he must appear, but under Dragon's Discipline. You've brought disgrace upon yourself, Nyal. You'll speak to no one, and you will be under guard until the end of the ceremonies. If you can't behave, I'll keep you under guard even for your engagement toast! Do you understand?

"Yes, sir," muttered Nyal, glaring at Adler.

Chapter 18

That night, Ruf fell into a sleep so deep that Cyna couldn't rouse him. The grooms left silently as darkness fell. By then she knew that Nyal would not return with Fallon and that she was quite alone. Fever soaked, Ruf Nab called out to Telerhyde and other friends who were not there, urging them on as though in battle. Cyna waged another type of battle, speaking soothingly to him in their voices, exhorting him to live, to walk, to be strong. The fear she'd felt during the afternoon was dissolved by anger and her anger became absorbed in the effort to keep the Dwarf warrior alive. She banished from her mind all thought of his dying. Rubbing her gold Healer's ring, she imagined him well and laughing, telling Fallon that she was a better Healer than he was. Toward morning the lamp flickered and went out. The stable was cold and dank. Cyna renewed the poultice and knelt beside the Dwarf. She healed him in her mind until she could feel her Healer's ring growing hot on her finger.

A rain-soaked morning light was lifting the gloom in the stall when his fever broke. His breathing became regular, his expression lightened, and he fell into a quiet sleep, curled up like a small boy, his hand beneath his cheek. For Cyna it came not as a relief or a surprise, but the only result she would tolerate.

He woke a little later. She helped him change his sweat-stained clothes and fed him gruel. When she was sure he was resting comfortably, she wrapped her cloak about her shoulders and went out into the courtyard.

It was overcast. To the west, the mountains which rose up from Harkynwood were shrouded in clouds. A cold breeze from the sea was like an invigorating tonic, clearing her senses, driving out the smells of horse and sickness. She climbed the steps to the top of the battlement wall and stood for a long time, listening to the gulls which clustered on the kitchen roof and the surf which pounded far below at the base of the cliffs. She closed her eyes, took three deep breaths, and silently thanked Kythra for Ruf's healing.

The castle was beginning to stir. From the battlements she watched The Eacon, resplendent in his crimson cloak, cross the courtyard to his chapel.

She checked Ruf once more. Satisfied he was sleeping normally, she left The Keep and hurried to Curlish Plot. The road was muddy from the rain and heavy traffic. A well-trodden path led down the slope to the grove. The followers of The Old Faith—a few badly hung over—wet from a night in leaky tents, were beginning to gather about The Stone.

She found Fallon kneeling at the foot of a giant oak across the plot from The Stone. His eyes were closed, his head inclined slightly. His left hand rested against the rough bark of the oak, as though he were touching a friend. At length he was finished and opened his eyes, which were bloodshot. He held out a hand, which trembled slightly. "Ah, Cyna, good morning," he said. He winced, delicately touching his forehead with his long, slender fingers. "One day I hope to discover an herb that will cure the aftereffects of Elfin brandy." Using the trunk of the tree as support, he pulled himself to his feet. "And how is the redoubtable Ruf Nab?"

"He was very ill, Master. Didn't Nyal find you?"

"Yes, he did."

"You should have come," she scolded.

"But you have healed him?"

"Yes, I have. His fever broke this morning."

"Wonderful! I knew you would do it. If you had truly needed me, I would have come at once."

Her anger softened. "He was near death, Master Fallon.

His body was poisoned. He was out of his mind with fever. Do you think this could be my Gift?"

"Your Gift? You *are* getting impatient, aren't you? No, Cyna, this was not your Gift, or at least, I hope not. Healing is a Gift we all have, every member of The Old Faith. And The New Faith, too, though they don't believe it, so they don't use it. But this has been a significant healing, and I'm very proud of you!"

"Thank you, Master! I prepared a poultice of arnica leaves for him, and black willow tea. I believe it was the arnica leaves that cured him."

"Oh, dear." Fallon clasped his forehead.

"Are you well, Master?" Cyna asked in concern.

"Well enough. But no sooner do I think you have taken a giant step forward when you turn and run backward. Herbs don't heal, witches heal."

"Of course, but . . ." At the edge of the meadow was a great fanfare and shimmering banners. Landes crossed the meadow toward them, followed by Nyal and the rest of the northern lords. "Good morning, Father," she called to him.

"Yes, Cyna, hello," he said brusquely.

"Didn't you hear? I've done a healing. Ruf Nab is mending!"

"What? Oh, yes. Congratulations, dear." He strode past.

"Ruf is better!" She smiled at Nyal, forgiving him for his desertion the night before.

Nyal met her eye, then looked away as he followed Landes. Only Adler, following with the rest of the lords, gave her a nod and a smile.

Fallon watched her confusion. "They're busy with politics," he said, gently. "Except for Telerhyde—and that was his brilliance—most Humans forget The Law when they begin to meddle in politics. Then, when they've muddled up everything, they come to us and want Magic to straighten it out. Remember, all we can ever do is help them work within The Law."

The Tribes gathered at The Stone. The Royal Others and the lords stood in a great circle around it. They stood where they had stood the morning before except, she noticed, Nyal. He was tightly wedged between Landes and Ned and avoided her eyes. He looked ashen. *Has he drunk too much?* she wondered, suddenly irritated. *Why did he never return last night?* Behind them, the families of Humans and Others gathered, excited and reverent. Fallon held out his arms to them.

"I thank you all, my friends, for helping make this Convention a successful one." Cheers and applause rang out. "I wish to speak to those of you who are younger than myself. Which is most of you." The Wizard smiled ruefully and was rewarded by a good-natured laugh from the crowd. "Each generation must find and define Magic in its own way. Each generation projects its own desires, beliefs, and expectations upon Magic and thereby defines itself and its age. It is not necessary to believe in Magic for this to happen. Today we face a time of unrest. It is important that you not look for solutions outside yourselves, for you are the living embodiment of The Law. *You* are the most Magic thing in all Creation." The applause was deafening. Fallon turned toward The Stone. The moment had come.

Cyna clasped The Meg's tiny hand in her right, Fallon's in her left, and closed her eyes. The sleepless night had taken its toll. Her shoulders ached and her head felt light. She waited expectantly for The Stone to rise.

She suddenly wanted it over, wanted to find a bed and sleep in it. Dreamlike, she summoned her memory of the millpond. Instead, she saw herself in the stall, frightened and alone, waiting for Nyal. The memory of her fear was so strong it made her gasp. She steeled herself and released it, remembering instead the surface of the water, reflecting the sky.

She heard a murmur behind her and knew that The Stone was moving. It must float up into the air, right itself, and float back into its hole. Her mind flicked again, worrying at Nyal's desertion of her and his attitude this morning. Her breath felt short. Even with her eyes closed she could feel The Stone shudder as it hung in the air. She tried to force her thoughts back to water. Water reflecting the sky. She looked through it to the pebble at the bottom of the pond—and all around her the air turned dark.

In the distance she heard a terrible screaming. Nyal rode

at a gallop, his chestnut stallion lathered and blowing. From
behind him came the sound of pursuing horsemen. Above her
loomed a tower, soaring against the sky. The screaming
grew louder. It came from a woman who fled through the
snow, looking over her shoulder. A soldier caught her arm.
More soldiers closed in behind him, faces leering behind
black shields. In vain, the woman twisted away, trying to es-
cape. Swords swung. As though cut by a razor, the scream-
ing stopped. Cyna struggled to awaken, but felt herself
pulled irresistibly away from everything she knew.

She was floating high above a rolling valley. On a distant
hill stood a huge standing stone. Behind it, the sun cast its
shadow across the valley toward a tumbled-down fortress.
Two armies faced each other. In one, ragged Peskies fin-
gered short bows, skinny Elfin folk unsheathed short bronze
swords, snugging wood and leather shields to their left arms.
Before them, the opposing force was huge, Human and well
armed.

"Cyna? Cyna!" Fallon was saying. "Little Gods, you're
sense of timing is appalling!"

She was lying on her back on the soft earth, Fallon bending over her. The screaming she had heard faded into the distressed wail of the crowd around her. Cyna sat up, holding
her head in her hands.

"Are you ill?" Fallon asked.

"I'm fine," she said. "What's happened?"

Around them, Others milled about, stunned disbelief on
their faces. Ur Logga openly wept. The Meg, supported by
her ever-present Husbands, was being led away, hysterical.

"The Stone broke, that's what happened! It slipped from
our minds."

Cyna looked up. The Stone was broken in half. Its edge
had fallen against another, smaller standing stone nearby. Its
upper half still rested upright against the smaller stone, the
lower half rested in the grass. "Oh, no," was all she could
say. "Oh, no!" She was shocked to hear herself wailing with
the Others.

"Yes, I'm afraid we broke it." Fallon nodded his head
rapidly up and down. "Perhaps there is something in what

the Ogres have been telling me. What happened to you?" He peered closely at her.

Still faint and shaken, Cyna shook her head. "I don't know."

"Well, *you* fell down first, then The Stone," said Fallon. "I thought there might be a connection."

"It was the strangest thing," she whispered, remembering. "It was as though I had a dream."

"You had a vision?"

"I saw a woman murdered," she said faintly.

Fallon said nothing, staring at her intently.

"And I saw Nyal fleeing. There was a tower—but Master, I saw a battle. Not a battle really—two armies. It was like a nightmare."

"Yes, yes," said Fallon. He gripped her hand tightly. "What else? Who was fighting?" His grip was so strong that she winced and pulled her hand away.

"Elves and Peskies on one side—I didn't see much." She shuddered. "They faced a large army of Humans," she added as an afterthought.

"But you didn't see the outcome? Still, that's quite good!" He looked at her as though he had never truly seen her before. "Congratulations. You have it now, Mistress, and you have my sympathy." He reached beneath his robe and pulled out a heavy gold chain, similar to the one which he wore. He placed it about her neck with trembling hands, although whether they trembled from the awe that was on his face or from the effects of Elfin brandy, Cyna wasn't sure. But she was alarmed. "What do you mean? Why do you call me Mistress?"

Fallon's smile held no humor. "You are no longer my apprentice. You have received your Gift. And how wonderful! What I would give to be young with the Gift of prophecy!"

"Prophecy? No! What I saw was a dream, Master," she protested. "I didn't sleep or eat last night. I fainted."

Fallon shook his head. "You must accept responsibility for your power, Mistress. Prophecy is the greatest Gift, and Morbihan has need of it. With prophecy one can unravel the tangled threads of cause, weave the future that one chooses."

"Master, this is not my Gift! You said I'd know, and this

didn't feel like it. I only felt sick and faint." The sounds of crying all around her brought Cyna to her senses. "The Stone! We must do something!"

As though he were very tired, Fallon sat on the ground beside her. "No, Mistress. There's nothing to do. It's only a rock, and it's broken for a reason. Great events have a way of foretelling themselves." He gestured to the frightened throng around The Stone. "The Bond of Silence is lifted from you. They *all* know now, even though they can't dream your dreams. Some will say The Dracoon is upon us, that this is the fourth of The Seven Signs of The Final Days."

Chapter 19

Tym was frightened. Something was terribly wrong. It was more than Ruf Nab lying weak and helpless in the stable. It was more than The Stone breaking, although to listen to the other grooms, that was bad enough. When Tym had seen The Great Stone quiver and topple over, almost crushing the Other Royals who stood beneath it, he had only nodded his head. The very first time he had seen the ceremony, ten years before, he had told friends that it would happen. "You can't go on picking up things, especially such big ones, with nothing at all," he had said, and been scoffed at as a nonbeliever.

But something was wrong. The realization came upon him gradually during the morning after the Stone Moving. At first he thought it was his own fault. He had a blinding headache and only a hazy memory of the night before, but he thought he remembered Nyal telling him to do something. He couldn't remember what it was or if he had done it, but he remembered being told. So the first thing he did upon awakening, after checking on Ruf Nab and taking a snort of Elfin brandy for his headache, was to find Nyal. When his master didn't appear as usual at the stable, Tym sought him out at the lords' tent.

"Are you a messenger from The Eacon?" asked Lord Benare as Tym stepped inside.

"No, sir! I'm Nyal's groom, sir."

"He'll not be needing you, boy," Lord Benare told him. "Go about your business and take the day off."

Tym was surprised. He felt bad, but he went about his normal schedule as best he could. He fed Avelaer and mucked out his stall. After three days with little exercise, the horse was restless. When he tore Tym's shirt off his back and chased him from the stall, the groom decided he would risk his limbs no further. Despite all the pageantry of the day, he would insist that Nyal take the stallion out for exercise. Tym went to The Stone Setting ceremony with just that in mind. Nyal approached, flanked by Landes and Nedryk.

"Begging your pardon, sir, it's that horse . . ." Tym said and stopped, dumbfounded, for Nyal strode past him without a word. Never before in Tym's experience had the mention of Nyal's stallion failed to bring total and complete attention. Jumping to the wrong conclusion, Tym raced after him shouting, "I'm sorry, sir, but I forgot. Tell me what you want again and I'll do it in a flash—"

But then another, well-armed gentleman stepped in front of him and said, "What do you want?"

"I'm Nyal's groom, sir." Tym snatched off his cap.

"He won't be needing you today, boy. He has things to do. Stay out of his sight."

When The Stone fell, he scarcely noticed it, he was so busy watching Nyal. It was easy to see that the young Human was in trouble. Somebody had taken his long sword and Landes and Nedryk never moved from his side. Twice Nyal looked longingly at Cyna as though to speak with her, and twice Nedryk had stepped between them. Tym was outraged.

With all the carrying on about The Stone, Nyal was escorted back to the tent of the Lords of the North. Tym had to leave to feed Avelaer his lunch and scratch up something for himself. In the stable he met Cyna, who was feeding Ruf Nab.

"Your Ladyship," Tym said, "something terrible's happened."

"I know," Cyna said. "We all feel awful about it. There's to be a meeting in the central tent where Fallon will explain everything. But till then there's nothing we can do but wait."

Tym nodded, mystified. "Have you spoken to him?"

"Who?"

"Nyal!"

Cyna compressed her lips. "No. When you see him, tell him I must talk with him as soon as possible."

Ruf was better, according to her, though Tym thought he still looked weaker than the stable cat. He decided not to burden the Dwarf with his concerns. Instead he haltered Avelaer and ponied him for an hour, riding the palfrey. Alternately dragging and being dragged by the energetic chestnut, he considered his master's problem from all sides.

It was at lunch that he found out how much trouble there was. Taking his place between Ur Baffet, one of his Ogre companions of the night before, and Wink, Benare's young groom, Tym glanced around the table. A few members of all the Tribes were there, picking through the remains of the feast of the night before. But the conversation was subdued and many of the tables remained empty. "Where is everybody?" he asked.

"Weeping and wailing still," Wink said, gnawing on a joint. "They's all gone daft about this stone." He nodded knowingly at Ur Baffet. "You look pretty under the weather yourself, Tym. Does he beat you about, too?"

"Who?" Despite his worries, Tym was ravenously hungry and glad the table was half-empty. He filled his plate and poured a large mug of beer.

"Your young sir." Wink leaned forward and said in a loud whisper, "He's a scrappy one, ain't he? Hardly a mark on him and they say Lord Adler's brains were rattled like he'd run into a unicorn!"

"What? Baffet, what's he talking about?" Tym asked. Yet he felt a prickling along his spine. The Ogre looked away in a manner that told Tym that he knew more than he wanted to.

Whispering loudly enough for everyone at the table to hear, Wink went on. "It's a singularly bad thing, to attack a lord, if you're not one yourself. And they say Nyal's not a

lord at all, he's a woods' baby!" Wink's eyes flitted over
Tym's face appraisingly. "How'll you serve him, Tym, now
that they say he's a bastard? Well, I can see by your face,
you never knew!"

Tym sat, dumbstruck, only slightly aware that Ur Baffet,
wracked with embarrassment, had begun talking about the
weather. All the eyes around the table watched him as he
rose from his seat and left the tent.

Cyna, who would have expected to know that something
was wrong, missed it altogether. Fallon's insistence that she
had received her Gift made her irritable. She became increasingly irritated with Nyal as the day grew longer and he made
no attempt to see her. An hour after The Stone fell, the leaders of The Old Faith apprehensively assembled in the green-
and-white-striped tent. Landes called the meeting to order.
Cyna glanced around the huge tent, but saw no sign of Nyal.
She frowned.

"Yes, what?" Fallon was saying.

"Master Fallon," Finn Dargha's clear voice cut through
the babble of voices, "tell us what this means."

"It means The Great Stone is broken, Your Majesty. Exactly as you saw. That's all."

Meg Dallo fluttered at Fallon's sleeve like a wounded but-
terfly. "It's simply an accident that we broke The Stone, isn't
it? It could happen to anyone, wouldn't you say? It was just a
matter of time, really. I mean, accidents *do* happen; it doesn't
have to *mean* anything."

"Sit down and let The Wizard speak!" snapped The Snaefid. "What about the Ogre prophecy?"

A roar of voices filled the tent and Landes had to rap the
center pole sharply with his sword scabbard. "Let the Master
Wizard speak!" he shouted sternly. "Save your questions till
afterward."

Fallon pulled his beard. "It's true, there is a prophecy.
Kythra prophesied that there would be a time she called The
Dracoon, The Final Days of The Old Faith. We would recognize it by a series of signs. Now, it's important to remember
that every year a certain number of the signs occur, because
they are natural happenings. According to The Kythrian Pre-

dictions, it is only when *all* seven of the signs happen within a single year that The Final Days will surely occur."

"Just what are the signs, anyway?" asked Landes.

Ur Logga spoke slowly, counting them off on his fingers. "In the first sign a traitor rises, in the second a hero dies. Then, there is the confusion of seasons, the Breaking of The Stone, and the Disappearance of the Heavens. That is followed by the Splintering of The Five Tribes, and, in the end, the Death of Magic."

"So you see," Fallon said, "it's rather complicated."

"Well, we don't have all those things," The Meg said excitedly. "We hardly have any of those things!"

"Despite the weather, there's no way of knowing if we are in The Final Days," Fallon went on, holding up his hands to quiet the Others. "And even if we are, it's a perfectly natural occurrence, not to be feared. Remember, like all things, The Old Faith had a beginning, a middle, and one day it will have an end. This is The Law. All things undergo this cycle, except The Law itself. So, my friends, whether The Final Days are upon us or whether we have just carelessly broken The Great Stone I cannot tell you. Each of us must discover this for ourselves."

"Stones have broken before, haven't they, Master Fallon?" asked Finn Dargha, his merry brown eyes intent and serious.

"They have, Your Magnificence," Fallon replied. "The Grandfather Stone at The Salis Circle broke into twelve pieces many years ago. I'm sure that many thought that was the end. It was not.

"Furthermore, eighteen years ago, a full five of the signs occurred. That was the year of The War. But as you will remember, on the day predicted by some to be The End, Telerhyde led us all in moving The Great Stone for the first time in generations. And since then we Keepers of The Old Faith have lived in peace and a certain amount of harmony."

The Meg pouted. "Why must Ogres make such a dreadful prophecy?"

"It's not the Ogres' prophecy," Cyna corrected her. "They only preserved what Kythra told them."

"But none of us here can begin to fathom cause and effect," Fallon said, addressing the company. "One thing is lost, another gained. At the very moment The Stone fell to the ground, Cyna received her Gift. Morbihan has a new prophetess."

All eyes turned to Cyna. "Is this true, My Lady?" asked Ur Logga.

"Cyna?" said Landes in an incredulous tone. At his side, Ned paled.

"Cyna," Fallon prompted gently.

She flushed, heat flooding her cheeks and hands. "Oh, no, I don't think so. I fell ill, that's all."

"Cyna has seen a glimpse of the future," Fallon insisted.

"Have you seen The Dracoon, Mistress?" The Ogre asked, worry making his eyes large and dark.

"I did not!" Her voice was sharper than she intended. "I had a bad dream."

Ur Logga turned to Fallon in confusion.

The Wizard frowned. "Take some time, Mistress, to think this over."

"I saw nothing!"

Fallon's eyebrows had risen as Cyna spoke. Now they crashed down, cutting a stern line across his face. "Very well, if that is what it is to be. Everything will be fine, if we have faith. If The Old Faith dies and Morbihan changes, as will certainly happen some day, The Law still goes on."

"Are you saying it's the end but we should do nothing, Master Fallon?" The Snaefid demanded.

"I'm not saying it's the end, or the beginning. And I'm not saying that you should do nothing, nor that you should do anything!" Fallon replied with mounting impatience. "I'm explaining The Law. It's a pity none of you has taken the time to understand it!" He glared pointedly at Cyna.

"Hear, hear!" shouted Landes above the babble of voices that followed Fallon's words. "Let's have some order here!"

Fallon shook his head and murmured out loud to himself, "They never want to learn about how things work until they fear things are breaking down!"

Nyal fumed in confinement. When he saw Cyna collapse, he tried to go to her, but was restrained forcibly by Landes and Ned. Even when The Stone fell, he had never taken his eyes from her, watching with dread as Fallon placed the golden chain of a Gifted One about her neck. He desperately wanted to be with her to find out what had happened, but Dragon's Discipline did not rely on personal honor. There were two large, steely-eyed fellows between him and the entrance of the tent to enforce it. Benare's men-at-arms, they regarded Nyal with dispassionate patience, as sheepdogs watch sheep. Whenever Nyal approached the tent flap, their hands stole to the hilts of their short swords.

At length, after the lords had gone to the main tent to hear Fallon explain The Stone's breaking, Nyal retired to a cot propped against the back wall. His mind racing, he feigned sleep as he listened to the rain and watched his guards. One guard snored gently on a cot by the tent flap. The other had stepped outside for a moment. Just behind him, Nyal became aware of a thin, ripping sound.

Rolling over cautiously, he saw the blade of a knife cutting through the canvas wall. There was a pause and a blue eye peeked through the slit. Then the knife appeared again, cutting more energetically. A moment later Tym slid his head through the hole. Silently he gestured for Nyal to follow him out. With a cautious eye on the dozing man-at-arms, Nyal arranged the blanket to look like a sleeper. Then he slid out through the hole on his belly.

Thick fog had poured in from the sea. Nyal could scarcely make out Tym crouching low and sprinting for the shelter of a nearby group of low standing stones. They met there and Nyal felt Tym's fealty in his fierce embrace.

"Thought you needed some help, sir. Those lords are spreading stories about you."

"Good man, Tym," Nyal said. "I have to find Cyna."

"She wants to see you, too, sir. She's in the stable with Ruf, last I saw her."

"Good, I need to see her, then get back before they find out I'm gone."

At Eacon's Keep the drawbridge was down and there was no one in sight except The Eacon's men-at-arms. They saluted properly and let Nyal and Tym pass. The courtyard was deep in mud, and they followed a pathway of planks which led to the stable.

Cyna was not there. Ruf Nab slept, his broad face pale beneath several days' beard. "We'll wait for her," Nyal said. But it was unsafe to wait in the stable, for several of the lords had their horses there and might appear at any moment. Just across the courtyard was a small stone building with a steeply slanted roof.

The finely carved wooden door opened at Nyal's touch and he stepped into the cold darkness of The Eacon's temple. A large altar surmounted by a massive stone statue of The Vorsai stood at one end. The draft from the open door made the candlelight flicker and pulse. The shadow of The Vorsai statue seemed to leap and crouch.

From a door on one side Nyal heard the low murmur of men's voices. With a silent gesture to Tym, he turned to find a more private hiding place. But the voices rose in laughter and something caught his attention. The Eacon's voice throbbed in sonorous cadence. The second voice was familiar.

Nyal stepped cautiously down the aisle, Tym following behind. At an open doorway at the side of the altar, he saw into a small room, its walls hung in tapestries, lighted only by a fire blazing in the hearth. Before it, reclining on chairs, two men sat talking.

A powerfully built man sat with his back to the door, sharply outlined by the light from the hearth. The Eacon saw Nyal first. "Yes?" He was surprised, struggling to rise from his chair.

"I see you have company." Nyal stepped boldly through the door, trying to see the features of the man who now turned his face to the wall.

"I do," said The Eacon, edging toward the door. "But if you wish to talk, we can be alone in the temple."

"I'd like to meet your friend," Nyal said, blocking his way. "I think perhaps we have met before—"

The powerfully built man turned around. Instantly Nyal recognized the dark stranger who had attacked him on the road. He jerked back and heard The Eacon cry "Seize him, Lothen!" He glimpsed a blade and ducked. The sword sliced through the bright tapestry beside his head. "I am unarmed!" he cried, scrambling for safety. In the dim light, he could barely see the flash of the sword as it cut again through the air. Snatching a heavy poker from the hearth, he defended himself. Lothen's first blow sheared the poker in half, numbing Nyal's arm. With a cry he retreated, dodging the cold fury of Lothen's blade.

Tym, his dagger naked in his hand, shouted a Northern Sea oath and charged through the door. With a roar, The Eacon seized a piece of firewood from the hearth. Surprisingly fast for his great size, he swung in short violent strokes, driving Tym to the wall.

"Let him live, Lothen, let him do The Vorsai's work!" The Eacon cried. "Save yourself and send the guards to help me!"

Lothen feinted and Nyal stumbled to the side. With a humorless laugh, Lothen bolted through the door.

"Stop him!" cried Nyal. The Eacon turned on him, eyes glowing like a wild animal's. Nyal swung the stub of the poker, splintering the firebrand in The Eacon's hand, showering the room with sparks. Tym slipped through the doorway and Nyal followed him, slamming the door shut after them. They dragged a bench in front of it, and Nyal braced it stoutly before he followed Tym up the temple aisle. As Tym opened the outside door, a blast of wind drowned the altar candles.

The courtyard was still fog shrouded. Nyal paused on the plankway, his ears and eyes straining for a sign of Lothen. He heard the sound of horses' hooves crossing the drawbridge.

"Let's get to the horses!"

"What about Her Ladyship, sir?"

"I swore to The Dragon I'd find the traitor! That man knows Telerhyde's killer, Tym, I know it!" A banging began within the temple. "Hurry!"

After Nyal had crossed the length of the first plank, Tym pulled it loose from the sucking mud and dragged it behind him. Together they destroyed the rest of the pathway, then struggled through the mud toward the stable. Tym lost his boot and Nyal glanced nervously back through the mist while Tym swore and dug and pulled it out. A loud bell began to toll. The horses were still saddled, cross-tied in the yard before the stable. They gathered up their swords and armor, and clattered toward the gate. At the drawbridge the gatekeeper was peering worriedly through the fog into the courtyard. He greeted Nyal.

"What's the problem in there, Your Lordship?" he asked.

"Problem?" inquired Nyal, trying to look unconcerned.

"He never rings the temple bell except if there's a problem. Oh, well. You'd better hurry on unless you want to get stuck here. I have to close the drawbridge when he rings like that. Gate-boy! Where's that cursed boy?"

When they were just out of sight of The Keep, Nyal took only time enough to lace on his helmet and breastplate and strap Firestroker to his side. Then he urged Avelaer into a ground-eating canter. Tym followed on the brown palfrey. The tracks of Lothen's horse stood out vividly on the muddy road before them.

Melloryth's cheeks and throat felt aflame. She had been in the darkness of the temple since early morning. She had never liked the temple before but lately it seemed the only place where her hopes might be saved. Each morning found her in the back row of benches wrapped in her dark brown cloak, praying. Sometimes she prayed for Cyna to die. Other times she prayed for Nyal to convert to The New Faith. Once she found herself praying to give up everything and marry him in a wild, frenzied ceremony at the center of an Elfin ring, but she quickly changed the Elfin ring to the temple and made the prayer proper again.

When Nyal came into the temple she was so overwhelmed she could hardly breathe. She had heard of prayers being answered but to see it happen right before her eyes affected her profoundly. He didn't notice her. Single-minded of purpose, he crossed directly to her uncle's conference room. She could not hear his words, but she could imagine what he must have said, for the uproar was immediate and very exciting.

"He must be caught!" Her uncle said when Tyrll had arrived and freed him from the small room. "But his own people must do it, do you understand me? Tell them that he attacked me, that he violated The Peace. Here, Melloryth, what are you doing here?"

Melloryth shrank back into her seat, staring at the floor stones. "Doing my devotions, Uncle," she said.

"Speak up, girl, I can't understand you when you mumble like that," The Eacon said. "What did you hear?"

"Nothing, Uncle," she said.

His light eyes seemed to pin her to the bench. "Nothing?" he said. "Nothing? I've warned you never to lie to me, girl! Come back with me to The Keep." He stepped out the temple door and began to sink slowly into the mire of the courtyard. "For Vorsai's sake, man, don't just stand there, find the planks!" And he cursed for a while longer until the gatekeeper came with the planks and they rebuilt the path back to The Keep.

"Excuse, me, M'Lady," said the gatekeeper, carrying another load of boards.

The Eacon turned around. "Here, girl, get out of the man's way! Go about your business!" He turned back to his conference with his men.

Melloryth glared out across the landscape of mud. She imagined her uncle sinking into the watery pool before her, struggling, pleading. She shook her head in denial and strode past him.

She walked in an exalted state, unaware of her surroundings until, too late, she found herself by the gate. With pomp, the drawbridge was again being lowered. As it groaned into place, the gate boy saw her.

"Melloryth the Brownie-lover!" he singsonged.

"No!" she cried. "Leave me alone!"

Delighted with her reaction, he danced a jig on the edge of the drawbridge where it crossed over the gorge above the sea. "Melloryth the Brownie-lover, Old Faither! The Vorsai will burn you! Old Faither! Troll!" he tormented her.

With a cry, she flung out her hands, thrusting him away to ward off his taunting words. He cried out as he fought for balance on the edge of the bridge. She pushed again and he fell backward, waving his arms as though trying to fly. She watched him until he landed on the sharp rocks just above the high tide mark. The tide was out and the gate boy lay still. Only a scrap of his sleeve fluttered, like the sleeve of a rag doll.

The main gate was open and she fled across the drawbridge. The road wandered before her, rolling across the meadow. To

one side the ground sloped gently down to Curlish Plot and the
tents of the Others. On the far side, orchards gradually blended
with this most westerly patch of Harkynwood.

A cart strained by, pulled by a skinny horse, slipping in the
mud, lashed by a dull-eyed farmer. Breathless, blinking back
her tears, Melloryth stepped off the side of the road. The way
was easier and before long she was running through the or-
chard, unmindful of the wet grasses which had grown up in
defiance of the late spring. Sometimes the memory of the gate
boy, falling backward, frightened her. He was just lying there
in wait, she told herself, tormenting her still with one of his
games. Mostly her thoughts were with Nyal, remembering the
firmness of his step, the strength of his purpose. He had come
for her. They had driven him away, but he had come for her
at last. She knew now that no matter what they did, no matter
how her uncle pretended, she would be his.

She was thinking this as the terrain gradually changed and
she stumbled deeper and deeper into the forest. She stopped
for a while where a crystal spring bubbled up beside a mossy
rock. She dreamed of him riding up and lifting her onto the
back of his charger.

Later she grew chilled and retraced her steps. Although she
walked for a long time, she recognized nothing. The Eacon's
Keep had disappeared from where it had been. The trees grew
taller, like the masts of a great ship. The land seemed strange,
almost bewitched, and not at all familiar. She was frightened,
but it didn't shake her faith that Nyal would save her. She
only wondered whether it had been her uncle or the witch
Cyna who was trying to dispose of her in this way.

Chapter 20

The bell at The Eacon's Keep had been tolling throughout
the morning. Although The Stone was broken, the followers
of The Old Faith roused themselves with their love of ritual
so that they might hold the closing ceremonies, regardless.

The ceremonies were by tradition a celebration of unity, but the rain-sodden group which gathered about the oak grove resembled a group of mourners at a funeral. Cyna stood between her father and Fallon, arguing before the shattered stone. The cold wind whipped the sky-blue cloak about her legs; the gold chain felt heavy about her neck.

"She has received an important Gift," Fallon objected. "She should be given time to think this over."

"I fainted from lack of sleep," Cyna insisted. "I have no Gift."

"Regardless," Landes counseled after a time, "she is no longer an apprentice and can make her own choices."

"Agreed," said Fallon, reluctantly.

"Cyna?" Landes said, gently.

"It is my wish to marry Nyal."

"Ned, tell the guards to release Nyal," Landes instructed.

"Guards?" asked Cyna.

"Well, yes, there's been some difficulty," Landes was explaining the brawl during the Council when Ned returned.

"He's gone! There's a slit in the back of the tent and he's gone!"

"The young hothead has violated discipline!" exclaimed Lord Bombaleur, aghast.

"Nyal has promised to be here for our engagement toast," Cyna reminded them. "He will come."

"I'll look for him," Ned said. "Perhaps he's with his Dwarf." He walked hurriedly toward The Keep.

The bell at The Keep began to toll again. "I wish they'd stop that!" exclaimed Fallon. "I keep thinking that Gleese is celebrating." Fallon seemed unusually distracted.

Cyna watched eagerly for Nyal, but Ned returned alone, out of breath from running.

"There's trouble," he gasped.

"Trouble?" demanded Fallon.

"The Eacon claims that Nyal attacked him!"

"What?" Fallon's eyebrows shot upward in surprise.

"And they say he's killed the gate boy—pushed him right off the drawbridge! The Eacon demands Nyal's arrest."

"But Nyal would never do such a thing!" Cyna objected.

"The ceremonies are ended!" thundered Fallon. "Everyone

go home and we will ponder what has happened here." He waved a hand at the assembled Others who, in turn, glanced about, startled and apprehensive. In a quieter voice he said, "My Lords, let's discuss this where we can have greater privacy."

Adler and Benare formed a delegation to go to The Keep. There they examined the temple anteroom and the body of the gate boy, after it was dragged up from the ledges beneath the drawbridge.

"It's very serious," Benare told the hastily reconvened Council an hour later. "The Eacon has scraped knuckles and a bruise on his arm. In the temple there are clear signs of a fight. The gate boy is dead and The Eacon's niece is missing. The Eacon is saying that Nyal has violated The Peace."

"What's happening?" cried Landes in an anguished voice. "First he attacks Adler, and now The Eacon. Killing an innocent child—has the boy gone mad?"

"He was always hotheaded," observed Benare, nervously stroking his greying mustache.

"Wait, My Lords," Fallon's voice cut through the excitement of the room with its heavy logic. "The only ones to profit from violating The Peace are The Eacon and his henchmen. None of us. Certainly not Nyal." There was a murmur of agreement in the room.

"Aye," said Lord Benare. "Whoever did this is a man who opposes Telerhyde's policies, a man who stands against The Peace."

"I agree, M'Lords," said Landes.

"But Nyal called for the end of The Peace," objected Adler.

"That's true," Benare said thoughtfully, "and if he truly isn't Telerhyde's son . . ."

"He is not," Landes said. "But that never made a difference to Telerhyde."

"My Lords," Adler said, his lips pursed in thought, "what if, in rage and chagrin at being a bastard, Nyal struck Telerhyde down? But no, that doesn't make sense. Then why would he attack The Eacon?" Adler frowned, defeated by his own logic.

"Unless he and The Eacon are in league with each other!" Bombaleur said.

"That's ridiculous!" Ned objected.

"Completely ridiculous!" Landes agreed. "I hardly think . . ."

"Suppose The Eacon had promised a prize for Telerhyde's death and then reneged. Then would what he's done make sense?" Farryl asked.

"I'm not even going to listen to this!" Fallon said in disgust and strode away toward Eacon's Keep through the rain.

"It's not as impossible as you might think," said Adler, glancing at Cyna. He went on eagerly. "Nyal arrived here days before we did, and we know he had at least one private audience with The Eacon. If The Eacon had promised him a prize, the girl for instance, and then reneged, that hothead might attack him as he attacked me!"

"And killed the gate boy as he fled?" mused Bombaleur.

"The rise of a traitor!" whispered Benare.

"This is insane," Ned declared. "Nyal would never do these things!"

"What you're saying is mad!" Cyna agreed.

"Then where is he?" demanded Adler.

No one spoke until at last Landes cleared his throat. "Well, I suppose it could make sense. If one didn't know Nyal. But delicate diplomacy is always called for at the Stone Moving. This year it is even more so. Forgive me if I am wrong, My Lords, but in Telerhyde's memory I can take no chances. We must find Nyal and discover what has happened. If he has betrayed Telerhyde, he will pay with his life. Cyna, I will not consent to your engagement until this matter is cleared up. And we'll need to protect Young Tel from his schemes. He can't have gotten far. Ned, get the horses." Landes reached for his long sword and buckled it on.

With a shrug to Cyna, Ned was gone, running out into the rain.

Landes went to her and took her hand. "You stay here. You may be in danger."

"How can you imagine that Nyal would hurt me?" Cyna wrapped her cloak snugly about her and followed her father outside.

"I don't, my dear. But how else can you explain what's happened? If he is who you think he is, why hasn't he come to pledge himself as he promised?"

"I don't know! But he's not a murderer!"

From beside her, Adler growled, "More than anything else, I hate him for hurting you, Lady Cyna!"

"Ned!" shouted Landes. "Where are the horses?"

"Here!" Ned rode up, riding his black charger and leading Landes's bay.

"Wait!" shouted Cyna. A gust of wind billowed her cloak around her and for a moment, standing in the middle of a muddy field, all the lords turned around to look at her. "Nyal did not do these things!"

"Don't worry, Cyna," Ned murmured. "I'll take care of it."

"I'm sorry, My Lady," Adler said, "but I'll not let the murderer of Telerhyde and the breaker of The Peace run loose." There was a murmur of assent.

"Wait a moment," Ned said. "We don't know he murdered Telerhyde."

"Lords," said Adler, his teeth set grimly. "Begging your pardon, but that's something we should discuss after we catch him. Right now he's on the road putting distance between us."

"Will you listen to me?" Cyna cried. "This is insane!"

"Cyna, stay in the tent!" Landes ordered.

"Will you listen!" she shouted.

"To horse," cried Landes. He swung up on the bay charger. "Let's not lose time, Lords, let's find him!" He was gone, the rest splashing behind him.

"By The Old Girl, you are wrong!" Cyna shouted after them, but her words were lost in the sounds of horses and men.

"Thunder and sour cheese!" she swore. Around her she became conscious of many eyes staring, watching. The royalty of the Others looked out from the large Peskie tent, where they had gathered on the far side of the meadow. The Snaefid, holding back the tent flap, shook his head. Finn Dargha frowned in concern while Ur Logga, who had been bending down to see, politely stared off in another direction. Cyna heard The Meg's voice carrying through the sound of rain, "But there's nothing in the signs about this, is there, Ogre King? That the hero is killed by his disloyal son? We really don't have anything to worry about, do we?"

Fuming, Cyna turned on her heel and strode toward the castle. Fallon was in his chamber, packing his few belongings in a sack. "Master Fallon, the lords accuse Nyal of being in league with The Eacon! Of murdering Telerhyde!"

"So that is how it is to be."

"Master, we must do something!"

"Yes, we must. Meditate with me, Cyna. Use your new-found foresight to tell us what will happen."

She stared at him aghast. "Master, we must help Nyal!"

"You must use your Gift!"

"But I have no Gift! I don't know what will happen any more than you. I wish only to marry Nyal and put this madness behind me!"

"Oh, dear." A look crossed Fallon's face and for a moment Cyna thought he would cry. Then, abruptly, he turned away to frown at a damp cloak hanging from the doorknob, a cloak he had forgotten to pack. He sighed, stuffing the damp cloak in with his dry ones. "I must get on with my studies. I'm leaving with The Snaefid and his troop this afternoon. Going up in the hills to study metallurgy with them. Enough of herbs with Ogres, heh? What will you do, now?"

Cyna shook her head disbelievingly, as though to clear cobwebs from before her eyes. "Master Fallon, don't you understand? Nyal is in danger! We must make the lords listen to us!"

"And what makes you think they will?" Fallon asked.

"Because we both know that Brandon was poisoned!"

His pale blue eyes seemed to glow with light in the dark room. "Still, that's no proof of Nyal's innocence. Strange events surround us. The Ogre prophecy seems too close to the mark. The lords are frightened, like everyone else in Morbihan, and frightened men will imagine anything that makes them feel safer."

"But if they catch him, they may hurt him!"

He looked at her appraisingly. "You saw this very thing in your vision this morning, remember?"

Cyna hesitated.

"Nyal fleeing for his life, that was your first prophecy, Mistress! Come true so soon. You have a great Gift. Now use it! I must know the outcome of the war you saw this afternoon."

She remembered the helpless feeling of falling. "Master, that was not prophecy. I was sick, I had not slept . . ."

He regarded her sadly. "For your own sake, do not reject your Gift, Cyna. It is your path to learning The Law."

She shook her head in exasperation. "Master, what good is The Law if we do not avoid the bad and make things better? Nyal could be hurt, even killed. If you have any compassion, help me to save him!"

"By trying to reason with Landes and those blockheads? No! Our tool is Magic. I will use every ounce of my poor powers to reach the bottom of all this, and I encourage you to use yours to see the future and foretell what will happen. Morbihan needs the Gift of prophecy! For too long has it been limited by my Gift of shapechanging."

"That was not my Gift this morning, Master!" she insisted stubbornly. "I have no Gift, only a lover who is unjustly accused. For the last time, will you help him?"

"Not your way. You're meddling. Use your Gift or else go about your business and let him and me go about ours." When Cyna only glared at him, Fallon sighed. "Ah, well. Mayhap it will all come together in the end. Be off, now. Say good-bye and leave me alone. I must leave this place."

"Master Fallon . . ." Cyna said, but he was busy arranging his possessions by the door.

"Go! Go! Do you never listen? If you will not prophesy, then there's nothing for you to do!"

Furious, she left him, climbing to the top of the battlement as she had that morning. The gulls were no longer perched on the kitchen roof. The breeze from the sea was harsh and the tumultuous sky was as dark as the granite walls of The Keep. Cold rain pelted down, soaking her to the skin.

The Dwarfin troop had gathered outside the gates. Curious inhabitants of The Keep braved the rain to watch the Others depart. They were sullen when finally Fallon appeared, riding on his Elfin pony. He doffed his cap and waved. Then the Dwarves turned and marched down the muddy road.

Cyna closed her eyes, took three deep breaths, and prayed to Kythra. She prayed for a sign. After a long time she heard her name being called. Finn Dargha and the Ogre king stood below her in the courtyard. "Halloo, Mistress Cyna!" called Ur Logga.

"Up here," she called back.

Finn sprinted up the battlement steps to her side. Ur Logga lumbered behind him. "The Eacon has just proclaimed that The Peace is broken. We're leaving, Mistress, back to the safety of Harkynwood. We're all traveling together, Elves, Peskies, and Ogres. We leave within the hour."

She held out her hand. "Have a wonderful trip, Your Magnificence."

"But you? Where do you go?"

"I must help Nyal."

Finn shook his head. "How can you do that?" he asked.

Cyna hesitated. "I will speak to my father . . ."

"I doubt he will return here, Mistress. The grooms have packed the tents and gone already."

"Then I will find him!"

Ur Logga nodded, deferential before her determination.

"What of Ruf Nab?" Finn asked.

A gust of wind swept across the battlement. A few large flakes of snow blew with it, plastering themselves to Cyna's cloak. She shivered. "He's not well enough to travel yet," she said.

"He can't stay," said Ur Logga. "When we leave there will be only followers of The New Faith here."

"He's right," Finn said. "It's not a safe place for a Naerlundg. He'll have to come with us."

"He's too weak," Cyna protested. "Such a journey would kill him."

"Come with us then, and save him," Finn said.

Ur logga's eyes lighted up in his shaggy face. "Yes, Mistress. Come with us into Harkynwood! You'll both be safe there."

"Yes, come with us, Mistress," Finn repeated. "I don't like this place."

When she still hesitated, Ur Logga bent down to stroke her hair. "Where else can you go?" he asked.

Cyna shook her head in bafflement. "Only until Ruf Nab is better. And I have news of Nyal."

They waited for her while she quickly gathered her few belongings from her room.

Chapter 21

After several miles, the single, muddy road that led from Eacon's Keep was so heavily traveled by the witnesses of the Stone Moving that it was impossible to make out Lothen's tracks. Nyal and Tym were forced to slow their pace, watching the sides of the road to be sure he hadn't turned off.

Nyal was not without thought for Cyna. When they had been on the road for an hour, he glimpsed a figure resting beneath a tree. "Ride on, Tym, I'll catch up. I need to give this small fellow a message for Cyna." He reined in Avelaer and called out, "Ho! Master Elf!"

Slipfit, who was traveling back to Harkynwood from the Stone Moving, was startled. One moment he was resting, musing about all he'd seen, and the next a large Human horseman was shouting at him. As any wild Elf might do, he ran.

Nyal swore in surprise and set his heels into Avelaer's sides. "Wait, fellow!" Nyal's stallion was far swifter than the middle-aged Elf, and caught up with him in a few strides. "Wait!"

"Na! I never did it, whatever it is! Na!" cried Slipfit, his back against a tree, ready to dodge Avelaer's nervous hooves.

"I wish you no harm," Nyal said, soothing his excited horse. "I need a favor."

"I can't give favors to the likes of you who has everything he needs already," Slipfit replied indignantly. "I'm a poor creature and haven't a thing of my own. Even this dagger," he offered as an afterthought, "isn't mine, but borrowed from an Ogre who lives near here. A big Ogre," he lied, "so don't you try to take it."

Nyal dismounted and tied Avelaer to a tree. He squatted on his heels and balanced his elbows on his knees, which brought him to eye level with the Elf. Slipfit was unnerved by this and rested one hand on his dagger's hilt. "Here, now, what do you want?" he shouted. "Go away! I never did a thing to you, leave me alone!" Nyal extracted two gold coins from his pouch and the Elf fell silent. He had not seen that much gold in many years. "What do you want, hey?" he asked again, more quietly.

"I am Nyal of Crowell," Nyal told him in Elfin.

"Telerhyde's Nyal?" The Elf asked suspiciously.

Nyal nodded. "I want you to find Fallon's apprentice, Cyna."

"Fallon the wolf," muttered Slipfit.

"No, Fallon the Wizard. I was to meet Cyna at The Stone and we were to pledge our love. But I've sworn to find Telerhyde and my brother's murderer. I follow him now."

"So?" the Elf demanded, made more nervous by Nyal's thick Human accent. "I know nothing of love or murder, let me pass."

"I need a friend," Nyal continued, "one who will find Cyna and ask her to forgive me for leaving as I did. Tell her that I'll return in a few days with the name of Telerhyde's assassin. She'll understand. I'll give these gold coins to that friend for finding her and telling her this."

"Where she be?" demanded the Elf.

"At Eacon's Keep. Ask any Old Faither there, they'll show her to you." Nyal jangled the coins in his hand.

"All that gold for just telling that?" Slipfit asked.

Avelaer whinnied, looking back down the road from which they had come. A group of horsemen rode into view, moving at a brisk pace. "The lords!" exclaimed Nyal. "Excuse me," he said to the Elf and vaulted onto Avelaer's back. The horse leaped eagerly out into the center of the road.

"My Lords," Nyal called, raising a hand in greeting. "A conspirator in Telerhyde's murder rides before us . . ."

Adler, riding beside Ned at the head of the column, lowered his lance and charged. Nyal never heard Landes say, "Now wait a moment!" for the fury of Adler's attack was so sudden he barely had time to react. His shield was tied to his saddle, his lance had been left in The Eacon's stable. He checked his horse abruptly and swung to the side, letting Adler career past him. Swearing, Adler swung around and prepared to attack again, throwing his lance down and pulling his sword from its scabbard. "Bastard!" he cried as he rode down on Nyal again. "Assassin!"

The other lords had drawn their weapons, fanning out in a ring about Nyal. "Adler, wait!" Nyal shouted, but Adler was upon him again.

The young lord was too eager. Swinging early, he missed Nyal's unprotected head and slashed instead against his breastplate. From the corner of his eye, Nyal saw Ned spur forward, his hand on his sword hilt. Nyal drew Firestroker and swung it in a wide arc, driving Adler back. But the ring of lords grew tighter, lined with swords and lances. Nyal was in the hollow center, surrounded. The faces of the men he had grown up knowing were unfamiliar, cold. Only Ned and Landes broke the circle.

"Wait!" Ned shouted.

Landes spurred his horse to take a place beside Nyal. "My Lords, listen! We cannot, in the name of The Dragon, compound evil with error. We came here not to kill this boy but to learn the truth!"

The attack hesitated, the lords paused. Adler swore and reined in his charger. Nyal sighed in relief.

"Nyal," Landes said, worry pinching his eyebrows together above his long nose, "you have been accused of Telerhyde's murder."

"What?" cried Nyal.

"Why did you attack The Eacon? The Peace is broken . . ."

Aroused by combat, Avelaer trumpeted his battle cry and bit Landes's stallion on the neck. Landes shouted, "Nyal, hold that animal!" But his own horse, twisting away from the chestnut's attack, slipped in the mud and fell. Landes screamed.

"Father!" cried Ned.

"Treacherous bastard!" shouted Adler and drove straight for Nyal, his sword swinging.

Nyal set his spurs to Avelaer's flanks. He met Adler directly, parrying as the enraged lord thrust at his unprotected head and legs.

"Murderer!" Ned cried as he joined the attack. Nyal dodged as Ned's blade cut through the air just above his head. Behind him another lord attacked and Avelaer flinched from a blow, squealing in rage. Ears flat to his head, he reared, striking out with his hooves. Nedryk set spurs to his horse, but the black charger wavered. Teeth gnashing, Avelaer crashed into the weaker horse, knocking him aside. The road was open before them and Nyal urged Avelaer into a full gallop.

Slipfit watched in horror from behind the tree. It had been many years since he'd seen Humans giving vent to violence, and as before, the sight filled him with fear and loathing. He remained very still while the horsemen gathered around Landes, who was moaning on the road. He watched as they lifted him tenderly and laid him on a pile of their cloaks. Some raced off after Nyal, others galloped back toward Eacon's Keep. After a long time, they brought Fallon the Wizard. Slipfit recognized him from that wind-torn night beneath the hollow tree.

"It's very bad," Fallon said after examining the wounded Human.

"Find Cyna and tell her what's happened," Landes groaned.

"Too late," Fallon told him. "She's left with the Others for Harkynwood. Don't worry, old friend, she'll be safe. It's you I'm worried about. Someone help me make a litter and get him to some shelter as soon as possible. We can't return to Eacon's Keep. Snaefid?" He turned to the Dwarf who had accompanied him.

"Aye, he'll come with us," The Snaefid said.

After a time, they all left and the road was empty again. Slowly, as though remembering how to move his limbs, Slipfit reached out and touched the gold coin that lay at his feet where Nyal had dropped it. "Na, I could not do that for you, Human-boy," he said clearly. "She's gone, you heard the

Wizard." As his hand touched the gold, it trembled slightly. An old memory stirred him. For the first time in many solitary years, an Elfin song came to his lips.

"Love is good when love is young
Before old anger turns the tongue.
But love is best when love is sung.

Love is grand when love is old.
Treasure your memories more than gold.
But love is best when love is bold."

He picked up the gold coin, hefting its weight and humming to himself. "I'll be your friend, Nyal of Crowell," he said at last to himself. "I'll find your lady and tell your tale."

Chapter 22

The cold rain settled into a steady drizzle as the parties of Ogres, Peskies, and Elves prepared to leave Eacon's Keep. The nomadic Peskies, used to living outdoors in all types of weather, were swathed in shalkskins and layers of felt. They protected their bows and arrows beneath wrappings of skins. The Meg was magnificent in a full-length cloak of wolfskin, which repelled the rain and swirled behind her like a grey cloud. Her Husbands donned rakish caps and short capes of weasel fur. Mounted on their massive unicorns, the Ogres relied on their own thick fur to keep them dry and warm. Shivering more in apprehension than with cold, Cyna wrapped herself in her heavy brown cloak, carrying the rest of her belongings in a sack. Her best boots of Elf-cured gongohide felt light and warm on her feet.

Ruf was very weak. Cyna covered him with a horse blanket and a waterproof shalkskin, which Finn Dargha thoughtfully provided. The Ogre Honor Guard undertook the task of carrying him gently in their arms as they rode in the rear of the caravan. The black walls of Eacon's Keep were manned by watchful men-at-arms who glared down at them as the procession left the campground where the broken stone lay. A few miles from the castle, they turned off the Human road. Finn Dargha led the way through Harkynwood, walking quickly and surely. Just as she had when she arrived at The Keep only three days before, Cyna rode a unicorn, sitting behind one of the Honor Guard. On her left, the sea seemed grey and monstrous. Behind her, The Keep loomed dark and forbidding against the wind-torn sky.

Deeper into the forest, the trees became larger. The conifers which had flourished near the seashore gave way to massive beeches, oaks, and walnuts. In a normal year, foliage grew so thickly it shaded the forest floor from the sun, and lush ferns made a soft carpet to walk upon. But in this endless, dismal spring, no leaves had appeared to grace the huge trees' branches. Wind swept unfettered through the barren groves. The sound of their footsteps was soggy and each traveler walked alone, thinking his or her own thoughts. Only the song of the Elfin Husbands united them, a persistent rhythm celebrating a more secure time.

They didn't pause for a noon meal. Finn continued to stride confidently ahead, his head lowered against the constant rain, busy keeping track of the Peskie scouts, who reported back to him with birdlike whistles and chirps.

An hour before sunset, they stopped to set up camp for the night in a sheltered glen. The Ogres tethered their mounts, quickly piling up branches and twigs for fodder. Ur Logga took his fire-sticks, meticulously wrapped in broad gambrin leaves, from his saddlebag. Squatting in the center of his Honor Guard, who sheltered him from the wind with their broad bodies, he plucked some kindling from the special sack he always carried hung about his neck and began to twirl a fire-stick between his fingers.

Finn Dargha shouldered his way through the solemn Ogres. "That's no way to start a fire, Your Majesty!" he exclaimed, pulling out the short steel dagger he wore on his hip. "I have flint."

"Thank you, Your Magnificence, but this is the Ogre custom," Ur Logga murmured. But Finn had already struck flint to steel. A spark leaped from the black stone to the pile of dried moss the Ogre king sheltered at his feet. Simultaneously, all nine Ogres reached down, pinching and slapping, to extinguish the glowing moss. "A true fire is kindled in the heart of the fire-bearer," Ur Logga reproved the Peskie king gently. Again he placed the brittle fire-stick against the dry kindling board and twirled it between his fingers. Closing his eyes, he intoned.

"Midnight Mother, you all-knowing,
Embers of your heart all-glowing,
Free us from the fear that binds,
Pierce the darkness of our minds."

He repeated the chant and the Honor Guard joined him, squatting in a circle, eyes intent on the tiny glow that was beginning to show on the kindling board, blowing gently on it, offering it bits of dried moss.

Finn shrugged philosophically and returned to the other side of the glen where his wife, Fir Dahn, was directing the Peskies to gather a pile of dead tree limbs. He rapidly struck the dagger to flint, creating a shower of sparks. "Ogres always have the driest tinder and the slowest fires," he complained. Soon both Ogre and Peskie fires blazed like beacons at either end of the glen.

When The Meg's gossamer tent proved too delicate for the heavy wind, Fir Dahn invited her to spend the night in the royal tent of the Peskies. There wasn't room for all her Husbands and, after some anxious tears and pouting, it was decided that Fir Dahn and The Meg would share a tent with no Husbands at all. Finn Dargha and the entire band of Elfin Husbands took the small tent while Fir Dahn and The Meg took the large one. Fir Dahn invited Cyna to share their comfort, but Cyna felt she should be near Ruf. It was crowded, but she found room in Finn's tent.

Several Peskies cooked rabbits and game birds, which they had shot during the day. The Ogres, trying hard not to show their disgust at the act of eating animals, gathered fist-sized stones and placed them on the coals. Ur Logga dug a large hole in the ground, lined it with a well-oiled skin, and

filled it with water. With forked sticks and cautious mutter-
ings, the Ogres transferred the hot stones to the water. When
the stones cooled, they tossed them back into the fire. Cyna
was used to Ogre customs and the patience they demanded.
Nevertheless, she sighed out loud and wished mightily that
they had thought to bring a pot, for she was tired and hungry.
At last, heated by the rocks, the water began to steam and finally to boil. After what seemed like a long time, the Ogre
porridge was done, steaming hot with dried fruits all
plumped out from the boiling water.

Cyna resisted the desire to wolf down her portion as soon
as Ur Logga ceremoniously handed her the wooden bowl. Instead she brought the share to Ruf, who lay, pale and weak,
in the driest corner of the tent. He roused himself and swallowed grimly, his nose wrinkled. "Are you not feeling well,
Ruf Nab?" Cyna asked, touching his forehead with the back
of her hand. His wound still seeped an ugly, greenish fluid.

"Nay, I'm much better, Witch," he said, his voice soft
with exhaustion. "It's just Ogre cooking. And the pace they
set. Lugged about in their hairy arms all day, lurching about
atop their one-horned beasts, I'm seasick. Unicorns should
be hunted, not ridden."

"Mayhap you'd prefer to walk," she jested, adjusting the
cloaks that covered him.

"Would that I could," he agreed, the trace of a smile shap-
ing his wide mouth. "Where are we going?"

"They all return to their homes in Harkynwood."

"And you, Lady Cyna?"

"I have no home," she said softly. "I am here to heal you."

"Then where shall I go?"

"I'm taking you to the Elfin palace. There you must stay
with me until you're healed. Then go where you want."

He sighed. "I am a warrior and I am no longer young. All
my life I have served the House of Crowell. Yet now, when
bad omens surround us, there's no Crowell to serve—my
lord is dead and young Nyal has gone off by himself on
some hotheaded scheme. He's in great trouble, I can feel it. I
want to be the first to defend him. Yet here I am helpless,
carried through the forest like a crying baby."

Cyna stared across the glen at the fire. She said nothing.

"I owe you a debt, Mistress."

"For what?"

"For my life. I was a dead man, till you cured me." He shuddered. "A warrior all my life, yet I fear my own death."

"Of course you do. We all do." Cyna bent to snug the horse blanket around him. "Be patient. You will join Nyal again when this is all over, I'm sure." Yet she was not sure. After he had eaten and dozed off, she took her own portion and found a seat at the mouth of the tent with Finn Dargha and Ur Logga. She removed her water-soaked boots and placed them near the fire to dry.

"Will you visit us in Urden Barrow?" Ur Logga asked.

Cyna shook her head. "I'll stay with Ruf Nab while he recovers at The Meg's palace."

Ur Logga nodded. The leaky, smoky Ogre den was no place for an ailing Dwarf. "I will be sad when we part tomorrow," the Ogre king rumbled.

"And I, Your Majesty," she said. "I'll miss you and your tribe."

"But you will see Harkynwood," he said. "It has been long since a Human witch learned the Harkyn. Perhaps you will even discover Kythra's Sanctuary."

"Kythra's what?" Cyna asked, frowning.

"An Ogre myth," Finn chuckled. "She's supposed to have lived with Ogres deep in Harkynwood."

"No myth," Ur Logga objected. "Many centuries ago she lived among the Harkyn Ogres and prophesied the history of the world to us. When each Tribe gave her an offering, the Ogres built for her a great home she called the Sanctuary."

"A tower of stone?" asked Cyna, remembering her vision.

"Of course!" Finn laughed as he leaned forward to place another branch on the fire. "But no one has ever seen the Sanctuary or remembers quite where it was supposed to be." He rolled his eyes upward and shrugged.

"I think some things can exist yet not be in plain sight," the Ogre grumbled.

"Why have I never heard of this?" Cyna asked.

Beside her, Finn yawned. "Ogre myths. I think our big friends have more legends of Kythra than the rest of us. It comes of spending winters holed up in the ground with nothing else to talk about. You know the sort of thing—she's supposed to have lived in a summit deep in Harkynwood, in a tall tower. It doesn't matter that there are no mountains deep in Harkynwood, for this is a myth. From the top of the tower she could see all the way to the four corners of the earth and forward and backward in time. Stories for children," he finished, smiling. "Or Ogres."

Ur Logga made a distressed sound. "His Magnificence, who is wise and knowing, is, of course, always correct, but the Ogre legends say she truly lived."

"I'm sure she did," the Peskie leader replied. "But myth tends to be what happens to the size of a fish when Elves sit around the fire and sing songs about it."

"What?" asked Cyna, sighing as the fire warmed her toes.

"It gets bigger. Tales have a way of growing like grass." Beside him, the Ogre pulled at the hair on his cheek and looked pained. "It's not so awful, Your Majesty," Finn said cheerfully. "You can disagree with me. We Peskies enjoy discussion and debate."

"The Ogre legends," Ur Logga said, articulating each word carefully, "tell of a Human woman who came to Harkynwood many generations ago. In those days"—the Ogre's voice took on the cadence of a master Ogre tale-teller—"Harkynwood was not inhabited by Others as we know ourselves now, but by separate tribes." Finn nodded his head. Ur Logga spoke on: "In those days, there was no Old Faith, only ignorant strivings. The Ogres, who once lived alone in this land, had been driven out of their seaside homes by Elves and Peskies. We would not touch metal then and built everything by stone. Then Humans defeated the Peskie warriors who had driven my folk away."

"According to our Peskie legends your own folk were very fierce, Your Majesty," Finn said. "And you attacked us first. Do you see what I mean about myth?"

The Ogre continued as though he hadn't heard. "From the south the Humans came in greater and greater numbers, driving even Peskies and Elves deeper into the forest. It seemed like there would never be enough room on the earth for all of us. War became our way of life. It was not a good time.

"Then Kythra came to Harkynwood. She was a young

Human and gifted in knowledge of The Law. She healed the great king of the Ogres, Ham Urbid The First, when he was terribly wounded by a unicorn. Then she lived for many years with the Ogre tribe and learned our ways."

"She lived with the Peskies, according to our version," Finn said dryly.

"And that is true. She lived with each of the Tribes and learned all our ways," Ur Logga said patiently. "Then she began to teach."

"Yes," said Cyna, remembering Fallon's lessons. "She taught that each of us is a part of The Law. That The Five Tribes are one, like fingers on a hand."

Ur Logga smiled. "Like fingers on a hand," he repeated. "And she was so strong that she convinced Ogres, Peskies, Elves, and Dwarves to stop warring and talk."

"What a great noise that must have been!" said Finn.

"And then she called upon the king of the Humans and even he came to listen. For the first time, The Five Tribes met together on Fensdown Plain, on the edge of the Longhile River. To prove the power of Magic, she led them in moving the great stone Argontell. Which is why we always move stones when we come together now."

Finn snorted again. "Have you ever seen Argontell? It's enormous! If they truly moved it with their minds, then they had better minds than ours! Besides, there was a use for all of that in those days. They built the Great Stone Circle of Salis, they say, and with it wizards can mark the seasons and foretell the movements of the moon. But now it's all a show, a wizard's trick to delight the children."

As though he hadn't heard, Ur Logga went on. "She created us as The Five Tribes and taught us our strength, which is in our unity. It was then that we Ogres built the Sanctuary, where every creature might be safe under her protection. And she looked into the past and told us from where we came. She looked into the future and told us where we would be going. She looked out into the heavens and saw how The Law worked and that one day we would see The Dracoon. When she died, all Five Tribes came together to celebrate the good fortune that had brought her to us. The Old Faith was born at that moment. That was many generations ago and the place has been lost, but not the gift of unity. Kythra's Sanctuary is still alive in our hearts as we pursue The Law."

"It's odd that the place would be lost," Cyna mused.

"There was much building after that. All the Tribes came out of Harkynwood together and built the Avenues of Power and the Stone Circles. It took generations. The Sanctuary fell into disuse."

"I wonder if we could find it."

Finn Dargha yawned. "That would take more than Magic!"

It was late. The fire was dying down. The Meg's Husbands were sleeping in a corner of the tent, nestled together like a litter of exhausted puppies. The rain had stopped and a cold mist clung to the tree trunks. Ur Logga rose and stretched. "Good night, my friends," he said. "May you rest in harmony with The Law." Cyna reached up and gave his hand a squeeze. He left the tent to sleep outside with his Honor Guard, who were already curled up together at the foot of the great oak tree.

"I never realized how orthodox Ogres are," Finn mused.

"They follow The Law," Cyna said.

Finn looked at her appraisingly. "Was Fallon wrong? You have no Gift?"

"Only the Gift of healing."

He nodded, his bright eyes watching her. "It must be difficult to be a witch."

"Why do you say that?"

"You have to uphold the tenets of The Old Faith. Yet you must see as well as I do that all around us The Old Faith is losing its essential quality. It doesn't answer the questions of our lives anymore. It's good for little more than the yearly stunt of Stone Moving. Not even that, now."

Cyna tried not to show her discomfort. "Fallon says The Old Faith can't stop working, Your Magnificence. The Old Faith is simply recognition of The Law. The Law doesn't answer questions about life because The Law *is* life. Or rather, it is to life what downhill is to water. The way of going."

Finn shrugged. "I have heard Fallon say that, too, Mistress. But no one can tell me what it means, can you?" Cyna was silent. "When you can use The Law to find your Nyal or to heal The Meg's sorrows, call me, and I'll be a believer again. Until then, I look to the sun to get me up in the morning and hard work to put me to bed. And pray for luck to keep The Eacon behaving himself now that The Peace is broken."

Before the sun was up, feebly burning its way through the thin cloud cover, they were traveling. Cyna felt disturbed by her conversation with Finn the night before. She wondered about The Meg and her mercurial moods.

It was true that The Old Faith no longer built the huge Stone Circles or traveled the Avenues of Power as it had long ago. The vital energy that had once focused the power of the earth had ebbed. The Tribes no longer came together to build and create, but went their own ways. Humans farmed and traded. The Others mined and hunted and spun. Despised by The Perime, they traded with it through their Human neighbors. The lords had grown rich as well as powerful, she reflected, even as they sheltered the Others from The New Faith's violence.

The New Faith seemed to be at the very heart of the problem. It seduced Human farmers in the south with a favorable rate of exchange and promises of a sweet life after death. It was easier for some Humans to follow The Vorsai and blame their problems on the Others than to find solutions to mutual problems according to the difficult Principles of The Law. The merciless rule of the vengeful Vorsai was easier than the relentless justice of The Old Faith. Too many Humans were tired of taking care of themselves and trying to understand The Law, Cyna mused.

The rain held off and everyone's spirits rose. Midday they halted at the huge oak tree that marked the turnoff to the Ogre tribe's den. Cyna said good-bye to each of the Honor Guard, accepting their shy smiles and ritual grooming as they bent down to run their huge hands gently through her hair.

"Good-bye, Your Majesty," Cyna said.

"Mistress Cyna," Ur Logga rumbled softly, "if this is The Dracoon, I hope you will always be in harmony with The Law." His gnarled fingers trailed across the ends of her long hair. "Good-bye," he said. She lingered for a moment to watch the Ogres and their unicorns silently disappear into the woods.

Ruf was transferred to The Meg's litter. Cyna took off her heavy cloak and walked with the Elves for a while, learning their songs. Her boots had become stiff from drying too quickly and they chafed her feet. With the rain holding off, The Meg shed her wolfskin cloak and gaily led her tribe through the woods, always singing, sometimes dancing complicated steps that wove the entire Elfin ensemble through the trees in the wrong direction. When that happened, Finn Dargha would halt his band of Peskies and wait, impatiently glancing at the sky. Cyna was grateful for the rest. The noble Husbands, unused to Ruf's weight in the litter, would sink to their knees and gasp for breath. Eventually The Meg would dance within sight and the whole caravan would set off again.

By afternoon the flat, tree-covered forest was broken by gentle, rolling hills and occasional streams. A footpath appeared and then broadened into a byway. The rain had swollen the streams and made them difficult to cross, but the new trail led to shallow fords and even an occasional bridge. Cyna noticed that the meadows along the streams had a well-cropped order about them, and the woods that grew in the shadow of the hills were brush-free and well maintained. The sun set on the wet and exhausted travelers as they wandered through a neatly groomed landscape where even the winter-swept thickets were orderly and seemed to exist in a harmonious balance with their surroundings.

Shortly after sunset the moon rose, silver and nearly full, casting sharp shadows along the side of the path. The Husbands had stopped singing hours before and now their labored breathing set a grim cadence for the march. The Meg led the procession, humming to herself, calling out encouragement to her tired followers.

Cyna was concentrating on putting one sore foot in front of the other, trying not to stumble on the shadowed path. Suddenly ahead of her she saw a firefly dart. The Meg laughed her silver tinkle of a laugh. Another firefly flashed and Cyna realized it was a lantern. All at once the forest at the edge of the meadow seemed to glow with light. The Meg began to sing and she was joined by a chorus of welcomers.

Elves appeared from behind every tree, laughing and singing their welcome to the weary travelers. Fresh, strong hands lifted the litter from the shoulders of the Husbands. Someone seized Cyna's sack of belongings and took her hand to lead her through a bewildering maze of thickets toward The Meg's palace.

The Elfin palace was within a peeled log stockade on the side of a mountain. The gates were open and the courtyard filled with revelers. At their center was the most beautiful creature Cyna had ever seen. An inch shorter than The Meg, dressed in fine gossamer, she stood with her arms raised over her head. A hush fell over the assembled Elves as The Meg and her entourage stepped inside the stockade. The beautiful creature began to sing. Her voice was clear and golden. She sang of the rising moon and The Meg's arrival as though each event had come from the same great source. The melody held a vibrant joy. Cyna knew without being told that this was The Megin, Phaedryn, Meg Dallo's eldest daughter and next in line for the Meghood.

To the tired Human witch, the welcoming ceremonies seemed to go on forever. The chorus of greeting was followed by The Meg's triumphal song and dance. Then, despite their exhaustion, the Husbands danced a whirling, rhythmic, pulsating dance, each offering himself to The Meg, each being turned away after much flirtation and lingering looks. At last Phaedryn sang a final "Welcome, beloved Mother," everyone cheered wildly and went inside.

The palace seemed modest from the outside. Its peeled log exterior, like the stockade, had weathered to a fine silver color and it soared three stories high. Narrow windows looked out into the courtyard and the steep roof blended into the looming mountain behind it. But once inside, Cyna realized, it was vast, indeed. The light-colored logs enclosed one great entrance hall, two stories high and surrounded by a balcony. The floor was polished stones, white alternating with deep blue. The far wall was of polished granite and it took Cyna a moment to realize that it was the side of the mountain, carved away. Two large doorways led down long corridors aglow with torches. On the wall between them was a large hearth with a blazing fire. High above Cyna's head, on the ornately carved beams which supported the roof, Elves danced and performed, heedless of the cruel distance to the stone floor. A group of Elfin musicians blew on reed instruments on a raised platform across from the hearth.

"Ah, my Meginette," said The Meg, enfolding her daughter in her arms. "My little dewdrop."

Phaedryn led them to the hearth where, on a raised dais rested an exquisitely carved chair draped in soft fabrics. The Meg reclined gracefully on her throne and the entire assembly seemed to go mad with delight, clapping, cheering, and singing half a dozen songs at once.

"My guests," sang out The Meg, "Fir Dahn and Finn Dargha of the Peskie folk, and Mistress Cyna, a Human witch. You will take them and their retainers to the guest chambers and see that they have everything they need. We are weary from our journey and need to confer with our advisors. Then you will all assemble here for supper. I have news which I must impart to you before this day is done." She clapped her hands sharply. "Now, do as I tell you. Instantly."

Cyna directed the quick Elves who sprang to assist her to help carry Ruf Nab to a quiet place. He had a chamber of his own, with dry sheets and a warm blanket. When he was settled, one of The Meg's Husbands led Cyna down the lighted corridor through twisting and turning avenues carved out of solid rock. When she had lost all track of direction and distance, he opened a door and gestured into the small room inside. A small bed stood next to a cabinet with a water jug on top.

"Will you call me if Ruf Nab grows worse?" Cyna asked him as she gratefully sat on the bed.

The Husband, too shy to speak, nodded, blushing furiously. He bowed low and left her, closing the door behind him.

Cyna rinsed her hands and feet in water from the jug. The bed was too short for her, but it was deep and soft. She slept fitfully, despite the fatigue she felt. A vague alarm, like a faint voice calling for help, wrenched her repeatedly from her dreams.

Chapter 23

When she first awakened, the little room was so dark that Cyna thought she was back in the mounds of the Ogres. The candle left by the royal Elfin Husband had sputtered out while she slept, and deep underground in the Elfin palace there was no natural light. But soon she found her way to the door, hailed a passing Elf, and borrowed a candle.

Curious about the surroundings, she strolled the corridors near her room. The ceiling was of smooth stone so low she frequently was forced to stoop. Each corridor was so broad that several Elves or even two Humans could walk abreast. Doors led off to sleeping chambers at regular intervals, each door looking much the same as the others. Several times the ceiling abruptly dropped lower and she bumped her head. Ducking to pass through a doorway, she encountered an elderly male Elf wearing a scarlet tunic and a worried expression.

"Aha! Mistress Witch!" he exclaimed. "I've just come from your chamber and I feared we had misplaced you!"

"Misplaced me?" Cyna was amused.

"There are so many chambers, that if Ronstelle the Coy had told me the wrong corridor, it would have taken all night to find you! But here you are, out exploring, how fine! I am," he stepped back and executed a deep bow, "Lypharch the Reasonable, Second Husband of The Royal Meg, Senior Father to the Royal Daughters."

"How do you do," Cyna bowed deeply to him and he blushed. "I am Mistress Cyna, a Healer."

"Welcome, Mistress. There is to be a Meg's Council shortly, and your presence is requested. Follow me!"

He set off briskly, walking precisely down the middle of the corridor. She hurried after him. Other Elves stepped aside

and bowed low as they passed. He acknowledged them with
a crisp wave of his hand or nod of his head. "Quickly, Mistress," he said and ushered her into the great hall.

The Elves were assembled, dressed in Elfin finery, chattering excitedly to each other. The Meg sat on her throne near
the hearth, a golden staff in her right hand. At her left side
stood Phaedryn, a heavy golden belt hanging from her tiny
waist, her nipples rouged bright blue beneath her gossamer
robe. Lypharch prostrated himself before The Meg. "Most
Splendid Mother of Elves, the Witch has come to do your
bidding."

"Come here, Human Witch-girl," The Meg ordered, frowning. "You must help me in this." She rose and the Elfin mul-
titude quieted, waiting expectantly for her words. "Usually,"
The Meg said, her voice ringing out in the crowded hall,
"usually We return from the annual Convention of the Peace
of Harkynwood to report to you that all is well. All is well
today, too, but We have had some difficulties. The Stone was
moved. High into the air. I saw it with my own eyes. The
Law rules supreme."

The assembly cheered politely, nodding vigorously to one
another.

"But, as I say, We had difficulties. There was an accident
with The Stone. And here to explain it all to you is Mistress
Cyna, a wonderful witch." She smiled, waved toward Cyna,
and sat down to thunderous applause.

Startled, Cyna faced the expectant Elves. "Well," she said.
"Well. The Stone is broken. It broke as it was lowered into
the earth. Fell, actually. It slipped our minds." A cry of dis-
may sounded through the room. Remembering her duty as a
witch, Cyna held her hands high until the voices stopped.
"Nothing exists outside The Law. You have nothing to fear."

"But if we live within The Law, Mistress," said Lypharch
beside her, "why should such a thing come upon us?"

"It is The Law," Cyna tried to explain. "Each thing has a
beginning and an end . . ."

"It's Mati," said a voice from the assembly. "Mati broke
The Law. He brought this upon us!"

"Silence!" The Meg was standing, her face flushed, a vein
throbbing in her temple. "Silence. You have heard the witch.

There is nothing to be concerned about. You are dismissed to begin the celebration of your Meg's return. At Once!"

Cyna felt the air of hesitation in the room. "At Once!" repeated The Meg. The Elves began to move to their places. Musicians raised their instruments and began to play. The double doors of the hall were thrown open and the procession began. Cyna walked with Finn Dargha and Fir Dahn, just behind The Meg's Husbands. The Meg was escorted by Lypharch who bowed low, and offered her his arm, a courtly suitor. On her other arm, Phaedryn seemed to glide without touching the ground. Behind them the Husbands strutted, their muscular torsos oiled and gleaming.

"You will be of great help to The Meg, Mistress," Fir Dahn murmured.

"At least Ruf has a place to heal," Cyna replied.

"I can't bear one more Elfin song," Finn whispered to his wife. "I hope it rains!"

But the Elfin ceremonies were greeted by a cloudless midnight sky. The full moon hung over Harkynwood, drenching everything in its silver light, dimming the stars which shone through the leafless trees upon the clearing before the palace. There was a chill in the air and Cyna shivered, drawing her cloak more tightly around her. Again she felt the faint voice of alarm that had disturbed her sleep. The entire community of Elves formed a large circle around The Meg and she extended her hands to them.

Each Elf reached out to her. "Behold, the moon is risen!" The Meg cried out.

"Risen and given us its wisdom!" chorused the Elves.

"The year is past! Twelve moons have watched over us, protecting us from our enemies!" The Meg waved her hand and Lypharch and the Husbands stepped into the middle of the circle. Lypharch began to sing in a high clear tenor. "I sing," he began, "of the royal house of Elf, of the saga of the powerful family of The Meg Triumphant!" The Husbands formed a strange rhythm and harmony behind him, taking the refrain of each verse and transforming it into the rhythm of the next.

Lypharch sang of the beginning of Elfdom. Untold thousands of years before, The First Meg had stepped upon the earth. She was the daughter of Briande and Luf, the Earth and the Sky. The Earth rejoiced in her daughter and issued forth the trees, the grass, the flowers, and the creatures of the earth so that The First Meg would have nourishment and playthings. Her father protected her, shining his one great eye on her that she might see during the day. He wept that he could send only his wounded eye, the moon, for her to see by at night. So the first gifts to The First Meg were all the plants and creatures of the earth, the sun and moon and life-giving rain, born of loss and regret, but nourishing all things that live.

Lypharch sang of the golden years of plenty and how The First Meg became lonely in her perfect world. Taking pity, her mother created The First Husband. The First Meg loved him and was happy. And so Briande created all the Husbands and The First Meg was even happier. Between them they created the whole tribe of Elves.

Yet while The First Husband was honest and loyal, He was heedless. One winter day while The First Meg was off inventing musical instruments, The First Husband showed The First Son how to throw snowballs. The son was headstrong. Despite his mother's warnings, he picked up a stone and threw it. It sailed through the air and shattered the harp his mother was fashioning. The splinters of the harp flew into The First Meg's hand and her blood dripped upon the snowy ground. Wherever her blood touched the earth, it became transformed into gold. Angered at what The First Son had done, Briande banished him forever.

Cyna stifled a yawn. The moonlight had dimmed, giving the faces around the Elf meadow a dull, rosy glow. She found folktales interesting, each one amusing in its primitive attempt to grasp and explain the nuances of The Law. Each said the same thing, she reflected, but made its tellers the center of the earth's history.

She listened to the deep tones of the Husbands as they chanted their litany. Then Lypharch was singing of the present Meg. He made no difference between them, as though The First Meg and her diminutive successor were the same. He sang praises of her beauty. The Meg giggled and preened, flirting with her Husbands, who were never too busy singing not to flirt back.

Lypharch sang of The First Husband, The Meg's beloved. Beautiful and endowed with a voice that rang with love and courage, but headstrong. He would not sing Songs of Praise, and broke Meg Dallo's heart. Cyna sensed a wave of unrest trickling through the Elves in the clearing. She squinted to see better through the gathering gloom of the night.

Then Lypharch sang of The Meg's two jewels, Phaedryn and Mati, daughter and son, fruit of The First Union. Listening, Phaedryn did not giggle and blush like her mother, but stood erect and proud. She looked out over the assembled Elves with a clear, somber gaze, the cold wind billowing her sheer garment around her. Phaedryn was a flower, Lypharch sang, a joy to the heart of Elfdom. Born knowing the magic of creation within her, she loved The Meg with all her heart and put no desire of her own before the royal mother's.

Mati was different, truly the First Son of a First Husband. When The First Husband denounced The Meg and was banished forever from Elfdom, Mati, although pure of blood and beautiful as an Elf prince should be, proved that he, too, had a headstrong, devious character. He thought himself better than Phaedryn and refused to sing and dance for his mother. He demanded to learn the magic of the dances which only his mother could interpret. When he was denied, he secretly learned them by himself. He began to weave spells. He gathered around him other young male Elves, restless like himself, who behaved in unmasculine ways such as drinking and staying out all night. They sang their songs for each other, not for The Meg. Yet The Meg still loved her son and would not believe that Mati stood against her. As time passed, his spells made her sickly. More and more she could not carry out the joy of the Meghood.

Then, backed by his male companions, Mati called together the entire assembly. His mother was too ill to rule, he declared, and took the throne for himself. It was so unheard of for a male Elf to rule that there was no word in the Elfin language for his title. Yet he ruled the community for the better part of a year. Then the Husbands overthrew him and his companions. They drove the rebels away, into the Trollurgh Mountains, never to return under the penalty of death. The Meg ruled again, triumphant. But, like The First Meg, her heart was wounded by her son.

As the assembly of Elves listened to their own tale, they were silent, stony faced. Some whispered among themselves, occasionally glancing up into the sky. The Meg wept, tears streaking her face, staining her eyes red, swelling her face. She raised her hands above her head and sang through her sobs, "I am the Daughter of the Earth and Sky, watched over and protected by the sun and moon."

The assembly and the Husbands joined in the chorus: "You are The Meg of Elf and Daughter of the Earth and Sky. Hail to your mother's bounty! Hail to your father's eyes!"

All the Elves dropped their heads back and stared straight up at the moon. There was a half breath of silence, then someone screamed, "The moon is dying!"

A glance told Cyna what had happened. A month before in Ur Logga's den she had predicted an eclipse. Excitement and concern for Nyal had driven it from her mind. Yet above her the moon had darkened, taking on a sickly, reddish cast. It dimmed even as she watched.

The panic that followed was immediate. Cyna held her hands over her head and called out that it was an eclipse, nothing to be afraid of, but she was nearly trampled by waves of rushing Elves. Finn Dargha protectively clasped Fir Dahn in his arms, seeking refuge behind the taller Human witch. The Meg waved her arms, screaming, "Stop! Stop! Listen to me!" but except for the Husbands, who prostrated themselves before her, and Phaedryn, the entire Elfin population disappeared into the woods surrounding the palace. A sudden silence settled on the place, broken only by The Meg's inarticulate sobs.

"Come, Mother, come inside." Still composed, Phaedryn took her mother by the arm. Cyna and the two Peskie leaders followed, jostled by the Royal Husbands, who glanced fearfully over their shoulders at the dark hole in the sky. Phaedryn led her mother to the throne.

"The end," The Meg was sobbing. "It is the end of us all."

"Your Majesty, no," Cyna reassured her, bending down

beside the throne. "The moon will return very soon! It is only an eclipse."

The Meg raised her head. Cyna was startled by the anger which leaped at her from the tiny, tear-stained face. "You knew of this?" she asked hoarsely. "You knew Luf's Eye would die tonight, the night of The Welcoming? And you didn't tell me? How dare you not tell me! How dare you humiliate me before my Elves and my Peskie guests! You liar of The Law!"

"Luf's Eye did not die," Phaedryn murmured. "If the witch is right, it merely winked."

"Your Majesty, forgive me," said Cyna, "but I've been worried about Nyal and with the breaking of The Stone I forgot to . . ."

The Meg's silver voice rose to an impossible pitch which made Cyna's ears ring. "You forgot! You have ruined me! What kind of false witch are you? You have plotted with the Peskie king to bring me down! They are banished! All of them!" she cried to the Husbands, who stood dumbstruck. "A pox on all Human witches! Take her from my sight! A pox on Peskies! Traitors! Take them away from me!" Phaedryn bent over her mother with a glass of brandy and gestured to Cyna to go.

It was Finn Dargha who led the stunned witch away from the great hall and the ranting Meg. He sent a lieutenant to rally his Peskie troop from where they still were sleeping in their rooms. "Mistress Cyna, you'll not be staying here, we'll leave tonight," he said firmly, and turned to Fir Dahn. "My love, go pack our things while I check the supplies. Cyna, find your wounded Dwarf and hope he can walk for himself. Otherwise we'll have to leave him to The Meg's tender embraces. If we hurry, we can be out of Elf country by midday tomorrow. I have my fair share of courage, but not enough to face Her Megship again tonight. Not after this!" The Peskies assembled quickly, moving silently in the dark as they hurried past the wooden gates of The Meg's palace. The moon was brightening again, casting a feeble light to show them the way.

Ruf was not strong enough to keep pace with the fleeing Peskies, Cyna knew this minutes after they entered the forest. Still weak, he leaned against her, his breath coming in short gasps. Before long, his forehead was plastered in sweat. The Peskies were too slight to bear so heavy a burden as a Dwarf. Cyna felt the stirrings of panic. She tried to think of what Fallon would do in this situation, but knew with a wave of despair that Fallon would never have forgotten to announce a movement of the heavens. And yet she was still a witch and protected by Magic, even if she had to return to the palace and face The Meg.

Suddenly the wonderfully nimble Finn Dargha stumbled and flew through the air. A large form exploded from the shadows of the trail, then blundered away. By the time everything was sorted out, Finn was fuming over being tripped by a tether rope and Fir Dahn was quieting the startled black-and-white pony tied to the end of it. "Who would tether a pony in the middle of the forest?" wondered Finn, rubbing his bruised shins.

"Only an Elf," said the Peskie queen. "What a dizzy tribe they are!"

Ruf had sagged to the ground during the halt, fighting to catch his breath.

"Get on the horse, Ruf," Finn Dargha commanded suddenly.

"This may be one of The Meg's steeds," Cyna cautioned. New Faith Humans were always complaining that Peskies were thieves and didn't respect private property.

"She's already banished you for your witchcraft," Fir Dahn said. "The penalty for horse stealing can't be much more." The pony whinnied and tossed his head as though nodding agreement.

Aided by the Peskies, Ruf struggled on top of the small, perfectly formed horse. His toes almost touched the ground. The pony's black coat was punctuated with large white patches that shone in the strengthening moonlight, giving the Peskie troop an easily seen center in the dark night. He moved with spirit and strength, yet seemed gentle and friendly. Cyna called him Bihan because he was so small.

A few miles from The Meg's palace, Fir Dahn began to sing a marching song in her high, clear alto. One by one, the rest of the troop joined her. They were still singing when the sun rose, moving swiftly and effortlessly through the forest, their song interspersed with whistles and birdcalls. Bihan trotted beside Cyna, seeming tireless despite Ruf's weight. His light blue eyes were bright with excitement. Occasionally he offered his own whinny to the chorus of voices around him, like the laughter of a young Elf.

Chapter 24

With Ned, Adler, and the rest in pursuit, Avelaer raced down the narrow road with wild-bred speed. He gained enough ground that Nyal eased him as the road wound into the foothills. Just over the first crest, Tym waited at the side of the road, waving from the palfrey. "Sir, follow me!" The groom turned away and disappeared into the dark pinewood that flanked the road.

Nyal pointed Avelaer's head toward the wood and the charger leaped a low hedge. Nyal found himself on a narrow path that ran along the side of a steep ledge. The path was thick in pine needles and the horses' hooves made no sound. Turning a corner, he reined to a halt in a small glen. Nyal leaped to the ground and seized his horse's head. It took all his strength to muffle Avelaer's challenge to the lords' horses as they thundered by.

"They attacked me, Tym," Nyal exclaimed when they were past. "They think I killed Telerhyde!"

Tym swore. "Lady Cyna told me there were strange things going on, and she was right! It gets stranger and stranger. With luck, they'll ride on for another mile or two before they see we've doubled back," Tym said. "I'll go brush our tracks off the side of the road. Sir, you're hurt!"

Nyal's sword arm was bleeding and he had no strength in his fingers. His horse had fared worse. The sword thrust was intended to sever the stallion's hamstring, but had missed narrowly, leaving a deep gash in his hock. Blood soaked his snowy white fetlock. Nyal bandaged the horse's wound while Tym covered their trail as best he could.

"We have to catch Lothen," Nyal said, gritting his teeth stoically as Tym wrapped a strip of cloth torn from his cloak around his arm.

"You can't travel like this, begging your pardon, sir," Tym told Nyal. "Your horse needs rest, to say nothing of yourself." When he saw that Nyal was going to ignore him, he shrugged. "Lothen came off the road back there. It looks like he's doubling north."

"To Elea, perhaps," Nyal said. "Let's follow."

"Yes, sir," Tym said. He led the palfrey out along a rocky outcrop. "Lead your horse for a bit, if he'll let you. We'll find a way down this ledge here and be off."

They moved slowly, for the cut on Avelaer's leg opened again with exertion. Nyal led him with his left hand, holding his right protectively against his chest.

The tracks of Lothen's horse stood out clearly on the soft forest floor. The trail followed the slope of the ground, so it was natural and easy. By late afternoon they crossed a narrow and rutted road, overhung with branches. The tracks led them down it, through countryside that was silent and deserted. Tym led the way. Behind him, he occasionally heard the impatient snap of Avelaer's teeth and Nyal's soothing "Easy, boy." When the stallion became fractious from the pain of his wound, Tym stopped and helped Nyal calm him.

The sky lightened momentarily at sunset and the moon rose, veiled behind a thin layer of clouds. When it became too dark to see the trail, Tym built a small fire by the side of the road, where they warmed themselves. They had no food, so they rolled themselves in their cloaks and slept on the ground.

By first light, they were leading the horses across rolling farmland. Lothen's tracks stood out boldly on the narrow trail until another road joined theirs, broader and well traveled. "We'll keep on," Nyal said. "We know he's going north. There aren't so many roads that we'll lose him." They passed occasional farmhouses, low and squat, hugging the ground. Dawn revealed farmers working in their barns by lamplight as they milked the cows and goats. Nyal stopped to ask if anyone had seen a horseman with a black shield. One thought he had, and gestured toward the north.

The mud of the road sucked at Tym's feet. Leg weary, he hauled himself up on the palfrey's back. He was still leading the way when they came upon a small inn late in the afternoon.

The innkeeper was splitting logs in front of the door. "Yes, sir?" he said.

"Have you seen a horseman?" Nyal demanded. "He wears a black shield. Probably would have been on the road last night or this morning."

"Aye. Grey horse, black shield. He was by last night. Had dinner, then rode on. I asked him if he was from the Stone Moving; he just laughed at me. Nasty fellow, if you don't mind, sir. I hope he's not a friend of yours."

"No friend of ours," replied Nyal, and Tym snorted in agreement. "Have you some food for us? And grain for the horses?"

"Just put the pot on, sir, the fire's not hot yet. Can you wait a bit?"

Nyal accompanied the innkeeper to the barn with the horses while Tym hauled their few possessions upstairs to a tiny room with one bed in it. Exhausted, he sat for a moment. Nyal would be upstairs in a few minutes, then Tym would go to his accustomed bed in the stable. His legs twitched as though he were still walking. His head dropped forward and he began to snore gently.

He was awakened by voices in the yard and feet pounding up the stairs. He half raised himself from the bed and the door burst open. Lord Benare strode in, his sword drawn, followed by the innkeeper.

"Here he is, Yer Lordship," the innkeeper was saying. "I should have known he was up to no good. But please, sir, kill him in the yard, so's you don't mess the blankets."

Tym gasped and pulled the blanket up to his chin. Benare glared blankly at him. "Who are you?" he demanded.

"Tymeryl, sir," Tym stammered, too frightened to lie.

"Where are you coming from?"

"The Stone Moving, sir."

Benare stepped cautiously into the room as though an assassin might leap off the wall at any moment.

"Do you travel alone?" Benare asked, poking with his sword tip at Tym's cloak where it lay at the foot of the bed.

"Yes, sir," Tym said.

The sword tip slowly lowered. "Sorry to bother you," Benare said. "We seek Nyal of Crowell, who has fled after breaking The Peace by attacking The Eacon and killing The Eacon's gate boy. If you see him, stay clear; he's grievously wounded Lord Landes."

"Yes, sir. Sorry to hear that, sir," Tym said, bobbing his head.

"Beggin' your pardon," the innkeeper said to Tym after Benare had gone. Relief spread across his face. "He's a fierce lord, he is. A bunch of them has rode in here and asked if I had any guests. I hope you don't take offense, sir. I knew it wasn't you, but I had to tell him, you understand . . ."

Tym flew downstairs. Ten horses were tethered outside the inn and from the small room where a fire gleamed in a hearth he could hear the sound of irritable voices calling for food. He crossed to the barn swiftly, pausing at the door for a moment to adjust his eyes to the dim light.

The barn was small and none too clean. The sharp odor of ammonia and dung bit at his nostrils. There were no stalls. The brown palfrey and Avelaer were cross-tied to heavy wooden beams, buckets of oats and water in front of each of them. Nyal sat dozing beside his horse.

"Sir!" Tym whispered, "you've got to get up." Nyal stirred and opened his eyes. "The lords is here, sir."

Nyal stared dully as though he didn't understand.

"Sea Prissies, sir! They'll kill us both if we don't hurry!" In exasperation and fear Tym dragged Nyal to his feet, shoving him toward his horse. "Find your saddle."

Tym had the palfrey saddled and ready to go while Nyal was still smoothing out the saddle blanket. Tym took over from him and saddled the stallion, keeping a watchful eye out for Avelaer to kick or bite. He did neither and Tym frowned in concern. He felt the stallion's wound. "It's fevered," he said. "And you don't look so good yourself, sir.

We'll find a good smith and get him fixed up. Can you hide your face? The lords don't recognize me, so just hang back and let me talk. Maybe they'll not notice you and we can get on the road again. Then we'll find him a smith and us some breakfast."

Within a mile the gash on Avelaer's hock had opened again. Nyal walked by the horse's head. Proceeding slowly, glancing fearfully over his shoulder, Tym led them into a small village.

There was a well in the center of town and a figure was busy filling a pitcher as they rode up. Tym took the figure for a child and had already said, "Here, son," when the creature turned around and Tym realized he was addressing a Peskie. "Excuse me, Master Acorn," he corrected himself with great respect. "Do you know where we might find a smith? And perhaps a bite to eat?"

The Peskie's golden eyes flitted over the two Humans' faces. "There's a smith out on the River Road," he said. "He's not Human, if that bothers you. He's Dwarf."

"Nay, Master Corncob, it pleasures me greatly," Tym replied before they rode off.

The smith was two heads shorter than Tym and almost twice as wide. He said little as he examined the stallion's wound.

Avelaer hated blacksmiths and kicked out with his good leg, narrowly missing the Dwarf's knee. "Here, watch it!" the smith barked. "Hold him, manling," he said to Nyal. "Don't let him get away with that! Move over, you big donkey." He whacked Avelaer sharply on the rump and seized the hoof of the wounded leg.

"Whoa!" Tym, Nyal, and the smith shouted as the horse threw up his head and struggled to free himself, his leg lashing out, the smith clinging grimly to it.

"Twist his ear!" shouted the smith, being shaken back and forth like a leaf in a storm. Tym seized the horse's ear and twisted it until the animal froze, his head high, nostrils flaring. "Hold him, now," the smith cautioned, "he won't like this." He pulled a red-hot iron from the coals of his fire and swiftly applied it to the stallion's wound. There was a sizzle and the smell of burning hair.

The horse squealed and erupted several feet into the air.

Tym hung on fiercely. The smith flew through the air into the muddy barnyard. Nyal held the reins and shouted, "Whoa, boy! Easy!"

At length the horse settled down again, angrily kicking out with his injured leg. Braving more commotion, the smith applied a dampened bag of herbs to the wound and bound it tightly.

"Now keep him quiet for a day or so," he said, breathing heavily. "Feed him oats, don't let him near clover. He'll have a scar where the hair'll be white, but fire takes the fever out, so he'll be good as new."

"We can't rest!" Nyal said. "We must be off."

"You've no choice unless you want to walk. And from the look of you, you won't be walking far. Let me tend to your arm," the Dwarf observed. His eyes fell on Nyal's sword. "Broderick's work, is it? I thought so. I can always recognize a master's work. You're welcome to stay here if you want."

"We're overmatched already, sir," Tym observed. "Lothen would make short work of us now, even if we found him."

Nyal hesitated a moment, then nodded in agreement. "We'll rest for a day, regain our strength."

They stayed for several days with the smith while Nyal and Avelaer healed. During that time, Tym found pleasure in the large, frequent meals and the deep hay of the barn. Finishing dinner, he would retire to the hayloft to nap. When he finished napping it was time for supper. In the morning he sometimes wandered over to the meadow, where a caravan bound for The Perime had camped while the smith shod his oxen.

He found some good fellows there. North seamen like himself, they were clever, hardworking men. He asked many questions and learned that the caravan was traveling to Elea and from there was sailing to Dnevre, the northernmost port of The Perime. The wagon drivers and guards were ignorant of the events that had transpired at The Eacon's Keep. And, Tym suspected, they were uninterested. They seemed to find the inhabitants of Morbihan amusing, not to be taken seriously. To them only the profits they would make trading with The Perime were serious.

The smith wanted Nyal to stay longer, but when the caravan prepared to leave, they said good-bye and joined the wagons as they started for Elea.

Nyal walked behind Tym, leading Avelaer. Avelaer's hock was healing nicely and both the palfrey and Tym had filled out from their rest. They were three weeks traveling, slowed by the wet roads. The wagons groaned under loads of furs and (a wagon driver whispered to Tym) gold ingots from the Dwarves in the mountains. Nyal groaned when he thought of Lothen escaping so easily from him. "He'll catch a boat to The Perime and we'll never find him!" he muttered.

Elea was an ancient city of Morbihan, but it was also the chief port of trade with The Perime. Many of its inhabitants were of The New Faith and had been citizens of The Perime before moving to what they thought of as the frontier. The largest house in the city was owned by the ambassador from Moer and the city was governed by an elected assembly which met in his living room. In Harkynwood, Elea was often referred to as "The Whore of The Perime."

Surrounded by a thick wall of reddish brown stone, Elea had three entrances. Two were on the land side, massive arches cut through the wall, flanked by watchtowers and sealed off by heavy iron gates, which rose and fell as caravans entered the left. On the sea side, where the walls followed the natural line of the harbor in a graceful curve, the triple-gated entrance was high and sculptured like a triumphal arch. The population seemed to be entirely Human. The men-at-arms who lifted the heavy iron gates stared coldly at the caravan. They wore the shields of Lord Adler, a red swan on a blue field.

Nyal and Tym followed the caravan, plunging into the mob of people who flooded the narrow streets. The aroma of raw Human and animal dung assailed their nostrils and seemed for a moment to blot out all sound. Tym choked for air. Many of the streets were not wide enough to accommodate the laden wagons and the caravan took a meandering course as it struggled toward the waterfront. Other caravans were moving back and forth through the city, often laying claim to the same street at the same time. Arguments broke out. Once the wagon leader of the caravan was struck over the head with a board in an altercation about right-of-way.

Passersby plastered themselves against walls and hurled curses while the wagons passed them.

At length the caravan came to the harbor. Between the city walls and the edge of the water was a broad expanse of level ground. It was covered with flat, wide slabs of rock, each as large as a wagon, carefully set into the ground. In front of the city gate was a tall, slender standing stone so ancient that its runes were almost entirely worn away. A few steps away was a spring of fresh water.

Ships were moored to stone docks. A constant stream of humanity surged back and forth from them, carrying cargo. The caravan drew itself together near the standing stone. The wagon drivers loosened their swords in their belts and stood vigilantly beside their wagons. Other caravans stood nearby. Flies swarmed over the horses and the odors alternated between the fresh air from the sea and a mixture of fish and manure.

Nyal led the horses to the spring and let them drink, loosening the palfrey's girth and brushing Avalaer's forelock out of his eyes. Flies buzzed around the horses' heads and Avelaer shook himself angrily.

"What now, sir?" Tym asked. "Do we chase him to The Perime?"

Before Nyal could answer, a bugle blew. A portly man flanked by two boys with golden trumpets made his way through the crowd, his face rosy and expectant with importance. Passersby greeted him with squeals of excitement. At the base of the standing stone he stopped and the trumpet sounded again.

"Hear me!" he cried in a high-pitched, penetrating voice. "The events and messages of the day!" The harsh sounds of the harbor quieted as all eyes turned toward him. He visibly swelled with pride. "The rains continue in the mountains! By order of the High Commissioner, the drains within the city must be kept open! Anyone who allows a drain in or near his house to become clogged will suffer the penalty of three pieces of gold or ten lashes at this stone!"

There was a gentle murmur as the city folk digested this piece of news. The clarion voice went on. "Be it known to all men that the murderer of Telerhyde has been identified! Nyal of Crowell is traitor and murderer. By order of the Lords of the North he has been stripped of his property and is declared a troll! If he is discovered within the city of Elea, he is to be bound and brought to the Council of Lords for execution!"

Nyal turned away, hiding his face. Blood was pounding in his head. He turned over his shield so that the dragons of Crowell were hidden. "Let's get out of here," he whispered to Tym. "Now we've no choice but to follow Lothen to The Perime."

They found a stable near the harbor which accepted the horses for a gold piece. "Robbers! Trolls!" Tym cursed after the horses were bedded down on skimpy straw. "City people are all thieves. Follow me, sir, and keep your head down. We'll be safe, you'll see. There's thieves and smugglers in this port, I can feel it. I'll find the worst of them and get them to take us across the Straits."

The ship Tym chose was an old sea galley. Her lines were graceful and The Old Girl carved on her bow was a lucky one. But the years and changing times had played hard with her. An awkward cabin bulged from her deck and her original steering oars had been replaced by a large, jury-built rudder that protruded from her stern like an obscene thing. She rode low in the water. Although tightly lashed to the dock, she had an odd, rolling motion.

From a stone tower at the end of the stone dock, Humans sang a hauling song as they pulled on a massive block and tackle, lifting large boxes onto the ship's deck. There grunting, cursing seamen lowered the crates down a narrow gangplank into her hold.

"Deep respects to you and your heroic ancestors," Tym hailed the captain. He was as much past his prime as the ship. His long, grey hair was tied back from his forehead while his beard, incongruously red streaked with silver, grew wild. His large, bare belly bulged over a wide belt studded with bronze disks. The sword which hung from the belt was steel, well honed and balanced as a north seaman's blade should be.

Nyal stood uncertainly to the side as Tym and the captain bargained. Tym seemed to know the captain's relatives and there was great backslapping and an exchange of gold.

"He's an old smuggler, as slippery as a serpent, M'Lord,"

Tym whispered as they walked across the gangplank. "He'd as soon slit our throats as look at us, so watch your step. He's carrying illegal cargo, and he's agreed to ferry us over the Straits for twice the going rate and not ask questions. You're to ride down in the hold with the cargo, whatever it is. Beggin' your pardon, sir, I know it's rough down there, but we can't have you recognized. Don't worry about a thing. We'll find your man and find out who killed Lord Telerhyde." A seaman passed them on the gangplank.

"We sail in two hours, with the tide," he resumed when they were alone on deck. "I'll keep watch up here, but you better get below. Sir, please!" His voice rose a notch as Nyal did not move. "They'll kill you, sure as Peskies got ears. Lots of Humans were at the Stone Moving last week. They know what you look like!"

"What about the horses?" asked Nyal.

"The horses!" Tym replied, slapping his forehead with the flat of his hand. "I'll go see to them. We'll have a nice stall made up in the stern. Get below now, sir."

A worn ladder led down into the darkness of the hold. Reluctantly, Nyal moved toward it. "I'll be back in no time!" Tym called to him.

Tym left the ship, moving quickly through the dockside crowd toward the stable. The purse was now empty. It had taken everything to buy passage on the timeworn ship. He dreaded facing Nyal, but Tym was sure he could sell the horses for enough to sustain them until they could find Lothen and return to Morbihan as free men.

Chapter 25

The stench that rose from the bowels of the ship was staggering. Sweat broke out on Nyal's forehead and he gripped the ladder tightly as his stomach heaved. His eyes adjusted to the hold's darkness and he descended again, carefully, for the rungs of the ladder were moist and slimy.

A narrow aisle ran through the center of the ship. On each side, piled high and haphazardly, crates were stacked and lashed together. Beside him, a crate shuddered as a frantic scratching sound came from it. Nyal stepped hastily away and bumped into another box. A deep growl sounded in the darkness.

"Hello," said a voice. "You one of the fellows who's crossin' with us?"

Nyal made out the figure of a boy dressed only in a torn loincloth. "Yes," he said and gagged again on the stench.

The fellow stepped forward extending a grimy hand. "I'm Slat, ship's boy. You'll get used to the stink!" he added with a laugh. "It's the apes that smell the worst. You got any stuff?" Nyal shook his head.

"Well, you'll ride down here with me. Stay out of the bow and stern—they pitch too much. Here in the middle's about as good as it's gonna get. You can help me watch during the crossing to see the cargo don't break loose and shift. Could sink this old scow, you know."

Nyal nodded. "My horses will be along soon. Where can I put them?"

"Horses!" the ship's boy laughed again. "The whole cargo's animals this trip. But there's room in the stern with the unicorns. Come look at the apes."

Nyal followed him into a dark labyrinth of bales and boxes. "It was a Perime galley once. They kept men down here," Slat explained. "Chained 'em to the sides by those big iron rings. A man in here would never see the light of day 'til he died."

"What kind of men were kept here?" asked Nyal, steadying himself as they came to a wet spot.

"Criminals—traitors from Morbihan or soldiers from the south islands. They capture a man and ask him if he wants to die or go on the galleys. If you're smart, you say 'kill me.' If you're a fool, you say 'let me live, I'll go on the galleys.' You get stuck on the galleys and you wish you were dead! You get an oar, that's the only thing you own. You're chained to it, then chained to these rings. You eat here, you live here, you die here. And all the time you just pull that big oar. We don't got oars on her now, though. Captain uses the room for cargo and we cross the Straits with the wind. Makes it slower sometimes. Here's the apes."

In the gloom Nyal could make out a wall before him. A low moan came from it.

"It's the brig. Used to be where they kept the ones who wouldn't behave, before they drowned 'em."

A familiar, musky odor reached out to Nyal from the wall. In the dim light he could barely make out iron bars and a stout lock. Something moved in the corner.

"Here! Get up, you great ugly thing!" Slat struck the bars with the handle of his dagger, making a sharp ringing sound. The shadow in the corner stirred. In another corner a smaller shape cowered back into the shadows. Slat turned to Nyal. "Stinks, don't they? The captain says they don't live long even though they're big; says he'll get a great price for these three if they live 'til we get to Moer. But the big one's sick, I think. It won't eat. Hey, don't you growl at me, you bastard!" He struck the bars again and the shadow shrank back.

"Don't do that!" Nyal exclaimed. "Dragon's Breath!" he swore, thunderstruck. He stepped forward and stared at the Ogre. In the gloom he could barely make out the tiny kit clinging about her neck. "Slavery," he said. "This is a slave ship!"

"We don't got no Humans." Slat objected. "Don't go callin' *me* a slave. I'm a free Perime seaman, 'cept for the captain, who'd kill me if I tried to jump ship."

"But these—apes. Do you often transport them?"

"I never seen 'em before. See, there's caravans come once a month or so, an' we always pick up unicorns and little spotted screechers. But this time we put into Flean before we come here and there's these three apes. They say we'll get little ones the next trip—Brownies who look cute and would cut off your hand as soon as look at you."

"There's more?"

"As many as we can get. There'll be a good market home in the Perime for Morbihan Brownies and apes, I tell you. The captain'll make a good profit." Slat gestured at the other crates and pens lining the hull. "They buy 'em for the games. Nothing your Perime man likes better than to see unicorns ate by wolves. Now he can see saber cats tear Brownies."

Nyal turned away from the ship's boy. His nausea was gone, replaced by a cold anger. "Where did you catch them?" he asked.

"We don't catch them, just buy them from the traders. They get 'em in the south, I think the man said."

"Fensdown Plain," Nyal said.

"That sounds like it. You know about apes, then?" Slat sounded disappointed. "I thought maybe you'd never seen them. Like me. I'm a Perime man; I thought they were just tales. I didn't think such things as these ape creatures really existed."

"I know of them," Nyal said, fighting to keep his voice calm, his eyes still on the Ogre.

A voice from the outside filtered through the gloom of the the ship's hold. "That's the captain. I gotta go. See you later." Slat disappeared toward the bright light of the hatch.

Nyal stood still. The Ogre breathed heavily, as though her throat was obstructed. It took Nyal several moments to realize that she was sobbing.

"Greetings, Clever One," he whispered, using the name which Ogres called themselves. "I am Nyal of Crowell."

There was a silence, then the creature breathed again, deeper, trying to control herself. "Who are you?" Nyal asked. "Why are you here?"

"Lord of Crowell?" asked the Ogre in a guttural whisper.

"No," he said patiently, "just Nyal." He could make her out now. She was young, her face swollen and bruised. Not much taller than he was, she had the ruddy hair of the southern Ogres of Fensdown Plain. "How has this happened?" he asked.

"While traveling to the Stone Moving, we were captured by Human farmers. Some of my family escaped, but my kit cried in fear, and they found me. They beat me and sold me like an animal. I am Rib Tonnan, daughter of Ur Banfit, king of the mountain Ogres in Fensdown Plain. This is my daughter, La Tonnan, and there," she gestured into the shadows, "is my little brother, Prince Nib Banfit."

"Princess, little Prince!" Nyal said, stunned. "I remember you well. We met at Telerhyde's funeral."

"Telerhyde! How he would grieve if he knew what was happening! How have you come to this awful place?"

"The Lords of the North believe that I killed Telerhyde. I've been stripped of my land and hunted like a troll. I'm pursuing a man, a New Faither, who knows who really killed Telerhyde. I go to The Perime in search of him."

The Ogre sighed. "What a terrible time! My father was killed protecting us, and many friends died on the journey." She suddenly began to cough, a thin raspy sound. Nyal knelt beside her, reaching through the bars, thumping her between her great shoulders. When the coughing stopped, she smiled at him. "It will be good to have you as a companion for the voyage."

Nyal shook his head. "My groom will be here soon. We'll think of a way to free you."

"Here! Boy!" bellowed a Human voice at the hatch. "Where's that damn boy?"

"Yes?" said Nyal, rising quickly and stepping away from the princess's cage.

The first mate hung head-down by his knotty arms, peering into the darkness. His lip curled with distaste. "The water cask's been loaded in the stern. See the apes and the unicorns have water. Anything left over, give it to the ones that are worst off. We'll be two days in the Straits. If we lose the unicorns, the captain will have your tail."

"Yes, sir," said Nyal, "right away, sir!" He held himself back in the gloom, glad the mate thought he was Slat. "A moment, Princess, and I'll be right back," he whispered.

He followed the narrow aisle up the center of the hold. Another bright patch of sunlight guided him to the rear hatch, where a leaking cask of fresh water sat. He brought a bucket back to the princess and prince and left them in privacy to quench their thirst and clean themselves while he tended to the inhabitants of the other cages.

From deep in the shadows of the stern of the ship he heard a familiar sound. There were two unicorns. They were not large for their kind, massive shoulders towering only a foot or so above the height of a good-sized horse. Feet like tree trunks shook the timbers of the ship each time they stepped. Their single horns rose from the bridge of their broad noses, almost touching the ceiling of the deck above. Tiny eyes, not good even in daylight, peered nervously in his direction. One gave a challenging snort. The sound echoed in Nyal's ears, reminding him of joyous afternoons spent hunting with his father and brother in the foothills of Crowell.

"Steady, fellows," he said, gingerly edging forward to slide the bucket through the side of the pen. The unicorn closest to him tossed its head in a challenging motion, its horn crashing against the deck above. Then it stepped forward to the bucket, nostrils flaring, testing the water. Its rich brown coat was matted, and ribs protruded from its sides. Above its stumplike feet, the skin was raw and bleeding from ill-fitting iron rings which shackled the beast to the base of the mast where it extended through the deck to the spine of the ship. The unicorn drank gratefully, its large, horselike upper lip curling in pleasure. The bucket was empty within seconds.

Nyal carried water until his arms ached. The cask was well below half-full when the unicorns finally stopped looking eagerly for him with their dim eyes. They stood, still shackled but momentarily content, like a pair of horses, switching flies off each other's faces with their ropelike tails.

The remaining cages were filthy. He could identify most of the captives by their strong scent. A shaggy saber-toothed cat, panting in fear, lunged at him as he poured water into her bucket. With a shout he fell backward, her claws just grazing his throat. Yelling and hissing at her, he drove her back, pouring her water hastily before she could attack again. A pack of small dire wolves growled but allowed him to fill their bucket, waiting until he had moved away before clustering around it to drink, their tails wagging. A cage full of spotted gongoes jabbered excitedly. A large, single timber wolf with surprisingly blue eyes watched him calmly and ignored the water. The aurochs were cheated. Nyal strained to tilt the huge cask and pour out the last drop, but the great bovines still looked eagerly after him as they drank their final drops of water.

When Nyal had finished, he saw that the princess had fallen into an exhausted sleep holding her daughter, her long auburn curls matted across her massive chest and shoulders.

He tried to smile reassuringly at the prince, who was huddled next to her. The young Ogre was only six or seven years old, staring at him with frightened eyes.

At any moment Nyal expected to hear Tym arrive with the horses. He wold tie them in the aisle next to the unicorns, he decided, but he worried about water. Two days was too long for any creature to go without a drink. Not many of the captives would survive the crossing unless there were a few extra casks loaded aboard.

Nyal climbed up on the crate nearest him, the one with the timber wolf, and leaned back against the ship's hull. His back and shoulders ached, and the half-healed sword wound in his forearm throbbed. The stench made his eyes sting. The ship was quiet. One of the hatches had been covered over and the hold was even darker than before. He thought of Cyna, wondered if the wild Elf had reached her to tell her what had happened.

Nyal of Crowell!

Nyal sat up hastily, peering into the darkness.

The voice seemed to have come from right beside him but there was no one. The timber wolf moved beneath him and he could hear the rough-coated saber-tooth's nervous panting. "I'm hearing things now," he said out loud to hear his own voice.

The only other sounds were muffled animal noises, the slap of water against the ship's hull, the dull boom as the ship gently struck the dock. She must be loaded now, for he heard no men or objects moving. Where was Tym with the horses, he wondered.

Nyal of Crowell! Listen to me! He could hear it clearly. The voice was deep and commanding, but strangely garbled, as though not the speaker's native tongue.

"Yes?" Nyal answered cautiously, his eyes searching the dark corners of the hold.

"The man you seek is not in the Perime. He has sailed round the island to Fensdown Plain," the voice said urgently. *"Treachery is at work! For the sake of Morbihan, you must go south to Fensdown Plain!"*

Nyal held his breath, his dagger drawn. "How do you know this? How do you know who I am?" he hissed.

"I know you by The Law." The voice was getting fainter, as though the speaker were moving away and calling back over a great distance. *"And by The Law you must go south to avenge the murders of your father and brother!"*

He listened for a moment. "Hello?" he said. The voice was gone. There was only the dull slap of waves against the hull.

"Hello," replied the princess, yawning. "Nyal?" she asked after a moment. "Are you still there?"

"I'm right here," he replied, his hand still tight on his dagger.

"I'm sorry, I was asleep. Were you talking to me before."

"No, a visitor."

"A friend? Is he still here?"

"I don't know," Nyal said. He slid off the crate and stooped to look at the blue-eyed wolf in the crate. The creature stared back at him, unblinking, its sky-blue eyes reflecting a strange light in the dank hold of the ship. Nyal turned to the cage which held the Ogres. "Princess, how would you like to get out of here?" he asked abruptly.

Chapter 26

The princess was startled. "But how? We are surrounded by sea and enemies."

"I'll need your help," Nyal said. He found a heavy, rusty rigging pin and used it as a lever to attack the lock. The lock gave way and the rusty hinges moaned as he pulled open the door. "Can you walk?" He helped the Ogre to her feet and steadied her.

The small prince and La Tonnan cowered behind her, clinging to the hair of her legs. She stooped so as not to bump her head on the low ceiling. "What are you going to do?" she whispered.

"Help me."

The sturdy loading ramp lay on the floor of the hold where it had been dropped. It was made of heavy timber and the princess and Nyal needed all their strength to shove and pull it into position beneath the hatch. Grunting with its weight, Nyal helped the princess to lift one end, then slid closed the iron pins that held it. Looking up through the hatch, he could see the sky coloring to a deep purple. It was almost sunset.

"All hands aboard! Move it, you Sea Prissies!" the captain bellowed from above them. "The pilot boat's coming."

"Quickly," urged Nyal. He led the way down the darkness of the narrow aisle to the unicorns. Catching his scent, one lifted its head and made a sound something like a cow. "Steady, now," Nyal murmured. The rigging pin was still in his hand. He slid it through the slats of the unicorn pen and found the ring that held the chain to the base of the mast. He pulled and pried, the veins of his arms standing out, sweat bursting from his forehead. The iron held.

"Throw us a line, you Morbihanian Elfwit! We've been waiting for your pilot boat all afternoon!" bellowed the voice above. And then Nyal heard him grumble, "If he makes us miss the tide again, I'll have him flayed and sell his pelt to a Moerian circus. Prepare to make fast!"

"Dragon's Breath! They're getting ready to sail!" Nyal swore, hurrying. He pulled so hard that his arms quivered with the strain.

"I can help," the princess said quietly. She handed her infant daughter to Nib Banfit and stepped into the pen. She extended her hand to the unicorn and make a low noise in her throat. The animal watched her warily. "Soooooooo, steady, soooooooooo," she crooned, sliding her hand along its neck and scratching behind its ears. "Maybe we can free its feet," she whispered. Nyal handed her the pin cautiously, for the awesome strength and bulk of the beast could crush them both with one casual gesture. The princess bent down, still crooning softly. The muscles in her shaggy forearms bulged as she twisted the pin. The shackle popped free.

"By The Law!" exclaimed Nyal. "Now this one."

That shackle was stronger and the Ogre finally ripped the chain from its fastening, splitting the base of the mast. When both unicorns were free, the princess took her place near the hatch as Nyal slid open the gate of the pen. "Shoo!" he whispered, waving his arms. But the beasts only stared at him.

"Shoo!" he repeated, louder. " Phsssssst! Both of you. Go home!"

"Prepare to cast off!" bellowed the captain from above.

The larger of the unicorns stepped out of its pen. Its mate followed, head lowered, nostrils flaring. A fresh breeze swept past the hatch. Again the unicorns stood, unsure. Nyal flapped his arms and ran at them, howling.

In alarm, they bolted down the aisle. As they passed the loading ramp by the hatch, the princess leaped in front of them, barking and growling. Aroused by the noises, the dire wolves began to howl. The unicorns turned in panic from the princess and blundered up the ramp to the deck.

"Quickly, Princess!" called Nyal as he flung open the crate of the yowling saber cat. "Free the aurochs!" Running down the aisle, he freed the wolves and the spotted·gongoes. The dire wolves streamed silently past him. As he flung open its door, the blue-eyed timber wolf paused to look into Nyal's face, a piercing look that brought gooseflesh to his arms.

The ship lurched. Nyal stole a glance out the hatch. On deck a unicorn had driven the captain and several crewmen up the mast. It paced below, threatening them with its horn and repeatedly ramming its head into the mast. The ship shuddered with each blow.

Sailors tried to distract the beast from its attack. From behind them the larger unicorn, goaded by their shouts and screams, lowered its head and charged. Sailors scattered, leaping over the side into the water to escape. The charge carried the unicorn along the deck, where it became entangled in a shroud. Struggling against it, it pulled the line tight and the mast bent, groaning. "Hey, watch it!" cried the captain as the smaller unicorn continued to ram the old wood with its horn. The mast splintered. Mast, sail, shrouds, and men toppled into the water.

As the animals ran for freedom, the loading area before the city gate, still crowded with workers and wagons despite the late hour, was transformed into instant chaos. Drivers deserted their wagons and horses bolted as wolves ran beneath their feet. Sailors fled from the pack of spotted gongoes that clambered over crates and cargo. The creatures would not run free for long, Nyal thought grimly, for the city walls cut off flight to the countryside. But the confusion might cover the escape of a fugitive and a few Ogres.

"Come on!" Nyal took the princess by the hand. The infant, eyes huge in her wizened face, clung to her mother's neck; the prince clutched Nyal's belt. Unnoticed in the twilight amidst the chaos, they sprinted across the deck onto the dock.

The saber cat disappeared around the corner of the wall and Nyal and the princess followed at a run. Out of sight of the marketplace, a small jetty reached out into the water. Above them the city wall was empty of men-at-arms. The smaller unicorn trotted up behind them.

"Whoa!" cried Nyal in alarm.

"Whoa, steady," soothed the princess, holding out her hand. "She's tame!" she cried as the beast nuzzled her fingers.

"On her back then," Nyal ordered. "Whups!" He lifted the prince up to ride behind her. The blue-eyed wolf turned the corner behind them and stopped, staring. Nyal picked up a rock and threw it. "Be gone!" he shouted. The wolf sidestepped the stone and watched them, unblinking. Nyal turned back to the princess.

"Where now?" she cried.

"I ride south to Fensdown Plain, but first I must find my man and get the horses."

"I'll go with you to Harkynwood, if I may. I would appreciate a companion."

Nyal took her hand and she pulled him up to ride behind Nib Banfit, who clung tightly to her waist. The baby, La Tonnan, wrapped her arms tightly about her mother's neck and bounced on the princess's shoulders. "The stable then, quickly!" Nyal said.

The unicorn's trot was a swift, jolting pace. Straddling the beast's wide middle, Nyal had no grip and was forced to grasp the Ogre's fur for balance. The beast obeyed the princess's commands eagerly, quickly covering the distance across the square to the gate.

The men-at-arms who had come out to watch the animals and laugh at the fear of the sailors and wagon merchants realized too late what was happening. They now ran in terror.

At the princess's urging, the unicorn broke into a bumpy canter, through the gate and down the narrow streets of Elea. Humans fled in horror before them, scrambling into doorways and leaping over walls.

"It's to the right!" Nyal called, and the princess guided the unicorn down the alleyway. "I only hope Tym's there. He went to get the horses hours ago!"

The unicorn cantered into a small square which faced the stable at one end. The moon had risen and added its silver light to the fading twilight. At the sight of the Ogres and the unicorn, the stable keeper uttered a New Faith oath and sprinted away, across the square. His groom followed, screaming.

"Tym!" called Nyal, sliding from the unicorn's back. There was no answer. Wasting no time, Nyal ran to Avelaer's stall. The stallion greeted him with a low-pitched whinny, lowering his head to accept the bridle and pawing the ground as Nyal threw on the saddle. A cry from the courtyard brought Nyal to the stable door.

The unicorn's nostrils flared and its weak eyes peered across the square to where torches flared. At the other end of the courtyard, firelight reflecting from their swords, the pursuing Lords of the North had drawn up a thin battle line. Ned rode at the head and Nyal recognized Adler and Farryl just behind him. The rest fanned out, blocking the small streets that spilled out from the square, their torches throwing flickering shadows across the cobblestones. "We have you now, traitor!" called Ned.

"Nyal, quickly!" called the princess.

Nyal vaulted onto Avelaer's back, drawing his sword. He was glad that Tym was not with him, for the odds were twenty to one and Tym, for all his seaman's courage, could hardly change that. "They want me," he called to the Ogre. "You race down that main street to the gate. Save the kits."

At that moment a great roar echoed in the courtyard. The unicorn's mate, bleeding from arrow wounds and maddened by the sight of fire, charged from a side street straight at Ned. The lords' horses shied and bolted.

"Follow me!" Nyal cried once more and set his heels in Avelaer's sides. Behind him, the unicorn's thundering

hooves drowned out the lords' cries of frustration and were
as a spur to Avelaer. Moments later they were at the great triumphal arch. The city guards, unaware of the havoc in the
square, looked up in surprise as a horseman and an Ogre
family on a unicorn raced through the gate.

In Harkynwood, Fallon, who seemed to be drowsing by
the fire, smiled.

Chapter 27

Tym had gotten a good price for the palfrey, and was well
pleased. But when Avelaer was shown to the stable keeper,
he had kicked out the side of his stall and bitten the man on
his thigh. After much searching, Tym found an out-of-work
wagon driver, more interested in the strength than stable
manners, who offered to buy the horse on the condition that
he could find a harness that would fit. Tym lied as he agreed
to meet the man the next morning, took half the price, and
retired to an inn near the waterfront. He didn't want to return
to the boat too early, for he would have to explain to Nyal
what he had done.

He came through the triumphal arch at dusk, the same
time the first unicorn emerged from the hold of the ship. He
watched openmouthed as the unicorn glared at the captain
and crew, then lowered its head and charged. A moment later
the second unicorn erupted from the ship's hold, followed by
a flurry of wolves.

"Nyal," murmured Tym in alarm. He ran toward the boat
only to meet a large saber cat slinking, belly low, up the
gangplank. Tym found refuge behind a crate. The air was
filled with the spotted gongoe's ear-splitting shrieks. Peering
out from behind the crate, Tym felt a soft nudge in the small
of his back. He whirled around to discover that he had been
joined by the blue-eyed wolf. He emerged from behind the
crate abruptly, running backward, shouting and waving his

arms. He scrambled for safety to the top of a stack of cases, warding off gongoes that shrieked past him, watching helplessly as the ship's mast toppled captain and men into the water. He was too busy to notice Nyal and the Ogre family as they ran across the square.

Finally, torn between his own survival and concern for Nyal's safety, Tym bolted toward the boat only to encounter two large aurochs as they galloped wildly across the shuddering gangplank, hooking their widespread horns left and right. He watched from behind another crate as one of the beasts pawed the ground, its nostrils flaring. It glimpsed the sailors who frantically hauled at the sail and shrouds that entangled the captain in the water. As a domesticated bull will charge a red cloak, the auroch charged the flapping sail, swinging his horns viciously. The sailors scattered, the sail settling slowly over the head of the struggling man in the water.

When the unicorns trotted over the gangplank and passed near him, Tym ducked between shouting and screaming humans, racing for the safety of the city gate. It was lowered and the guards firmly refused to raise it again. A small riot which ensued as frightened sailors tried to force the gate was broken up by the approach of the larger unicorn.

"Shoot!" screamed a guard from inside the wall and a hail of arrows swarmed like bees. A sailor near Tym was struck in the buttock and fell into the unicorn's path. Most of the arrows struck the bars of the gate and fell back, but several flew free and one found its mark. It glanced off the unicorn's head, leaving a deep gash. The creature roared in pain. It glared about, trying to see. A movement caught its eye as the archers strove to nock their next flight of arrows. It lowered its head and charged.

Tym, caught between beast and gate, leaped over a broken wagon wheel and landed running, searching desperately for safety. Behind him he heard the enraged animal strike the gate, peeling it back. Tym ran toward the dock, glancing back to see the unicorn shaking its huge head, forcing its entrance into the city. Although an auroch lowered its horns menacingly, he dodged it, racing to a small ship docked there. He climbed the mast and, relatively safe at last, rested there with several other nimble fugitives.

Tym could hear screams and curses from inside the city gates. His eyes anxiously swept the dock and the deck of the demasted ship. "Did any passengers get off that boat?" he asked.

Next to him a young boy shook his head. "There was just one and he's down in the hold, he is. Squashed flat, I'll bet. Serves him right. He must have let them unicorns loose. Lost me my first ship, he did. He should drown forever, he should. Hey, look, there's the captain drowned there, tangled up in the shrouds. First mate's sunk somewhere in there. They can't swim, you know? Over their heads and they're dead." He shook his head again, enjoying the carnage thoroughly.

Tym slid down the mast. No one noticed when he slipped aboard the old galley. The gangplank had been torn from its pins and teetered precariously as he slid down it. "Sir? Nyal?" he called. The hold was silent except for the sound of bilge water lapping at the timbers. He searched behind and beneath crates, his fear gradually giving over to relief. "Nyal!" he shouted when he emerged back on deck into the sunlight. He searched along the dock all the way to the gate.

Inside Elea, the screams of the populace had reached a frenzied pitch. There were no guards by the gate. Wounded men moaned, lying where they had fallen, and sailors rushed to their aid. Tym raced on, crossing deeper into the city itself. There he found the streets deserted, an occasional splintered door giving testimony to the passage of the unicorn.

He followed the street that led directly to the stable, dismayed that the monster seemed to have followed the same route. He moved cautiously in the gathering gloom of twilight. Humans began to appear, some crumpled to the ground, others tending them. The shouts and screams told him that the beast was close. Cautiously he stepped into the small square that fronted the stable. It was lighted by torchlight and there, facing a row of armed men, the big unicorn stood, dying.

Three lords faced it across the distance of the square. Two others wheeled their horses behind it, as they would do if they hunted in the wild. Already one leg was dragging behind it, hamstrung, unable to bear its weight. Blood flowed from great gashes in its neck and shoulders. It roared, a strange sound midway between a bugle and a bull, and lowered its head to charge its tormenters.

The charge was a slow, crippled stagger. The lords closed in for the kill. From behind, one man spurred his horse in close and severed the tendon of the good leg with one stroke. As the great beast abruptly sat down, two other horsemen closed in from the front, looking for the death blow. A lord on a black gelding leaned far out over his horse's pommel as he balanced his sword blade across his forearm, intent on the most difficult blow of all, a clean strike between the creature's shoulder blades into its heart.

As the horseman began his thrust, the unicorn bellowed again and swept its head to the side. It caught the black charger just behind the girth and threw it high into the air. At the same moment, the lord's companion struck at the unicorn's unprotected throat and blood gushed out upon the pavement. The huge beast shuddered for a moment, then fell slowly onto its side.

Twenty feet away, horse and rider crashed to the ground in front of Tym. The horse, panic-stricken, struggled to regain its feet, striking out at Tym as it rolled upon its armored but helpless rider. "Whoa!" shouted Tym, grabbing the horse's head to save himself from being trampled. "Whoa, boy, steady." The horse fell back for a moment and Tym promptly sat on its head to keep it quiet. He looked at the rider and froze as his eyes met with Ned's.

Tym flinched away, looking for the best alley to escape to. The blood of the unicorn ran across the pavement and surrounded them in a dark pool. Abruptly the charger began to struggle again and Tym leaped off, slipping in the blood beneath his feet. The horse struggled to his feet and Ned rolled clear.

"Well done, sir!" A strong hand seized Tym's shoulder.

Other lords helped Ned to his feet. "I'm fine," said Ned, cautiously stretching out a leg. "I'm fine." He turned toward Tym. "You've saved me a maiming, sir," he said. "I am Nedryk of Fanstock. I am in your debt."

"My Lord," stammered Tym.

"Your name?" boomed the man holding his arm. It was Lord Benare. "Where are you from?"

"I am of the north sea . . ." Tym whined, fear thickening his Northern Sea accent, making him stammer.

"Here, what?" said Ned. "Norsea? I'm pleased to make your acquaintance. These are my companions, Lord Benare, Lord Combin, Lord Adler, Lord Bombaleur. That's Lord Farryl there with the horses."

Tym nodded to each one.

"You look familiar, Lord Norsea," Benare said. "Have we met before?"

"Yea, mayhap," Tym fumbled. "But probably not. I've just arrived from Dnevra where I live with my aunt."

"Here for a visit from The Perime?" asked Farryl.

"Adventure."

"Well said," said Nedryk, limping to a doorway to sit down. "We are on a mission of vengeance. We seek a man who has killed our leader, but just as we were about to take him, the unicorn came charging at us."

"It's a big one," said Lord Adler.

"A good blow you struck," Lord Combin said to him.

"I was made lucky by Ned's noble attempt," Lord Adler said, modestly.

"And I was made lucky by Lord Norsea, here," said Ned.

"The man you hunt is gone?" asked Tym, relaxing as they failed to recognize him. "Who is he?"

"A bastard and Lord Telerhyde's murderer. We'd best be on our way," Ned grunted as he rose to his feet. "He's not many minutes before us."

"You need a horse, M'Lord," Tym lied. "Your charger is on three legs."

Ned swore. "He looks fair to me," he said.

Tym shook his head. "His fetlock swells. You'd not be half an hour on the road before you'd be walking. I also need a horse. Let us find a stable and buy ourselves mounts. And then, My Lords, if you will have me, I would ride with you. I would like to share this adventure, if I've good companions."

Ned smiled and nodded. Farryl slapped Tym on the back. "It seems the unicorn has joined you with our adventure."

Chapter 28

Cyna traveled with the Peskies for several days. On the last day, the whistles and chirps of the Peskie scouts who led the way became louder and more insistent. Finn Dargha stopped frequently to listen, each time changing the course they traveled through Harkynwood. High near the foot of the Trollurgh Mountains, the thick forest was broken up by large lakes gleaming like silver beneath the overcast sky. Natural meadows lined the sides of the lakes, covered by last year's grass, which lay over the meadows like a brown blanket. Soft bogland sucked at their feet and thickets of pricker bushes tore at their clothing. Toward evening, Cyna was beginning to stumble from weariness when Finn led them through a thick barrier of brambles into a broad meadow.

Four great shalks, the giant elk of the Harkyn, raised their heads and stared at the new arrivals. Their shoulders taller than Cyna's head, the three females chewed contentedly as they gazed at the Peskie troop. The male flexed his muscular neck, his velvet-covered antlers circling the top of his head like a massive crown. He snorted in halfhearted challenge to the weary group of travelers, then lost interest and followed his wives as they wandered toward the far end of the lake. Just beyond, the low tents of the Peskie tribe were pitched beside the shore of a large lake and cooking fires made thin columns of smoke in the air.

"Finn's back!" cried an elderly Peskie emerging from the nearest tent. A cry went up as the travelers spilled into the meadow. Small dogs barked and bounded to greet the travelers. Babies were held high so that returning parents might admire their growth of the past few weeks. Everyone was hugged. Cyna was introduced to half a dozen Peskies who stood on tiptoe to kiss her soundly on both cheeks. Eager

hands lifted Ruf from Bihan's back and carried him away to
a tent to rest. The pony was tethered where hardy grass was
showing beside the lakeshore.

With great ceremony, Finn took an arrow from his quiver
and dipped it in a small bag of white crystals. "We are grateful, great shalk, for your gift," he cried, pulling back his
bow. The tiny arrow bit deeply into the haunch of a nearby
shalk buck. The large elk kicked impatiently as it would at a
fly. In a short time it knelt down and fell asleep. Murmuring
gently, an old Peskie woman stroked it as she cut its throat
with a keen stone knife, catching its blood in a fire-darkened
clay pot. The shalk didn't flinch, although Cyna shuddered.

Over well-roasted shalk steaks, Finn told his tribe of the
breaking of The Stone and the Ogre prophecy. The smiles of
welcome and gladness fell from the firelit faces and their cel-
ebratory songs died, leaving only the crackling of the fire
and Finn's urgent voice.

"The Ogres' superstition insists things will get worse, that
this is the end of The Old Faith. According to them, this is
how it adds up now," he tallied on his fingers to emphasize
his point. "A hero dies and Telerhyde is murdered. The confusion of the seasons—well, there's no grass for the shalk yet
and it's past the Ides. I forgot! A traitor rises. Well." Finn
glanced for a moment at Cyna and went on. "The Lords of
the North are convinced that Nyal, Telerhyde's foster son,
has turned traitor. They say it was he who killed his father."
A horrified whisper swept through the assembly. "So," and
Finn raised his third finger, "a traitor rises. The Breaking of
The Stone I've already told you about. The Disappearance of
the Heavens might well have been the eclipse the other night.
Those are the first five of the Ogres' final signs."

The old Peskie spit into the fire. "Aye, but we've had hard
springs and eclipses and broken stones before. Even had heroes murdered by those they love." He shook his finger at the
Peskie king. "Ogres and Elves might be superstitious, that
don't mean we Peskies got to call it the end of the world."

"Of course not," Finn agreed.

"And if it is, we'll think of some way to make a profit on
it," the old Peskie added, a twisted grin skewing his face. He
was rewarded by a few appreciative chuckles.

"What's the rest of the signs?" asked a husky young Peskie clad in shalkskin.

Finn raised his other hand extending two fingers. "The Splintering of The Five Tribes and the Death of Magic. Before you think further, you should know that Her Megship has banished myself, the entire community of Peskies, and Mistress Cyna from Her Megdom." The Peskies looked at him in stunned silence.

"What about our water rights?" demanded a skinny Peskie near the fire, her two Peskie children clinging to her skirt.

"Nobody tells us we can't cross the River Dark in the summer if we need to water our shalk!" cried someone in the back of the crowd.

"We'll not need to water our shalk anytime very soon, thanks to this awful weather," Fir Dahn said. The others nodded, grumbling.

The ancient Peskie turned to Cyna. "That's six signs, sure," he said. "In five hundred years no Meg has ever refused us the right to pass through her territory with our herds. Is this the Death of Magic also, Mistress Witch? How did we lose the moon and not have the warning of a Human sorcerer?"

Cyna blushed. As she measured her reply, Finn rose to his feet. "This is the only light moment in this whole, dismal year," he said, and raised their spirits telling how the eclipse had interrupted the Elfin ceremonies the night before.

"The Ogres' seven signs may well be upon us," the old Peskie said when Finn was finished. "I've never seen a spring like this—no grass for the shalk, the water level of the lakes so high, and the mountains not thawed out yet. There'll be floods soon. We've never been so far from the mountains so late in the year. And feel how cold it is?" His breath was turning to vapor in the cool night air. "We might have to move farther still if this keeps up."

"Wherever the great shalk are, I'm content," Finn replied, leaning back against a large pillow and looking up at the sky. "I've seen so many Human and Elf *buildings*," he made the word sound like a prison, "that I'd be happy to follow the shalk herds through endless winter, just so I'm outdoors and free."

Later, when Cyna was preparing for bed in the tent which had been strung for her, Finn stopped by. "I have received bad news about your father. He's been sorely injured," Finn said gently. "He was hurt trying to capture Nyal."

"Hurt by Nyal?"

Finn nodded. "Nyal cut down his horse and your father's leg was crushed."

Cyna stared apprehensively into Finn's eyes. "He isn't dead?"

"I don't think so, Mistress." Finn shook his head. "Master Fallon came where your father lay on the road and took him away. He's with The Snaefid in Snaefid Hall."

"At least he's with Fallon," Cyna said with relief. "Fallon can cure him! Is Nyal . . ."

"Nyal has fled. Your brother has sworn to capture him."

She held her face in her hands. "I never should have left."

"What else could you have done?" Finn asked.

A shalk doe gave birth to twins that night and Cyna was awakened by the noise and excitement. Fir Dahn was the shalk midwife, doing little more than murmuring praise to the animal and shooing the Peskie children away. The birth happened quickly as they do in the wild. Soon two shalk calves stood shakily on their feet, their huge brown eyes regarding their Peskie helpers without fear. The children steadied the absurdly long legs and helped the calves find their mother to nurse. Several young male Peskies lit fires and drew lots to see who would stay up to watch the herd. As Cyna finally settled down to sleep again, she heard the distant howling of a wolf.

Sleep did not return. The thought that her father lay in pain tormented her. If Fallon were right and prophecy were her Gift, why had she felt no inkling of her father's injury? Why was she as mystified about The Final Days as everyone else? She had seen Nyal pursued, true. But she had also seen a woman attacked, a tower, a war. Even if these were prophecies, how could she tell them to anyone when she didn't understand them herself?

The shalkhide was twisted and uncomfortable beneath her, a poor protection from the hard ground. She was weary of traveling. She was fond of Finn and Fir, grateful for their kindness and generosity to her. But the Peskies lived an athletic, outdoor life, a stark contrast to the lives of the Elves. Peskies were governed by the migrations of the great shalk, following the herds to the highlands in the summer and to the shore when snow spread down from the Trollurgh Mountains. It was not the sort of life that would speed Ruf's recovery.

At dawn another shalk lay down and began labor. Calving season had begun. The weather might not be following its natural course, Cyna noted, but the biological seasons were intact.

Despite the rugged journey, Ruf was feeling a little better by morning. Using a Peskie herding staff as a cane, he slowly followed Cyna as she wandered down to the edge of the lake. The clouds parted a little and occasional sunshine illuminated the meadow and forest. Several shalk grazed a short distance away. The sound of their hooves pawing at the dried grass and their rhythmic chewing made a pleasant backdrop to the brooding silence of the surrounding Harkynwood.

Across the lake, the forest spread out in all directions, flat and grey. Far to the south, Cyna could make out the peaks of the Trollurgh Mountains, snowcapped and rising high over the forest. To the west the forest closed in, dark and foreboding. Cyna explored along the lakeshore. The meadow widened there and the herd of shalk raised their heads to watch her pass. Nearby the Elfin pony searched the dried stalks for morsels of green grass.

"Isn't he beautiful?" Cyna stroked the little horse's head, then took the tether rope in her hand. "Get on, we'll go for a stroll," she said to Ruf, who had been limping painfully behind her.

"As though you hadn't done enough walking!" he exclaimed. But he pulled himself onto the pony's back and they walked along the shore of the lake. A flock of geese resting by the lakeside parted before them, grumbling in goosey sounds.

"It's the magic of the Harkyn," Cyna told him. "The wild animals have no fear of harm from other creatures."

"Some magic," Ruf snorted. "They'd move a little faster if they knew that I ate goose pie with a Peskie family this morning!" He suddenly yelped as Bihan laid back his ears and snapped at his toes.

Cyna smiled. "He doesn't like you scoffing at Magic." She walked along the edge of the water.

Ruf slid off and found a comfortable seat on a moss-covered log.

"Look!" Cyna cried.

He was quite out of breath from the mild exertion and the sound of falling water drowned out her voice. "What?"

"It's a river!" The lake, fed by the glaciers above, was the headwaters of the River Dark. Clear and cold, the water ran over a ledge of bedrock and then tumbled in a roaring waterfall into a large pool below. "There's a path," Cyna pointed to a narrow track that clung to the bank above the river.

The black-and-white pony whinnied and the tether rope slipped from her fingers as he trotted down the path.

"Whoa!" shouted Cyna and Ruf Nab together.

"He'll break a leg!" exclaimed Cyna.

The pony stopped and looked back, shaking his head.

"Easy, Bihan, come here." Cyna edged down the steep slope toward him.

Surefooted as a goat, Bihan trotted on ahead of her to where the River Dark had cut a steep ravine into the bedrock of the Harkyn. Here the sides of the path narrowed and thick moss made the rocks slippery. Stones slid under Bihan's hooves and showered over the edge, falling for a long time before they splashed into the river far below. "Whoa!" cried Cyna as she reached for his halter. Her footing gave way and she slid down the gravel slope. She grabbed at a sapling which clung to the side of the ravine. She was frightened and yet aware of a strange exhilaration. The gravel beneath her slid slowly toward the edge as the roots of the slender tree gave way. She heard a boisterous whinny and the roar of falling stones. For a moment she tumbled through space, then the icy water of the churning river closed over her.

The cold water took her breath. She struggled to the surface, reached for a gulp of air, and heard the roaring of the river. Then she was dragged down again into an icy green silence. She felt herself rolling over and over, losing all sense of what was up and down, just whirling faster and faster in the silent greenness. All at once she felt at peace. Her body was dragged and spun in the torrent of the river, but her mind, and with it her sight, became clear and she could see far beyond the river and Harkynwood.

Cyna was floating now, high above the earth, looking down on mountains and valleys. Glaciers, feeding the very river she was drowning in, gleamed white. She glimpsed the outline of Morbihan beneath her, the snarling wolf's snout, its curling ruff.

Then before her rose a tall tower. It was gone in an instant and a woman fled through the snow, looking over her shoulder. A soldier caught her arm, other soldiers closed in behind him, swords swinging. For a moment snow swirled in a thick blanket, and then the air was clear.

Before an old fortress, in the shadow of a standing stone, rows of Peskies and Elves held a battle line. They braced against charging horsemen with black shields. The Others' line surged, held, gave way.

They were urged on by a Human. The horse beneath him plunged and whirled, its ribs showing with hunger and exhaustion. Cyna knew the leader's eyes were grey with faint streaks of color, like a dawn sky, yet she could not see his face. Dwarves beat their drums and Ogres charged on galloping unicorns.

She struggled to escape the sounds of war and rage. Dimly before her, she glimpsed a huge standing stone quivering in the air.

Cyna lay on her stomach and there was a great weight on her shoulders. Something tasted sour in her mouth and she realized she had been sick. She gulped for air.

"Here, she's breathing!" said a voice.

"Don't stop!" said another and the weight on her shoulders grew greater.

She coughed, gagged, and was sick again. It was clear water, cold like the river. She lay on a sandy bank which curved along the river's edge not a stone's throw from where she had fallen in. She struggled to sit up.

"Lie still, Cyna," Finn said firmly. "You were dead a

minute ago, till this Dwarf of yours squeezed the water out of you."

She caught her breath and sat up, looking into Ruf Nab's worried eyes. "Bihan?" she asked, dreading the answer.

"He's fine, he's run off," Ruf grumbled. "You risked your life for a worthless pony."

They brought a tent and pitched it by the riverbank, built a fire, and warmed her by it. Ruf, who had dragged her from the water, was chilled too. Together they shivered by the fire, wrapped in shalkskins and blankets, sipping tea brewed by Fir Dahn.

Later that evening Finn visited her. Still shaken by what she had seen, she said softly, "I saw a vision while I drowned."

He regarded her curiously.

"I saw a war," she continued. "Humans attacking Others. And a tower."

Still Finn watched. Amusement and doubt played at the corners of his generous mouth.

"I also saw a woman murdered . . ." Cyna added reluctantly.

An elderly Peskie woman who had come by to offer Ruf a nasty-tasting tea, chuckled.

"Why do you laugh, Gunnar?" Finn asked.

"Mayhap the murdered lady was Mistress herself when The Meg catches up with her!" She leaned back, laughing in resonant clanks like a broken bell.

"Madam!" scolded Finn. "Apologize to the witch!"

The old Peskie barely concealed her smile as she looked at Cyna. "Well, of course I apologize, Mistress. I'd not hurt your feelings, to make fun of your bad dreams. I just can't resist a good laugh after all that's been going on. Forgive an old Peskie, Lady, and say you took it in good fun."

Cyna smiled and nodded her head. She had meant to ask Finn's advice about what she had seen, but she couldn't risk more Peskie humor. She turned her face toward the pillow.

"She's exhausted," she heard Fir say. "Let her sleep now."

A few days later, the great herds of shalk began to move. The Peskies packed their tents and followed them as they had for countless centuries.

Finn said nothing when Cyna refused to go farther with them. Instead, he directed his Peskies to gather a store of firewood for her. Cyna said good-bye officially at a small feast and party given by Fir Dahn. The next morning she watched the tiny caravan's departure, smiling and waving as the Peskies staggered under their loads of tents and cooking utensils.

She turned back to her tent. That morning Ruf Nab had tested his new strength by chopping wood with a slender Peskie axe. Now he lay exhausted in the tent. Bihan had reappeared just that morning, trotting down the path and whinnying a greeting. Firmly tethered, he grazed on the few blades of grass that the shalk had overlooked. By the edge of the lake, Cyna had found a modest selection of hardy spring flowers and a few herbs she might use in her work. Nearby, a half day's journey away, there was a family of Ogres who had a sick kit. Finn's messengers had located them and now Cyna had another patient who needed healing.

It was a far cry from the comfort of Crowell, a far cry from what any beginning Healer would hope for. She was lost in the middle of Harkynwood, with rustic Ogres and empty space for a practice.

It seemed to prove the fallacy of Fallon's thought. How could she possess the Gift of prophecy when never in all her dreams had it occurred to her that she would heal in utter obscurity? And yet, deep inside, she feared he had been right. Even as she denied the Gift each day, each night her dreams were flooded with visions of events. Most were of folk she had never known—a blond girl, a ragged Elf. But sometimes her visions were of Nyal. She often awoke crying out, the horror of the dream driving her to deny that her Sight was true.

BOOK FOUR

The Eacon dictated to Fryd as he ate, chewing rapidly on morsels of newborn lamb left over from the night before.

"Your Supreme Majesty, Holiest of Holies, Most Excellent Seventh Tyrant of The Perime of Moer:

"The pieces upon the board have moved and the advantage is ours.

"Your most estimable servant Lothen has left to begin the campaign in the south. The Peace—that hateful tool of Telerhyde—is destroyed and the fabled might of Morbihan is scattered. As I suspected, the Lords of the North are easily misled and have no real power with Telerhyde gone.

"Magic still stands in our way, but even it is weakened. My agents are everywhere. I confidently expect that soon it will be my pleasure to report that Magic is destroyed utterly and the justice of The Vorsai reigns over this island.

"I remain your obedient servant, et cetera, et cetera."

He waved Fryd away with a flick of his wrist. He tore at the leg of lamb, pausing only to wipe his mouth with the back of his hand and brush crumbs from his vest. He felt a cautious optimism.

A flock of sparrows pecked at his leavings. One sparrow stood a little apart from the others. It cocked its head, watching The Eacon, not his crumbs. The Eacon paused in his chewing, frowning at the tiny bird. It was brown with dark-banded wings like its fellows, but its bright eye was pale blue.

"Fallon?" cried The Eacon, and even as he said the name, he threw his mug. He missed and as one the sparrows rose in alarm, soaring like tiny arrows over the wall of The Keep.

Chapter 29

Melloryth was lost in the forest for a long time before she was found by the wild Elf. She searched for The Keep for days, but the witch had concealed it well and she never found it. It made her weep to think that each hillock she saw might be her home made unrecognizable by the witch's spell. For she had come to believe that it must be Cyna who had dispatched her so.

All because Nyal loved her and had requested her hand in marriage. Because the witch would lose him now. Yet Melloryth never lost hope that Nyal would come on his huge red war-horse and rescue her. She determined to find what she now thought of as his lair in the mountains. But it rained often, and she found it increasingly difficult to stay warm. This too was a part of the witch's spell, she was sure. She had no comb and branches became tangled in her long golden hair. She caught occasional glimpses of the mountains through the trees. Serene, secure, they called to her.

She was very hungry the first few days, but then she wasn't. Her body felt light and she realized that her uncle was just and true. He had always said that when she didn't pay attention to her desires, she became more spiritual. She felt very spiritual when she found a meadow surrounded by dark green pine trees.

Not a proper meadow with grass, but a clearing filled with shrubs and berry bushes. Crossing it was difficult because stickers and burdocks became caught in her hair and held her fast. Repeatedly she had to stop and free herself. The bushes were bare of everything but black-tipped thorns, but the shrubs held some old seedpods and withered fruit from the year before. These she ate. When she became sick, she realized that she was all spirit now and that this was her punishment for feeding her body.

It rained and she could feel each raindrop as it struck her. It was foolish to go on. Nyal would find her here in the middle of the berry bushes. He would ride into the thicket and find her in the center, asleep. He would kiss her lips and she would awaken and rest in his arms and he would care for her and take her to his grand, high-towered castle, where everything was white. When she was strong, he would marry her and she would show him how spiritual she had become and they would be happy forever. Together they would foil the witch's plot to kill Melloryth and win Nyal back.

Cyna had studied Magic because she wanted to heal. It had never been her dream to understand how the wheels of the universe spun. She never wanted to be one of the educated few who could give those wheels a nudge, set them spinning in another direction. She had only wished to master herbology and marry Nyal. Yet now, day by day, as she denied her Gift, the cosmic wheels of The Law ground her down.

Nothing was working out as she had hoped. Except for her nightmares, she had heard no word from Nyal since his abrupt disappearance. What little she had heard about him seemed violent and foreign. He no longer sounded like the golden youth she had fallen in love with the summer before, or the sad, intense young man who had come to her at Eacon's Keep.

Days lengthened into weeks until she lost track of time. She practiced alone in a remote corner of the Harkyn while Ruf Nab made his slow recovery. Her infrequent clientele were isolated Ogres and Elves, creatures who would, by their own desire, never play out a larger destiny. The Ogre Family had a cow which they pastured by the river. Cyna recognized the compliment when they entrusted its freshening to her. She had become a midwife to livestock.

And so one part of her desire was answered in a way she had not expected, she became a simple Healer in the depths of Harkynwood. She practiced herbal remedies for the creatures who limped to her door. Only Ruf, his leg wasted and sore, reminded her of more powerful cures of which she was somehow capable. Although the shadows under his eyes still held the exhausted look of one who remembers traveling for a time with death, every day he grew stronger. If he had not constantly been before her, it is possible that she might have forgotten that the power of The Law worked within her.

As it was, when she saw the small Elf, she thought only that one more wounded creature had come to her, too desperate to know of another Healer.

He flitted like a shadow near a rock by the pool where she had fallen in. For a moment Cyna thought her eyes were playing tricks. Only by remaining very still and narrowing her eyes could she see the dim outline of the motionless Elf against the rocks. "Ruf," she said softly, "someone's here."

Ruf Nab moved casually, reaching out his long arms to find the handle of his bronze battle-ax. "Where?"

But Cyna was already on her feet. "Hello," she called. "Can I help you?" Ruf limped after her, wary.

"Hello?" repeated Cyna, for the Elf had remained motionless, like a wild thing that hopes to remain invisible. She could see him clearly now. He was old for an Elf—his hair had lost its curl and hung about his face in grey wisps. He was dressed without regard to fashion, but in scraps of blankets and ill-fitting hand-me-downs. His green felt boots, made originally for a large Peskie, were cracked and leaking, their too-long toes curled up at the ends. But it was his face that drew Cyna's attention. It was long, as though stretched by years of sadness, and his eyes were large and dark.

Slipfit had traveled far through the forest since he had taken Nyal's gold coin. He was tired and wished for a meal and a warm fire. But his Elfin shyness overtook him and he ducked his head and muttered, "Na, Mum."

"I beg your pardon?" Cyna asked.

Flustered by having to talk with a female, he darted back among the large rocks that banked the side of the river. He appeared a few moments later dragging a large sledge behind

him. It was heavy and he dropped the haul rope with a sigh
of relief. "Be you Cyna?" he demanded. He knew she was,
for he had been watching the campsite and heard Ruf call her
by name. He didn't wait for her reply. "Na, Mum, where you
been; I been looking ALL OVER!!" Cold, exhaustion and relief combined to make his Elfin dialect thick as good soup.
"My friend say you'll be in the grove. WHAT grove, I ask?
All this time I been looking, and looking, and finally I find
you and is this a GROVE?"

Ruf Nab stepped closer, made cautious by the Elfin out-
burst, his hand resting on the handle of his ax. Slipfit took no
notice of him, fairly hopping with righteous fury. "Na, Mum,
you must never NEVER do that! Not to be in the grove has
made me travel all over this forest! Not for the wolf, an' I
never find you! An' I did it for my friend who be gone and
back in a few days!"

"What?" said Cyna, shaken by his fury, not comprehend-
ing his meaning.

"Good morning, I be Slipfit," he went on, regaining his
manners, his tongue finding more readily the Harkynwood
dialect in which all the Tribes spoke with each other. He
doffed his felt hat and gestured toward the sledge. "See what
I got here. She's daft and a goner but I found her in the briars
all thistled. I thought you might want her, since she's one of
your own. She has a strange hat, hey?" On the light, well-
crafted sledge lay a Human girl. Only a few tattered rags
covered her body. Every part of her exposed flesh was covered with scratches, scrapes, and insect bites. Her hair was
thickly matted, tangled with twigs and looking, as the Elf
noted, like a grotesque hat. Her eyelids were half-open, revealing senseless, staring eyes, a shocking blue, the whites
yellowed and stained.

"Ruf!" Cyna cried as she stooped over the pathetic figure.
"Bring me water! And my herb chest, quickly!"

The Elf watched curiously as Cyna lifted the girl from the
sledge and carried her to a bed of soft skins near the flap of
the tent. Her hands probed gently, searching for a pulse and
finding it, swiftly examined her wounds and scratches.

"She's not badly injured," she told Ruf as he hobbled from

the riverbank, carrying a bucket of water. "She's starving and freezing and has had nothing to drink."

"Will she live?" Ruf asked.

"Yes." Cyna was surprised by her own certainty.

Despite the girl's appearance, there seemed to be nothing wrong that couldn't be cured with the right herb and a little care. After some broth, Cyna would wash her and do something about her hair. As Ruf and the Elf helped carry the girl into the tent, Cyna wondered who the young girl could be and why she was so far from Human habitation. "How did you ever find her in the forest?" she asked the Elf.

"The wolf finds her." Slipfit said matter-of-factly. "He shows me how to go. I be out in the woods to bring a message from my friend. He wants me to tell Lady Cyna where he's going."

Ruf tapped a finger on his temple, and Cyna nodded. The Elf seemed daft. "And where's your friend the wolf going?" Ruf asked in tones that he would use to humor an idiot or a small child.

"Blue-eyed Elf eater be no friend!!" Slipfit exploded. "He be doing wizard work, that one! My friend, he be a big strong Human."

Ruf took a step back, tightening his grip on his ax. "And who is your friend?"

"Nyal of Crowell."

"Nyal?" Cyna almost dropped her herb box. "You've seen Nyal?"

"Yea, I seen 'im. He gives me this gold coin, see?" Slipfit exhibited the coin, hung like a pendant about his neck with a frayed cord.

"When did you see him? Where?"

Slipfit told her of his meeting with Nyal and repeated, with great care, Nyal's words.

" 'Return in a few days,' " Cyna repeated. "Oh, Ruf, what's happened to him?"

"Finn heard that he fought with your father."

"I see that, too!" Slipfit exclaimed and told them of the terrible fight with the lords. "An' I come as quick as I could, Mum, but I don't know where you be. Hard it be to find you! The blue-eyed wolf, he help me, but I not like wolves—they make good dinner of Solitaries. He finds the weird one," he added, nodding at the comatose blond girl, "but he eats her not and leaves her to me. I ask you, what I do with an odd Human girl?"

"You did wonderfully well, Slipfit," Cyna told him. "To find anyone in this forest is a wonder." His Elfin dialect was thick and he had been alone in the woods for so long that his speech was erratic and hard to follow. Cyna barely understood what he was saying, except that he had brought her news of Nyal. She beamed at him.

The trace of a smile split the solemn length of the old Elf's face. "I be here sooner, but I bring along the raggedy girl."

His news buoyed Cyna's spirits. As she tended to the blond girl, Slipfit was happy to tell her again and again of his meeting with Nyal. His Elfin imagination embellished the story as he recalled small, delightful details.

When Melloryth awoke she was in the abode of the witch. It was dark and smoky. Naked, she lay on the skins of wild animals and her whole body felt like it was on fire. She cried out in pain and fear.

"Hold still! We won't hurt you," a voice said sharply. Melloryth felt a searing pain on the side of her head. "Hold her, Ruf."

Melloryth struggled, but strong hands pinned her arms to her side. She panicked. Her head was held firmly despite her thrashings and the pain came abruptly, as though a giant were ripping out her hair. She ceased struggling and began to pray.

At length the pain stopped and her arms were released. She kept her eyes tightly shut lest she see what fate had befallen her. A foul-tasting fluid was forced between her lips. She struggled again, feebly, choking, sputtering, but the strong arms overpowered her once more.

At last they left her alone and she lay on the skins and sobbed. After a time it seemed as though she were running down a long tunnel. She realized with a start that she was naked. And then she heard the gate boy behind her. At the end of the tunnel, Nyal, sword in hand, called her name. The gate boy's footsteps pounded behind her and something terrible had happened because she couldn't run. The bright light at the end of the tunnel faded. It was dark and smoky again. The warmth of a nearby fire soothed her. When she turned toward it, a red-haired demon shouted, "She's awake!"

Melloryth shrank back in fear. The witch appeared before her, touching her, lifting the skins which covered her to see her body. "No fever," the witch said. "What's your name, girl? Don't look like that, no one's going to hurt you."

But she hid her face and prayed for them to disappear. Later, when the witch tried to touch her again, she screamed and kicked out, knocking to the ground a bowl of loathsome brew. The witch looked at her strangely. Melloryth shivered and looked away. She didn't want to become captured by the witch's eyes. When a new bowl was placed near her, she ignored it. She was not going to be poisoned. When her captors weren't looking, she stole some of their food from the kettle that hung over the coals of the fire.

When Melloryth was stronger, the witch allowed her to wander the campsite. Her dress was gone and she refused to wear the cloak the witch offered her, but she didn't want the evil ones to see her naked. Finally she covered herself with the skins that she had lain on near the fire. She had no idea where she was or how to fight the witch's enchantment and find her uncle's castle again.

But each day she grew stronger. Her confidence that Nyal would save her never faded. She saw him thundering down from his abode in the mountains, his sword drawn, his great horse rearing high. The witch, about to torture Melloryth again, fell to the ground babbling in fear. Her demons were slain with one sweep of Nyal's gleaming sword and then he lifted Melloryth up and held her in his arms.

She prepared for his coming. She listened for the sound of distant hoofbeats, watched for his reflection in the surface of the water where the river ran quietly by the bank. Hope burned fiercely in her breast until the day she bent over the still, clear water to drink and saw her own reflection. She gasped in horror.

Her clear, milky complexion, her sky-blue eyes, her golden hair were gone. Her skin was dark and rough, her eyes were dark and fevered, bulging out above her sunken cheeks. The pink dome of her skull shone through ragged tufts of fuzz. A cracked sound, like the moan of a mortally wounded animal, escaped her lips.

She fled the clear pool and fell upon the sandbank, tearing at her scalp and beating her hands against her face. The witch came then and held her in her arms until she stopped screaming. A bitter brew was forced between her lips. The world grew softer. The witch guarded her now, rarely leaving her side, forcing vile fluids down her throat, watching every move.

But it was not necessary. Melloryth no longer planned escape. She no longer dreamed of Nyal's triumphant rescue. Her prayers had been too weak. There was no hope now; she'd realized that the moment she had seen her reflection. The witch had won, the dream was over. Melloryth had been turned into a frog.

Chapter 30

Because The Peace was broken, travel was no longer as safe as it had been in the past. Nyal and the Ogres frequently saw bands of homeless Humans from Elea on the road, hunting for unwary travelers and lonely farms, carting spoils and firewood back to Elea. For safety's sake they often traveled through the woods or on back roads, for they feared that Ned and the lords were not far behind them. But they had no provisions and travel was slow. Two nights in a row they camped with no fire.

The rain clouds blew off and a warm breeze beckoned them south. One evening they stopped at a Human farm. Nyal told the grizzled farmer and his apprehensive wife his name and asked for shelter. The farmer offered a meal to all of them in exchange for work. In the morning they worked for several hours, using the unicorn and Avelaer to haul large stones and logs to finish a stockade the farmer was building around his home. "It's not like Telerhyde's day," the farmer observed. "In these times, you never know who's out there, wanting to take what you've spent your life getting."

Unable to tell followers of The Law from New Faithers, nor even who might be the lords' allies from marauders on the road, Nyal and the princess stayed away from Human travelers. It never occurred to them to avoid Others. As they drew closer to Harkynwood, the road was well traveled. Traders carried their wares between the forest dwellers and Human farmers of the plains. Fabric and mead of the Elves, wool and hides of the Peskies were carried by horse cart and caravan to be exchanged for Human grain and Dwarfish gold and iron. Searching for shelter, Nyal and the Ogres happened on a small Peskie caravan just at sunset.

"We are tired and hungry," Nyal told the Peskie leader, who watched him, head cocked, amber eyes bright. "We need shelter for the night, but I have no coins to pay."

Still the Peskie regarded him silently. Then he gestured to the small field where the caravan's oxen were tethered.

Gratefully, Nyal and the princess led Avelaer and the unicorn to the field, unsaddled and hobbled them. The princess took the kits to a private place behind some trees to groom them and share the meager supplies the Human farmer had given her.

Nyal sat by the fire as the Peskies prepared a dinner. No one spoke a word as the leader prepared a mug of warm, foul-tasting tea and presented it to him. He drank, wrinkling his nose. With a flush of self-consciousness he realized that every Peskie in the camp was watching. "Good fortune," he toasted them and courteously drank the rest of the brew.

He sat leaning against a tree. Weariness swept over him. His arms felt leaden and his eyelids fought to close. His head nodded and fell to his chest.

"Get the ropes," the Peskie leader said quietly to his followers. "If he moves, hit him with your cudgel. Nedryk of Fanstock will reward us for this."

Nyal's eyes would not open. A hand seized his wrist and he felt the rough bite of rope. He struggled to move, shaking his head, his arms too heavy to lift.

"Watch it! He's thrashing!" a Peskie voice cried, and he felt a dull blow on his forehead. The pain was piercing, driving a barb of consciousness through his drugged mind. Roaring, he lurched to his feet.

"Throttle him down!" cried the Peskie leader.

Two ropes encircled his neck, a third was looped about his right wrist. Even as he fought to gain his balance, the ropes tightened about his throat, muffling his cry. He gasped for breath. Illuminated by the campfire, the feverish Peskie faces began to dim. His right hand was pulled behind him, the rope tearing the skin of his wrist. Desperately, he reached with his free hand for Firestroker's hilt. It came free, light and humming in his left hand. He slashed wildly, clumsily, falling to his knees. The keen blade sliced through one rope, arched through the air, slashing the other.

Nyal took a great gasp of breath and his vision returned. At the other end of the rope attached to his hand, a Peskie turned and fled. Weariness swept over him again but he fought his way to his feet. "I am a traveler!" he shouted. "Are you trolls? By what right do you attack me?" An arrow struck the tree by his head. "Eacon's Breath!" he swore and stumbled across the darkened campsite.

"Nyal, this way!" He felt the princess's hand guide him in the darkness and heard the soft sound of Avelaer's welcoming snort. Another arrow whistled past his ear. There was no time for saddle and amenities. A stroke of his sword freed the stallion from his hobbles, with another the unicorn was free. "Run!" he cried, handing La Tonnan and the prince up to the princess. He turned and swung Firestroker menacingly at the Peskie leader. The Other nimbly sidestepped and two younger Peskies seized him about the waist from behind. He shook them off and grabbed a handful of Avelaer's mane. The horse was already running, Peskies scattering before him, as Nyal vaulted onto his back. Nyal swung his sword to clear them more quickly and felt the blow from an arrow striking his back. Then the stallion brought him safely into the darkness of the road and stretched out in a pounding gallop.

Nyal had no control over Avelaer, no saddle, no bridle, but he clung tightly to the horse's mane and urged him on. He rode through the darkness until the chestnut was lathered and blowing. Pain spread gradually through Nyal's back and into his chest. His breath became shorter as the pain grew more intense. Numbing weariness spread into his arms and legs. He forced himself to focus on the pale edge of moon that struggled to shine through the fast-moving clouds above him.

It seemed like hours had passed before he was aware of his horse slowing to a stop. He did not know that the princess touched him anxiously, feeling for signs of life, strapping him to the horse. For a while he talked to Avelaer. Branches and brush tore at him and slapped at his face and he swore at the stallion's choice of path through the woods. Sometimes he could hear the whistle of the unicorn's breath as the princess urged her mount forward, leading the chestnut stallion. "Good Old Girl," he murmured, dreaming that he rode The Dragon.

Near morning, the princess pulled her unicorn to a stop beside a low hill in the middle of the forest. Nyal awoke for a moment. He could no longer feel his legs to urge his horse onward. "I'm coming, Telerhyde," he muttered and leaned forward to say something encouraging in his stallion's ear. He was only moderately surprised to find himself collapsed on the ground beneath Avelaer's feet. "I hope he doesn't kick me," he thought and then again forgot where he was as the princess gathered him up in her arms. He only felt relief that now he could sleep.

Chapter 31

Ur Logga had not been sleeping well since the day both Stone and Peace had been broken. He worried about The Dracoon. He also worried about Ur Banfit, his brother king in Fensdown Plain. No word had returned from the messengers he repeatedly sent south. Some evil had befallen his relatives, he was convinced. Never before had they not attended a Stone Moving. Troubled, Ur Logga often listened late into the night to the Peskie network of birdlike sounds which rang through the Harkyn.

On this night he was roused by a dull pounding on the barrow door. He left his wife slumbering peacefully, comforted by the sounds of his tribe sleeping and dreaming all around him. He was not alarmed, for there was nothing in Harkynwood that would attack a full grown Ogre in his den. He walked across the huge assembly hall, empty at this hour in the morning. The thudding noise was fainter here, but he heard it again as he mounted the steps and opened the huge door.

Princess Rib Tonnan fell into his arms. He saw the frightened eyes of the kits behind her. "Cousin, help us! Nyal of Crowell has been wounded!" She turned and ran through the trees that surrounded Urden Barrow. He scarcely took time to gather his thoughts before he raced after her.

He saw the unicorn first, tethered to a large oak. The huge beast's coat was dull with dried sweat and he tore hungrily at the slender branches and the dried grasses that grew at the top of the barrow mound. Tied to a tree nearby was Nyal's horse. Avelaer shied and snorted a challenge as the Ogres trotted up in the dim morning light. Ur Logga stretched out an open hand to him, caressing his fear with concern. The horse stood still as he approached.

Ur Logga could see that Avelaer had come many hard miles since he pranced in the parade around The Eacon's Keep. He was leaner now, the muscles of his flank and chest hard beneath the matted red coat. The Ogre king saw the healing wound on the horse's hock and the exhaustion and hunger in his eyes. "Whoa, Nyal's horse," he addressed the stallion formally, with the respect that Ogres showed all living things. "How came you here?"

"Cousin, over here!" He saw the princess kneeling beside Nyal, who was lying lifeless on the ground.

When all was tended to and the princess had told him all she knew, he called for an Assembly and closed himself alone in the bare King's Chamber to prepare. The single stone lamp flickered. He reached for it, patiently picking at the wick, pulling it out until the flame burned pure again. There was nothing to keep him from stepping across the threshold of the doorway before him, but still he waited. His heart hammered in anticipation of the wisdom that must possess him now.

He felt within himself the fear of confusion, but as Fallon had advised him many times, he must not let complex problems befuddle his tribe. He had always felt kindly toward Telerhyde's youngest son. There was a deep bond between Nyal and Cyna, another, more unspoken, between Nyal and Fallon. These were his special friends within the Human tribe. An Ogre did not take such relationships lightly. He also took very seriously his relationship with the Lords of the North, Guardians of The Old Faith. Yet, the lords now sought Nyal for Telerhyde's murder. If Nyal were guilty, Ur Logga had no doubt that Human justice would be harsh. He let out a sigh, making the lamp flicker again. He stepped through the doorway.

At the end of the long stone corridor, another doorway opened into the Assembly Hall. There the corbelled ceiling arched high over head, polished granite soaring up into darkness. Before him, sitting on the low, flat-topped Stones of State, waited his tribe.

They rose as he entered. "Greetings Ur Logga, king of the Elder Tribe of Clever Ones," they greeted him formally. He reached his hands out to them. Bin Laphet, the eldest, the fur across her shoulders snow white, took his right hand and led him to his stone. Ur Nelse, the youngest adult, his dark eyes shining with pride, took his left. The den joined hands.

"By Sky, Earth, Water, and Fire,
By our beloved ancestors,
By our children to come,
I call forth Wisdom to
Consecrate this Assembly,"

Ur Logga intoned. He closed his eyes. It was always frightening for just a moment, the feeling of Opening, the letting go. He felt their minds reach out. Because he was king, he opened fully and let them know him. There was the gentle shock as their minds met his. The fear slid away, like a stone which covered a vault, and the tribe was in him and he was open to them. Now they knew what he knew, felt what he felt.

When he was finished, the twenty Ogres sat in silence and stared off into another part of the chamber, a few with tears on their cheeks. Ur Logga took his mind back, felt the welcome stillness of solitude. He crossed to the central Stone of State, piled high with rushes and soft mosses, and sat.

"So?" he said aloud.

"It is The Dracoon," murmured Lods Gramin, Ur Logga's wife. Her anxious expression stirred him to pity, for she always had a cheerful demeanor. "The Tribes have splintered and now Humans again hunt Ogres. Oh, poor Ur Banfit! Thank The Law his sweet daughter and the kits have survived."

"How long will any of us survive?" asked someone.

"We are protected here in Harkynwood," Ur Logga said.

"But they are attacking the forest! Humans with axes were cutting down trees when they attacked Ur Banfit and the princess."

"New Faith Humans with axes have attacked the forest near Elea," said someone else. "The Peskies said so."

"It may well be The Dracoon," Ur Logga said slowly. "But our den will live with honor as we always have. We will notify the Lords of the North that Harkynwood is in danger and what the Ogre tribe has suffered in Fensdown Plain. Now, we must decide what we must do with the Human, who some say is an assassin."

Bin Laphet shook her head, her brow furrowed. "But it is little Nyal, Your Majesty. He is Telerhyde's baby." The word she used in the Ogre tongue also meant "adopted son." In Ogre there was no word for bastard.

"A sower of chaos," growled a husky Ogre from the corner by the door. "The murder of Telerhyde began the cycle of The Dracoon."

Ur Logga bared his teeth, sucking in a long breath through his canines. "I offer, Clever Ones," he said to his tribe, "the thought that both of those things cannot be true." They stared at him blankly. "Fallon himself has told me that Nyal of Crowell is an upholder of The Law. Mistress Cyna was to marry him. Can this man also be a murderer?"

"He's Human, remember," someone cautioned.

Ur Nelse raised his eyes to his king. "Your Majesty," he said, voice quavering with the strain of speaking in an Assembly, "what shall we do?"

Ur Logga winced. He had hoped the Assembly would decide a course of action and he would be entrusted only to follow it. Now the decision had come to him. "Will he live?" he asked Bin Laphet.

"I know not, Your Majesty. His wound is not severe, but he sleeps and will not wake. He needs a Human Healer."

Ur Logga saw a glimmer of hope and seized it. "Then we will take him to a Healer first," he said. "If he dies, we will bury him with all the honors due to a friend. If he lives, we will notify the lords and let them do what they must do." A relieved smile broke over his face as he remembered what Fallon had told him. "First Magic, then politics. That way we know we have it right."

Chapter 32

Though Cyna did not ask him to, Slipfit stayed on, helping in many ways about the camp. He restrung Cyna's tent so that it seemed larger and more sturdy. When he wasn't talking with her, he gathered more firewood so that there was always enough. One day he disappeared for a few hours, then returned with a knapsack full of provisions and a few belongings. Cyna guessed that he was moving in when he set up a small tent along the riverbank a short distance from hers. He was a hard worker and made Ruf's life easier by his eagerness to carry out any task, whether it was staggering under an armload of firewood or dragging a bucket of water from the riverbank. In the evenings he sang Elfin songs and exchanged stories with Ruf, telling of the awful days of the Brownie Roasts and the Magic that he had seen with his own eyes which had brought about the Victory at Harkynwood.

"I be happy now," he told Cyna one evening as they gathered in her tent about the small but merry fire.

"I'm glad, Slipfit," Cyna said. "I'm happy that you've come to stay with us."

"You be not like Dallo, Mum, you be a good one," he said seriously. The lost girl appeared at the tent flap and Slipfit rose to his feet. "Na, Mum, I be looking after her. Used to coping with difficult females, I be."

The lost girl began to recover physically, but in the beginning, Cyna did not recognize her symptoms and attributed the girl's odd behavior to a nasty nature. But after a time, unlike her initial modesty, the child would forget to cover herself. When she began weeping uncontrollably for long periods of time and hopping about on her hands and knees making peculiar sounds, Cyna realized she was dealing with a case of lunacy. The more she tried to take care of her, the more upset the girl became. Eventually Cyna just left warm skins available and let the girl go about as she wished. But what with her making croaking sounds all night and running about naked, Cyna often found her patience tried.

The mad girl refused to eat with them. In the evenings Cyna would prepare an evening meal, dishing it out in three huge portions. Then, after Ruf, Slipfit, and she had eaten and lingered by the fire, the mad girl would creep up behind them and steal the rest of the food. She always ate on her hands and knees, dipping her face into the bowl, tears running off the tip of her nose and flavoring her dinner with the salt of her mad grief. Her constant weeping and croaking made it hard to think.

Bihan was another distraction. Cyna worried that wolves would find and eat him, for the spirited pony constantly slipped his tether and disappeared for days at a time. Ruf Nab grumbled that Bihan always knew when wood needed hauling. No matter how cleverly the Dwarf tied the pony up, an empty halter often greeted him in the morning. With all the commotion, it took great effort for Cyna to be able to meditate each morning.

On a particularly noisy morning, Bihan chose to reappear after an absence of several days. He trotted about the campsite whickering greetings to everyone. The river was raging from the last rainstorm and the mad girl was sitting beside it, croaking rhythmically. Ruf Nab was busily sawing a log with Slipfit who sang a sawing song. Cyna had to look farther away for a private place.

Beside the river it was always gloomy and dark in shadow. But a little distance behind the tents was a cliff which rose steeply, crisscrossed with fissures and ledges. Standing at its base, Cyna looked longingly upward and saw that a sliver of light highlighted a narrow crack in the rock which led upward. High above the ledges the sky was brightening. Cyna wrapped her skirt about her legs and began to climb.

The crack widened, zigzagging up the cliff face. In places it was almost as though steps had been carved in the grey rock. The higher she climbed, the quieter and brighter it became. Small plants, herbs, and wildflowers began to appear. At the top, she threw herself down on a large flat surface of bare rock, breathing hard from the climb. This side of the ravine was higher than the opposite side and she could see across the tops of the trees to the Trollurgh Mountains.

When she had caught her breath, she cautiously ventured back to the edge of the ravine, where it plummeted to the river below. Looking down, she could see the edge of the tent and hear the distant, rhythmic sound of sawing. She found a comfortable spot away from the edge and sat, her eyes closed. She prayed, as she always did, for the wisdom to be a good Healer. As the sun rose over Harkynwood, she sat composed, trying to quiet her mind and find the rhythm of The Law. But a flood of problems swam before her.

The Ogre's cow's milk was off. The Ogre's wife had been saying so for a week, but Cyna could find nothing wrong. Now the Ogre kit was sick again and the milk seemed the likely source. The blond girl had proven more difficult than Cyna expected. Madness was something that Cyna had little experience with. Beyond seeing that the girl had enough to eat, Cyna was at a loss about how to help her. She spent some time wishing good on everyone she knew, as Fallon had taught her. And then her thoughts moved to Nyal. Her mind began to race again, as though to flee from the nightmares of judgment and punishment that had punctuated her sleep.

She opened her eyes. A small breeze was up, scattering last year's leaves over the edge. They floated out, slipping gently down to the river. She urged her mind to follow them, to slip gently on life's currents. But it raged ahead and even as she watched the leaves, she cursed Fallon, worried about Nyal and thought of a new brew to try on the mad girl.

Giving up her meditation, she glanced around. The Harkyn grew almost to the edge of the chasm, tall pointed-topped evergreens forming a dense, green wall. Yet higher up, almost invisible through the trees, Cyna glimpsed the dull gleam of stone, as though a part of the ledge continued. Intent on finding the top, she stepped into the shadows and fought her way through tangled brush and overhanging limbs.

The trees were old and their roots formed an uneven surface on the forest floor. Large stones were strewn about. *They almost look like toppled standing stones,* Cyna thought. She caught her foot on an exposed root and nearly fell, but as she caught herself she glimpsed the ledge again. It was not a ledge at all, she realized, but a tall finger of piled stones, wrapped in dead vines. Intrigued, she pushed her way through the tangled brush. Coming closer, she could see that the stones were carefully joined together. *Like the work of stonemasons!* she thought in amazement. She traced the fine joint between two stones with her finger. *But no one could join stones together this tightly. At least, not anymore.*

Pulling back a thick vine, she examined the structure more closely. It was round and quite large, curving out of sight into the edge of the forest. She followed the curve until vines and underbrush blocked her way, then turned and followed it in the other direction. Her heart began to hammer violently in her chest. She took another step and saw before her an opening in the rocks.

Only a little higher than her head, it was narrow, overgrown with vines. She fought through them, driven by a frantic energy that seemed to pull her into the darkness within. Inside was a circular chamber, crumbling and littered with old birds' nests. Two small, arched windows allowed a faint light to penetrate. Cobwebs hung from the corbelled ceiling above her. Along one side, a set of stairs curved up along the wall and out of sight. The handrail had long since rotted away. On the opposite wall was an astonishing fireplace. Small and low, its opening was carved to represent the open mouth of a stone Human face, its cheeks puffed out as though it were blowing a great breath into the room. The workmanship was exquisite throughout, the finest Ogre masonry, but on a Human scale.

She was startled by the sound of loud cries from outside. Reluctantly, she passed through the arched doorway and fought her way back through the underbrush to the edge of the ravine. "Hello!" she called. "Who's there?"

"Hellooo!" came the cry again. "Hellooo!"

"Over here!" she cried. "Who is it?"

On the opposite back of the ravine tree branches shook. A moment later, a group of Ogres appeared, waving at her from across the chasm.

"Wait!" Cyna called. "Wait, we'll find you and guide you to the camp!"

It took some time for Ruf Nab to follow the path along the River Dark back to the shalk meadow, locate the Ogres, and lead them down to the campsite. Cyna could not restrain herself and embraced Ur Logga as he formally groomed her hair with his fingers, murmuring, "Mistress, it is good to see you safe and well."

"Your Majesty, you're just the one I wanted to see! I have discovered something wonderful up on the edge of the bluff! I must show you!"

"Yes, I wish to see whatever it is. But first, I must request Magic from you." Ur Logga's face was seamed with worry lines. "I would not have bothered you, but Master Fallon is too far away to reach quickly." He gestured toward one of his companions. The Ogre stepped forward and gave his king a large bundle, drawing the covers back. Cyna cried out, for it was Nyal cradled in Ur Logga's huge arms, so still that at first she feared he was dead.

"He has a wound in his back, Mistress," Ur Logga explained. "We have not touched it. But it is two days since he came to us and although he breathes, he never wakes."

Cyna ran ahead of the Ogre to her tent to clear a place before the fire. The Ogre gently laid Nyal down and Cyna examined his wound. The broken shaft of an arrow protruded from just below his shoulder blade. Ruf was already boiling water and Slipfit brought the herb chest.

"I must be alone," she said. "Your Majesty, please wait outside. Take the girl, too. I can't concentrate with her clucking." The mad girl crouched by the tent flap, her eyes wide, staring at Nyal. She shrank away from Ur Logga as he approached her, then ran from the tent on all fours.

Alone, Cyna examined Nyal more closely. His pulse was slow and light, his breathing so faint she could hardly detect it. His skin was pale and cool to the touch. When she pinched the soles of his feet, he didn't flicker. By then the water was boiling. She prepared a poultice to remove poisons and turned her attention to his wound.

She worked gently, for the flesh was swollen and inflamed. By pressing her fingers around the wound she could feel the arrowhead anchored in the bone of his rib. She pulled. Nothing happened. Taking a small dagger from the herb chest, she carefully cut around the shaft, opening the wound farther. She hated the sight of blood and had to stop several times. Cautiously, she worked the arrow from side to side, loosening it. It came out suddenly in her hand. She laid it aside while she cleaned the wound and applied a poultice. When she was done, she called for Ruf to help her roll Nyal on his side and cover him with skins. She poured a little willow bark tea between his lips, but he didn't swallow. Beneath his lids, his grey eyes were dilated and black.

"How is he, Mistress?" inquired Ur Logga as she emerged from the tent.

"The wound is festered," she said.

"Does he awaken?"

"Not yet."

The Ogre Honor Guard had started a fire and they clustered about it, making lunch. They boiled water in their customary way, scooping a hole in the ground and dropping hot rocks into the water. A hearty lunch of gruel was cheering after so many days of watery soup. Even the mad girl ate with them, squatting near the tent and mouthing the lumpy gruel between her lips as though she had no teeth. Ur Logga glanced at her curiously, then quickly looked away as she hopped to the riverbank to drink from the stream. The Ogres had been traveling day and night to bring Nyal to Cyna and, after lunch, they slept.

Slipfit was tidying up the tent when Cyna looked in on Nyal. Again for a moment she feared he was dead. The wound had cooled but his pulse seemed a little lighter, his breath a little slower.

"Hey, Mum," said Slipfit, "shall I burn these?" He held out the bloodied dressings and the arrow shaft.

"Let me see." Cyna took the arrow from his hand. The splintered shaft was slender, wrapped with sinew to a flint arrowhead. The edge was meticulously chipped to chilling sharpness. "A Peskie arrow, wouldn't you say?"

"Aye, Mum," he agreed. "Small and keen, like its maker."

As she examined it, light from the fire illuminated a tiny crystal entrapped between the flint and the sinew by the shaft. Cyna touched it to her finger, then to her tongue. Her tongue grew numb and in a moment she could not feel the tip of her finger. "Nightshade!" she exclaimed.

"Hey?" asked the Elf.

"When I was with the Peskies they showed me how they kill the great shalk with arrows tipped in an herb called black nightshade. The poison spreads through their system and they slumber, making it simple for a small Peskie to slay the huge beast."

"Be my friend slain?"

"Not if I can help it." She scrambled across the piled blankets to the herb chest. "There must be an antidote here. But what?" She surveyed her collection of pouches and jars, each prominently labeled.

Like Fights Like was the law of medicine that she used most often. Fallon had taught her how to reason out cures by using this principle. As heat and fire cured fever, as cutting and surgery cured wounds, so herbs could cure poison. *"Black nightshade,"* Fallon had told her long ago, *"is one of the most powerful herbs. It can kill as well as cure if you use it carelessly. There are few herbs which require such respect."* But one which did was green hellebore. "Like fights like," she said aloud and removed some hellebore leaves from their pouch.

She removed the poultice from Nyal's back and replaced it with a paste made of hellebore mixed with hot gruel so it would stick. Then she crushed more leaves. She soaked them briefly in warm water and made a paste which she placed under his tongue. "Call Ruf please, Slipfit," she said when she had finished. "If anything happens, I'll need him." But nothing happened. For hours she kept watch. She worked as Fallon had taught her. Eyes closed tightly, she imagined him healthy, laughing, the joy of feeling his strong arms around her. Nyal continued to lie, barely breathing, cool and lifeless to the touch.

Her back stiff from crouching beside him, Cyna stepped out of the tent. The Ogres lay scattered about the campsite, snoring softly. The air had the thick feeling of approaching rain. It was dark at the bottom of the ravine and the chill of the afternoon had settled on the stones. Cyna bent down beside Ur Logga's sleeping form and touched his shoulder. "Your Majesty, I have found something I want you to see. Follow me."

The Ogre awoke instantly. The mad girl fled like a startled chicken as Cyna led the way to where the path started up the steep bank. Ur Logga followed, cautiously shambling up the path.

The steps were thickly shrouded in mist. Cyna had to move cautiously, holding on to outcrops of rock, for the path was damp and slippery. At the top she paused. An eerie silence lay upon the stones. Even the sound of their footsteps was muffled. Behind her Ur Logga breathed deeply from the climb. "It's here" she said, gesturing toward the trees. She bent the branches aside and stepped into the forest. Behind her, for all his great size, Ur Logga followed her with as little sound as an Elf's breath.

She found the arched door of the tower. The Ogre king had to stoop and twist sideways to enter. He looked about him with amazement. He examined the fireplace with its strange face. He reached overhead to trace the joint in the stones over the doorway. He examined the high corbelled ceiling and followed the curving stairway until it was choked with rubble. Cyna waited for him in the main hall before the fireplace. When Ur Logga returned, cobwebs covered the top of his shaggy head and his hands and knees were black with dust.

"It's strange, don't you think?" she asked.

The Ogre's voice was harsh with emotion. "Mistress Cyna, you are truly Gifted. You have discovered Kythra's Sanctuary!"

Chapter 33

The frog kept a vigil by Nyal. When she had first seen him, pale and lifeless, a terrible despair overcame her. The witch seemed to have won so totally that there was no hope left in the world. The frog wished only that she could join the rhythmic croaking of her fellow frogs who thronged the riverbank, and be lost in oblivion. But the witch had won even there. For while her green cousins swam and sang and hopped as she did, they knew that their froggishness was a natural thing and they were happy. But the frog who had once been a Human girl named Melloryth could remember her other life and she mourned it.

So she kept a vigil by Nyal. After she was first driven from the tent, she crept behind it. In frog posture she sat so close that she could feel the cloth of the tent against her rough skin and hear the witch talking to her demons and mixing loathsome brews. Even though she couldn't see him, just being close to Nyal gave her a feeling of poignant joy. Then she returned to the secret place behind the tent and watched the Ogres—huge and horrible—as they bustled around fixing breakfast. She listened to the sounds of Nyal's breath. In the early evening a demon found her.

She had dozed off and dreamed she was a girl again. She heard the demon calling "Mistress! Mistress!" and struggled into wakefulness just as he spied her squatting beside the tent.

"You poor thing," he said. "So here's where you've been. Go on. Shoo now. Go down by the fire and get some dinner."

She hurried away before he could touch her. Later she stole some apples from the Ogres' supplies, for even though she was a frog, she grew tired of eating flies and water bugs. But by then the witch had returned.

Slipfit's voice brought Cyna and Ur Logga running and stumbling down the path to the campsite.

"Mum! Hey, Mum!" Slipfit cried, hopping in a frantic jig to attract her attention.

"Is it Nyal?" There was dread in Cyna's voice as she arrived, out of breath, at the foot of the path.

"Yea! My friend, Mum!"

"Mistress!" called Ruf Nab, sticking his head out of the tent. "I think he's coming around." There was a murmur of pleasure from the Ogres.

Inside the tent, Nyal lay on his back, a rosy flush coloring his cheeks. Cyna knelt beside him and touched the side of his throat beneath his jaw. His pulse was stronger and his skin felt warm.

"He's been taking deep breaths," Ruf told her. "First I thought they were his death rattle and I tried to find you. Then he spat out the poultice and I saw his breath was coming back. He's been sighing. Groaning, too."

She slid her hand beneath his back. "The wound is cool, no fever," she said after a moment. "You're right, Ruf, his breath is coming back. And his heart, too. Give me that pillow so I can raise his head." As her arm encircled his head and shoulder to lift him, Nyal sighed again and opened his eyes. "Nyal. Nyal, it's Cyna. Can you hear me?"

A tear slid down his cheek and his mouth contorted with grief. "Dragon Fire," he gasped.

"Ruf, quickly, get a lamp so I can see! Nyal, where does it hurt?"

"Dragon Fire," he repeated. A great sob convulsed his body.

She held him tightly. "Nyal, Nyal, please! Don't move, just tell me where it hurts and let me fix it."

After a moment his sobs stopped and his hand rose weakly and touched her hair. "Cyna?" he asked, bewildered.

"Yes, it's me. I'm not letting you die," she said fiercely, "I'm making you well. What hurts?"

"Nothing," he said after a moment. "I'm so tired."

She sighed in relief. "You've been poisoned and you're feeling the effect of the herbs."

"Like Brandon?" he murmured.

"Yes, my love," she said. "But what killed him has saved you."

He closed his eyes again and she held him tenderly while he fell asleep. The chill of the night clung to the sides of the tent and the fire burned low, the green wood sputtering. Slip-fit brought her a blanket before going to his own tent to sleep.

Cyna rested her cheek against Nyal's forehead, feeling his warmth returning as the poison left him. His breathing became deep and rhythmic. Occasionally he stirred and murmured something in his sleep.

In the morning, the bustling of Ogres awoke Cyna. It was just dawn and only a dull light filtered into the bottom of the ravine as she emerged from the tent. She assured herself that Nyal rested peacefully, then pulled on her battered green boots and wrapped herself in the long brown cloak. Despite his improved condition, she felt a strange urgency, a sense of dread. A thick mist was rising from the river, clinging to the rocky face of the cliffs, making the stones along the river-bank damp and slippery. She followed the path upward.

With almost childlike enthusiasm, the Ogres had begun the task of clearing the ground around the tower and removing the rubble from the stairs. Ur Logga supervised the work, giving guttural orders to his Honor Guard. "Good morning, Mistress," he greeted her. "Nyal is better?"

"Much better. He will live," Cyna said.

His long teeth gleamed as he smiled in pleasure, nodding his head emphatically. "I was sure he would be well when you showed me what you discovered in this place. The Sanctuary where Kythra worked is very powerful. We will stay a while. It will honor us to return the tower to something of its former grandeur. It is significant that Kythra's place has come to light now, in The Final Days of The Dracoon."

Cyna looked up at the tower silhouetted against the rosy

dawn sky. "Kythra stood here, didn't she, Your Majesty?"
she said. "Many years ago she stood here and saw much that
we see. And so much we don't."

He grunted. "She saw much that was different, also. She
saw the snowcapped mountains, certainly, although some say
the snow was closer then, that the ice is retreating. She saw
Harkynwood, too, for it was here. And she saw what was
going to happen, while we can only guess. Yet she taught us
much. Why have we forgotten so much of what she taught
us?"

"I don't know," Cyna said.

After the Ogres' first flurry of enthusiastic work, it was
time for breakfast. They left her alone and descended the
path to make porridge. Cyna promised to join them, but a
strange lethargy seized her and she sat for a time, staring
across the chasm of the River Dark to the forest on the other
side. When at last she turned back to the tower, the sun had
risen behind it and it seemed taller than it had the day before.
The Ogres had cleared away the vines that clung to its sides.
Naked rock, it rose above the surrounding trees to a commanding height.

Cyna shivered and drew the ragged cloak more tightly
about her. She knelt to meditate, but her teeth began to chatter. Feeling faint, she retreated from the edge of the bluff to
the tower's door. Inside, the Ogres had cleaned and swept.
The rubble that clogged the stairwell was cleared and neatly
piled outside the door. The cobwebs were gone and a small
fire smoldered in the fireplace.

Cyna stepped inside and groped for a handhold as her
whole body began to shake. A sudden roaring in her head
deafened her. She felt herself falling and closed her eyes,
crying out in protest, feeling the nightmare beginning again.

*In the shadow of the tower, Nyal glared defiantly at accus-
ing fingers. A noose drew tightly about his throat. He struggled violently but with failing strength. His face grew red,
then blue. His eyes bulged, then glazed with death.*

*From the dark, she heard screaming. It pulled at her and
she was drawn unwillingly, fighting to get free, fighting to go
back to Crowell, back to her life with the Ogres, back to any-*

where but from where that shrill and mindless scream sounded.

A woman ran, fell, got up and ran again. Behind her, armed men with black shields followed. A horseman was before her, cutting her off. She scrambled for a way to escape, but there was none. The soldiers formed a ring around her, light gleaming from their sword tips. The swords fell.

And as the woman screamed again, Cyna understood. It was she who fled from the violence of the blows. The woman was—had always been—Cyna who writhed in pain, twisting away as the blades struck again and again. The screaming stopped as though the sound itself had been cut by a sword. She saw herself lying still, even her blood ceasing to flow as her heart lost its struggle and she died on the ground surrounded by strange men.

But the dream would not end. She was falling down into a place long shielded from the sun, where she heard voices murmur in the distance. She recognized her mother and father walking hand in hand. Ned danced as a small boy, delighted with his father's praise. She heard the clash of war and glimpsed a young Fallon riding beside an even younger Telerhyde. Whirling farther still, she saw her father's birth and her grandfather's. Generation upon generation fluttered by as she fell through them, beyond them, into the dark abyss of the past. She saw the Tribes emerging from the forest, building the Avenues of Power, joining together to move the great stones. Down, still down, she spun. Then abruptly she felt the doorjamb beneath her hand and realized she hadn't moved from where she stood. Except that the wood beneath her hand was freshly cut, the stones of the tower new, their edges sharp in the bright sunlight.

Cyna cried out in fear. Something vast was before her. She could see and she could not. It shifted, ever-changing. Tall, short, male, female, it whirled before her. It seemed to be a glittering Human, a glowering Dwarf. She cried out again as it came closer. Now it was a woman, slender and intense, dark in a spinning cylinder of light. "What are you?" Cyna gasped.

When she heard the voice, it was as though it came from

*within her own head, resounding the way a deaf person
hears music.*

"I am Kythra.
You have called to me and
I am here as I have always been."

*The form shimmered as it spoke, lighting the inside of the
tower, casting flickering shadows about the room.*

"The time of The Dracoon is at hand when
Fools abound and the Tribes splinter
Apart. It remains only for Magic
To die
Before all the signs
Manifest
    "Cyna, you must
Accept your Gift.
You can no longer delay.
You have the Sight, you see
Truly.
    "If the Tribes and
The Old Faith are to be
Saved,
You must step forward and take
Your place.
Prophetess!
No matter what you
See!"

"No!" Cyna cried.

"You must!
The knives will butcher
Or the Knife will be the bridge.
Your destiny is your choice.
Cyna! Do not run
From your own Sight!"

The form pulsed more rapidly, whirling closer, a heatless light. Kythra's words echoed in Cyna's mind.

"I once lifted a stone
With my friends.
A huge stone,
We lifted it high,
Lightly as a fire log,
Easily as a cat
Is brushed from a chair.
        "A great love,
An unfaltering conviction,
A passionate desire
Will burn with white heat,
Will move mountains,
Will move stones,
Will part the sea.
        "I once lifted a stone
Off the crypt of the old gods
And set them free
In the guise of The Law.
The One Law.
The Law of Thought,
The Single Principle.
        "Your thoughts
Are all you have,
All there is anywhere.
If you do not use them
To set you free,
They will chain you to your illusions
Forever.
        "I once lifted a stone, a huge stone.
You are the same as I.
You see Nyal's face with love.
It is your own.
You relish Fallon's wisdom.
It is your own.
Your father's manhood,
Your children's innocence.
They are all your own.

More accurate than your mirror,
The world all around you
Is your own reflection.
   "I once lifted a stone.
You are the same as I."

As though light flowed through the room, the air about
Cyna grew brighter. It swirled about the changing form of
Kythra, and reached out to envelop Cyna's body. It grew
brighter and brighter, until she was blinded by its brilliance.
Then, as suddenly as it had appeared, it was gone, winked
out like an ember when a fire dies.

When Cyna returned to the tent later that morning, she
moved hurriedly, barely greeting the Ogres whom she met
on the path. The dread she had felt upon rising had height-
ened and she paused to glance apprehensively about the
camp. Bihan, loose again, snorted a greeting and trotted toward her to have his ears scratched. She hurried past him.

Nyal was dressed and sitting up, finishing a bowl of Ogre
porridge as he talked with Ruf Nab. He rose and took Cyna
in his arms as she stepped into the tent.

"Excuse us, Ruf," Cyna said after a moment.

"Of course, Mistress."

When they were alone, she took Nyal's hand. "You're better."

"I'm fine! I'm starving. I could eat a unicorn!"

"Sit with me. We have to talk."

He watched with concern as she crossed the tent and drew
the herb chest from under the pillows. She was pale and her
hands shook slightly. She poured steaming water into a mug,
then added a pinch of woodruff from the herb box. "Here,
this will strengthen you." She made a mug for herself and the
tent filled with the sharp aroma of the herb.

"What's wrong?" he asked.

She didn't look at him directly, but reached out to take his
hand. "We must leave Morbihan. I want to go to a new place
with you where we can be safe. We must sail to the Outer
Isles if we are to live our lives together."

He frowned as she spoke. "Leave Morbihan?"

"As soon as possible. We can leave for the coast today. We'll find a ship to carry us far away, far from The Perime and The New Faith."

"Cyna, don't let The New Faith frighten you like this! Morbihan is our home."

"It's not just The New Faith. It's The Old, as well. The Ogres tell of The Final Days of The Dracoon . . ."

"I know. Princess Rib Tonnan told me. But folktales are no reason to give up one's home. Not without a fight. You mustn't be frightened!"

She leaned closer to him, her eyes imploring. "Please."

"You're being unreasonable. I can't leave Morbihan at a time like this!"

She kept her voice steady. "Nyal, I have received the Gift of prophecy. I've seen what the future holds for us here. Believe me, my love, we *must* leave. Come with me to some quiet place where you can raise your horses and I can heal our neighbors and we can have some happiness."

"I have sworn before you and on Telerhyde's grave that I will find Telerhyde and Brandon's killer! I know the man who can tell me who the killer is, and I heard a voice telling me I will find him on Fensdown Plain!"

"Nyal, with my Sight I have seen you dead!" Her words rang within the close confines of the tent.

The fire had burned low and its smoldering coals reflected as red pinpoints in Nyal's eyes. "One can't measure the cost of an oath."

Cyna felt as though the ground were sliding away from beneath her feet. "I have seen Kythra. She has told me that The Old Faith is dying! This *is* The Dracoon! Only the Death of Magic remains before the very end. Please, Nyal, come away and let's save our dreams!"

He rose to his feet, his face stony. "No. If that's my destiny, I'll pay the price."

She turned from him and leaned against the tent-pole, remembering the horror of the prophecy. Her voice was a hoarse whisper. "You will strangle, Nyal. And I will die by the swords of strange men. Is that what you want? Both of us dead? What good will oaths be then?"

"Your death—Cyna . . ."

"Oh, Nyal, come away before we lose everything."

Shock and fear played across his face. He reached out for her, held her tightly in his arms and for a bright moment Cyna thought she had won him.

When he finally spoke, his voice was gentle. "I heard a voice telling me I must go, yet you see Kythra and foresee that we must leave. You say you have the Gift of prophecy, but how do you *know*? Can we leave everything we love, forsake everything sacred, because you *think* something bad will happen?" He held her away from him by the shoulders, staring intently as though trying to see past her eyes. "What if you're wrong?"

"I'm not," she said.

A motion at the tent flap caught Cyna's eye. Slipfit stood there, gesturing frantically. "They be bad ones! Coming nigh! Run, Mum! Run, Friend! Hey, an' get out!"

"Cyna?" Outside, Ruf was running as best he could, bounding with his good leg, stumbling on the boulders that bordered the riverbank. "Cyna! Nyal! The lords are coming!"

Nyal tore himself from Cyna, lunging for the pile of pillows by the fire where Firestroker lay in its scabbard. But the poison had weakened him. Outside the tent, he sank to his knees, his face white, his sword slipping from his shaking hands. Cyna knelt beside him, wrapping her arms protectively about his shoulders, waiting for what she had been dreading.

It seemed only moments before Ned stood before her, his face haggard and grim, his sword drawn. "Sister, stand aside so there'll be no trouble." Someone took her by the arm and pulled her roughly away. Ned rested his blade on the side of Nyal's neck. "We've chased you all over this cursed island," he growled. "Make trouble and I'll end it right here." At his signal, Lord Adler bound Nyal's arms behind his back.

Drawn by the sound of horsemen, the Ogres had gathered. Ruf Nab, grim and pale, hefted his bronze ax in his hands. Behind him, Slipfit glared defiantly at the ring of lords who surrounded them.

"Ned, don't do this!" Cyna implored.

Her brother ignored her. He raised his hands. His voice was emotionless and flat. "In the name of the Dragon's

Council, I have apprehended Nyal of Crowell. Charges will be made as soon as a Grand Council is called together. Take him to that tower we saw at the top of the bluff. Keep him there."

As they led Nyal away, Ur Logga cracked his knuckles nervously. "I'm sorry, Mistress. It is given in The Peace that I had to tell them where Nyal was. I sent word by Peskie as soon as we found him."

"Then you never should have asked me to save his life," Cyna whispered. "You have killed him."

Chapter 34

When a lord or Royal Other was accused of a serious crime, tradition demanded that a Grand Council be called. Each Tribe was required to send a witness whose rank was equal to the one accused. Because the charges against Nyal included Telerhyde's murder, only the highest-ranking Others took part. Because Nyal was Human, only Humans could judge him. The Others were there to guarantee that the proceedings were fair and conducted according to The Law. Several days passed before everyone arrived and the Grand Council could be convened.

Kythra's Sanctuary had become a prison. Nyal was locked in a tiny room near the top of the tower. A window looked out over Harkynwood, and through it he watched the sunset each evening. The tower was guarded by the Lords of the North, for they were the accusers. Lord Benare, widely respected because of his years and his devotion to Morbihan, was in command and posted the formal charges, nailing them to a tree at the edge of the clearing, where all could read them.

The long pursuit of Nyal had taxed the endurance of the lords and their horses. Lord Norsea had been a welcome companion, invaluable to Ned and his followers because of his knowledge of horses. Ned had grumbled when the stranger insisted that a slower pace would save their mounts, swearing coarse oaths when it seemed that Nyal had disappeared from outside Elea. But then word had come that Nyal had been found, and amidst the celebrating and the forced marches, Lord Norsea's caution had become beside the point. But the shy, good-humored stranger had no part to play in a Grand Council, so Lord Benare courteously showed him to a place from where he could watch the proceedings and learn about Morbihan's justice.

Tym despaired when Nyal was captured, for he had traveled with the lords for many miles and he knew their anger and vengefulness. And he was frightened for himself, as well. If the lords learned they had traveled with Nyal's groom, the groom would suffer his master's fate. He was glad to see Cyna and Ruf alive, eager to catch a glimpse of Nyal, but he held back, afraid he would be recognized. When he joined the crowds that began to throng about the base of Kythra's Sanctuary, he was careful to keep his distance from his old friends, drawing the cowl of his cloak about his head. Something told him that traveling unnoticed among the lords was an advantage that could help Nyal.

He hid in the considerable group of curious Humans and Others who had come to witness the proceedings. He was near the front of a group of curious Human farmers, Peskie traders, and rough-talking wood Elves when Cyna stepped out into the clearing by the riverbank. She was dressed in her best woolen dress of barberry yellow. From his vantage point at the edge of the cliff far above her, it seemed to Tym that her sky-blue cloak fluttered about her like a banner in the breeze. But moments later he pulled the hood of his cloak down over his eyes and watched, frowning, as a small procession made its way up the long path to the tower.

The friends who he had been hoping would help to free Nyal now seemed powerless. But Ruf Nab, looking thin and ragged, limped beside Cyna. He led a group of Dwarves who carried Lord Landes on a litter. Telerhyde's old right hand had aged. At the top, he winced as Cyna embraced him, reluctantly accepting her help as he struggled to his feet. "My hip," he explained as he leaned heavily against a knobby cane. "It's broken, thanks to Nyal's horse. Fallon tells me it's mending, but it doesn't feel like it." Tym had hoped most for Fallon to fix things, but The Wizard stood aside impassively, his face grim. He barely acknowledged Cyna as she bowed before him.

Because of the constant arrival of more Peskies and Dwarves, as well as the already substantial number of Elves, Ogres, and Humans, the broad rock ledge before the tower was crowded and spectators filled the woods at the edge of the forest. Tym found a toppled standing stone with a good view of the proceedings and sat on it, crowded by a family of argumentative Peskies. They smelled of woodsmoke and shalk sausage. Excited by the occasion, they made good companions.

The weather, which had been mild in the previous weeks, had turned harsh again. A cold breeze swept down from the mountains. A fire was built in front of the tower to signify the beginning of the Grand Council, and space was made so that Landes could watch the proceedings as he reclined beside it. Like everyone else, he had only his cloak and muffler to protect him from the occasional bursts of icy rain.

The Council was held at the foot of the tower. Behind Lord Benare, Adler, Farryl, and the rest of the lords sat on the tower's stone steps as Nyal's judges. Across from them, the Royal Others gathered together at the top of the path to witness the proceedings. By craning his neck, Tym had a good view of the broad expanse between lords and Others, where Ned paced. Soon Cyna appeared at the top of the steps, flanked by Ruf Nab and a ragged wood Elf. Ned stepped forward to greet her.

"Nedryk," she said. Her brother ignored her hand and leaned forward to kiss her on the cheek. Beneath his green cloak, he had lost weight. His handsome face was gaunt, there were shadows beneath his eyes, and deep lines curved downward across his forehead and beside his mouth. His serious blue eyes regarded her with shrewd appraisal. "Mistress," he said, giving the word an odd twist.

"No one has let me see Nyal. How is he?" she asked, her voice barely loud enough for Tym to hear. He bristled at Ned's reply.

"He's well enough, for a murderer."

"Ned, how can you believe he did those things?" Cyna exclaimed.

"He crippled our father. How can you believe in his innocence?" Ned replied evenly, taking her by the hand and leading her to a place beside Ruf Nab.

Benare drew his sword and laid it across the ground in front of him, signifying that the Council had begun. "We, the Lords of The Dragon, have demanded a Grand Council on this day," he cried. "Before you see Lord Nedryk of Fanstock, our appointed Accuser. The Accused is Nyal, seneschal of Crowell. Are you present and do you see that this is so, Murdock, Snaefid of the Dwarves?"

"I'm here and I see it," The Snaefid replied. His knotty arms were folded across his chest and his lips compressed into a thin line.

"Are you present and do you see, Dallo, Meg of the Elves?"

"I am here; I see," The Meg responded.

A motion caught Tym's eye. As The Meg spoke, the wild Elf beside Cyna trembled violently, staring at the ground between his feet.

One by one, Benare called each leader of The Old Faith and each one responded. "Fallon, Seventh-Degree Wizard, known as the Shapechanger, the Twice-tested, are you present and do you see?"

"I am and I do."

"Before proceeding, does anyone wish to address the Grand Council?" Benare inquired, raising his eyebrows to peer at the assembled Others.

Cyna rose. "My Lord, I beg permission to speak."

"As Nyal's fiancée?"

"No, My Lord. As a believer in The Law."

"Speak."

She rose. "This is a difficult time. Many of us are confused by the events that have happened and frightened by the predictions of what is to come." Cyna gestured toward the tower. "I believe that the place upon which we stand is the tower of Kythra, the place where she prophesied, the place where she lived out her days." The Peskies beside Tym leaned forward, attentive despite the cold gusts of wind that ruffled their clothing. A murmur of wonder rose from the crowd. "I propose that we take a moment to dedicate ourselves here where The Old Faith began. That we remember the love and friendship that has governed us in the past. And I ask you," she turned toward where Benare sat, flanked by the scowling lords, "to listen carefully. With Kythra's wisdom, find the truth."

"Liar of The Law!" The Meg stood, face twisted with anger. "You who would not predict the heavens for me! I'll not participate with this false witch! She has conspired to heap shame upon me!"

"False witch?" exclaimed The Snaefid, looking shocked.

"She plotted to make me look the fool!" The Meg cried. "Concealed from me the death of the moon so that my tribute was darkened by the mighty eclipse! Frightened my people, so they have lost faith in their Meg! I denounce her!"

The wild Elf leaped to his feet, striding with short legs to the center of the rock. "Me, me, me!" he shrieked. "Denounce yourself, Dallo! You be the same as ever in your disgrace!"

"Husband!" gasped The Meg, her face going ashen at the sight of him.

"Yea, Husband I be! Slipfit I be!" he cried, pounding his chest, his Elfin shyness swept away by his rage. "It be I, First Husband, who asks you again, as I did years ago: WILL YOU NEVER CHANGE? Will you never see that Dallo be just an Elf? It be the Meghood which binds our people together, not Dallo!"

"Take him away!" cried The Meg imperiously to her Husbands, who were gathered near the top of the stairs where they might hear the proceedings. They obediently started up toward Slipfit.

"A fight!" observed the grizzled Peskie beside Tym. "Mind the children, them Elf-boys can get terrible violent!"

But quicker than the Husbands was a small and lovely Elf who ran across the clearing, stopping the Husbands with a gesture of her hand.

"Father!" she cried and knelt before Slipfit. The Husbands stumbled over each other and wrung their hands in confusion.

"Vile daughter, touch him not!" The Meg shrieked. "I am The Meg! Seize him, he who wounded your Meg's heart! Traitors! Deserters! Plotters all!"

"Who's that young one?" Tym whispered, standing up for a better view.

"Phaedryn, The Meg's spawn," the Peskie said. "Will you move a bit? I can't see."

Hesitating between them, Phaedryn looked from The Meg to Slipfit, quivering like a bowstring. Slipfit smiled at her, his long face lighting up like a Spring-Day candle. Blushing, Phaedryn looked away toward her mother, but when she glanced back again, Tym thought he saw Slipfit wink.

"Your Megship, if we could come together just for now, I'll make it up to you . . ." Cyna pleaded, but The Meg turned away from her and threw herself into the arms of her Husbands.

Benare pounded the handle of his sword against the steps to restore order. "Silence! I convene this trial and I'll tolerate no more outbursts while on the Grand Council's business! Lords, bring out the prisoner." Tym steeled himself to make no sound. Nyal appeared, his hands bound behind his back and no cloak to protect him from the chill in the air. He stumbled on the steps as he was dragged by two men-at-arms to a place before the lords.

"Nyal of Crowell," Ned said solemnly, "it is charged that you are a murderer, conspirator, liar, coward, and traitor."

Nyal's voice was low and Tym had to lean forward to catch his words before they were lost to the wind. "I am neither murderer nor traitor nor any of the things you say I am."

"May I address the lords?" Landes said, rising with effort and speaking with great respect.

"I recognize Landes of Fanstock," Ned acknowledged.

"I know the lords' thoughts on this matter, and I know that they hold Nyal responsible for my injury," Landes said. "But you must know that I do not. It was an accident. I warned him to train that horse."

Frowning, Ned paused to whisper with Benare before turning to address the assembled witnesses. "We were witnesses to the outrage. We will not remove that charge," he said tersely. "Nyal of Crowell, you are accused of the murders of Lord Telerhyde, the gate boy at Eacon Keep, and the captain and crew members of The Perime ship *Witsyn*. You are accused of holding secret meetings with enemies of Morbihan. You are accused of attacking Lord Landes and The Eacon Gleese. You are accused of the destruction of the *Witsyn* and the loss of all her cargo. You are accused of breaking Dragon's Discipline. Will you speak?"

Nyal had been watching Ned closely. He had a black eye, Tym saw, and his lower lip was swollen and split. "Are you crazy, Ned?" he said. "You know I didn't murder Telerhyde!"

"You will address the Council with respect!" Benare ordered. "Answer the charges."

With an effort Nyal controlled himself as he turned to face the assembly. "I am no assassin," he said. "When Telerhyde was murdered, I was cutting hay with forty companions. Finn Dargha will speak for me! He saw me there!"

"True!" Finn Dargha's voice was high and clear. "I went to get his help to find Telerhyde! He was on the east side of the Manor, at least four miles from where we found the body."

Ur Logga's face softened into a smile. "He could not have been in two places at the same time," he said to The Snaefid beside him.

Benare pounded the heel of his sword on the rock before him, the clash of metal breaking through the murmur that was starting among the onlookers. "With respect to you, Your Majesty, and to you, Your Magnificence, but you must be silent. This is the lords' Grand Council and it is our custom that only those who are recognized by the Council may speak."

Ur Logga ducked his head, blushing, but Finn Dargha muttered "Ask me then, and I'll tell you!" as he sat down.

Lord Adler, who had been listening with a slight frown playing across his face, rose. "Lords, as I have heard it told, Nyal was the first to find Telerhyde's body, am I right? As though he knew just where to go."

"He was on the road in plain sight," Nyal responded. "My horse was faster, I got there sooner. And Telerhyde's body was cool. He had been murdered an hour or more."

"By a Peskie spear point," Adler said smoothly. "If you conspired with Gleese, could you not have conspired with trolls to have Telerhyde killed?"

"Why would I do that?" Nyal argued. His voice was rising, and Tym could see, even at a distance, that a vein throbbed in Nyal's temple. *Steady,* he pleaded silently, *don't lose your head!* "I loved Telerhyde. He was my father!"

"He was *not* your father," Adler flashed, his voice like a whip. "Your birth betrayed Telerhyde, you bastard!"

"He didn't seem to think so!" Nyal flared.

"It wouldn't be the first time," Adler sniffed. "History's filled with stories of bastards who wanted a title and killed for it."

Ned stepped between them. "Can anyone speak to this matter? Can any say that they know with certainty that Nyal did not conspire to kill Telerhyde?"

"You know I wouldn't do that, Ned!" Nyal cried. *"You* speak for me! You know me. You were my brother's best friend, you can't pretend to believe I killed Telerhyde!" He covered the ground between them with two strides.

Benare nodded at the two guards and they drew their swords. "If you didn't, who did?" he demanded. "We know you met to conspire with Eacon Gleese."

Nyal turned to him. "Your Lordship, in my whole life I've met with New Faithers three times. Once to battle a bigot on the way to the Stone Moving. He was a rider with a black shield who spoke as though he knew who killed Telerhyde. Ruf Nab will witness that!"

Ruf nodded in silent agreement.

"The second time," Nyal went on, "I was welcomed by Eacon Gleese in his Keep. I accused him of knowing the bigot who attacked us, but I have no witness to my words. The last time I *did* fight with Gleese, because he was sheltering that same bigot! I tried to ask him questions, but Gleese let him escape. I pursued him to learn the truth about Telerhyde!"

"Now you're charging that Eacon Gleese is the traitor?" Benare asked. "Is there anyone who can speak for you about your meetings with him?"

Tym shifted uneasily. "No," Nyal said finally. "There is no one here to speak. You must take my word."

"He admits he met with Eacon Gleese," Adler said. "Should we listen to the excuses of an assassin?"

"Because the real assassin is among you!" Nyal flared.

"Will someone restrain him?" requested The Meg. The guards seized Nyal and he struggled against his ropes until he saw their naked swords.

Benare had grasped his own sword. "Silence, prisoner. Will anyone speak for the accused?"

The representatives of the Tribes shivered and drew their cloaks more tightly about themselves. Cyna stepped forward. "Lords, hear me."

Ned paused, conferring again with Benare. "You may speak as the Lady of Fanstock, Cyna, but not as a Magic-Keeper."

"Then I must be content with that. I know Nyal better than anyone here. I know he's incapable of such acts . . ."

"Of course he's capable," snapped The Meg, wiping her eyes. "He's the ambitious son of a great ruler, a usurper! There was no one to save poor Telerhyde as my Husbands saved me." The Husbands, clustered about her at the edge of the ravine, collectively blushed and looked modest.

"You be not saved, Mum, you be ruined!" shouted Slipfit. "That witch be a good Human! You listen for a change!"

The Meg ignored him, oblivious to Benare's pounding sword. "It's as though Mati killed me and then poisoned poor Phaedryn," she wept.

Cyna was appalled. "Your Megship, you have no right to say that!"

"I'll not speak to that witch!" The Meg declared.

"You're not in Elfwood now, Meg Dallo," said Finn reproachfully. "Show a little courtesy."

"A footloose Peskie tells me how to behave?"

Ur Logga had risen to his feet. "Respected friends, trustworthy companions . . ." he began.

"If you please!" Benare interrupted impatiently. "Your Megship, this is not the forum to air your personal difficulties. Please sit down! Lady Cyna, we require proof that Nyal did not do the things with which he is accused. Have you proof?"

"No," Cyna admitted.

"Then let us finish." He leaned forward and conferred with his fellow lords. At last, nodding, each lord took his place again. "Nyal, in view of the fact that you have admitted to the attack on Eacon Gleese, and it's the only way to explain what happened," Benare said, "the charge of conspiracy stands. The charge of murder likewise stands, as you offer no proof of innocence."

"You fools!" Nyal growled. "I had no reason to kill Telerhyde. Though I only wish I had killed Gleese!"

"There are also the murder charges regarding the gate boy and the captain and mate of that ship."

"I don't know what gate boy you're talking about!" Nyal shouted. "And if the captain died when the cargo escaped, I did kill him! I'm glad I did!"

"Oh, no!" Cyna said aloud.

"Guilty by his own words," Ned said simply to Benare.

"He sailed a slave ship!" Despite the naked blades of his guards, Nyal whirled on Adler, his lips curling in distaste. "Your city, My Lord, is a slave market!"

"Watch your tongue, bastard!" Adler warned.

"Elea is a slave market!" Nyal repeated, turning to the assembled Royal Others, "where kidnapped Royal Others are sold for sport to The Perime!"

The Snaefid clutched his battle-ax in his knotty hands. "Is this true?"

"Ask Ur Logga! Ask yourselves if starting the slave trade again is reason enough for someone to have murdered Telerhyde!" Nyal shouted, adding "Get away from me!" to the guards as they seized him and dragged him back to the safer spot in the middle of the bare rock before the tower.

Still standing, Ur Logga anxiously flexed his hands into massive fists. "It is true," he bobbed his head, his voice the deep timbre of Ogre formal speech. "Nyal, foster son of Telerhyde, freed my niece Rib Tonnan and her daughter and brother from the bowels of a ship. She says her father, my brother king, the Most Honored and Wise Clever One of Fensdown Plain . ."

"Oh, spit it out, Your Majesty!" Finn Dragha cried. "Just say it!"

The Ogre went on, allowing no one to interrupt what he knew to be an Ogre's sacred formality of a public meeting, ". . . renowned as Keeper of the great stone Argontell, was murdered by Humans, who then adbucted the princess and children, sold them into slavery, and were about to ship them to The Perime with a cargo of wild beasts . . ."

"Slavery?" quavered The Meg. "Others in slavery?"

Benare spread his arms wide, as though begging. "My friends!" His voice was so filled with pleading that everyone stopped and looked at him. "We will deal with this problem, if it's true, be assured! We know that there are evil things afoot—this is an evil time. But we have come here for one thing, and one thing only! To try Nyal of Crowell for his crimes! And we must finish with that before we can do anything else!"

Ned nodded energetically. "Nyal distracts us with these charges. He's charged with murder and conspiracy, and he's confessed!"

"Some pirates drowned when I freed a cargo of slaves!" Nyal raged. "I loved Telerhyde, you idiots! But someone here is trading in slaves and had a reason to see him dead!"

"Silence him!" Ned said to the guards. The Others were glancing nervously at the lords and talking among each other so loudly that Ned could hardly be heard. He drew his sword and laid it on the stone, the sharp tip pointing at Nyal. "I call him guilty!" he proclaimed. Ferryl and Bombaleur hastily stepped forward and laid their blades beside Ned's, followed by the rest. With a sigh, Benare turned his. "Nyal, once of Crowell, now a troll: The Grand Council of your peers has found you to be a traitor, conspirator, and murderer. You are condemned to die tomorrow morning at first light." He turned to his companions. "We will draw lots, Lords, to see who performs this deed."

Cyna had struggled forward through the crowd to hear the Lords' words. Now she choked back tears. "Don't do this! I forbid you to do this!"

"Sit down, Mistress Cyna," Benare said hurriedly.

"Guards, take him to a safe place where he will await our vengeance."

The guards stepped forward and took Nyal's arms. He wrenched himself away and turned to the Others. "If they kill me, the real killer goes free!" he shouted.

"Nyal the patricide!" The Meg hissed.

A guard seized Nyal from behind, wrapping an arm around his throat. He was dragged, struggling, into Kythra's Sanctuary.

"Free Nyal!" Tym shouted, too outraged to observe his usual caution.

"Free Nyal! Death to the slave traders!" cried a Peskie beside him. The uproar was general now, everyone on their feet. Peskie hands stole toward their dagger hilts. Ur Logga lumbered protectively to Cyna's side. At a nod from The Snaefid, the Dwarf troop withdrew to the head of the stairs, watching the rest warily.

The lords had drawn their swords and stood resolutely before the tower's door, but they were outnumbered and for a moment Tym thought that there was a chance. He was shocked to see Fallon stride forward and stretch out his arms. "Put your weapons away. The Grand Council has spoken!" he cried. "No one has a right to overthrow their will!"

"But Nyal is innocent!" Cyna wept in frustration.

"Then trust Magic!" Fallon told her sternly. "All of you, trust The Law! Don't shatter the remnants of Unity and lay waste to everything we have built! Each of you listen to the counsel of The Law within you!"

For a moment a tense silence gripped the assembly. Then Finn Dargha unnocked an arrow and returned it to his quiver. The Snaefid lowered his ax. Even Ruf Nab stepped back respectfully and, although his eyes were filled with tears, he bowed his head as Fallon swept past him. Tym groaned silently, then groaned again out loud as Benare ordered the guard on the tower tripled. Nyal's trial was over.

Somehow Cyna rose to her feet as Benare spoke the ritual words that dissolved the gathering. While some returned to the warmth of their tents, Cyna paced the edge of the cliff overlooking the ravine. Half a dozen lords guarded the gate to the tower and Adler, who was in charge, politely but firmly refused to admit her. At length a Peskie found her and gave her the message that Fallon awaited in her tent.

The Wizard sat on the pillows and blankets that surrounded the fire, sipping from a mug. He made no gesture of greeting as Cyna entered. She crossed to him, not bothering to perform the ritual courtesy of bowing. "Master Fallon, you must help me now!"

Fallon fixed Cyna with his bright blue eyes. "I do not wish to speak about Nyal. The Council has acted and it is not my right to contradict them. He will live or die without my help."

Cyna shook her head, tears filling her eyes. "You are wrong, Master. Without help he dies tomorrow."

Fallon waved an impatient hand. "That's politics, Cyna. I'm most worried about you."

"Me?"

"You have forsaken Magic. You continue to refuse your Gift. You imperil us all."

"Master, Nyal is the one in danger right now . . ."

The Wizard shook his head. "Cyna, for once will you listen? It's one thing to be modest in your desires, it's quite another to refuse to serve when you are needed. Do you want to become to Magic what The Meg is to Meghood?"

"What does this have to do with Nyal's life?"

"If you truly care about him, use your Gift!"

Cyna shook her head as if to shake off bees. "My Gift? How can I use prophecy to save Nyal? What good is it, Master Fallon? All around us Magic fails. What can I do but predict death and perform tricks at festivals?"

"Tricks?" Fallon rose, his voice quivering like a harp string. "You understand Magic as tricks?"

"Master . . ." Cyna began.

"Silence!" He turned away from her. It took him a moment to regain his composure. When he turned back, he spoke quietly, glaring at her from across the fire. "If your study of The Law has taught you only 'tricks,' what will you do for Nyal? Let the sentence of the lords take its course?"

"I will ask Ruf and Slipfit to help me free him. Ur Logga will back me, and perhaps The Snaefid. The Ogre Honor

Guard and the Dwarves are strong enough to hold off the lords. I don't expect any problem from the Elves, and even the Peskies may join us."

"And if you succeed?"

"I will spirit him to the port of Flean. For enough gold we'll find a boat to take us to some remote place."

"Ah, Cyna, what a general you would make." Fallon shook his head and gazed into the fire. After a moment he said, "Do you have any brandy?"

"Of course." She brought him Elfin brandy in an earthen mug.

He held it in his hands a long time before he sipped. "If your goal is to save Nyal, it's a gamble, but a brave plan."

Cyna felt a flicker of hope.

Fallon went on. "You can flee with Nyal, and perhaps you will both survive to escape. But what of your friends Ur Logga, Finn, and The Snaefid? If you ask them, I'm sure they will battle with the lords for Nyal. But they have families and tribes; they can't leave Morbihan with you. They must try to live here, at war with the lords. How long do you think they will last before the onslaught of The New Faith? It will be The Final Days of The Dracoon and *you* will have created it."

"But I can't let him die," she insisted.

"You can't stop him from dying!" Fallon snapped. "You can heal, but you can't overcome death!" His tone softened. "You will die. I will die. But no one knows when, despite what the lords decide."

"But what else can we do?" she asked despairingly.

"It upsets me that you have not used the power that you have. I hoped that you would become my finest student, but I'm afraid that you are your father's child. You have become a well-meaning politician, as he is. But you are not as good as he is. Landes, were he well, could have saved Nyal."

He drained his brandy. "Be quiet and listen closely to me. I will tell you this once and then you must know it, for I'll tell you no more." He cradled the empty mug in his hands. "Magic is the informed use of The Principles of The Law to achieve the magician's goals. It is a power, you cannot accept it or refuse it like a suitor. It is a Gift that each creature partakes of, and none can deny. The power of Magic is awesome! Life, death, time, space—all these can be overcome by Magic. And are, daily. *But you cannot control Magic by your will.*"

"Master Fallon, with all due respect, I know . . ."

"No, you don't! If you did, then Nyal would not be facing his death nor Morbihan her Final Days. Think on this: your father has a broken hip. With all my power of Magic, I could heal him, I *have* healed him in the past. But he no longer believes I can—he believes he's getting old and all his friends are dying. So he limps about, pain-ridden, while important business falters along without him. Out of his fear and ignorance spring all the miseries of his life. Does that tell you anything? Be quiet!" He waved his hand impatiently at her as she began to speak.

"On the other hand, Ruf Nab should have died. Not only was his leg festered, but the poison had spread to his blood. Few see death that closely and return to describe its face. But he believed you could heal him, and you desired to heal him. So you did! No matter what you say, I have to believe that somewhere, in some deep recess of truth within you, you *know* that it was not your beloved herbs that saved him. It was *your desire and belief.* You cannot stop The Law from working, Cyna. Out of desire and belief spring Magic, but you must choose. Will you let cause and effect trample you in the dust? Or will you use Magic and trust The Law to create good?"

"Good?" Cyna blurted. "How can I create good when my Gift foretells Nyal's execution? When all I see left are my own murder and Morbihan at war with itself?"

"All that?" asked Fallon.

Cyna told him her visions.

"Yes, I see," The Wizard said at last. "How terrible. Of course you fled from all that. I understand. I wish I had known sooner." He rested the fingertips of each hand together. "Cyna, like it or not, you are Gifted with the profound understanding of cause and effect. But prophecy can only tell you the most probable event. Change a root cause, and you change the entire effect. Change even the intention, for intention is the thought . . ." There was a scrambling sound. He turned toward the entrance of the tent. "Who's there?"

Cyna lifted the lamp and its flickering light picked out the figure of the mad girl cowering in the shadows. "Go away," she said. "Shoo." She waved her hand and the naked figure began to hop away.

"Wait," commanded Fallon. "Who is this?" He rose from the pillows and bent to examine the girl more closely.

"She was found lost in the forest. She won't wear clothes. She only eats stolen food. I've found nothing that will make her better. Her mind is gone."

Fallon frowned. "Here, girl, what's happened to you?" The mad girl made a hoarse croaking noise and fled through the entrance of the tent.

Fallon sighed and turned back to Cyna. "I haven't time to teach you more. You must learn for yourself. But I would hate to have my last apprentice be known as a blundering politician who ended an era. You refuse your Gift, so give me your witch's chain."

Slowly, her arms leaden, Cyna lifted the heavy gold chain from her neck and handed it to him. "You are not fit to be a witch. You're no longer a Magic-Keeper," the old Wizard said sternly. "I must leave you now. But I advise you strongly to act as though you have faith in The Law. Spend the night in meditation. Or at least reflect on the consequences before you do whatever it is you are going to do."

He turned to go, but his steps faltered at the tent flap. He turned back to her, and she was shocked to see that his eyes were bright from tears. "My dearest Apprentice," he said, his voice gentle and soft, "find courage if you can. Even when everything seems lost, I beg you to trust Magic, as frightening as that may be. Trust The Law as I do right now, as frightened as I am. That's the best you can do for Nyal. For us all."

The frog had climbed the slippery stairs and heard the death sentence for Nyal as she clung to the grey stones. Now she lifted her voice in song by the riverbank. Her cousin frogs sang in celebration that the rain had ended for the day.

and a thick mist rose from the river. The frog sang a song of loss and grief.

In the twilight, lighted by the campfires that burned near the tents, she saw a figure approaching her. It was the ancient Wizard, cloaked in sky blue, gold chains hanging from his neck, seeming so old and frail that his footsteps made no sound. He was almost upon her. She sprang away, but found herself trapped against the ledge. She trembled, broken frog sounds coming from her throat as she cowered against the rock.

"Here now, what's this?" The Wizard said. She turned her eyes from him so not to see his face, but his voice was kind. "What's the matter, girl, where are your clothes?" A croak of panic escaped her lips and she made an effort to dart around him but he put out a hand. "Here now, settle down, I won't hurt you. I have my own business to tend to and I'll not be meddling in yours." He stepped aside and let her hop by him. He continued to make his way down the riverbank. The frog, attracted by the kindness of his voice, paused to look after him.

He stopped, breathing hard from climbing over the rocks. Impulsively the frog hopped after him. He took a few more steps and the frog followed him. After some minutes of climbing, they came to a place where the river formed a torrent as it poured over a huge rock and dropped into a pool below. Here the old Human paused and looked out over the pool. Shivering in the cold, the frog stopped beside him, looking up into his face. Some deep instinct told her she had no need to fear him.

"What's wrong with you?" he asked. "Are you mad? Bewitched? A lunatic, surely, a child of the moon."

His deep voice made her feel warm. She did love the moon. To sing in the moonlight with her green cousins had been the only time she could forget the horrible curse upon her.

"But surely you were happy once," he went on. "You must have known the friendship of other Humans, been important to someone, even known love."

The frog wept, terrible, shuddering sobs. When she regained her composure she looked up.

"Ah, poor creature." The Wizard cocked his head and looked full into her face, his brilliant blue eyes looking past her frog exterior, looking deep into Melloryth's being. "You will know love again, if you wish."

The frog listened, her heart beating rapidly. "You are under a spell, a delusion," he said. "If you wish to return to yourself, it is very simple. Do a service for someone you love. It doesn't matter if the service is large or small, or whether the one you love even knows what you have done for them. You may perform it in your heart if you are unable to perform it any other way. You will become a girl again by this act. Go now, you have made me late. I must act, quickly."

Moved by his kindness, the frog hopped away, then stopped and stared back at the old man. The Wizard reached beneath his cloak and pulled out a small leather bag. From it he took a fine dust and spread it on the ground around him. He murmured strange words. When he was done, he traced symbols in the air with his slender fingers. Finally he stood still, a Master Wizard in full regalia waiting beside a riverbank.

Through the rising mist she glimpsed the river tumbling in foamy abandon over rocks and ledges. A loud crashing came from the woods beside the river. The frog started, terrified.

Fallon turned toward the sound. "Ah, you have come," he said. The frog saw another Human emerging from the forest.

"Yes," the Human said. "Did you think I wouldn't?"

The voice was cold, so cold the frog shuddered. She turned and hopped swiftly away. The Wizard had given her hope and she knew what she must do.

Chapter 35

Shaken by Fallon's words, Cyna performed the simple ritual by which all witches and Healers dedicated themselves to Magic. She spent the night alone by the riverbank, deep in meditation, her body shivering from the cold. Again and again she heard Ned's hollow voice, saw The Meg's face twisted by emotions that made her Elfin beauty coarse and brutish.

And always she heard Fallon's voice. More than once she rose to call Ruf Nab to a last, desperate gamble to free Nyal. Each time it was not the thought of impossible odds which stopped her but Fallon's warning. "Trust The Law," she repeated again and again to herself. "Trust Magic."

She came to a decision. If Nyal died, she would die. The destruction of the one she loved would make the slash of strange men's swords a welcome release. She wished she could go to Nyal and tell him that since he would not follow her to the Outer Isles, she would follow him. The thought gave her a sense of peace.

But the thought of what the morning would bring was unbearable. It was only with a kind of desperate discipline that she drove thoughts of death from her mind. She remembered the few golden days they had shared in summer. She remembered what they had dreamed of together and built it in her mind like a monument. She forced herself to see Nyal laughing with delight at the frolic of a field of colts. Again and again she called to him and willed herself to see him turn to her with a look of pleased surprise.

Yet, despite her tricks, the morning came. "Trust The Law," she said once more to herself, seeking comfort in the unyielding words.

It took Nyal a long time to free himself from the ropes that held him. He twisted his hands, painfully tearing the flesh of his wrists, creating more slack until there was enough room for him to pull a wrist free. Moments later he stood up.

The window looked out over the chasm and was too narrow to allow a grown man to pass through. The door was as solid as a stable gate, made of thick oak. The wood was not well seasoned, he noticed, probably taken from dead branches and trees which the Ogres had found nearby. The green wood would shrink and crack but not, he thought grimly, until long after there was no Nyal of Crowell to notice it. He prowled the chamber, examining every crack, pulling on every stone

within his reach. The tower was solid. It had stood for un-
countable years and would last many more.

He wrapped himself with his cloak and sat, leaning against
the wall. He wondered about how it would happen. He
would ask for a trial of arms. Better to go with his blood hot
and a chance to leave an impression. But the lords were not
fools and ritual execution by strangulation was the probable
choice. A shudder shook him as he coiled the rope that had
bound him. It was a poor weapon, but he would fight.

The chamber had grown dark and chilly when he heard the
sound of metal being dragged across stone in a strange, hopping rhythm. He sprang to his feet, pressing his ear against
the door. The sound came closer, ominous in its slow,
painful progress. He shrank back, his heart thundering in his
chest. With a last rasping thud, the sound stopped. Something scratched at the door. Whatever it was did not sound
Human or of the Others. The scratching grew stronger and
with it, odd grunts of effort. A creature was trying to get in.
He held his breath.

He felt the sudden rush of cool air as the door creaked open.
He saw nothing, for the inside of the chamber was as dark as a
cave. He raised the coil of rope in his hand, poised for flight or
battle. Metal scraped the floor and something touched his foot.
He leaped back, but the creature retreated, snuffling and
croaking. Nyal bent down cautiously and touched the weight
on his foot. It was Firestroker. Drawing the sword from its
scabbard, he felt the joy of its perfect balance, home again in
his hand. Before him, in the impenetrable darkness, he heard
the creature move. It croaked again, a squeaking urgency in its
tone, and he followed it through the doorway.

The bottom floor of the tower was empty, the door open.
Outside men-at-arms slept, snoring gently by the embers of a
dying fire. Nyal stepped over them, sword ready. Ahead of
him, the creature moved quickly in strange hops and lurches.
In the moonlight he could see that it was a nude young girl.
She crouched at the top of the path, gesturing excitedly. He
followed her down the rocky stone steps of the path into the
even blacker darkness of the ravine, where the roar of the
river sounded.

The bottom of the path skirted the tents and campfires as it followed the course of the river. Rocks and boulders were slippery under his feet and he slid and skidded, his boots soaking, deafened by the sound of the roaring river.

The girl plunged into the water. He tied the rope to his belt so that he had both hands free and dived after her. The cold water numbed his body as he struggled to the opposite bank. The girl hopped before him, croaking excitedly, leading the way up the steep bank. Nyal felt grass beneath his feet and heard the startled snort of Avelaer. Relief and gratitude flooded him. Black in the moonlight, the stallion tossed his head and pawed the ground. Nyal tied one end of the rope around Avelaer's neck and looped it about the chestnut's nose.

"Madam," he whispered in the darkness, "we may never meet again, but let me say thank you. I will try to deserve your trust." He reached out into the darkness. She emitted a sharp, high-pitched sigh. His hand encountered cold, rough skin. In revulsion, he snatched his hand back. "Thanks," he mumbled and vaulted onto Avelaer's bare back.

The sky was lightening at his back as he skirted the side of the lake to take a westward course. Avelaer was fresh and eager. Nyal rode with barely restrained fury. He rode on until night turned into morning and morning gave way to late afternoon. All he had once valued had been stripped away. Crowell, Morbihan—even Cyna was lost to him. He was a dead man, tried and sentenced. He possessed only his horse, his sword, and now, a little time. But this short reprieve was all he needed, for the thought of vengeance drove him south like a stiff wind.

Chapter 36

Ruf clattered down the path, his cheeks flushed. "Nyal's escaped!"

"Oh, Ruf!" Cyna rose from the side of the riverbank to embrace the Dwarf. Together they whirled in a kind of dance of joy. "How?"

"I only know that when the moon was dark, I went to get him out of there. I meant to free him if it meant my life. But he was gone already! The lords have just found out!"

From high above her on the ledges before the tower, Cyna could hear the sound of cursing. "I must tell Fallon!"

Fallon lay by the bank of the river, as if resting from the walk back to his tent. His head was turned and he seemed to be gazing out at the pool where Cyna had almost drowned. A light mist rose from the dark water and shimmered in the cold light. Beaded moisture gleamed on The Wizard's face and hair.

"Master," Cyna said softly, for he seemed to be asleep. "Nyal is free! He escaped in the night!"

When he did not move, she touched the old Wizard's shoulder. He was gone. Brushing his hair from his eyes, she found a wound on his forehead, a bruised and purple gash. Clasped in his stiffened hand was a large gold ring. Tears sprang to her eyes and broke her voice. "My teacher, just when I am beginning to understand." She was silenced by his stillness. Fallon's body was cold, empty.

Finn found her near the path. She told him that Fallon had been murdered and he brought Peskies to carry the body up to the tower. As word traveled, the Tribes gathered. They built a huge pyre on the rock ledge where Nyal had been condemned. Cyna dressed The Wizard in his finest sky-blue cloak and carefully combed his hair and beard. He appeared thin and unreal as his body lay on the pyre, as though Elves had made a clever model.

All the Tribes gathered. The Honor Guard stood beside Ur Logga, exchanging ritual grooming and guttural murmurs. Finn's boisterous followers, subdued for once, bared their heads of their thick felt caps and stood in silence behind their prince. The Meg, pale and quivering, stood with her hands nervously touching now her hair, now her lips or breasts. Beside her, a stark contrast, Phaedryn was still and poised. The Husbands prostrated themselves on the stone of the ledge.

Landes leaned on his crutch beside Benare, who was armed and mufflered for the road. Ned looked hollow-eyed as he stood impatiently by the steps. The Snaefid and his Dwarves beat a mournful rhythm on their drums. By the tower, Ruf Nab stood stolidly beside Slipfit, his eyes on Cyna's face. Beside them, wrapped in Cyna's ragged brown cloak, was the mad girl.

Landes, leaning heavily on his crutch, shook his head. "I always liked the boy. How could he kill Fallon?"

"Nyal didn't kill Fallon as surely as he didn't murder Telerhyde," Cyna said.

Landes glanced at her strangely and sighed. "I loved that boy, aggravating as he's been."

"Can anything get worse?" The Snaefid asked of the air.

A small fire was started at the top of the path. The wood, wet from two months of soaking rain, sputtered and resisted the flame. Ur Logga, grim and silent, patiently spun the firestick between his fingers until the flame flared to life.

Benare, as leader of the lords, stepped to the small fire. He carefully ignited a pine torch and turned to the pyre. "It is the Death of Magic," he said, laying the torch on the shavings and pine resin beneath the corpse.

"It is the death of The Old Faith." Finn Dargha, crying openly, coaxed his torch to flame. "Telerhyde and you, Fallon, both gone in half a year. Old and tired with holding back time and the cutting edge of The New Faith. You are gone and the rest of us are swept away in the confusions and passions of a new time."

The Meg began to weep with an agonized, high-pitched sound. Her Husbands reached out to her as her knees buckled. "What will happen now?" she cried. "What will happen to me now?" The Husbands, stroking and cooing, led her away. Alone, Phaedryn stepped forward, kindled a torch, and cast it on the pyre.

One by one, the leaders of the Tribes stepped forward and lit their torches. Ur Logga, shrunken inside his great frame, fumbled his torch and it fell short, flickering on the wet stone of the ledge. Smoke and steam rose as wood resisted fire, hissing and snapping, flickering and fading out.

Cyna stepped forward. "To Magic, Master," she whispered. "To Gifts." Her torch flickered and went out. "No!" she said aloud. She snatched up Ur Logga's fallen torch and rekindled her own. The clump of resin-filled pine twigs smoked feebly. Cyna knelt and breathed on them. The flame wavered. She leaned closer and blew. The shavings glowed faintly. Cyna sprawled on the ground, heedless of the damp or the surprised looks on her fellow mourners' faces. She blew gently at first. The thin edge of ember spread across the sticks, leaving ash in its wake.

She blew harder. The embers seemed to dance before her. They took on brief life, flared and were gone, spreading across the kindling. Like Fallon's life, spreading across Harkynwood, rekindling The Old Faith. The ember dying out, but the fire going on, spreading. Like her own life, receiving the fire from him, flaring up and soon dying out. She glanced for the last time at Fallon's face. Without the flush of life he seemed transparent in the glow of the fire.

With a roar, flame burst out and raced through the loosely piled wood. For a moment smoke obscured the pyre, then Cyna saw it was ablaze, fire reaching high, brilliant against the dull grey morning sky. "Farewell, Fallon," she called out, casting her torch into the inferno. "Thank you."

She turned away abruptly and crossed the expanse of bare rock to the head of the path. Finn put out a restraining hand. "Wait, Mistress. You must stay and read the coals to tell us what the future holds."

"No," Cyna replied. The Others turned startled eyes toward her. "I know the future, Your Magnificence, and there's no time to root about in the ashes of my old Master. Ned, wait for me."

"But Morbihan needs prophecy," Finn reproved her.

"It will have to make do without mine," Cyna said. Her brother had paused at the head of the path, watching her. "Do you remember, Ned, how Fallon always said he was no prophet? Well, now I've become one! But prophecy is not my Gift, it's my curse."

"But the custom," Ur Logga rumbled apprehensively. "We must follow the custom and read the coals . . ."

"Look into the coals yourself, Your Majesty," Cyna said gently. "You need no witch to see what you need to know. Wait, Ned! We need to speak."

But Ned had turned away, buckling on his sword. "There's no Magic left, you fools," he snapped. "Let's recapture Nyal."

"Show a little respect, My Lord," Benare said. "The Wizard is still hot and you're hurrying off in vengeance."

"Would you have me cool my heels with worthless ceremony while The Wizard's murderer runs free?" Ned demanded. "I must get my men on the road."

"My Lord," growled the Snaefid, "a Seventh-Degree Wizard has just passed. If we are to maintain unity, custom decrees that we remain by his pyre to read the future and await a sign. At a time like this we must follow The Law in such matters."

But Ned hurried from the bare, windswept expanse of rock to the path.

Cyna watched him, a strange prickling sensation in her forearm. "Brother," she called out formally. "Wait." She hurried after him. He paid no attention to her call, and she gathered her skirt up, taking two steps for his one. "Wait, Ned!"

"I have no time, Cyna, the traitor must be caught."

"I agree. Where is your ring?" Ned paused near the bottom of the path to glance back at her. "Your Healer's ring that Fallon gave you. You were a Healer, remember, Ned?"

"Yes, I was." He turned away again.

Cyna followed him. "As a Healer you know herbs, what heals and what kills. I found this ring in Fallon's hand when I found him dead this morning. He must have pulled it from the finger of his murderer." She held it up. "It's yours. Why, Ned? Why did you kill your teacher?" She was aware that he had drawn his sword, but she went on. "Brandon was your friend, yet you poisoned him with wolfsbane. That was easy for one schooled in healing. Telerhyde would have trusted you behind him. Did you kill him, also? Why?" Her voice echoed back upon her from the sides of the ravine.

Ned's lips curled back, his eyes burned darkly in his gaunt face. "Fallon was not my teacher! He worked for Telerhyde, who cared for nothing but the power to control this whole island! I have never had anything of my own—even a father, for mine played toady to Telerhyde all his life! Giving away the forest, coddling Others! Cyna, if you could listen for just a few moments to Eacon Gleese! *He* is my teacher!"

"Ned, that's foul! He's made you sick!" Cyna reached out

to him, unafraid even as she saw him raise his sword. *It is not Ned I fear, but The Black Shields* . . .

Hurrying to catch up with her on the path, Slipfit had no time to cry out a warning, for it was a deathblow and Cyna was too close. She never even raised her hands to ward off the steel. Direct as an arrow, the Elf sprang forward, taking the full blow. With an oath, Ned struck again and Cyna fell.

Chapter 37

Three Others, Ur Logga, Ruf Nab, and Phaedryn strolled along the top of the chasm. Why Phaedryn sought Ruf Nab for counsel was a mystery to her, but the Dwarf's honest comments did much to strip away the troubled Megin's confusion.

"In Dwarfin terms, it's the principle of honor," he told her. "We honor mother and father equally. But if there is a conflict, we must honor the larger community of Dwarves."

"But what of yourself?" asked Phaedryn. She glided beside him, little more than half his height, her bright golden eyes anxiously searching out his craggy face for nuance of meaning.

"I live my life and enjoy it as best I can. But when the hammer hits the chisel, my life is nothing compared to the Dwarfin community as a whole."

"But you are a great leader, son of The Snaefid."

"All the more reason, for a true leader serves his followers. Or hers," he added. "My father is as devoted to his community as I will be one day. What is it, Your Majesty?"

The Ogre had stopped at the top of the path down to the river. "Something is wrong," he said, standing suddenly motionless, nostrils flaring.

Phaedryn followed Ogre and Dwarf as they descended the long path, their strides hastening with growing alarm as they neared the river's bank. Ur Logga cried out when he saw Slipfit and Cyna lying on the bloody ground beside the tent.

Phaedryn gathered Slipfit to her chest, running her hands over his body, looking for signs of life. Her golden eyes dark with grief, she murmured, "He is dead." She rocked him gently as though to comfort him, knowing there was no comfort left. She clasped the Ogre's hand for comfort. "He is dead," she repeated again and again. "My father is dead."

"Mistress?" Ruf knelt beside Cyna, brushing away sand and hair from where they crusted the bloody wound just above her left temple. She stirred. "Ned," she whispered. Ruf leaned down to hear her. "Traitor . . ."

Ur Logga called the Others, his voice a stentorian roar.

The Elves came first, trembling at the sight of Phaedryn as she bent down to straighten Slipfit's body.

"Touch him not!" shrilled The Meg. She fell to her knees, and the odor of Elfin brandy lingered about her. "Oh, no! The only one I have ever loved!" The Husbands, fearful and alarmed, cowered behind her. The Meg turned to them as they prostrated themselves upon the ground, raging, striking them with her hands. "Worthless fools! Take me home! I want to go home!" The Husbands cowered away from her, covering their faces. She lashed out at the nearest one. "Get up, you Elfin-drone! Help me, you impotent baggage carrier!" The Husbands stumbled to their feet.

Phaedryn took no notice, gently smoothing the folds of Slipfit's ragged jacket and straightening his cap. Ned's gold ring fell from where it had caught in a fold of his sleeve. Phaedryn stooped and took it up.

"Touch him not, Phaedryn! Come away!" The Meg stamped her tiny foot.

Holding the ring in her hand, Phaedryn rose and turned cold eyes on her mother. "He was my father. I will honor him."

The Meg gasped. "Ungrateful Elf-spawn! How dare you talk that way to your mother!"

"Mother, be quiet!" Phaedryn turned to the Husbands. "Mourn the best of Elfdom, Elves! His devotion to the Meghood was greater than his devotion to his wife. Spurned by his own kind, my father found a family with the Human witch, Cyna. He has given his life for Cyna. It is in the highest tradition of Husbands and Fathers to sacrifice themselves for their family. Who among you is as brave, as deserving of the title 'Husband'?"

The Husbands stood and bowed their heads. "Take him up gently, Fathers. Let us bear him to the pyre still hot from The Wizard's passing. When the coals have cooled, we will help him in death as we never helped him in life. There he will make his final passage." She began to sing The Mourning Song, her clear golden voice broken with emotion. Silently and with great care, the Husbands lifted Slipfit and carried him up the stony path. Even The Meg followed, choking back her tears.

Ur Logga helped Ruf as he gently carried Cyna to her tent.

While the Elves attended Slipfit, the Other leaders met by the river in front of Cyna's tent.

"Benare and Adler are faithful to The Five Tribes. They ride in pursuit of Ned's traitors," Ruf reported. "They plan to ride straight to Elea, for Benare believes Ned will make for The Perime. But the lords' ranks are riddled with New Faithers. Farryl, Holbein, Bombaleur—more than half of them ride with the traitor. Who could have believed that so many were rotten? Sorry, Lord Landes, but that's the word that comes to my mind."

"Rotten it is, Ruf. And my own son is the worst."

"I must prepare to ride south," observed Ur Logga. "The rest of my cousin's tribe lives there. I must try to find them."

"Your Majesty, that's madness!" Landes exclaimed. "The mountain passes are crawling with trolls. Mati Redcloak maintains his forces there."

"I have no quarrel with rebellious trolls."

"They may have a quarrel with you," The Snaefid observed. "That charming Honor Guard of yours is no match for a troop of angry trolls. You'll be combing each other's hair while they fill you with arrows. I think you need Dwarfin protection. It's been many years since I saw Fensdown Plain."

Pale and exhausted, Cyna stepped out from the tent. Ur Logga helped her to a seat beside the fire. "I'm coming also," she said.

"No, Mistress." The Snaefid shook his head. "You have

been injured. And it will be dangerous. You must stay here and tend the Sanctuary until Ned's been caught and all this settled. Remain safe."

"Safe?" said Cyna bleakly. "Our world is crumbling, Snaefid. How can I expect to remain safe? Nyal travels to Fensdown Plain. I have foreseen a great battle there. I must find him and warn him."

"Foreseen?" Ruf repeated, looking at her closely.

"Don't be silly, Cyna," Landes said with an air of finality. "You'll stay here with me until you're well enough to travel." He raised a finger to his own temple, in the same spot where she had been hurt, and cocked an eyebrow at the Others.

"He's right, Cyna," Finn said. "You mustn't upset yourself."

"Of course," she said after a moment. "You're right." No one found it strange that she agreed so easily.

Ur Logga reached out in Ogre fashion to touch his companions' hair. "The Death of Magic," he said softly. "The Splintering of The Five Tribes. Who would have believed they would cause so much pain?"

"Dying is difficult, I suppose," Landes said.

"No," said Cyna, her eyes searching the distant peaks of the Trollurgh Mountains. "Dying is easy, I think. Living by The Law is difficult."

As the sky darkened, Cyna felt stronger and climbed the path to witness Slipfit's funeral fire. She held on to her father's arm, her head pounding dully. When it was her turn, she lit a slender torch and cast it into the blaze. "Farewell, little friend."

The wind was rising. The day was dull grey and an occasional snowflake fell, making the coals hiss and steam. Cyna circled the coals and crossed to the tower steps, where Ruf stood with the mad girl. "You must not stay here with me, Ruf Nab," she told him. "Rejoin your tribe and give The Snaefid your help."

The mad girl gazed up at Cyna. "I certainly won't stay with you, either," she said, "and I would rather not return to my uncle, for I have never liked him. I will find Nyal of Crowell, who has asked to marry me."

"You can talk!" Cyna said in astonishment.

"But I won't talk to you. You are truly a wicked witch," Melloryth said. "You had that nice old man killed and burned just because he freed me from your spell."

"Ruf, can we find someone to care for this one? She's better, at last, but she's still too mad to wander free. She might harm herself."

"You will never capture me again," said Melloryth. She turned and ran to the stairs. With a sigh, Ruf started after her.

In her tent Cyna packed her extra cloak and the herb chest.

"The pony's back," Ruf announced later that night. "You should keep him here with you. I've tied him up securely this time so he can't run off again."

BOOK FIVE

"Lothen,

"The most dangerous time lies before us, for now we need to destroy Magic to conquer Morbihan. My trusted disciple Nedryk knows the risks and has undertaken to try to kill Fallon. If that is done successfully, he will join you in the south."

Lothen folded the letter and placed it inside his breastplate, next to his skin. Smoke obscured the horizon, but the warmth of the blaze attracted him. He favored the full armor of The Perime regulars and insisted that The Tyrant's Guards, the finest soldiers of The Perime, wear it also. But in Morbihan's chill winds the armor felt cold and he had come to enjoy a good fire.

The Eacon was too cautious, Lothen thought, not a true man of The Vorsai. He spoke of "if" and "try" as though he were frightened of the powers of demons and old men. Ned was stronger, daring more action. When Lothen next spoke with The Tyrant, he would make his observations known.

Fensdown Plain was quiet but for the sounds of burning. Too quiet! His eyes were keen and he saw nothing out of place in the army before him. "Roth Feura," he greeted his lieutenant and mounted his horse. The lords were scattered and ignorant of danger. The Others . . . he spat in disgust. This was a boring campaign, a waste of disciplined troops, chasing farmers. There was no one in Morbihan, no one in all the Outer Isles, who could put an army into the field to face him.

Chapter 38

Cyna left for Fensdown Plain in the dead of night, while her father and the rest were still sleeping. She meant to travel alone, but after several miles a familiar whinny made her turn around. Bihan trotted after her, his milk-white tail streaming behind him. She called his name, holding out her hand to him. He laid back his ears as he approached, arching his neck and bucking joyously.

"Whoa now!" she said sternly, stepping back. "Behave yourself."

But the tiny spotted pony continued to frolic, arching his neck as he trotted beside her, snapping his pearly teeth. Yet he was gentle enough when she paused to tie her herb box and sack of clothing to his back. She rested at midday, eating sparingly of bread and Dwarfish sausage. Bihan sighed contentedly as she scratched his ears and that night he slept standing close to her like a black-and-white sentinel in the darkness.

She felt a new freedom as she traveled the wide trail through the Harkyn and her dread of what she faced faded. Although the path always wound upward toward the mountains, she walked boldly, the pony trotting beside her.

Late the next day, she came across a weathered old inn, grown shabby with the years. The innkeeper, who rarely saw anyone but Peskie traders, set out a great feast of heavy, dense loaves of hot acorn bread and a spicy shalk stew for his only guest. He sat with her, eager for news of the outside world.

"What can you tell me of the trolls?" Cyna asked. "Are they of The Old Faith?"

"No, not even of The New Faith," he laughed. "They live with the old gods of the sky and mountains. And they eat horseflesh. Peskies trade with them, and for a price they let the caravans through. They're as fast as horses and they've noses like bloodhounds." He paused in his drinking. "You know, my great-grandmother was not a Human at all, but a wild mountain girl. Half-Elf, half-troll, they say." He wagged his ears in a startling way and winked at Cyna. "If anybody could deal with them, I can. But I'd rather take my chances with New Faith Brownie Roasts than spend a minute with a troll."

"You may have your chance," Cyna said. "I have the Gift of prophecy, and I have foreseen that a great battle is coming. I believe it is between New and Old Faith."

As Cyna spoke, his wide face melted with amusement. Burping softly, he smiled at her. "If it's prophecy that you're seeing, good luck to you. If it's going to be the end of everything, we might's well enjoy it while we got it," he said, and burped again. "To tell the truth, there's not much to end up here. Nothing the world will miss."

When Cyna left the inn the next morning, she kept an attentive eye out and traveled as swiftly as she could. Bihan trotted at her side, a steady companion. As the land rose toward the mountains, the forest thinned. She was walking through rolling foothills, thick in gorse and heather when she saw the first troll.

The pony snorted at the scent and stopped, nostrils flaring. The troll stood silhouetted against the sky on the top of a hill. A slender figure, his hair was long, tied back with a thong. A dark fur covered his shoulders and he carried a bow in his left hand. He stood for a moment, then was gone. Later, when the pony snorted again, Cyna knew the trolls followed her.

On the third morning of her journey, she awoke in predawn gloom, prodded into wakefulness by the keen edge of a sword at her throat. An Elf stood over her, but he lacked the docile smile of appeasement she was used to attributing to the males of that tribe. His teeth were clenched, his lips

urled in a sneer of hatred. He prodded her again with the
lade of his short sword.

"Up, Human woman! Slowly!" Two fellow trolls stood
ust behind him. One was also Elfin, the other Peskie, an
rrow nocked in his bow. All three were skinny and raggedly
ressed. Hunger had carved deep lines of desperation on
heir faces.

She rose slowly, made awkward by the sword at her throat.
ven though the Elves were tall for their kind, they came only
o her shoulder. "Are you Mati Redcloak? I wish only to pass
rough your country to Fensdown Plain on the other side. I
ill give you whatever I have if you let me pass."

The blade at her throat never wavered. "Tie her!" the
ader ordered his fellows. "Mati will decide what to do with
er. What's this?" He kicked open the herb box that lay on
e ground beside Cyna's cloak. Precious herbs were caught
y the fresh morning breeze and scattered across the ground.

The Peskie and the smaller Elf roughly seized her arms,
ut she felt no fear. These were not the horsemen she had
en in her visions. With a cry, she shook them off and
ulled herself to her full height. "I am Cyna, Healer, daugh-
er of Lord Landes. I read your future as well as my own,
roll. I shall not die at your hands! But your own life will be
hort and miserable unless you free me!"

With a swift blow of his hand, the Peskie pushed her. At
e same time, the Elf behind her kicked at the back of her
nee and with a cry, she abruptly sat down, more surprised
an hurt. "Tie her!" the Elfin leader repeated. "And catch
at horse. We'll have horse steaks for dinner tonight!" They
ere rough, pushing Cyna ahead of them along the narrow
ountain trail. Bihan was surprisingly easy to catch and he
llowed docilely behind, led firmly by the Peskie troll.

They came upon the encampment after several hours of
eady climbing. High near the top of the pass, snow had set-
ed in deep drifts. A few tents took what shelter they could
om the overhanging lip of a great ledge. They were battered,
eathered structures that had once been Elfin gossamer, but
ow were patched with animal skins and tree branches. Like
e trolls, the camp had a look of wasted exhaustion.

At the center of the ragged cluster was a tent with a flap

strung in the front of it like a small porch roof. There stood
fair Elf wrapped in a wolfskin. Cyna knew instantly he w
Mati by his red cloak and the strong resemblance to H
mother and sister. Light hair cascaded down his back, he
back by a leather thong. He was perfectly proportioned, b
like his companions he looked wasted and thin. Dark sha
ows circled his eyes. They were bright green like h
mother's and haunted by the same sadness. He held on to
pole before the tent's entrance as though without it he wou
fall. "What is this?" he asked.

The taller of the Elves bowed low. "A fat horse for dinn
and a Human woman, Majesty."

"The horse is welcome. Who's the woman?"

Cyna stepped forward. "I am Cyna of Fanstock. I was
friend of your father's, Mati. I have an urgent errand th
takes me through your mountains . . ." She broke c
abruptly as Mati sagged and collapsed, falling senseless
the snow before the tent. The taller Elf knelt in the snow b
side him, cradling Mati's head in his arms.

"Untie me!" Cyna commanded. "I may be able to he
him. I'm a Healer trained by Fallon." Bihan whinnied a
nodded his head.

"Untie her," the taller troll said to the Peskie. "What ha
can it do now?"

As the troll untied Cyna with trembling fingers, the rest c
ried Mati into the tent. Inside, it was surprisingly warm. T
belongings were weathered and worn, the air dark with a th
smoke from a small fire in the center. A ragged group
Peskies and Elves clustered by the fire, some too weak
stand. Their green and amber eyes observed Cyna's entran
with no surprise, only the dull-eyed look of hunger past cari

"What has happened to you all?" Cyna demanded.

"The caravans haven't returned from Fensdown Plain," t
tall Elf said. He was grey with exhaustion as he knelt besi
Mati's still form. "We always allowed them to travel into t
Plain freely, then extracted a toll of food and hides and me
goods as they returned. Four caravans have passed us, b
none have returned. We have been without food or suppl:
for weeks. We are dying."

Cyna moved swiftly, checking Mati's pulse, peeling ba

an eyelid to examine his green irises. "Go at once to where you found me. Bring back the box you were so rude as to kick over. And don't touch that pony!" she added as the troll rose to do her bidding. "He's not going to be your dinner!"

Before her, Mati lay near death. His pulse was feeble and irregular, his breathing shallow. *Nay, Elf-Prince,* she thought, *don't fail me now! I need you and your little band of friends.* Beneath the thick wolf pelt, his hands and feet were ice-cold. Cyna rubbed them gently and felt a sudden heat spring to her hands. She threw off her cloak and rested both hands on his shoulders. "You must awaken, Mati," she said. "Awaken and heal."

She closed her eyes and felt her eyelids flutter, felt energy and strength coursing down her arms. For a frightening moment she was afraid she would faint, afraid that another vision was falling upon her. She breathed deeply and felt the heat from her hands warming the skin of his shoulders. She remained motionless for several minutes. When the feeling of energy and purpose passed, she opened her eyes. Mati Redcloak stared back at her, his face flushed with color. "Hello," she said and smiled.

The tall Elf returned with the herb box, but the carefully cherished compartments were empty, the herbs blown away by the harsh wind.

"What food have you left?" Cyna asked him.

"Only a few roots and some dried berries," the Elf said.

"Put your biggest pot on to boil," she ordered. "Slice up your remaining roots. And take heart," she added. "There's no end here unless you wish it!"

In the bottom of the herb box was a cleverly hidden compartment. From it she pulled a long length of Dwarfish sausage and a bag of Ogre porridge which she had brought from Kythra's Sanctuary. Mindful of their shrunken stomachs, she made a gruel with a little porridge and roots for the weaker trolls. She sliced small chunks of sausage for the stronger ones. While the gruel cooked, she went from troll to troll, touching each gently with her hands, letting the heat of her body flow into theirs, marveling even as they did at the sudden burst of strength and energy she was able to give each one.

"Who are you?" Mati asked as she spoon-fed porridge to a

bandy-legged young Dwarf who held the edge of the bowl
with one hand as though she might snatch it away.

"Cyna of Fanstock. I was once Fallon's apprentice. I am a
Healer and I travel to Fensdown Plain to warn Nyal of Crowell that there will be a great battle there."

"A battle!" Mati exclaimed. "So why do you travel alone?
Aren't you afraid?"

Cyna dabbed the Dwarf's lips with a cloth. She smiled
ruefully. "I travel alone because no one believes my prophecies except Fallon, and he's dead. I've been a betrayer of
Magic, Elf-Prince. I'm a creature of The Dracoon."

"The Dracoon?"

So Cyna began at the beginning and told him all that had
happened. When she finished, the night had given way to the
thin light of early morning. Trolls of both sexes crowded
within the tent, listening gravely as they savored remnants of
their meal. They were from all Tribes except Human, all
ragged, thin, and young. When she told of her brother's
treachery and Slipfit's death, Mati's cheeks colored and his
green eyes filled.

"Come with me to Fensdown Plain," she said when she
had finished.

At first light, the trolls broke camp. The porridge was finished and they boiled the remaining roots, dividing the
sausage among them. Mati sent scouts ahead, young Peskie
who quickly outpaced the main troop. Cyna walked beside
Mati in the vanguard, flanked and protected by Handyl and
Syrd, who had captured her the day before. Their spirits were
high. Mati knew the mountainous terrain and was a gentle
but strong leader. His followers obeyed him instantly, their
eyes following him with an expression which Cyna had seen
on puppies following Nyal about the stable at Crowell.

Bihan became a great favorite of the young trolls, although at first there had been some grumbling when Mati ex-
pressly forbade anyone to eat him. The pony's sharp teeth
and arrogant disposition quickly won the trolls' respect,
while his persistence in following them up the steep, twisting
trails over the mountain won their hearts. The climb was difficult and the descent even more perilous, for the path clung

o the side of a precipitous cliff. Snow lay over the trail, blown away in spots to reveal blue ice. Cyna clung to what handholds she could find and blindly followed the trolls in front of her. One misjudgment or unexpected gust of wind could tear any of them from the path to a sudden death on the rocks below.

As it grew dark, the scouts returned to tell Mati that the passes ahead of them were choked with snow, but passable by daylight. They were forced to camp where they were, hungry and wrapped in cloaks as they clung to the narrow path that zigzagged across the face of the cliff. The cutting wind awoke Cyna during the night and she was comforted to find Bihan standing above her, his tail turned to the wind, snoring gently.

They made Fensdown Plain late in the morning, reveling in the comparative warmth of the lowlands. A fog hung over the Plain and the snow of the night before was melting off. Mati sent trolls ahead to scout for supplies.

"How can they see?" asked Cyna, peering into the heavy mist.

"They can't," Mati replied, "but they can hear. They're good fellows; they'll find something for us to eat. If I remember correctly, this road passes a large farm a few miles down the road. Perhaps there we'll hear news of the caravans or of Nyal."

The thought of a warm hearth cheered Cyna as nothing had in weeks. A few miles' walk and she thought she caught the smell of burned wood. The smell became stronger, hanging in the damp air. The scouts returned, huddling with Mati, whispering, casting worried glances in the direction from which they'd come. The vanguard pressed forward until round the edge of a hill they came upon the farm. It had been as large as her home in Fanstock, but now no warm farmhouse welcomed them. Cyna could see by the expanse it had covered that the fortified buildings had been a large and prosperous farm, but now only charred timbers loomed up against the grey sky.

"How terrible!" Cyna exclaimed, standing with Mati beside the blackened beams.

"Where are the farmers?" Mati muttered, almost to him
self. "And the livestock?"

"Perhaps they've been taken in by neighbors," Cyna sug
gested.

"Perhaps," Mati agreed. "Keep an eye out, now," he or
dered his trolls. "Don't straggle."

Bihan walked beside Cyna, his ears pricked, alertly sur
veying the countryside.

A thin morning sun gave the landscape a disquieting glow
The sun grew stronger, shredding the fog into patches. Ther
was no sign of the scouts. "Close ranks!" Mati barked. "Cyn
faire, Phastro, I want you to scout ahead. Follow those hors
tracks along the road, but be cautious. Let no one see you
We follow, but slowly."

Cynfaire and Phastro nodded grimly and melted into th
bushes by the side of the road. "I have a bad feeling," Mat
said.

The air had cleared enough to show that the road followe
close to the banks of a river, winding through hilly meadow
and patches of woodland. Cyna had never heard a silence s
complete. There were no voices of insects or birds, only th
muted sounds of the trolls' passage.

By midday the scouts had not returned and Mati sent tw
more off to find them. "I don't like this at all," he muttered
He led them off the road toward a woodlot that crowned
nearby hill. "You should ride, it's faster," he told Cyna
"Where's the pony?" But Bihan was gone again.

At the top of the hill, Mati posted guards and set lookouts
They spent the rest of the afternoon nervously watching th
road.

Fog again shrouded the hill at dusk. There was no sign o
the scouts or Bihan. The puzzled party lit no fires that nigh
They finished the last of their sausage and slept fitfully, fre
quently changing the guard.

Cyna awoke at dawn. She lay huddled beneath her cloak
cold and stiff from sleeping on the ground. The only sound
were the snores of the trolls and the drip of moisture from
trees and rocks. A soft whinny reached her from somewher
in the mist.

"Bihan," she murmured, rising to her feet. She stepped over the somnolent bodies of Mati and his retainers to the edge of the wood. The meadow before her was still. A guard held his finger to his lips and she nodded, stepping silently out of the covering trees into the open meadow. The rising sun glowed through the cloud cover like a large, dim lantern.

Another whinny reached her. She followed the sound. Her skirt made a soft rustling sound as it brushed the dead grass of the meadow. She walked toward a small grove of trees at the foot of the hill, avoiding the patches of snow on the ground. She was almost at the wood when she saw a flash of movement in the corner of her eye. A black-and-white dot gleamed on a nearby hill. Lost for a moment in fog, it emerged again and she recognized Bihan racing toward her. She whistled to him. Then the whinny sounded again from the wood just in front of her. She turned.

Almost hidden from sight, a group of horses stood tethered to low-hanging tree limbs. Behind them lounged armed men. Even before they turned toward her in surprise, she knew they would be holding black shields. Panic fluttered in her throat.

A high-pitched grating sound filled her head as they drew their swords. She fought the impulse to turn and flee as the men ran toward her. They formed a half circle about her, the sun's dull light gleaming from their sword tips, their faces twisted in cruel marvel at finding her here. She lifted her arms toward them, glad to feel the energy of prophecy begin to vibrate in her body. She closed her eyes, summoning Falon's words, CHANGE THE CAUSE . . . CHANGE EVEN THE INTENTION . . . *I will not run, not scream,* she thought. *I will defy the prophecy.*

A blow spun her around. A black-and-white fury was beside her, teeth bared, black hooves flashing. Bihan bit the sword arm of the nearest soldier, wheeled and kicked another. The man roared in pain and sprawled in the snow.

"Get on!" Bihan said, his voice an excited squeal.

Cyna stared, openmouthed. "What?" she gasped.

"Get on! Get on!" the pony whinnied angrily. "Must you always question everything?"

He kicked out at a black shield and snapped viciously.

Cyna threw herself onto his back and wrapped her arms around his tiny neck. He leaped over a fallen soldier and raced up the hill. The armed horsemen thundered behind them but Bihan's legs were a blur and he burst into the troll camp shouting, "Help! Wake up! Help!"

Already aroused by the commotion, the trolls stood ready. A swarm of arrows flew from the wood and the Human soldiers beat a retreat.

"Stand fast now! We'll fight them off!" Mati shouted.

"We haven't a chance in this wood!" Bihan trumpeted, prancing excitedly in a circle. He paused before her. "Cyna! Remember your visions! What did you see?"

Strangely calm, she closed her eyes and let the memory of the visions sweep over her. "I see an old fort . . . a standing stone . . ."

Bihan arched his neck and bared his teeth at Mati. "The witch sees the old fort at Dunn Naire! Go, quickly! We can travel through the woods."

The trolls gaped at the talking pony.

"Hurry," Cyna pleaded. "Do as he says!"

They moved swiftly, reaching the bank of the Longhile River and following it southward. The thick growth of trees slowed the horsemen's progress and Cyna felt a surge of hope. Bihan was everywhere, leading them forward, pushing them from behind. A score of trolls wore the bright semicircular marks of his teeth and ran as much in fear of the shouting, demanding pony as of the Black Shields who pursued them.

At last they came to Dunn Naire, where the Longhile emptied into the Straits of Kythra. The ancient, round fort stood on a high cliff overlooking the sea. Crossing a narrow, crumbling spit of land, they closed the fort's weathered gate behind them and fell to reinforcing it with branches and decrepit furniture.

"It will never hold!" Mati groaned.

"The approach is narrow, they can attack only one at a time," Bihan panted. "Fill them full of arrows as they get to the gate, then pull the arrows out and use them over again. You don't need Magic for this, young man, only common sense."

Breathing heavily from the long chase, Cyna watched the spotted pony and the troll argue.

"How is it that you speak?" Mati demanded. "And what's going to happen?"

"I speak when I have something to say," the pony snapped, his velvety lips curling carefully around the words, as though he were speaking a foreign language. "And what do you think I am, a fortune-teller?"

Cyna sank to her knees before the small horse. "Master Fallon!" she exclaimed. "I thought you were dead! I lit the pyre myself!"

Chapter 39

Nyal turned off the rutted mountain road and spurred up the slope toward the mouth of The Old Girl's cave. He knew the lords were only hours behind him, for he occasionally glimpsed the flash of Ned's banner far below on the zigzag road. Avelaer was exhausted, his explosive energy worn down to numb-legged struggle. Yet that was not why Nyal stopped here. He stopped for Brandon. It was the custom in winter deaths to wait until spring to climb the mountain to announce the warrior's passing. Brandon had never been given a Leave-Taking, and without it his spirit could not sit in the Hall of The Dragon. And only next of kin could perform the ceremony.

Near the entrance of the cave, Nyal tied Avelaer to a tree and walked the last yards. The banners left from Telerhyde's Leave-Taking were frayed and faded from the long winter. Wet snow choked the narrow trail, but the flat stones in front of the entrance were warm and the foul steam of The Dragon's breath issued forth from the dark entrance.

Nyal knelt on the warm stone. He did not know the sacred words. What fell from his lips was a jumbled litany. He told The Dragon that Brandon had been murdered. That he died foully but still a warrior in a battle that raged silently with an unknown enemy. That evil had befallen Morbihan, that stealth had replaced courage, treachery had replaced honesty.

He raged and he was glad to be alone, for he also wept. So intense became his feelings that he had lost all sense of time when he heard Avelaer snort a warning.

Three men on horseback blocked the trail behind him. He rose, swearing at himself for being a careless and sentimental fool. Already their swords were drawn. He had barely time to draw his own, no time to reach Avelaer. He recognized Faryll and Combin as they rode straight at him.

Ducking under Faryll's first blow, he threw a handful of dust and pebbles into the face of his horse. The beast shied away. Combin loomed above Nyal, shouting curses and swinging his heavy sword. Nyal parried, moving to his right, away from the horseman's shield to attack Combin's sword. The third horseman charged toward them at a gallop and Nyal struggled to retreat to the shelter of the cave entrance.

Faryll rejoined the fight, cutting him off. Attacked on both sides, Nyal stumbled on a loose stone and fell, sprawling helplessly on the rocks. Faryll bent low over his horse's neck to give the final deathblow. In midswing, without warning, he gave a hoarse cry and fell beside Nyal. The man was dead, his spirit fled, before he touched the ground. Nyal rolled to his feet, whirling to face the other horsemen.

"Sir, to your horse!" a familiar voice shouted.

Nyal recognized the third horseman as he parried Combin's sword. "Tym!" he shouted.

"Treachery!" Combin screamed as Nyal cut him down.

"To your horse!" the groom repeated. "The rest are not far behind!"

Nyal caught Faryll's charger and vaulted on. He led Avelaer behind him, glad that for once the chestnut was too weary to challenge another stallion. Tym led Combin's horse and they hurried, single file, up the twisting road. It felt good to Nyal to ride in a saddle again.

The road turned downward, following the banks of the Longhile River. Here waterfalls and cataracts churned the river until the water turned white. Over the river's roar, Tym told Nyal how he had become Lord Norsea and ridden in the lords' vanguard. As the road leveled and the rapids quieted, Nyal related the strange voice he'd heard in the ship's hold and of his decision to come to Fensdown Plain. They were on the Plain now, moving at a brisk pace down a gently rolling road.

"We'll go straight to Rathmere's Manor," Nyal told Tym. "He'll know of the trolls' doings and keep us safe for as long as we need." Nyal rose to his feet, standing in the stirrups, fist clenched triumphantly over his head.

But a mile later, the smell of charred wood reached them. On either side of the road, not a bird chirped or creature stirred. Tym glanced nervously around him, his hair prickling at the back of his neck.

" 'Tis strange," he said.

The first house they saw was the home of one of Rathmere's tenants. Nyal might have missed it but for the flash of motion of a single, tailless chicken which pecked in the bare ground that had once been a barnyard.

"Burned to the ground," Tym observed. "That's what we smelled."

Nyal shook his head. "These ashes are old. See, there's a vine growing up from them." Nyal remounted, concern replacing the elation he felt an hour before.

Rathmere's farm was a rubble, the great house a blackened pit in the ground. Searching the burned timbers of the barn, Nyal found the remains of Rathmere and his family.

"Is there no one here to bury their dead?" Tym wondered out loud. Shaken, they left the exposed valley of Rathmere's Manor and concealed themselves in the wood that grew along the crest of the nearby hills. There Tym saddled Avelaer, careful to smooth out the sweat-soaked blanket of the strange saddle. He was so happy to be back with Nyal that he hardly minded when Avelaer halfheartedly nipped his arm. "Where to, sir?"

"Hafelmajor the horse dealer lives across the valley. We'll go there."

The smell of burned wood grew stronger and Nyal knew what he would find even before they skirted the steep hill that once sheltered Hafelmajor's horse farm.

"The Final Days have come to Fensdown," Nyal murmured.

"Sir, let's run for the coast." Tym's voice was muted with dread. "It's not too late to find another ship and . . ."

Something moved on the nearby hillside and with a cry Nyal was off. When Tym caught up with him, he held a raggedly dressed Elf at sword point. Blood ran from a gash in the Other's arm. A short sword lay at his feet.

"Kill me, you thieving murderer!" the Elf raged. "You'll get nothing from me! Mati and the witch will have their revenge on you!"

"Let me kill him, sir," Tym said, sliding from his horse. "You shouldn't have to bother with trolls."

"Wait," Nyal said. The point of Firestroker was pressed hard at the Elf's throat. "Is it your kind that have done this?"

Tears sprang to the Elf's eyes but his back stiffened and he thrust out his jaw. "Just kill me, Human, don't jest at me! I know it's you and your Black Shields who have wasted this land."

Nyal eased the pressure of the sword. "I am Nyal of Crowell, Elflet. Where have you seen the Black Shields?"

The troll's voice rose an octave and color rose again to his face. "Nyal of Crowell! The witch told of you!" He fell to his knees before Nyal, then thought better of it and rose to embrace him. "The witch Cyna seeks you!"

They sat on the wet hillside above the ruin of Hafelmajor's horse farm while Phastro the troll told Nyal and Tym how he had come to be there.

"Cyna has come to Fensdown Plain," Nyal mused when the troll had finished.

"Oh, sir, she's a wonderful witch!" Phastro gushed. "She healed Mati of a wasting sickness and saved all of us. And she's followed everywhere by a magical black-and-white horse!"

"The Black Shields," Nyal pressed. "What do you know of them?"

"I found an Ogre," Phastro gestured toward the east. "He's hiding in an old bear cave, poor fellow, with a family of Human farmers. They told me that shortly after news of Telerhyde's murder reached Fensdown Plain, a few outlying farms were raided and burned down. There were no survivors to tell what happened, and everyone assumed that trolls had come down from the mountains. We didn't do it, sir! I swear to you, on my mother's life!"

"I believe you," nodded Nyal. "Go on."

"A rumor started that local Ogres and Peskies had joined forces with the mountain trolls. Local farmers banded together to rid the countryside of the Others."

"Fools! How could they do that?" Tym was outraged.

The Ogre had told how a merchant from The Perime struck a bargain with Hafelmajor. The merchant would buy all the Ogres and other predators they could supply. At first many of the farmers were reluctant to join, but the profits were great. Rathmere spoke against it, but suddenly he was killed and his manor burned. Ogres were blamed. The outrage was great and all the farmers of Fensdown Plain joined in a great Brownie hunt. Because the farmers feared that the Lords of the North would disapprove, the policy was kept secret. By the time they realized they had falsely blamed the Others, it was too late.

"When the generous merchant came to pay them, he brought with him the Black Shields instead of money. The farmers were raided, burned and pillaged. The few survivors became refugees, begging the Others to protect them. They say that New Faithers are coming over the sea to settle on the farms along the coast."

Tym bit his lip. "It's The Final Days, it is for sure."

Nyal struck a hand with his fist. "It's treachery and murder, that's what it is! Who leads the Black Shields?"

"He is called Lothen the Terrible."

"The turd who attacked us!" Tym exclaimed.

"How many men has Lothen?" Nyal demanded.

"Hundreds, I think, possibly more," the troll said. "I've not seen them all together to make a judgment."

"How many trolls follow your king?"

"Ninety-seven, sir. Each with short sword and bow."

Tym shook his head. "There's no fight there, if that's what you're thinking, sir. It's field mice against tom cats."

"Dragon Fire!" Nyal swore. "Are there no farmers left?"

A strange look came over Phastro's face. "Hush! Beg your pardon sir, but listen!" He held his hands in the air.

A chilling howl reached their ears. Phastro threw back his head and replied with a similar howl of his own. A few minutes later an exhausted Elf panted up the hill. Phastro ran to

greet him, hugging him, lifting him high in the air. "Cynfaire! I thought you were dead!"

"Nay," said Cynfaire after introductions had been made.
"But we'll all be dead if we don't get out of here. There's
horsemen on all the roads!"

"Can you lead us to where the troll force is camped?"
Nyal demanded.

"In a snowstorm at midnight!" Cynfaire boasted.

Chapter 40

Dunn Naire stood on a headland with its back to the sea.
Less than a mile inland, the standing stone known as Argontell—"The Great Knife"—towered from the summit of a
small hill. Between them the ground sloped down across a
stony, gorse-grown meadow to the banks of the Longhile
River. The river was narrow here, and the current was swift,
raging as though frantic at being pinched so tightly by the
land. Even in the normally dry summer months, there was no
ford at this place, no way to cross the river. So while the fort
and Argontell were within eyeshot of each other, they were
actually separated by several days' journey.

Although the fort was huge, Argontell's mass dwarfed it,
dominating everything in sight. Heavy with legends, it had
loomed over the plain for centuries. According to the Ogres,
Kythra and The Founders of The Five Tribes had raised Argontell from the riverbank to its place on the hill at the very
first Stone Moving.

At the fort, Cyna sat on the top of the outer ramparts wall,
hands locked around her knees. Bihan paced close by her, his
flinty hooves making sharp sounds on the stones. The first
attack of the Black Shields brought Cyna to her feet, her
hand gripping the pony's mane as he tossed his head defiantly and shouted encouragement to the troll archers.

If the Black Shields were startled that a small black-and-
white horse commanded the defenses of the fort, they gave

no sign. They had performed a New Faith ritual, burning effigies of their enemies and chanting their terrible cry, before they rode toward the fort. Now they hurled lances, probing, testing the wall. The trolls were disorganized, used to ambushes and skirmishes on open ground rather than the defense of a fort, and they shot their arrows randomly.

"They shouldn't shoot at any old thing that catches their eye!" Bihan scolded Mati when the attackers had withdrawn. "They must wait for a signal, then release their arrows all at once at an agreed upon target." Mati conveyed The Wizard's wishes to his troops and they nervously awaited the enemy's next move. It was not long in coming.

The Black Shields attacked two abreast, whooping and yelling across the stony field. As the ground narrowed, they neatly switched to single file and thundered toward Dunn Naire's rickety gate, broadaxes swinging. The trolls were massed atop the wall, arrows nocked. They stood quivering, awaiting Mati's command.

"Now," said Bihan as the first rider was a horse length from the wall.

"Shoot!" Mati cried.

The effect was devastating. Both horse and rider bristled with arrows. The horse fell thrashing before the gate, the rider slumped beside him. The second horseman was upon them before the archers could renock. The horse reared high, shying away from its dead companion. The horseman swung his broadax at the gate and the old wood splintered under the blow, leather hinges tearing.

"Again!" Bihan said.

"Shoot!" Mati screamed over the shouts and cries of the trolls.

Horse and rider tumbled down the steep slope, end over end, into the ragged surf below. The trolls cheered.

"Heads up! Heads up!" the pony shouted. "Here they come!"

A third horse and rider crumpled before the gate and the Black Shields withdrew. For an hour they galloped their horses back and forth, playing a game of nerves, but never coming within range of the quick, stone-tipped arrows of the trolls.

Mati checked with his men. "We've about five arrows

apiece," he reported to Bihan. "Four or five more charges, that's it."

The pony shook his head. "More than we need for now. Look!" Well out of arrow shot, the Black Shields were making camp. Tents sprang up and Cyna could clearly see the long rope to which they tethered their horses. "It's a siege. They mean to starve us out."

"And well they might," Cyna said. "We've no supplies left."

But a few trolls slipped through the gate while their fellows stood guard on the fort wall. They recovered the arrows which had not been lost or splintered, then set about butchering the horse carcasses that lay before the gate. The corpses of the men were left before the gate as a warning not to trifle with trolls.

The inside of the fort had been used as a holding pen for cows and sheep by the farmer who had owned the land. Now the trolls gathered the dried animal dung, built a fire, and spitted horsemeat roasts over it. As evening grew into night the diminutive warriors jested and told each other repeatedly how well they had performed during the attack. A frenzied good cheer hung in the air.

Bihan watched, his pale blue eyes pensive. Beyond the walls, the fires of the Black Shields blazed, illuminating their camp. The sound of hundreds of voices chanting the name of The Vorsai kept up a steady, nerve-shattering rhythm. At the edge of the meadow, New Faith sentries patrolled with torches.

"Will we be saved, Master Fallon?" Cyna asked when the moon had risen and seemed to balance on the top of Argontell.

"I don't know," the pony replied gently. "But Magic is alive here, Cyna. Don't you feel it?"

Cyna did. Despite the smoke and mist, the landscape glowed with a strange light. The air was fairly crackling with energy.

"How is it that you live, Master?" she asked. "Fallon the Shapechanger was killed. I lit his pyre myself."

Bihan's soft lips formed the words carefully. "Believe me, I was as surprised as you. I had been in and out of this pony and the wolf for weeks, keeping an eye on you, Nyal, and that little Elf. And Bihan has always been one of my favorite creations. So when Ned struck me, I reached for him even as I fell. And in that instant, he was there! My body was ruined as you saw. I couldn't go back. So I'm stuck here, in this little horse. I lost my Gift even as it saved my life."

Cyna remembered Ned's cold, expressionless face and reached up to touch her bruised and swollen temple. "Ned must be mad," she said, shuddering.

"He always needed to excel, you know."

"He's excelled in hate."

"Yes. Well, we all make choices," Bihan sighed, although to Cyna it sounded more like a grunt. "He learned to hate where some of us have learned to love and rejoice, right here in Morbihan. But how is it that *you* live, Mistress?" he asked, his horse lips curving up in what might have been a smile.

"I'm not sure," Cyna replied. "In dreams I saw the Black Shields so often, so vividly, just as it was yesterday, yet . . ."

"Yet like me, you mastered your Gift, so you live a while longer."

"Mastered my Gift?" She shook her head, her eyes as dark as the night around them. "I've mastered nothing. Perhaps Kythra had visions—*I* have nightmares. Sometimes they happen, sometimes they don't. They rule me. They keep me from sleep. How can I master that?"

"Oh, Cyna." She clearly heard Fallon's tones in the pony's odd high-pitched voice. "I wish I were a better teacher. You have always looked for solutions outside of Magic, outside of yourself. You healed Ruf, and praised the herbs. You predicted an eclipse, and praised your figures. You thought to save Nyal through politics and violence." The little horse laid back his ears and shook his head in frustration. "What will it take for you to understand?"

She was silent.

"But you are doing better, aren't you?" His nostrils flared, but he quieted, speaking in a gentler tone. "You changed your destiny and the destiny of Morbihan when you lived through that attack yesterday. But you still don't understand the whys and hows of it." He tossed his head with urgency.

"All Gifts deal with one of The Seven Principles of The Law. My Gift, shapechanging, deals with The Principle of Vibration. Your Gift, make no mistake, is the great Gift of prophecy and it deals with The Principle of Cause and Effect. You are Gifted to see the future—or what the future will be if present circumstances continue. Do you understand? *All things being equal,* you have seen the future. And that is the key to Cause and Effect—'all things being equal.' " He watched her, blue eyes willing her to understand.

"All things being equal," she repeated. "Yes, I understand."

"Then come one step farther, Cyna," the pony implored. "Remember the final step of healing."

"To see the patient well in my mind's eye."

"Even more," the pony admonished, "to know it, to believe it!"

"Yes," Cyna agreed.

"And prophecy gives one the ability to heal not just creatures, but events. Your Gift is to foresee the illness or the difficulty, but your *discipline* must be to cease believing what you have foreseen. This is not as easy as it sounds, for thought is the fuel of effects and it is very difficult to change one's mind. You foresaw the breaking of The Stone and believed it. You even told others of the possibility and they believed it, too. Even *I* believed it, for I was frightened by the idea. So we created it, all of us, with our belief."

Cyna shook her head emphatically. "But I believed that Nyal was going to be killed, that I would be murdered. I had foreseen it far more clearly than I imagined The Stone breaking. I was terrified! Yet those were just bad dreams, they never happened."

"But they would have happened! No, Cyna, something changed, something broke that prophesied chain of events. What *probably* would have occurred, had events and thoughts continued as they were going?" Bihan asked after a moment.

She didn't hesitate. "All things being equal, Ruf and I would have tried to free Nyal and take him to the coast."

"And created a war between lords and Others? Yes. And I suspect that by doing that, you would have planted the seeds for Nyal to be recaptured and executed, and for you to be a fugitive. With Nyal dead, what would you have done?"

"If my plans had killed him?" Her eyes clouded. "I don't know."

"Would you have tried to finish his mission?"

"I might. It would have seemed a time to finish things."

"So it's possible—probable—that you may have been here, alone. You might have faced the Black Shields, as you did this morning. And you would have died a witch who was rather good at healing but never mastered her Gift."

She turned back to him, her green eyes now steady. "Instead, I took your advice and rededicated myself to Magic that night."

"Yes."

"So you think it is *I* who have changed."

"You have. And that is what you had not foreseen. Now things are no longer equal."

"Does that mean we will win this battle?"

"Not necessarily. It only means that we are together here to fight it. But that is different from anything either you or I have prophesied. Perhaps it will be different enough to help."

Bihan trotted to the edge of the rampart and peered over into the darkness. Even from a distance, the light of the Black Shields' bonfires was bright enough to silhouette the fine lines of Bihan's head and curly mane. The deep, throbbing rhythms of New Faith invocations pulsed in the air. Cyna felt uneasy. The unnatural sounds seemed to permeate everything about her.

"They invoke The Vorsai," Bihan said, seeing her discomfort. "Don't listen. Their voices can rob the will."

"Do you think they'll attack tonight?" she asked.

"You're the prophetess, but if you're uncertain, let's ask our troll prince," Bihan said.

Mati was patrolling the rampart and came forward at Cyna's call.

"In the morning, I would guess" the troll leader replied shortly. "We can't hold out against an all-out assault. We haven't enough food or arrows."

The pony turned to Cyna. "We need your Gift," he said simply. "Tell me your vision again. Trolls face the Black Shields, yes?"

"Yes," she answered, her memory slipping back to the day when The Stone broke, to the vision of ragged, skinny Elves and Peskies. She understood that part of it now.

"In the daylight or at night?"

"Daylight. Wait, the shadows were long. Early morning or evening. On a flat plain."

"And their leader?"

"A Human man, bearded, so I couldn't see his face. But I remember something about his eyes . . ."

Bihan blew through his lips and paced back and forth. Mati watched him, frowning so deeply that his eyebrows formed one furry line above his eyes. "What does all this mean?" he asked Cyna. "When did you see this?"

"At the Stone Moving I had a vision. I didn't understand it then."

"But if you saw it, why did we not avoid this place?" Mati demanded. "It's bad enough to be trapped, but to know ahead of time . . ."

"No!" Bihan shook his head, his heavy mane falling over his eyes. "Fighting to avoid fate only makes it that much more certain. We must yield willingly and use our wisdom to change it. But we must leave this place now."

The troll leader threw up his hands. "Because we have no water, little food, and only a few arrows apiece? I see your point."

"No," said Bihan, "because I have glimpsed—and Cyna has clearly seen—where the crucial battle will take place. It is not in Dunn Naire. This place has sheltered us, but we must escape to open ground. And we are not all together yet." Ignoring Mati's puzzled stare he went on. "Tell your trolls to ready themselves. We leave as soon as the moon sets."

"Oh, surely, most magic horse," and Mati bowed low before him, the darkness unable to hide the gleam of irony in his amber eyes. "We can just tell those murderers across the way that we've changed our minds and we're leaving now, thank you very much."

"Listen to The Wizard," chided Cyna gently. "He's gotten us as far as this."

"Well, I suppose that's true," the troll grumbled. But his mood seemed to lighten with the thought of escape. "The Black Shields don't seem to want anyone to sleep tonight, anyway. If we're quiet, perhaps the trees by the side of the riverbank will afford us some shelter to slip around them in the dark."

He and Cyna went around to each group of trolls and told them what they must do. First, the fire was built up and torches were set at the top of the wall on either side of the gate. Mati asked the name of the young Dwarf who carried his ancestor's black oak drum.

"Garth Olem," the Dwarf replied.

"Are you brave?" Mati asked solemnly.

"I was a Naerlundg before I disgraced my home and became a troll," the Drawf said crisply. "I'll do till you find one braver."

"Then conceal yourself from the light of the torches and beat your drum," Mati said. "Beat it loud while each of us crosses the open space between the fort and the Black Shields' camp. But don't beat it for too long. Beat it and stop, then beat again. Don't let them get used to the sound. That way they'll not notice so quickly when you finally stop and join us."

"You'll have to cross alone, in silence after the rest of us have gone," Cyna added, to make sure he understood the risk.

The Dwarf was pale in the torchlight but he didn't hesitate and the tone of his voice was confident. "Done!" he said with a flourish.

"Do you know Ruf Nab?" Cyna asked.

"My uncle," he replied. "He would lay his hammer shaft about my backside if he knew what I have become."

"I think he would be proud of what you are about to do," Cyna said.

As Garth Olem began a steady, warlike rhythm on the drum, Cyna, Bihan, and the trolls gathered by a low part of the wall some distance from the gate. The Black Shields' fires threw long shadows across the sloping meadow toward them, and by the fire's edge Cyna could see black-robed sentinels watching the fort.

"Each one of you will climb down and hug the side of the wall," Mati instructed. "Then skirt the edge beside the neck of land to the meadow. Stay belly-down across the meadow all the way to the riverbank. No talking, not even a whisper. No stopping for anything or anyone."

"What about Bihan?" Cyna asked.

"How do you propose to get yourself down the wall?" Mati asked the horse. "Can you fly?"

"I'll manage," Bihan answered curtly.

"We trolls have much experience in moving horses up and down precipitous heights," the troll said. "We would be glad to help."

Bihan looked relieved. "I'd be grateful."

"Then get ready," Mati said. "We mustn't all cross together at the same time. First, Brathskyr, take a party of twenty-five to assure the way and scout the riverbank. Garth and the rest of us will give you noise aplenty to cover your going. When you've had time to reach the trees, Cyna and the horse will cross with a band of twenty-five more. I'll come across with the last group.

"If you are discovered, decide for yourself whether to flee or return to the fort. I will support you if you are attacked and must retreat. But any who remain in the fort are doomed when morning light comes. My advice is to scatter and make it back to the mountains as fast as you can. Let Others know what has happened here, and maybe something can be saved. Garth, beat your drum. Whendel, Quiberon, help me to make a sling to lower the magic horse over the wall."

There were no ropes or stout sticks, but the trolls each loaned a belt or strap and soon a harness encircled Bihan's round belly. With much grunting and straining, they lowered the pony down the wall until at last his hooves touched the chalky turf in the darkness below.

"You're next, Mistress!" Mati whispered.

"I'd rather climb," Cyna whispered back.

"I've seen you climb in the mountains and I wasn't impressed," Mati said curtly. "It's dark and we're in a hurry." When she still hesitated he said, "You listen to the horse about Magic, because he knows. Listen to me about climbing in the dark, for *I* know."

Sitting in the sling as though it were a chair, she felt as though she were being lowered into a hole. When the faint torchlight receded and the ground touched her feet, she knew the blinded isolation that a hooded falcon must feel. She stepped away from the sling and heard it being swiftly drawn back up. Reaching out into the darkness, she felt something round and soft. From the sharp intake of breath she recognized

Bihan and patted his rump. He stepped aside and she followed her hand along his back until she stood beside the pony's head.

Overhead, the scuffling sounds of trolls fumbling for handholds in the darkness sounded like faint whispers. Garth's steady rhythm masked their passage. Her back against the wall, Cyna made herself as small as possible as they passed. Bihan's breath was in her ear.

The trolls still within the fort began to sing "Hammer of Montyk," the Dwarfin marching song. After numerous choruses, the drum ebbed. The fort fell silent and Cyna could only hear the pulsing drone of the Black Shields' invocations. Then came a sharp cry, like a bird disturbed in its nest. "They're at the river!" Cyna heard Mati whisper triumphantly from the top of the ramparts. Within the fort, the news was passed on in touches and whispers until everyone knew and had exchanged hugs and handshakes in the dark.

The next group of trolls silently descended the wall and gathered on either side of Cyna and Bihan. Garth's drum began again, a rhythm Cyna did not recognize. "Follow us. Not a word!" hissed a Peskie voice. She rose to her feet, stretching the stiffness out of her joints. Her eyes had adjusted to the darkness and she recognized Whendel.

She stayed close to the side of the wall, her hands brushing its mossy sides. It was lighter by the gate, where the torches gleamed, but dark shadows shaded the narrow path. A stone's throw from the gate, the trolls slid over the sharp edge of the land that hung above the river.

Then it was Cyna's turn. Two trolls gripped her wrists as she swung her feet over the edge and let herself down.

She was dizzied by the sense of height until she felt steeply sloping turf beneath her feet. By clinging to the face of the cliff, she was able to walk, crouched, just below the ledge, following the trolls as they skirted the narrow, torchlit causeway before the gate. Behind her she could hear grunting and a shower of stones tumbling down the face of the ledge, but she didn't dare look back to see how Bihan was doing. She hoped the trolls were helping the surefooted pony along the path.

A cautioning hand touched her. "Be especially careful here," whispered Whendel. "The ledge falls away to the river right before you. So we must climb up and we will be in sight of the sentries. Be careful where you put your feet. Don't rattle a stone or break a twig. The riverbank is downhill fifty horse lengths. Use the gorse bushes and stones for hiding."

Cyna nodded and gathered up her skirt, tucking it into her wide leather belt so its hanging folds would not catch a stray pebble or twig and betray her. She could hear the percussion of Bihan's hooves on the ground. Groping for handholds, she scrambled up the path.

Stooping low, she ran toward the shadow of a low stone and paused, surveying the route she must follow. On either side of her, trolls swept silently forward, moving from shadow to shadow. Cyna stifled a panicked impulse to hurry in order to keep up with them, telling herself to find her own pace, to keep silent, to move with care.

Halfway down the stony meadow, she froze at a sharp hiss. An enemy sentry crossed before them, hardly a horse length away. Cyna pressed herself against a large stone and closed her eyes, holding her breath. The pulse of the Black Shields' litany was drowned by the pounding of her heart. Sweeping his torch high, the sentry peered into the darkness of the field.

Suddenly a shout rang out. The sentry turned, starting toward the sound.

"Sea Prissies!" roared a voice and almost instantly Cyna heard the clash of swords. In the bush before her, she saw Whendel raise himself to look in the direction of the uproar. Following his eyes, she saw a Human horseman fighting off several sentries on foot. Torches blazed as Black Shields raced toward the beleaguered Human.

"Run!" cried Whendel, waving his troop to use the commotion as a cover for their escape toward the river.

"Wait!" cried Cyna. She was louder than she had intended, for several sentries turned back at her voice, their eyes searching the dark meadow. "It's Tym!" Cyna exclaimed, rising to her feet, oblivious to the danger. Whendel and the trolls looked at her aghast. "Help him!" she implored.

Another horseman galloped into the light to take his place beside the first. "Nyal!" Bihan shouted, leaping forward to stand beside Cyna. "Do as the witch says!" he commanded the trolls. "Save them!"

Whendel and his troop had little choice now, for some of the sentries had turned back and were searching for them, beating the gorse bushes with their swords, holding their torches high.

"Rally, trolls!" cried Whendel and the trolls drew their weapons and raced forward.

"Cyna, run back to the fort!" Bihan shouted. "We're discovered now, we can't escape. Go!" He plunged forward, shouting orders to trolls who raced before him, each one reaching over his shoulder to pluck an arrow from its quiver.

The clash of arms behind her was horrifying, voices crying out in surprise and pain. "Hold! Hold the line!" she heard Bihan cry. "Nyal, over here!"

Cyna ran, obedient to Fallon's words, dismayed that she had come so far from the fort. Fear gave her strength and she flew up the steep path that she had so painstakingly climbed down. "Mati!" she cried, "Mati, help! Nyal is being attacked! We are discovered!"

Mati passed Cyna at a run, running toward the fighting, brandishing his knife. His trolls, shouting threats and warlike oaths, followed him.

Chapter 41

Cyna reached the fort and seized the battered gate, straining to open it wider. The leather hinges were stiff, and the heavy logs dragged on the ground. She pulled with all the strength left within her. "Dragon Eggs!" she swore aloud, but she managed well enough that the first rider rode through with room to scrape by.

"Cynfaire!" she cried to him. "Help me!"

The Elfin troll vaulted from his horse and leaped to help her drag the gate open all the way. Phastro was next, and then, bleeding from a cut on his forehead, came Tym, reeling in his saddle.

"Whoa!" Cyna cried to his excited horse.

Phastro leaped to grab the panicked animal's reins, heedless of his own danger. The horse dragged him for several strides before steadying under his touch.

"Tym, are you badly hurt?" Cyna demanded.

The groom swayed drunkenly in his saddle and crashed to the ground at her feet. In the dim light his face seemed stained black, but when she bent to touch him, her fingers felt the sticky heat of blood. Searching upward, she found a wound on his temple, just above his receding hairline. Blood ran freely and the contour of his skull suddenly changed, like a cracked egg.

A shriek behind her made her whirl around. Garth Olem staggered into the gate, clutching his arm. Blood flowed from his forearm and his nose. His black oak drum hung from the strap about his neck in shattered ruin. "Ahhhhh!" he howled in pain, "Aaaaaaaaaaaah!"

He seemed blinded in his agony. Cyna reached out to help him, but he struggled to pull away. "Phastro!" she shouted, but the Elfin troll was already running to help. Together they calmed the bleeding Dwarf. Cyna knew at a glance that his arm was shattered, and she wished again for the pain-deadening herbs lost in the Trollurgh Mountains.

But there was no time for regrets. Trolls streamed through the gate in retreat, stumbling in panic, dragging wounded and dead comrades with them. Those who could swarmed up the wall to the top of the ramparts and shot volleys of arrows into the ranks of the attacking Black Shields. Those who still fought outside the fort gave ground slowly, moving together and protecting their companions as one by one they fell back through the gate. Bihan, Mati, and Nyal were the very last.

"Close the gate!" shouted the pony, but trolls were already leaning on it, grunting with effort as their combined weight finally swung the old gate closed.

"Shoot!" shouted Mati, but those on the ramparts were already shooting tightly disciplined volleys into the attackers ranks.

"Here they come!" shouted Bihan as the old wood of the gate splintered under a blow. A mounted warrior on a heavy boned, Perime-bred stallion crashed through, a companion at his heels.

Nyal met him head-on. Firestroker whistled as it ripped through the air. The enemy warrior parried, feinted, and grunted in surprise as Nyal's sword found a path beneath his shield into his heart. Nyal spun his horse around, sword poised, but a troll arrow had found the other horseman and he fell from his saddle like a slaughtered ox. "By the Dragon!" shouted Nyal as Avelaer reared and sprang forward, blocking the narrow gateway. Beneath the onslaught of arrows, the vanguard of Black Shields retreated back across the narrow neck of land.

A weary cheer rang from the ramparts. "Greetings, Nyal!" called Mati. "I am the prince of trolls and I welcome you to Fort Hopelessness!"

Bihan cantered up the ancient staircase to the top of the ramparts. "Brace yourselves!" he shouted. "They're regrouping!"

"Everyone to the ramparts!" ordered Mati.

"I'll hold the gate!" Nyal called. "Cynfaire, Phastro! On your horses! Stay just behind me. Tym!"

"Tym's down," Phastro said breathlessly.

Nyal barely hesitated. "Someone take his horse. Join us at the gate."

"Light torches! The brighter it is, the stronger we look!" called Bihan, rearing high.

The ruse worked, for the Black Shields again withdrew across the meadow to their camp. They left mounted sentries, who cantered back and forth, taunting the trolls just out of arrow range. Mati posted a double watch at the walls as trolls crawled across the dark meadow, retrieving what arrows and other weapons they could, whispering death rituals beside the bodies of their comrades who had fallen in the retreat.

"Tym? Has anyone seen my groom?" asked Nyal as he was relieved at the gate by a squadron of Dwarf and Peskie trolls.

"Over here." He followed Mati past the fires at the gate into the shadows of the inner fort. The dead and wounded were laid on the grass by the old wall. Cyna straightened up as they approached.

"Cyna!"

There before the eyes of Mati and the wounded trolls she did not embrace him, but simply stood for a moment, her eyes locked on his. Then she took him by the hand and led him through the rows of wounded young Elves, Dwarves, and Peskies who lay on the ground. Some lay silently, others thrashed back and forth, moaning in pain. Still others lay terribly still. Tym was lying senseless on the ground before the rampart wall. Blood covered the groom's face and had soaked through the collar of his jacket.

"He took a hit bareheaded," Nyal whispered.

"He's very badly hurt. He lies like a dead man since he fell from his horse," Cyna told him. "Are you injured?"

Nyal shook his head dumbly.

"Then give me your cloak."

He barely had it off his shoulders before she started tearing it into strips. But the heavy embroidery of the green leaves resisted her and he took it back, tearing it until she had the strips to bind wounds and splint shattered limbs. She left him standing in the dark beside Mati.

"You were trying to escape the fort?" Nyal asked.

"Yes," Mati said. "We have no chance here—the Black Shields have only to wait for starvation to defeat us. Half of us were already across when the commotion started. What happened?"

"We were coming to join you. One of the horses whinnied and alerted their sentries, who attacked us. We would have been dead had you not come out to save us."

"Many are dead now, and the rest will be soon. There'll be no escape now. Perhaps they'll attack us in the morning."

"Perhaps, perhaps!" Bihan interrupted, trotting up from the direction of the gate. "We don't know what happens next, that's what we've all come to find out."

Nyal held out his hand to Bihan's muzzle. "How does this horse talk?" he asked. He stroked the pony's ears.

"He is the great Wizard," Mati told him, "Fallon the Twice-tested."

"Thrice-tested," Bihan said.

"Master Fallon!" Nyal snatched his hand back and managed a courteous half bow. "I'm sorry, I didn't know . . ."

"Of course not," Bihan said. "As I keep trying to tell everyone, none of us knows much, we're all advancing on faith."

"We *know* we have barely an arrow left apiece," Mati objected. "We *know* we can't hold the fort against them."

"Ned and the lords followed me," Nyal said. "Ned will join us when he sees what's happening . . ."

"I'm afraid not," Bihan said. "Ned is the traitor. He tried to kill Cyna and me with the same heartlessness that led him to murder Telerhyde and Brandon."

"Ned!" Nyal was stunned.

Bihan's ears were laid flat to his head and his eyes flashed in the moonlight. "How far behind you is he?"

"Barely two hours," Nyal replied.

"Oh, dear," said the pony.

Throughout the night the fort hummed with activity. The last of the horsemeat was roasted and the used arrows rechipped to lethal sharpness.

Cyna tended Tym and the wounded trolls in the fort's courtyard, where the horses were tethered. Dawn had colored the sky a faint slate grey before she finally paused and sought the solitude she needed after healing. Avelaer caught her eye and she stopped beside him to pat his neck. The stallion had changed. Despite the flickering torches and frantic activity that surrounded them, he lowered his large, arrogant head as gently as a pony and accepted her caress. Had Nyal not ridden him into the fort, she would never have guessed it was the same horse who had plunged like a wild thing about the courtyard at Crowell. She wrapped her arms around the stallion's neck and buried her face in his tangled mane. In all her prophecies, she had never seen beyond this day, never seen the end that they were about to fashion.

"Cyna." She turned at his voice.

Nyal rose and stepped from the shadows. She reached out to him and he took her hand, holding himself away from her with an odd formality. "I never had the chance to congratulate you on receiving your Gift. It's prophecy, you said."

"Yes."

"I'm happy for you."

"I'm so sorry, Nyal. I tried to deny it for us, but I cannot. Not any longer. I didn't want this. I only wanted you." She felt his hand tighten around hers.

"I should have run away with you when you asked me."

She smiled. "It wasn't possible for *you* to run away."

"All the worse for you and Morbihan, then."

"Nyal, that's not true!"

"I've killed us, Cyna. If I hadn't come blundering in here in the dark, you all would have escaped."

"Nyal . . ." In the faint light she could see that he, too, had changed. He was thinner, and several days of beard shadowed his face. His grey eyes were dull with grief. But, above all, he was alive, and his life gave her strength. "You don't understand, my love." She took her hand from his and reached out to him with her arms, seeking to break the distance between them.

He turned away from her, anguish tightening his voice. "The Dwarf who forged my sword said Magic and betrayal would be the light and shadow of my life, Cyna. Well, you are my light. But I've brought betrayal down on all of us."

"That's not true," she replied sharply.

His laugh was short and harsh. "I thought that *I* would be betrayed, and I was strong enough for that. But everyone I love has been betrayed. Betrayal has shadowed everything—Telerhyde, Brandon, Morbihan. And now the Black Shields are going to kill us. They're going to destroy Morbihan and there's no one left to stop them."

"Shhhhhhh." She closed the distance between them and covered his mouth with soft kisses. "Don't say that," she said gently. "Don't think that." She had felt him slip away from her once before, but never like this. It was as if he were far away from her grasp, sliding down into a dark pit.

He took her hands and held them against his chest. "You heard Mati; there's nothing we can do! Because of me, Tym is dying, those trolls are dead. Whoever my father was, I curse him. He sired the whelp who's ruined everything!"

"Nyal, stop it!" Cyna said sharply. "Don't talk this way. Don't think this way!"

Bihan whickered from the shadows. "Gently, Cyna, gently," he said. "He can't hear what you're saying." He trotted forward, his ears alert, his eyes on the tormented Human. "Nyal, if you could have anything you wanted what would it be?"

"To be dead!" he cried in anguish. Cyna recoiled from his words.

"Attack! Attack!" Mati shouted. A troll screamed. Mati ran to the ramparts, reaching over his shoulder to nock an arrow in his bow. "To the ramparts!" he shouted. "The gate is breached!"

A party of Black Shields had crossed the meadow on foot and taken the gate by surprise. Two trolls lay dead, others ran in confusion. The leader of the enemy warriors strode forward, his companions at his heels.

Nyal drew Firestroker as he raced for the gate and his momentum drove the first attacker back a step. The leader thrust out to defend himself, unprepared for the raging fury before him. Nyal hacked and stabbed, swinging Firestroker in hard, short arcs, and blood gleamed on its blade like a jewel.

With a roar, another warrior joined the combat, his sword thrusting, seeking Nyal's throat. The rest encircled him. Nyal whirled, swinging Firestroker in an arc, clearing the ground around him, felling Black Shields left and right. His rage was blinding and he felt nothing when a blade gashed his thigh. He fought on until another blow staggered him and he stumbled. In a moment he was down, struggling beneath their blows.

"Mati! Quickly!" whinnied Bihan. He bolted for the gate. The first Black Shield was ill prepared for a maddened pony, and cried out in pain as Bihan's hooves hammered him to the ground. Kicking and biting, the little horse fought his way to the center of the melee. On the ground, Nyal still raged and fought with bare hands. Bihan seized Nyal by the collar and dragged him backward toward the center courtyard.

"Shoot!" cried Mati as soon as the pony was clear. A devastating volley brought down the invaders. "Strip the bodies of arms and armor," the troll leader ordered tersely. "Then pile them by the gate. Give their friends a barricade they'll think twice about crossing."

Bihan still dragged Nyal, making directly for Cyna. Nyal braced his feet and wrestled the pony to a stop as Mati caught up with them. "That was either the bravest or the stupidest act I've ever seen a Human perform!" Mati exclaimed, handing Nyal his sword. "Are you all right?"

Wrenching himself from Bihan's teeth, Nyal staggered to his feet. "I'm fine," he said.

Cyna, her skirts gathered about her legs, hurried to them. "Nyal, what happened?"

"The Black Shields attacked," explained Mati.

"Then Nyal attacked *them,*" Bihan chuckled, with a sense of humor Nyal thought was entirely inappropriate. "Twenty at once!"

"You're wounded," Cyna exclaimed. "We need you, Nyal. You should be more careful!" she chided.

"I'm fine," he insisted.

"Then why are you bleeding?" She knelt to examine his thigh. Blood ran down his leg, soaking his boot.

"I'm all right!" Nyal exploded.

Cyna jerked back her hand in surprise. "Nyal, you've a sword wound . . ."

"Leave me alone, can't you? What difference does it make, anyway?" He pulled away from her and strode across the courtyard, away from curious eyes.

"By The Law!" Cyna watched him in astonishment for a moment, her hands clenched at her sides. Then turning on her heel, she strode away in the opposite direction. "Trust Magic, trust Magic, trust Magic . . ." she repeated under her breath. Ever since the night of Fallon's murder, these had become her only words of power. They had brought her great clarity of mind, helped her focus her powers during Fallon's funeral and with the trolls. But now anger flowed through her chest and constricted her throat. The same rage that had attacked twenty men had evoked her own. She stopped and tried to clear her mind, her eyes closed tightly as she stood in the midst of the wounded. "Trust Magic, trust Magic . . ."

Tym made a soft, gurgling sound. She knelt beside him, her fingers lightly exploring the sudden cold of his limbs, the monstrous swelling above his temple. His right arm had begun to shake violently, his breath turned into a strangled gasp. "Ah, no," she pleaded. "Tym, no." Rage still flowed through her. "Live!" she hissed in fury. "Don't die, Tym!" She held her hands just around his forehead, close enough to feel his life's faint heat. "Tym!" she called loudly, and felt a slow surge of power flow into her arms and hands. "Tym!" she demanded, as though summoning him. Energy and heat flowed through her in a joyous ache. Something within Tym flickered, then steadied. "Tym," she said once more, as though they had recognized each other across a great distance.

Bihan followed Nyal like a gnat. "If you could have anything you want, what would it be?" he asked again as he caught up with Nyal along a deserted length of the inner wall.

"This is not the time to play games!" Nyal snapped, stopping to remove his belt and twist it tightly to stop the bleeding of his leg.

"Of course not. But if this weren't so serious a time, and you could have anything you want . . ."

"I don't know!" Nyal exclaimed in exasperation. The thought crossed his mind that Fallon—the pony—had gone mad. "I told you. To die."

"Yes, what else?"

"To know the name of my real father, so I could curse it!"

"Is there anything you would wish for someone else?"

"For Tym to live," Nyal said reluctantly.

"That's good!" Bihan nodded his head vigorously. "Anything else? Remember, you can have anything!"

"For Cyna to live and be happy. For those poor trolls . . ."

"You don't have to die for them to live," Bihan said. "In this game you don't have to exchange anything. You just get what you really want."

"Then I would wish for an army. An army of Others and the faithful lords to drive the Black Shields into the sea! An army with the strength to drive The Perime out of the Outer Isles forever!"

"And who will lead this army?"

"Telerhyde and Brandon!"

"Ah. Well, suppose they couldn't, who's your second choice?"

"Me!"

"But you wished yourself dead! But then, I suppose if Tym and Cyna live, and a great army arises, you'd rather live?"

Nyal smiled. "If I could just take back all the blunders that brought me here, I would rather live."

"I see. What will you do if Tym lives?"

"I'd wish him everything he wanted. His own room, a boat. To get breakfast in bed."

"Oh, he wouldn't be happy with that for long," Bihan chuckled. "He'd be up and in trouble in no time. He'd want to be with you."

Nyal laughed. "Yes, and complaining every step of the way."

Cyna strode across the deserted courtyard toward them. Her step was purposeful and free. "Mati is looking for you both," she called. "He wants advice on assembling his forces."

Nyal's face hardened. "I'll go at once."

"Many of the wounded will be able to join the fighting," Cyna added. "They're recovering quickly."

"Tym?"

"Tym is eating raw horsemeat for breakfast and demanding that we find him his sword. He wants to see you."

"He lives?" Nyal demanded incredulously.

"And complains," Cyna said. "He gains strength by the minute."

Bihan pranced in a circle, his long tail lashing from side to side in excitement. "Well, it seems you've been granted your first wish, Nyal! Let me grant you another," he continued quickly, before Nyal could reply. "I've wanted to tell you for years, but I couldn't, for many reasons. You wished the name of your father, and now is clearly a time of reckoning. But before I tell you, you must know that although your mother loved your father, she never dishonored Telerhyde, not by her lights. It's difficult to explain, especially since to you I seem to be this creature rather than Fallon the Wizard." He hesitated, then plunged on brusquely. "For you see, Nyal, *I* am your father."

"You?" said Nyal and Cyna almost simultaneously.

"Yes. Your mother was the only woman I ever truly loved. But it's hard to love a Magic-Keeper, as you may find out. She left me and returned to Telerhyde. He took you as his own and raised you, as I never could. Your mother and you were the great sacrifices I have made for Magic and Morbihan. Don't stand there looking so stricken! It's not so terrible, being a Wizard's son."

"A Wizard's son . . ." Nyal repeated.

"A Master Wizard, at that!" the pony added. Cyna clearly saw a tear roll down his cheek.

"Horsemen!" cried a troll. "Horsemen have just crested the hill!"

They ran to the ramparts. "It's Ned!" cried Cyna, spying the Fanstock banner fluttering in the breeze.

"The Black Shields outnumber us by five to one," Mati observed.

"But you have *us,*" The Wizard exclaimed. When Mati raised his eyebrows, he went on. "We're all supposed to be dead, you know. Nyal, Cyna, me—and you, Mati. But here we are, afloat in a sea of possibilities. Perhaps together we can change this. Cyna, tell me your vision again."

She closed her eyes, remembering. "A battle."

"Yes, but who? Who fights?"

"Humans with black shields against Others. The Others are led by a Human." *The horse beneath him trembled, its ribs showing hunger. The leader's face was bearded and his eyes—grey with streaks of faint color, like a dawn sky.* "Nyal!" she said. "Of course! Their leader is Nyal."

"Yes," the pony could not mask his relief. "Yes, that's good, you saw truly. What else?"

"A standing stone."

"Argontell. Go on."

"Peskies, Elves, Dwarves."

"Do you mean the trolls?"

"Ogres charge on unicorns."

"Ogres!" he said softly. "How do you see that?"

"The armies clash together."

"Go back. Ogres on unicorns?"

"Look!" The troll lookout was pointing past the line of Humans who were gathering in the valley before them, at the hillock across the river. "Look! Look!"

The glare of the morning sun made Cyna's eyes blur but she could make out figures gathered at the base of Argontell. Even from the distance, she recognized the shape of the unicorns. "Ur Logga!" she cried.

"No!" cried Bihan. "Oh, no!"

Cyna looked at him in shock. The Master Wizard of Morbihan trembled in despair. "But they cannot be your vision," he wailed. "They're on the wrong side of an unfordable river. If they are what you foresaw, then all the doomsayers are right! We are lost!"

Chapter 42

"I wish to go home," The Meg repeated petulantly. "Will no one listen to me? What has happened to common courtesy? To obedience or devotion to your Meg?" The Husbands wavered, their eyes, by habit, imploring The Meg's happiness.

Phaedryn sighed and rose to her feet. Her legs were so tired that they trembled, for she had walked every step of the forced march and the pace set by the unicorns had taxed her to the limits of her endurance. She stepped between The Meg and her Husbands. "Royal Fathers," she said softly, "honor the great traditions of Elf. Stand firm for Harkynwood!"

Relieved, they turned their eyes to her, and The Meg fell again to her ceaseless wailing. Phaedryn turned away toward the river.

Melloryth watched her from nearby. Now that she was a girl again, she liked to observe the Elfin princess, small and dainty, always lovely in her soft, gossamer gowns, no matter how hard the march or how dismal the weather. Melloryth wanted to be like her, feminine but strong, dozens of husbands obeying her instantly.

Bem Gammin, the Ogre who had carried Melloryth on his unicorn through the mountain pass, bent down beside her. "Eat, pretty little one," he said, offering a wooden bowl of porridge.

"Thank you, demon," she said to him.

Everyone watched the river. It was high, flooded from the thawing snow of the mountains above them. Ruf Nab had led a party of Dwarves to examine the banks and now they straggled back, their boots muddy, their wide shoulders slumping.

"It's hopeless," Ruf announced, tugging off his helmet to

wipe the perspiration from his forehead. "The river is too wide to be spanned by any of the trees along the bank."

"The only way across is a two-day march back to the mountains," The Snaefid added.

"We cannot stand still and watch Others slain!" Ur Logga rumbled, anxiety thickening his accent.

"Your Majesty, even your unicorns would be drowned in that riot of water," Landes said. He moved slowly, sore not only from the nagging ache of his hip, but from days of riding in the arms of an Ogre. Ur Logga turned from him, frustration swelling the veins of his massive neck and forehead.

Landes patted him on the shoulder and turned toward the river. He stumbled and reached out for balance. Startled, Melloryth steadied him as he caught her arm. "Thank you, My Lady," he said. Looking across the river to the opposite bank, his eyes again sought Ned. The Fanstock banner fluttered in the morning breeze, but the men who carried black shields all looked the same. A heavy mist was rolling up from the river, blotting out the meadow, and he could only see tiny figures defending the fort. Squinting, he could make out the bright chestnut of Nyal's stallion fretting before the fortress gate. Above it, he saw a patch of sky-blue moving back and forth across the ramparts. Most likely it was Cyna. The slight forms of trolls looked like ants crawling about the walls.

A low groan went up along the riverbank as the enemy across the river began to move against the fort.

With no food and only a limited supply of arrows, Mati and Nyal agreed it was not wise to defend the fort any further. Instead, they would seek to create the chance of escape for at least a few, and meet Lothen and the Black Shields on the flat ground between the sea and the river.

They assembled before the gate. Mati led the right flank, which was made up of archers and the strongest trolls. Tym insisted he was able to lead the left wing, mostly wounded trolls who had recovered enough to fight. "My head's too hard for those Sea-Squirts," he had argued earlier when Nyal had tried to insist he remain with Cyna and Bihan. "I can still swing a sword." His crippled troops would guard the fort's gate.

Nyal would lead the center.

"Good-bye, Father," Nyal said awkwardly to Bihan. "I'll win you what time I can."

Bihan nodded, tossing his head. "I know you will, Nyal. Remember, you are a Wizard's son."

"Wait until we've engaged them," Nyal told Cyna, "then make for the river. Try to hide in the hedges along the bank with Father until the river goes down. Ruf will find you."

"I don't want to leave you," Cyna said quietly.

"Please, Cyna. I'll do the best I can, but no matter what happens, Morbihan needs Magic now. You must save yourself."

She nodded numbly, knowing he was right. She reached out to him and he held her, the cold steel of his helmet bruising her cheek. A bugle sounded. She stepped back and with a quick movement Nyal was on Avelaer's back. She held the horse's bridle while Nyal settled himself, loosening Firestroker in its sheath, setting his heels deeply into the stirrups. She stroked the horse's velvet muzzle. "Carry him bravely, Wind Thief," she whispered.

"Is there no Magic, Witch?" asked a troll in a quavering voice. "Can you not save us as Fallon saved Telerhyde in Harkynwood?"

Bihan raised his head to watch Cyna. "There is always Magic," she said in a steady voice that carried to each one of the ragged band of warriors. "Do you desire to win over The New Faith?"

"Yes!" several trolls answered. Mati turned to listen.

"Then hear me when I tell you that desire and belief are the foundations of The Old Faith. They will sustain us today."

"All things being equal, I don't see much chance of that," Mati told Nyal as they rode through the gate. "I'm afraid you've ridden a long way to join a dying cause."

"There is no other place I could be," Nyal replied as he turned Avelaer and took his place before the fort. "I was joined to this cause when I was born. And now I know that I was born joined to Magic and always will be." Drawing Firestroker and holding it up before him, he spoke in a deep voice that carried throughout the fort. "I dedicate this sword and my life to the destiny of all the tribes of Morbihan, Other and Human, mighty and despised." Trolls cheered, banging on their shields to make a defiant drumming sound.

Avelaer tossed his head, fretting at Nyal's restraining hand. Around them the mist swirled in the morning light. As the trolls' cheers died away, it was strangely silent. The air seemed charged, like a bowstring that has been drawn tight. Then Avelaer pricked up his ears at a faint sound and whinnied. An answering whinny came from somewhere in the fog before them. The mist on the meadow shifted, blown aside by the fresh morning breeze, and the silhouettes of armed horsemen, silent, waiting, loomed before them. Horses pawed the earth.

"They hold the high ground," Lothen told Ned, "but that is no real advantage as they are vastly outnumbered by battle-toughened troops. I will not commit my elite corps to this, only the regulars in the vanguard. You and your fellow lords will support them. It will give you a chance to prove your worth before the army. Assemble your followers."

At Lothen's command, the vanguard of the Black Shields began the attack. Ned and the traitor lords were poised behind them, waiting to strike. Whooping and yelling the vanguard came, proud to lead the attack, waving swords and lances, eager to fall upon the slender line of trolls. As they thundered up the slope of the rocky, gorse-grown meadow, their tight formation loosened slightly, flowing around the stones and thickets.

As they passed the low bushes that studded the valley, skinny trolls sprang out from behind stones and brush where they had been concealed. A few were crushed by the galloping horses, but others succeeded in seizing a strap or stirrup. With lightning thrusts of their knives, they cut through stirrup leathers and girths. Blood flowed from the horses' bellies, reddening their legs and making the ground slippery. Horses shied in terror and Black Shields cried out as their saddles slid to the ground. The battle line staggered.

"Shoot!" cried Mati. From the trolls standing firm before the fort, arrows flew like a cloud of deadly hail. Humans and horses fell thrashing, the ground soon slick with blood.

The vanguard wavered and fell back to regroup.

"Order them to charge again!" commanded Lothen, furious.

"Stand fast, now!" called Nyal as Avelaer wheeled and pranced in eagerness.

Ned led the second charge. Mati cried "Shoot!" once more and the last of the arrows swarmed out to thin the Black Shields' ranks.

"For Morbihan!" cried Nyal and Avelaer thundered forward, teeth bared. The trolls followed behind him, armed with stones and short swords. Mati, his large ears blue with excitement, waved his cloak beneath the nose of a bay charger. The horse shied from the sudden flash of red. With a well-timed flick of his arm, Mati bounced a rock off the horseman's helmet. "Harkynwood Forever!" cried a young Dwarf as he unhorsed the dazed rider with a thrust of his staff. Another horseman plunged past Mati, pursuing a screaming Elf. Mati seized the horse's tail and twisted it. He hung on fiercely as the war-horse squealed and bucked, throwing its rider to the ground.

The trolls held their ground, making the Black Shields pay a price in life for all they hoped to win. Yet there was little hope in the trolls' hearts. The sheer numbers of Humans in the vanguard seemed overwhelming. And at the far end of the meadow were Lothen and the main force, waiting for the moment to strike the final blow.

"We must run for the river!" cried Bihan. "Quickly, it's time!"

Cyna still stood on the ramparts where she could see the sweep of the battle. The thin line of trolls bent before the onslaught of the Black Shields, held, faltered, and held again.

"Cyna, quickly before it's too late! Get on my back; I'll carry you!"

"Wait." She was looking past the battle to the far side of the river where the Others were gathered about the base of Argontell. She had envisioned this scene many times before, but now it was clear and moving about her with the sharp edge of the urgent present. As the morning sun reflected off the slashing blades of the horsemen, it seemed as though the battlefield were glowing with a murderous light.

The knives will butcher or the knife will be the bridge.

"Cyna!" Bihan called, pawing the ground impatiently.

"No. Wait!" She seized the pony's mane, holding him close to her. "She spoke of this."

"Who?" demanded Bihan. "Cyna, what have you not told me?"

I once lifted a stone, and you are the same as I.

"Argontell!" Cyna cried. "That must be what it is!"

Chapter 43

"The Black Shields are attacking!" cried a Dwarf running up the hill toward the group of Others clustered on the rocky Argontell Plain.

Ur Logga turned away, unable to watch, while The Snaefid and Ruf Nab ran to the edge of the riverbank, swearing and crying out, urging on the trolls as if their words could turn the tide of battle. Landes was ashen, watching in silence.

Her sea-green robe billowing around her, Phaedryn climbed to the top of a low stone to gain a better view. Ned's gold ring felt cold and heavy between her breasts, where it swung gently from its chain. Even from this distance, her keen Elf eyes easily picked out the red cloak of her brother, Mati. She saw familiar faces she knew among the trolls, faces she thought never to see again. And wherever the battle was thickest, she saw Nyal on his chestnut stallion fighting the Black Shields, rallying the trolls. Yet again and again her eyes were drawn to the still figure in sky blue who stood with the spotted pony high on the ramparts of the fort. Cyna seemed divorced from the carnage beneath her, focused upon something on this side of the river.

Others surrounded Phaedryn, thronging the riverbank. She looked about her, trying to see what the witch must be seeing. Sunlight glared and blinded her for a moment, so she stepped into the shadow of Argontell. As she did, her eyes focused on the top of the great stone.

"Argontell?" she murmured, gazing at the weather-smoothed runes that stood out boldly in the early morning sunlight, cascading down its sides. As she said its name, she felt the Healer's ring grow warm. "Argontell!" she said again. She walked toward it, climbing up the steep hill and away from the scene of battle. The Royal Husbands and Fathers followed her by habit, confused but faithful.

The sun was rising behind the standing stone and it cast a long shadow that cut across the assembled Others, pointing directly at Dunn Naire. As he watched the company of Elves climbing toward The Stone, a chill took Ur Logga, making the hair stand straight up from the middle of his shoulders to the crown of his head. "The Standing Stone!" he exclaimed as though he had never seen it before. Fallon's words came to his mind. *Magic is not dead as long as we dare to love our lives.* "Ogres!" he cried, lumbering up the hill after the Elfin princess. "A Stone Moving! Finn! Murdock! Bring the others! Come quickly!"

The Peskie leader shook his head. "Give it up, Your Majesty!" he called, hopelessness twisting his lips.

The Snaefid turned to watch the Ogre king shouting orders to the Honor Guard and Husbands who clustered at the base of the huge stone. Ruf Nab started up eagerly. "Come, Father, let's give it a try. Anything's better than watching Others slaughtered." At a nod from The Snaefid, the Dwarf troop hurried after Ruf.

"Your Magnificence!" called The Snaefid, scrambling up the slope after them. "Finn, quickly!"

Rolling his eyes toward the sky, the Peskie prince motioned for his troop to join him as he followed, slow with disbelief. "Fallon is dead!" he shouted after The Snaefid. "You'll never raise a pebble without a Master Wizard! Even if he were here, Fallon and ten like him couldn't budge Argontell!" But he followed and reached out to take The Snaefid's hand.

The assembled Ogres, Elves, Dwarves, and Peskies clustered about the base of the stone. They gripped each others' hands and pulled as hard as they could, trying to narrow the large gap in their circle.

Landes lagged behind them, using his cane to drag himself up the hill. "Here, what are you doing?" he panted. "Wait for me!" He inched up to take Ur Logga's hand.

"Pull!" panted the Ogre, straining to complete the circle.

Landes dropped his cane and balanced on one leg, reaching across the space to Ruf Nab.

"Stretch!" demanded Ruf, but their sweating palms only slipped apart.

"Try again!" Phaedryn begged. Between her breasts the Healer's ring grew hot. The gap was closed within an arm's length. "We must!" she cried. "Try again!"

Only half understanding, Melloryth had followed them up the hill. She smiled up into Landes's desperate face as she took his hand, then reached out and shyly clasped Ruf's, completing the Magic circle of The Five Tribes.

Phaedryn screamed as the ring began to glow.

Chapter 44

For a moment Cyna quailed at the task that lay before her. A familiar dizziness seized her. "Not now!" she commanded. "No prophecy now!" She seized Bihan's mane firmly, her eyes focused on the very top of Argontell. Bihan steadied himself beside her and she felt Fallon's energy quivering in the pony's silken hair. "Argontell, lift!"

A loud roaring filled her ears and it seemed as though her mind shuddered. Steeling herself, she seized her senses roughly, casting them into the past. She remembered the millpond, saw the pebble in the water. Gathering all the elements together—stone, water, sky—she held them lightly in her mind's eye.

Beneath her hand, the pony pulsated with a brilliant light. Cyna's body shook so violently that she could barely stand. With her last strength, she tore her mind from the past and hurled it into a future where children played with leggy colts. "I love you!" she called to the future as well as to the man who fought only a short distance away, ringed by enemy swords.

The Others in the Magic circle stood, their hands joined, for what seemed a long time. Finn was shaking his head at the uselessness of it all when he was startled by a distant crack of thunder. The mists had risen and the sun shone brightly in the blue sky, casting a glare on the faces of those gathered around the stone. Melloryth smiled at the faces around her, her eyes vibrant and blue, her short blond hair gleaming in the sun. Beside her, Landes balanced precariously on his good leg. Phaedryn was staring up at the very top of Argontell, her head thrown back, her face twisted with pain. Between her breasts, the Healer's ring pulsated with heat. Finn closed his eyes in horror. "Lift," he implored. "If there is a Law, then lift. For that poor Elf, for all of us, lift!"

A crack of lightning shook them all. The Snaefid glanced about nervously and Ur Logga's lips curled in alarm. A sound like the hissing of a flock of geese filled the air.

"Look!"

High above them at the very top of the stone, a web of lightning played. It flared and flickered, crackling like a dry branch on hot coals.

"Dragon Fire!" exclaimed Landes. A wind swept across the hill, whipping at their clothes. As though assaulted by a storm from all directions at once, clouds gathered, sweeping in from the far edges of the sky, surging over the top of Argontell.

Finn's hair stood on end and he felt a prickling in his fingers. "Lift!" he implored as the ground shivered beneath him. "Lift!"

The sky darkened and the ground began to quake. Finn clung to The Snaefid's hand, struggling to stay on his feet. Dust rose up on all sides, turning the air thick and black. "Lift!" cried the Others all together.

With a crack of a thousand thunderbolts, The Stone came loose from the ground. It thrust above the circle of Others and hung in the air for an instant. Eyes wide, they watched while clods of earth pelted down upon them. Melloryth cried out, her feet sliding toward the cavernous hole that Argontell had left in the middle of their circle. Landes pulled her back, groaning in pain. "Hold the circle!" Ur Logga roared.

Free of the earth for the first time in a thousand years, Argontell floated, obedient to their thoughts. It made for the river. Geysers of water erupted beneath The Stone, shattering against the rock in a thick spray. Droplets of water caught the glaring sunlight and danced away in a million tiny rainbows. Wind howled, filling the air with sand and mud. The circle of Others, still tightly gripping each others' hands, craned their necks to watch as the huge stone settled. Argontell came to rest with one end on each side of the river, forming a mighty stone bridge.

And as it did, the silken mane beneath Cyna's hand ceased its shuddering and disappeared. When Cyna opened her eyes, there was no sign of Bihan or Fallon.

When the wind began to blow and the clouds clustered over Argontell, Lothen paused, looking back over his shoulder at the group clustered at its base. "Brownies and their Magic!" he spat.

When The Stone came free from the earth, the men who followed The Vorsai heard Lothen's trumpets and turned to face the new threat.

Melloryth was delighted by the Stone Moving. She had glimpsed the odd goings-on last spring from Eacon's Keep, but this was finer, louder, and far more satisfying. She laughed out loud as she imagined her uncle scrambling in terror before her.

Beside her, Landes had fallen to the ground. "Ur Logga!" he cried, "Bring the unicorns! Snaefid, prepare your troop for attack!" He seized Melloryth's hand and painfully pulled himself upright. "Move! Move! If we're not quick, they'll take the head of the bridge!" He shouted his orders, smacking a fist into his palm, showing how to strike, how to drive the enemy back and secure the bridge. Even as he spoke, the heavily armed cavalry of Lothen was galloping toward the opposite side of the riverbank. Melloryth gasped. The hooded figures all resembled her uncle's secret visitors, gathered together like a waking nightmare.

A ledge beside The Stone formed a ragged ramp. Ur Logga's unicorn shied, alarmed by the noise and dirt. The Ogre steadied the beast with a growl and it galloped forward, sensing the horsemen across the river. The unicorn's great, branching horn swept from side to side, seeking its enemy. Three abreast, the Ogre Honor Guard followed, waving branches and short clubs, urging their unicorns forward with harsh cries.

They were followed by The Snaefid and Ruf Nab, leading two phalanxes of Dwarves, who stormed the ramp and charged across the bridge.

The Peskies had already nocked their arrows and now they raced across the stone. In the middle they paused, released a volley of arrows at the enemy horsemen gathered at the river's edge, then ran on.

"Your Megship!" cried Landes. Without hesitation, Phaedryn ran up the ramp, the Elfin Husbands and Fathers behind her, waving their jeweled daggers. The Meg scrambled behind them screaming, "Kill the traitors! Slay them! Avenge the Beloved Husband!"

"Hold the riverbank!" Landes shouted, limping up the ramp. He gasped and nearly fell again. "By The Dragon!" he appealed to Melloryth. "Girl, help me!"

She obeyed, letting him lean on her shoulder, enjoying the feeling of her strength holding him up. Together they climbed the ramp. "That's it! Drive them back!" Landes shouted.

The Black Shields had formed a line of horsemen, two deep, to repulse the initial attack of the Ogres. Although the Ogres had the advantage of size and strength, Perime discipline and naked steel held fast.

Yet within moments, the charging Dwarves struck the enemy's flanks, broadaxes swinging. Here, Dwarfin determination penetrated the mercenaries' line.

"Yes!" cried Landes triumphantly from the middle of the bridge. "Yes!"

Ur Logga waved his club. "Clever Ones!" he rallied his force, "For the Harkyn!"

"For the Harkyn!" echoed the Honor Guard, laying about them with mighty wallops of their clubs. The enemy's horses shied away from the lunging unicorns. Finn's troop unleashed a volley of arrows and the Black Shield line began to fold.

The riverbank was secured when Landes reached it. Black Shield warriors fled up the slope and Ruf Nab's force charged after them. The center held a few moments longer, then seemed to melt before the Ogres' attack. "Hold!" cried Landes. "Wait!" But in their eagerness, the Ogres drove on, their blood-maddened unicorns carrying them up the slope after the retreating cavalry.

"No! They'll cut you to pieces!" Landes took a step to run after them, but his hip was too weak and he hobbled to a stop, crying out in pain and frustration. From where he stood he could see the danger that the Others could not, but they could not hear his warning over the clash of arms.

Although the attack of the Others from across the bridge divided Lothen's troops and forced him to fight on two fronts, the army of Morbihan still held no advantage. Lothen ordered his forces back, stretching the Others out in a thin line, dividing their forces into smaller groups. He watched carefully, enjoying the waiting as another man might enjoy the moments spent anticipating a hearty meal. Then he ordered The Tyrant's Guards into the battle. These elite troops, roaring their faith in The Vorsai, charged down on the strong right flank of The Snaefid's phalanx.

When the bugles sounded for the Black Shields' attack, the forces pursued by the Ogres turned and stood their ground. Steel against wooden clubs, disciplined mercenaries against a clan of brothers, they fell upon the Ogre Honor Guard.

It was sometime later that a messenger brought the news that a phalanx of Dwarves had stopped short of entrapment. Lothen struck out and the courier fell at his feet. "And where are they now?" he roared, slashing with his sword long after the boy had stopped moving. His lieutenants were silent, some staring fixedly at a distant point, some staring at the ground before them. The messenger, who might have known, lay mute.

"Fools!" Lothen needed to see what was happening about him. At his command they brought his horse and assembled behind him. He ordered the bugles to sound the attack and spurred his horse up the slope toward the fort.

* * *

It was not a brave thing to do and Tym felt ashamed, but the trolls he commanded were limping and carrying their own wounded. Although he knew the strategic value in holding the ground before the fort, Tym remembered all too well the cold power of Lothen's strength-robbing blows. So when the enemy commander galloped toward him, Tym knew at once that he would let him take the fort. "Follow me, fellows!" he called and ran down the hill to fall in behind Nyal's embattled forces.

By the time Lothen had taken the high ground, Tym was too busy in the thick of the battle to wonder if he'd done the right thing. Encouraged by the unexpected reinforcements, Nyal's forces surged forward, fighting down the hill toward the river.

Landes reminded Melloryth of her father. She struggled to hold him up as they staggered together along the riverbank in the direction that Ur Logga's troops had gone. A cow path twisted through the gorse bushes. Ahead Melloryth could hear the sound of fighting. "Snaefid!" Landes shouted. "Ur Logga! Finn!" Horsemen were galloping toward them. "Quickly," he said to Melloryth. "Follow me!"

Using his sword as a cane, he scrambled into the tangled center of a gorse thicket. "Shhhhh," he cautioned the girl who, filled with curiosity, parted the bushes to peer out. "Stay right here, no matter what happens."

Riders approached beating the bushes with the flats of their swords, looking for Others. When they were almost upon them, Landes dragged himself to his feet. Old warrior that he was, his sword flashed out with perfect timing, smooth and precise. A horseman tumbled from his horse without a sound. But still more rode behind him. It occurred to Landes that his one hope was to create enough distraction to save the girl. He hopped forward.

"Hold!" commanded a voice familiar as his own, yet strange, too.

"Nedryk!" Landes exclaimed. The banner of Fanstock streamed from Ned's lance. "Strike the banner down! Fanstock is no traitor while I live!"

Ned's eyes were dull, showing neither surprise nor regret.

"Well, you can't live long, can you, Father?" he said, lifting his sword.

In the instant that Ned raised his arm he was unprotected, the vulnerable edge of his breastplate exposed. Landes meant to strike him down, but his hand refused to move. "Nedryk!" he cried, his voice filled with grief.

And for this blink of an eye Ned's blade froze as father and son faced each other. "Nedryk!" Landes cried again, trying to remind the boy of who he was, of what he had betrayed.

Ruf Nab, leading a scouting party purposefully along the cow path, saw father and son frozen in their moment of reckoning. His Dwarfin nature respected the sanctity of family relations, so he stood for a moment and watched. Then Ned's sword began its swing at Landes's unprotected head.

Ruf threw his broadax overhand. It spun through the air and struck just below Ned's shoulder, splitting his armored breastplate. Ned cried out in pain and his sword fell harmlessly to the ground.

"Dwarves, attack!" Ruf shouted, charging weaponless toward the Humans who followed Ned. The attack on their leader shook the confidence of the traitor lords and they turned and raced back toward the line of battle. Ned's horse ran after them, with Ned barely hanging on to the saddle.

"M'Lord!" said Ruf to Landes. "We've broken through the enemy line and rejoined the Ogres. The Peskies have made contact with Nyal's forces! You must follow me, quickly! Girl!" he added sternly to Melloryth. "Follow closely; don't go hopping off!"

Melloryth clutched Landes's hand as they hurried toward the sounds of fighting. Bronze and steel rang like angry bells and the battle line was a swarm of confusion. Grunting Dwarves threw themselves against their Human enemies as Ogres regrouped and prepared for a desperate charge. Melloryth cried out, amazed at the fierceness of it. All the demons around her seemed to raise their voices in a thunderous roar. It was splendid and she nearly wept in joy.

"For the Harkyn!" chorused the Dwarves.

"For Morbihan!" cried Ur Logga.

"For Nyal!" shouted Melloryth, who heard the love in

their voices and responded with her own. "For Nyal and the mountains!"

Armed with desperate strength, Dwarves and Ogres carved a corridor through which the Elves, Peskies, and their two Human companions passed to join with Nyal and the trolls.

Now Lothen, his lieutenants, personal guard, and a few squads of regulars held the high ground before the gate of the fort. The Tyrant's Guards held the riverbank.

Between them, Nyal reorganized the united forces of The Five Tribes. Facing The Tyrant's Guards, he placed the Ogres, still growling and savage in uncharacteristic battle-fury. They were flanked by Elves. Facing Lothen, he called upon the Dwarves, supported on one flank by the remaining trolls, the other by Peskie archers with their poison-tipped arrows. Using rocks and boulders as a shield, Peskies and Elves made quick sorties against the heavily armed Black Shields, then retreated back into the jumble of boulders. It was difficult for the horsemen to follow while Peskie arrows riddled their ranks. Phaedryn led her followers with the War Song of Elf and the Husbands' short blades and strong hands guaranteed that no fallen Black Shield lived to rise again.

From the height Lothen was reassured. The joining of the Other forces was not a threat—indeed, it seemed to have been a master stroke. Now the entire force of Others lay between The Tyrant's Guards and his regular troops like a hare between the jaws of a wolf. He had only to snap the jaws together.

Yet he lingered. As a wise winner in chess will examine the board one last time before checkmate, Lothen examined the battle lines spread out below him. Leaving nothing to chance, he ordered a squad of horsemen to check the fort behind him to be sure the Others had left no surprises.

When The Stone had settled and Bihan had disappeared, Cyna had fallen senseless, facedown, with her arms outstretched at the top of the ramparts. She had lain that way a long time when rough hands seized her. "Wait," she murmured. "I just need a moment," and was dimly aware of being dragged by her arms. She struggled to free herself, jolted awake by a familiar fear.

"We will try to fight our way back to the bridge," Nyal said. "If any make it across, flee into the mountains. Spread word of what has happened."

The Others nodded, reaching out to grip each other in pledges of final unity, the Ogres roughly stroking everyone's hair.

"Did anyone see Cyna and Fallon escape to the river?" Nyal asked.

"I never had the time to notice," Mati said, his hands locked in Phaedryn's. "But Bihan is a tough pony; he would have made it."

"Oh, no!" Landes groaned. Nyal whirled, expecting to see that the final assault had begun, but the enemy's troops still stood silently. Then Phaedryn lifted her golden, moonstruck eyes toward the fort and pointed. On the ground between two of Lothen's personal guards fluttered the sky-blue cloak of Morbihan's Magic.

Although Lothen had never seen Cyna before, there was something in her that he recognized as his soldiers dragged her from the fort. He reined in his horse, glaring down at her. "That blue cloak is a magician's badge," he said accusingly.

On her knees where she had been thrown before him, Cyna said nothing.

"You are Magic!" he accused. "You Brownie lovers boast that Magic is Morbihan's might, yet you are delivered to me, The Tyrant's tool."

Cyna steeled herself to look into his eyes. They were black, like wells of darkness. She gasped as though he had struck her. Why had Fallon never told her that in The New Faith lived a sort of twisted magic? All around The Tyrant's minister hovered a shadow filled with terrifying power.

As though they shared a secret, Lothen leaned forward and whispered to her. "You who have the power to throw great stones about, do you know why you cannot win in war?" He pressed his blood-streaked sword blade against her neck, forcing her to raise her eyes again to face him. *"Because you blaspheme!"*

"We live by The Law and try to learn its workings," Cyna said, fighting to keep her voice steady.

"You have defied the will of The Vorsai and his servant, The Tyrant of Moer!"

"And I always will!" Cyna flared back.

Lothen smiled, lips curling like a wolf. *"No, I think not, Lady. It is your destiny to be slain for the gratification of The Vorsai. All Magic will die and this heretical land will be burned and cleansed!"* At a nod from him, two soldiers dragged her toward the battle line. Lothen spurred his sweating horse forward into the narrow space that separated the opposing forces. *"Morbihan!"* he roared. *"Morbihan! See what I have taken from you!"*

Before him the line of Dwarves was silent. Ruf Nab hefted his broadax helplessly and said nothing.

"Watch how easily the common soldiers of The Vorsai slay Magic," Lothen sneered, turning his back on the arrayed Others and nodding to a lieutenant. *"Sacrifice her."*

The lieutenant unsheathed his sacramental dagger as the soldiers jerked Cyna upright, one twisting her hands behind her back, the other wrenching her head back by her hair.

There was a sound of rage from Morbihan's ranks. *"Lothen!"*

At his name, Lothen turned back. For a moment he did not recognize the rider before him. Then the horse's nervous prance struck a chord of memory. *"The woods bastard? Telerhyde's puppy has grown a beard! Have you come to watch me kill Magic? Or to teach me manners again?"*

"I am no woods bastard, Lothen," Nyal mocked him. *"I am the son of a Wizard, born in the Harkyn! All that is Magic is right here before you!"* His sword stroked the air with a keen humming sound.

"I'm your match, New Faither! Release the witch and try me!"

Wizards and sons of wizards! Like insects they propagated! Lothen shuddered. To win he had to take Morbihan's heart. "I will keep the witch and have you both!" Lothen spurred his horse forward, attacking straight on, confident in his strength.

All sense of time fell away from Nyal. He circled, looking for an opening in Lothen's defense, a weakness in his strength. Lothen charged him, sword swinging. Avelaer danced and whirled away, responsive to Nyal's wish, at one with his will. Nyal circled again, dodging, feinting.

Once more Lothen attacked. Nyal parried, warding off the huge man's power with the edge of his blade. The shock staggered him but he fought on. Despite hours of battle, Nyal felt no pain or exhaustion and his arms were quick with his own strength. Firestroker grew hot in his hand. The sword began to sing, vibrating and pulsing with energy. Its tip glowed crimson, then blue, then white. Once more, as he had at Broderick's forge, Nyal seemed surrounded by a silent chord of music, shining with clarity.

White-hot sparks flew from Nyal's blade, while Lothen's own dark sword was nicked and burned. Lothen's strength still drove Nyal back, yet with each stroke Lothen felt a blade of ice cut through him, as though his body heat were being drained away. Nyal pressed the attack and Lothen retreated, step by step. His eyes widened in horror. His arm weakened and his hands grew numb as Firestroker pulled the temper from his larger blade.

The end was quick. Firestroker slashed through armor and flesh. Lothen grunted, sagging in the saddle. "Vorsai damn you!" he choked out. His sword fell from his fingers. Nyal struck again, like a woodsman felling a tree, and Lothen slid to the ground. Phaedryn sang her song and the Husbands did her bidding.

"Magic is half the battle," Fallon once said.

When they saw their chief fallen before a wizard's son, the name of The Vorsai on his lips, the Black Shields and the traitor lords broke and ran. The Ogres and Dwarves chased them down, trapping them by the riverbank. Some threw themselves into the raging waters, most died beside the river. Telerhyde was avenged when Ned died there, trying to bargain for his life with an Elf.

Chapter 45

The victory was at great cost to The Five Tribes. Many had sacrificed their lives, and as many were terribly wounded. Phaedryn and Melloryth worked beside Cyna as she labored throughout the day and into the evening, bandaging, healing, commanding wounded Others to recover and live.

Late in the evening Cyna found Nyal inside Dunn Naire talking with the Other leaders before a council fire. She came looking, as she usually did, for peace after so much healing. She paused at the edge of the firelight.

As Nyal spoke to the Royal Others, his voice had the ring of authority, the same grave cadence as Telerhyde's voice once had. But now for the first time she heard a deeper resonance, the echo of an impatient turn of mind. *He sounds like Fallon* she realized, surprised by the hot rush of tears that followed the thought. She wondered if she would ever see the Master Wizard again. Suddenly aware of how tired she was, she entered the council circle and sat silently beside Nyal. He wrapped his arm around her shoulders as he spoke to the Royal Others.

"We must trust Lord Benare and the loyal lords to hold the north while we secure the cities on the coast. Finn, your scouts will leave immediately to tell Benare what's happened. He is to lay siege to Eacon's Keep and capture Gleese. We'll join him when Fensdown Plain is free. We must move quickly, before The Tyrant sends reinforcements."

Cyna listened to his voice, gathering her strength as he drew up plans with the Others. At length she withdrew her hand from his and left him. Nyal caught up with her just outside the fire's glow.

"I must look after the wounded."

"I know," he said. "And I must leave at first light. The ports must be taken quickly so that no word of our victory reaches The Perime."

Down by the bank of the river, a Peskie began to sing.

"The sky will thunder
The earth will shake
If you dare
A marriage make
Of a Wizard's son
To a Gifted One!"

"Listen," she said. All around them, voices joined the refrain, gathering volume and power.

"For power will
To power breed
As might and Magic's
Passions feed
And fall like rain
Upon the seed
Of Kythra's plan
For Morbihan!"

"I'll be back soon, I promise," Nyal said. "When this is over, you and I will return to Crowell and raise the most beautiful children and the best horses in all of Morbihan."

"I know that," she said, kissing him lightly. "I'm a fortune-teller, remember?"

But we haven't much time, she thought, as they held each other in the darkness. She had truly seen the children and the colts, but she had seen dark clouds on the horizon, also. Morbihan was the guardian of the riches of the Outer Isles. It would need all their strength and Magic if it were to survive. "I love you, my darling," she said, and left him silhouetted against the fire to go about her work.

THE END

ABOUT THE AUTHOR

Patricia Mullen lives in New York City. She has published short stories and taught voice to actors at Smith College, American University and Circle in the Square Theatre in New York. A cofounder of the Meisner Extension, an acting studio at New York University, she has also taught horseback riding, managed a ski area and forepersoned a construction crew. In the quest for livelihood she has been an office manager, a technical writer, an actress, and a director. When not writing or teaching, she can be found on her pocket cruiser, *Tache*, sailing in search of the wilder reaches of Long Island Sound.